# Riyati Ripple

## Book III of Riyati

Kai Zeal

Aquakat Publishing

Published by Aquakat Publishing
PO Box 656
Pinson, AL 35126
aquakatpublishing.com
First Edition: November 2025

Cover Design by Kai Zeal
Cover Glyph Illustration by amagren
Edited by Isabelle

ISBN 979-8-9923922-6-5 (eBook)
ISBN 979-8-9923922-8-9 (Paperback)
ISBN 979-8-9923922-7-2 (Hardcover)

Human Creativity Badge by Conrad Altmann

To those who continue to press forward,
even through the fear, even through the doubt:
Stand tall and never surrender.

# content warnings

The viewpoints and actions in this book do not necessarily express the viewpoints of the author. **The following are depicted, described, or implied within this book:**

*Alcoholism, blood, body horror, bullying, child abuse, classism, death, decapitation, emotional abuse, emotional manipulation, extreme violence, fear of abandonment, gaslighting, gore, homelessness, human experimentation, kidnapping, misogyny, mass murder, parental neglect, physical abuse, poverty, school attack, self-harm, stalking, strong adult language, substance abuse, suicidal ideation, torture, trauma-induced nightmares, trauma-based responses, and victim blaming.*

**Reader discretion is advised.**

# CHAPTER
## Thirty-Five

TRACEY HAD EXPECTED Dr. Peter Zhang to be a suit-wearing, scholarly, soft-spoken man.

She'd thought wrong.

He turned out to be a slightly built Asian man with a wide smile and a thick Brooklyn accent. He always wore dark wash jeans with a designer t-shirt beneath a blazer, spoke to them as if he'd known them for years, and opened every session with a prayer to invite in the healing presence of the Holy Spirit.

His office was a small loft on the third floor of a brown brick building in Manayunk. Everything in the office was pristine. Not so much as one book or magazine out of order on the bookshelves. It smelled like eucalyptus leaves and was bathed in beige. Beige Berber carpet. Beige walls. Beige-colored cushy chairs and wooden tables. Beige boxes of tissues placed in different spots throughout the room.

By the time Tracey and Brian traveled to Dr. Zhang's office for their fourth session, they'd been on four dates. In their first session, Dr. Zhang directed them to take time together each week, no matter what. So Tracey found a babysitter for Brianna and off they went. To dinner. To the movies. To an outdoor concert at the Mann. They had a picnic and took a long walk

around the Horticulture Center in Fairmount Park. Their conversations grew tense every so often, but at least they were trying. The dates proved one thing: Tracey could make time for Brian and Brian could make time for Tracey. And they were learning to laugh together again.

"Did you make your way through chapter four of *Walking Together Again?*" Dr. Zhang asked them.

"Yes," Brian nodded.

"Good. Keep reading. I'd like you to go through chapters five and six this coming week." Dr. Zhang checked off something in a manila folder, then turned back to them. "Before we end tonight I want talk to you about some guidelines for your marriage, since we haven't touched much on infidelity prevention in our past sessions."

Tracey flipped opened her notebook.

"The first concept is radical honesty," Dr. Zhang said, sitting down in a chair across from them.

"Radical honesty?" Brian repeated.

"Yes. Christianity itself teaches that when you speak, you should tell the truth. No lies. But, there can still be a great deal of deception going on in your marriage if that's all you do. Radical honesty has to do with sharing information with your mate, which could potentially damage your relationship if you kept it to yourself. Secrets may not appear to hurt your marriage outwardly, but they can eat away on the inside."

Tracey glanced over to Brian. He had a pained look on his face, like the concept made him uncomfortable.

"What's this supposed to look like?" Brian asked.

Dr. Zhang answered, "Let's imagine you had used this guideline in your marriage in January. The very first time the young lady asked you to drive her home, you would have called Tracey and told her, giving her the chance to respond. And the next time. And the next time."

"Isn't that kind of overkill?" Brian asked.

"Yes. It's the type of overkill that keeps a man or woman out

of a cheating situation. Had Tracey known about those rides, she might have intervened by talking with you before the affair started, and you might have thought differently before cheating," Dr. Zhang explained.

Tracey looked out of the huge plate glass window. Rain slid down in long rivulets. Had she known about Lisette earlier, would she have worked on growing closer to Brian? Or would she have passed it off as nothing?

"The second concept is something called 'friends of the marriage.' It works like this: Any friend you have must support the health of your marriage. The person can't be willing to undermine your relationship. Dr. Jones, I'm going to use you as an example again."

He nodded. "Go ahead."

"The moment Lisette asked you if she could have you over for coffee, your immediate response would have been to invite your wife along. If you detected Lisette had a problem, then you would know that she was a person who did not see your wife as your life partner. You would have then terminated your friendship with her."

Tracey thought about that. Nope. Uh-uh. She didn't know one man who would do anything like that. Except maybe her brother-in-law Ricky, but he and Charla were on another level with their union. Maybe guidelines like these were how their marriage flourished.

She shifted in her seat. "Couldn't he have just ended the relationship as soon as he felt the need to hide it?"

"Maybe. Dr. Jones, what do you think?" Dr. Zhang redirected the question.

Brian laced his fingers together. He glanced from the doctor's face to Tracey's. "In the beginning, I didn't think anything at all. We were just friends."

"That's the reason for guidelines like this one," Dr. Zhang pointed out. "Have you ever heard the phrase, 'you teach others how to treat you'?"

"I have," Tracey said.

"This is teaching family, friends and co-workers how to treat your marriage."

"So, how do we do the homework this week?" Brian asked.

"I mentioned two types of guidelines to protect your marriage from infidelity. Get together and create more. I'm not going to ask you to etch them in stone, just list them. We'll go over them next week."

"Sit around and make up rules? No offense, but children need rules, and I'm not a child. I can govern myself," Brian said.

Dr. Zhang directed his words straight to Brian. "When did you accept Christ as your Savior?"

"My first year in medical school."

"And when you did, did you have a problem with accepting God's commandments and following them?"

"No."

"Do you think God's guidelines help to keep you safe, and perhaps lead you to blessings?"

"Certainly."

"Then I'm sure you'll agree God created the guidelines for his relationship with man out of love. You protect what you love. So if you love your wife, you'll make and follow guidelines to protect your union with her."

Brian glanced over to Tracey. She returned her gaze to the window. Balking at guidelines? Seriously? They had a DNA test coming up for a baby in the near future and he's sitting around resisting the type of counsel that could have prevented them from being in counseling in the first place? Unbelievable.

"A list of guidelines. Got it," Brian said.

"Your own list. Remember, you will come up with what works for you," Dr. Zhang stated.

BACK AT THE HOUSE, after they'd paid Chablis—their new babysitter—and checked on Brianna, they opened up their notebooks in the house office.

Tracey stretched her legs out in front of her as she sat on the futon. "This radical honesty thing is designed so we'll always share information that could become secrets. Especially things with the opposite sex. But I guess radical honesty could also extend to things like money, household purchases, and anything else you could keep a secret."

Brian slouched in the office chair. "I guess," he said, and then paused for a moment. "You know, my Dad had a couple of affairs. One of them ended right before I got accepted to UMDNJ. I think it lasted a few years."

"Why are you telling me this now?" Her eyes widened.

He shrugged. "I don't know. I never knew if my mother discovered his infidelity. If she did, she never told us. They never broke up."

"But, what we've learned—it contradicts all that nonsense."

"I know."

Were they deluding themselves, going through counseling and mending their relationship? Brian didn't drink or smoke or eat junk all day long, but what if women were a coping mechanism for him? What if they were something he could rely on to soothe him when life became boring or rough?

"Cut it out!" he said as he leaned over and tapped her on the leg.

"What?"

"I can practically hear the wheels grinding in your head right now. Stop worrying. I just shared something I knew."

"Good," she sighed. "Because I'm not living my life turning a blind eye to a whole bunch of mess."

"You won't have to."

She swallowed hard. Radical honesty meant she had to play along as well. "I need to tell you something."

His eyes narrowed. "Go ahead."

"Remember when we met at Rise. We'd gone out twice I think."

"I remember."

She sat up straighter. Her mouth, dry as cotton. "Well, in September, Kyle had come down to visit Tyler for a few weekends."

"Yeah?"

"The two of us were kind of learning how to deal with each other for the first time in years. He'd finished his business degree by then. He was taking a larger part of Tyler's life, supporting him financially and learning how to be a real dad to him, something I'd been praying about since I forgave him after he abandoned me. Anyway, I let him stay over in my apartment some of those weekends, and couple of those times, we got together."

"Got together?" He raised an eyebrow.

Tracey lowered her eyes to the floor. "It wasn't exactly a secret, because you and I hadn't gotten serious yet, but it happened after I'd met you. And I never mentioned it."

"Why didn't you?"

She looked at his face again. "Because I wasn't with him again. It was something that just happened and I didn't—"

"See it coming." He crossed his arms as he finished her sentence. "And you probably figured I'd stop calling if I knew you had your son's father visiting your house for sleepovers."

"Yeah."

Brian whistled as he sat back in his chair. "Robbed me of the chance to make a decision, huh?"

"I guess." Tracey searched for the right words.

He ran a hand across his face, then turned and grabbed his notebook from the desk. "What can I say? If you kept it to yourself because you wanted to be with me, well . . ."

"You don't care?"

"Oh I care a lot. But it's history now, so we should drop it. We need to focus on our future." He pointed at her with his pen. "No more secrets."

Tracey thought about the dance she'd had with Kyle at Crimson. Right then she felt she would burst with gratitude because she'd done the right thing pushing her way out of that. God only knew where her relationship with Brian would be headed if she'd had something else to confess.

She reached over and softly gripped his hand. "No more secrets."

# CHAPTER
## Thirty-Six

"SUNDAY NIGHT? WHAT TIME?" Tracey dropped the boxes in her hand to the floor then grabbed a pen and a blue notepad from the desk.

"Pick me up from 30th Street at 8:45. The Keystone arrives at 8:35," Tyler said with crunching sounds between his words.

She placed the pen back in its holder and dropped the pad on the computer desk. "What are you eating?"

"Chocolate-covered pretzels. From scratch, too. Granny made some and put 'em in a big tin to take back to Philly with me."

Tracey shook her head. Granny Addison makes her own chocolate goodies too? Kyle's never getting married. "How's your dad?"

"First he wasn't real happy about me going back home to Philly, but we talked about it and he's cool. We drove around a lot while I was here, and I'm taking my license test when I get back. So as soon as Dad buys me my BMW, I'll come back and forth every other weekend," Tyler laughed.

"Uh-huh," Tracey smiled. "Bye Tyler."

She hung up. Her son? Spoiled as rotten as a four-month-old tomato. What did she expect? Living with Kyle every summer,

he'd have to inherit at least a teensy bit of his materialism. God help him.

It was a regular Saturday. How long had it been since she'd had one of those? She'd hit the remote to turn down the music when Tyler called, so she swept up the remote control again and pressed the button to crank up the music on the SoundDock. Smooth jazz. Relaxing. Now back to work. Where was she? Oh yeah. Gathering up the old magazines and papers. She'd tote those down to the recycling bin when she finished in the office, so she put the stack outside in the hallway. The most boring hobby in the world to some people but Tracey loved it. Re-organizing. Moving furniture. Putting things in neatly-designed spaces. All she needed was some music to listen to and time to excavate and she'd get in the zone. Not just cleaning. This was therapy.

Tracey wiped sweat from her brow. The office needed new curtains to replace the sun bleached ones. She'd go out and buy a brighter color like springtime green, and maybe a few accent rugs to pick up on that color. And she'd seen some leather magazine holders at the Container Store. She could get some of those too to organize the periodicals she wanted to keep. Thank goodness Brian was out at the gym. He had plans to run a marathon next spring. Tracey guessed the extra exercise kept his stress level down. So the gym owned Brian, and Brianna would be at a birthday party until four. Tracey could take her time cleaning.

The futon? Hmm. It had seen better days. She could get a new cover for it and big fluffy pillows in green and white. And put it back into the couch position. Of course, that would only be wise if no one would be sleeping on it.

But Brian slept there now.

She placed an empty box on the office chair and stood and stared at the futon. One thing never came up in counseling. When were they going to start sleeping together again? Brian hadn't brought up the subject and neither had Tracey. Since

they'd managed to live in the same house without fighting for almost two months, she didn't want to rock the boat.

In May she'd been the one who had started the ball rolling in their physical court again. It had felt so good to get back together with him. That was back when she figured they'd moved past the indiscretion and it was time to forgive and forget. She'd played music and lit vanilla scented candles. Skin to skin satisfaction. She'd even brought out the heels and danced sexy for him.

She glanced at the futon again. He could stay there for now. Trust would be hard earned this time. If God wanted to take control of their sex life, she was open to that. Until then, the dancing heels would stay parked in the bottom of her closet.

Tracey glanced up at the shelves again, then plopped down in the office chair. Who was she kidding? She needed to reconnect with her bestie. She had to call Monica.

The phone rang three times before Monica answered. "Hello?"

"Hi." Tracey tapped her fingers on the desktop, letting a feeling of nervousness pass. "They say if you miss someone, you should pick up the phone and call. I miss you. I'm calling."

"And I didn't block your number, so you know I needed to hear that."

"So how are you doing? How's everything in your world?"

"I got a promotion. I'm the head of the project management team."

"Wow! Congratulations, you deserve it. I mean it, Monica."

"Thanks."

A moment of silence passed. Tracey didn't want to launch headlong into a description of how she came back home, or deciding to work things out with Brian, or anything self-centered.

"Go on . . ." Monica said.

"What?"

"You want to tell me what happened don't you?"

Tracey's best friend knew her well, but that didn't matter. She refused to focus on a personal story that seemed to be working itself out day by day. She wanted to *be* a friend rather than just *have* a friend.

Tracey said, "You know what I really want? To tell you I wish I'd called you sooner than this. There's been some changes going on here, but before I even get into all that, you know what *you* need?"

"What?" Monica sounded puzzled.

"You need your best friend to come pick you up for lunch and we can celebrate your promotion and you can tell me how *your* life is going. Can we do that? Please."

"Since you put it that way, one of my co-workers raved about the lobster rolls at Luke's Lobster in Rittenhouse. Treat me to some seafood?"

"I'm gonna take a shower and I'm on my way," Tracey said, excitement in her voice.

"See you soon," Monica said, and hung up.

Tracey put her phone down, stood up and looked around the room. Later for cleaning. It could wait.

Relationship mattered more.

RACE TRAINING INCLUDED Brian's diet. Tracey didn't mind cooking the quinoa, but she turned her nose up at eating it. She piled it on Brian's plate right before she slid it over to him.

"You're only having salmon and spinach?"

She swallowed a sip of ice water. "Yep."

"But quinoa is great for you."

"Yeah, and as far as I'm concerned, the only people who need to eat it are people in training."

"Speaking of which . . ." He picked up his fork and shot her a look.

"Yes, we are going with you when you run tomorrow."

He smiled. He looked better and better as the days progressed. The training made his already fit body look even more striking.

The phone rang. "Saved by the bell." Tracey said as she glanced at the caller ID. Unknown. She answered, "Hello?"

Silence.

She looked the caller ID then repeated, "Hello?"

Nothing.

Brian's strong hand swooped the cordless away from her. "Who is this?" he demanded.

His face changed as he sat back in the dining room chair. He listened for a few moments. "You need to go see your personal doctor—I can't help you."

"Who is that?" Tracey raised an eyebrow.

"Hold on," Brian said, placing the phone on the table. "It's Lisette."

"It figures."

He grabbed her hand. "Radical honesty? I'm putting her on speakerphone." He pressed the center button and left the phone standing on the table in front of them. "Lisette."

"Yes," Lisette's voice echoed in the kitchen.

"My wife is here on the phone with me. Say what you have to say."

"She's there with you now?"

Brian gazed into Tracey's eyes. "Yes."

The voice in the phone spoke again. "Look, whatever. I'm not feeling well this week. I thought you could help me."

"I'm not your obstetrician. Have you called your OB to report your symptoms?"

"Yes, I have."

"What did he suggest?"

"I told the office about the pain on my left side and they said I can take Tylenol for my discomfort. The pain is under . . . under my rib cage."

"They didn't ask you to come in?"

"No."

"And everything looked normal during your last visit? All your tests?"

"Yes."

Tracey took a deep breath and kept listening. She looked down at the smooth dining room table. Pregnant and alone. Could she blame the woman for reaching out? *Yes.* She should call 911, or better yet, call the doctor's office back and demand to be seen. Why did she think of calling Brian?

"When's your next visit?" Brian continued.

Lisette's voice sounded weak. "Tuesday, but I'm feeling really tired, and I get up and I have to keep laying back down. My side is killing me. I wanted to know if maybe you could come check me out. I wouldn't call you at home if I didn't need help."

Brian squeezed Tracey's hand. He cleared his throat. "If I do that Tracey is coming with me."

"I don't know about that," Lisette's voice squeaked through.

"I'm sorry. Your next choice is to either phone your OB and tell them it's an emergency, or call 911 to have them take you to the hospital."

"I thought maybe you'd just help me out," Lisette whispered.

"I understand you're in pain, and I'm sorry you feel so bad, but if I come check on you, Tracey comes with me."

"You know what, forget it."

Click.

Brian reached over and hung up the phone. They sat there for a minute staring down at their plates before Tracey squeezed Brian's hand back.

"Maybe we should go see about her?" The words tumbled out before she could take them back. That was not the suggestion of a hurt wife. That suggestion came from the back history of a scared, broken-hearted, twenty-one-year-old, lonely pregnant lady.

"She's a smart young woman. If her pain is that bad, she'll call 911," Brian said, looking down at his plate.

"But shouldn't we do something?"

He looked up. His words cascaded slowly. "She will call 911."

# CHAPTER
## Thirty-Seven

TRACEY WAS CHANGING clothes Monday afternoon when the house phone rang. She pulled a fresh shirt down over her torso before answering it.

"Where's Brianna?" Brian's voice sounded shaky.

"She's in the kitchen having a snack. Why?" Tracey switched the phone to her other ear as she straightened out her bra straps.

"Tyler?"

"He's around here somewhere. Last time I saw him he was on his phone trying to track down Jonathan so they could go hang out."

"So you're alone?"

Her pulse jumped. "Yes. What's going on?"

"I overheard Janette talking a few minutes ago. Lisette gave birth last night."

Tracey's heart beat fast and her skin grew hot. She eased down on the edge of the bed. They'd just heard from Lisette on Saturday. Now, it was quarter after four on Monday afternoon, and the baby had arrived.

"Last night? Must be at least nine or ten weeks early."

"Yes . . . I don't know the timing . . . but . . . uh . . ."

"What are you thinking?"

He stayed quiet for so long she thought the call had dropped. "Brian, are you there?"

"Yeah."

"So . . ." Tracey said, waiting for him to speak.

"It turns out she had preeclampsia."

"Aren't women put on bed rest for that?"

"Sometimes. If the doctors catch it before it gets out of control." He exhaled a loud sigh into the phone. "We had a patient, two years ago–I believe she was from South Africa. She developed an extreme case, with liver and kidney failure. She collapsed in her home, and her family rushed her to the hospital. She survived, but she was in a coma for three months and had to relearn how to walk. Her child didn't make it."

Tracey bit her lip and started to tremble. For so long this had been an event off in the future somewhere. Now, a premature baby. A sick mother. Did Tracey and Brian have any business talking about it? And who was responsible for this woman? She must have friends and family around Philly. Why hadn't they been taking care of her?

"Early birth?" Tracey said.

"Early means challenges. For her and the baby."

Tyler ambled past Tracey's bedroom door. A second later, he came back around, peeking his head through the crack.

"What's up?" he mouthed, his hand on the edge of the door, his eyebrows raised.

She held up her hand and nodded to him, pantomiming that she was cool.

He waved back then closed the door slowly behind him.

"Well . . . uh . . . we've got back-to-back patients here, so . . ."

"Yeah, uh . . .yeah." Tracey rubbed her arms. "Listen, I'll come pick you up today. Wait. Did you hear what she had?"

"A boy." Brian said.

💔

### COMPLICATED.

Tracey sat in the Volvo outside of Germantown Family, waiting for Brian. A light breeze blew bits of paper down the street like dingy confetti dancing in the fading sunlight. She'd waited only ten minutes, till just past seven-thirty, when he emerged. She studied his slumped shoulders, his head bowed as he walked out of the building.

Way complicated.

She climbed out of the car, calling and waving to him. "Hey."

Brian looked up. She shrugged, leaning against the car door, facing him as he trudged toward her.

"Kids?" He stopped in front of her.

"Ty's holding the house down. They don't need me. At least not like you do now." She jerked her thumb toward the backseat. "I've got your gym bag, running shoes, t-shirt, and shorts. You could use a good run to clear your head, right?"

"You have what I need." A smile settled on his tired face.

"I sure hope I do." Tracey opened the door and retrieved the gym bag, handing it to him. "Take this, go back in and get changed. Forbidden Drive is calling your name."

She watched his eyes take in her white t-shirt, black mesh shorts, and Nikes. "You're running with me?"

"I'll start with a walk. Then I'll jog. At some point I'll run." She nodded toward the building. "Go on."

THEY TOOK KELLY DRIVE, past the Falls Bridge, over to Ridge close to the Art Museum. Tracey parked the car and the two of them walked to the start of the Forbidden Drive. By the time they approached the thin paved path, Brian started talking. "Tracey, I don't know what our is role in this situation," he admitted. He walked faster.

"I know," she sighed.

"I can't get my brain around it."

"I know," she repeated, kicking a black rock out of the pathway. "Don't try."

They walked faster.

"I still don't think I'm the baby's father, but if I am, what does that mean?"

A light wind blew across Tracey's face. She smelled dry grass and earthy moss. "It means neither of you had any idea this would happen."

She hustled to keep up as his pace quickened.

He breathed harder. "And what do we do with all this?" His fists were clenched at his sides.

Tracey had no business trying to walk faster than a turtle. By the time they took the first turn she was practically wheezing. She did a quick step forward and grabbed his arm. He stopped moving.

"We pray," she said, reaching for his hands.

Brian paced in a slow circle. He ran a hand over his face, turned, and walked around again. Tracey stood still, watching. He dropped his arms to his side and stilled his legs. Alone on the pathway together, orange sun rays washed across his face coloring the brokenness.

"For?" he wondered, looking skyward.

"Lisette," Tracey sighed. "Because you and me, I think we just might be all right. But that young lady needs something and I don't think it has anything to do with you. And the baby needs all the prayer he can get."

They walked off the pathway and joined hands under the treetops. She leaned her head toward him and agreed with his whispered words to the Lord.

Together. Talking to God.

Closer than close.

# CHAPTER
## Thirty-Eight

ON THE FRIDAY following Labor Day, Tracey and Brian enjoyed dinner together at the Chestnut Grill and Sidewalk Cafe. That was when Tracey learned it was important for the health of her marriage that she not ask Brian about Lisette or her baby. Bringing up the subject disturbed him and upset the balance of understanding and growth in their shaky relationship.

Right after he ordered coffee, as soon as the waiter walked away, Tracey leaned across the small wooden table toward him. "Have you heard anything?"

"Heard anything?" With a curious look on his face, he reached for her hand, grasped it, and gave her warm smile.

"About Lisette and her son?"

His smile vanished. A dark look took its place. "Tracey, no."

"No, what?"

He spoke softly, rubbing her fingers. "No, I haven't heard anything, and I don't want to talk about it. Tonight is about you and me. Can we relax and enjoy our evening?"

"Of course, I was just asking."

He shook his head. "I know, but it's not something I want to talk about now. They're in our prayers. So, please, this is our

time." He brought her hand to his lips, kissing the back of it. "Just you and me—we need this."

The waiter came back then and delivered their coffee. It's warm rich scent teased her nose as she sat back in the chair, watching Brian as he sipped from his mug and signed the charge receipt. The determined set of his shoulders communicated everything he didn't say—which was, "Until we can establish paternity, there's nothing we can do, and I refuse to talk about it."

No way. Not good enough.

There was a child out there potentially belonging to Tracey's husband, and she wouldn't pretend otherwise. But she wasn't going to push him about it. At least not that night. She finished her coffee and pondered her options.

Because of security, HIPAA law, doctor-patient confidentiality and who knew what else, getting information about Lisette and her baby would be next to impossible for Tracey. The next reliable source of info? She hated to go there, but it was true. The gossip grapevine among the nurses at Germantown Family. The same grapevine Tracey had tugged on to get information about Brian's affair in the first place. She'd have to summon up the courage to talk to Ruthie about it. Brian might find out she asked her, but that was a risk she had to take.

FROM JANETTE'S MOUTH, to Ruthie's ears, to Tracey. In less than a two-minute phone conversation with Ruthie on Monday afternoon, Tracey found out all she wanted to know. Then she quietly asked Ruthie to not mention their phone call. Ruthie murmured her understanding, then hung up.

Baby Elijah Santana weighed in at less than two pounds at birth. The doctors had worked on him extensively to help him breathe. An hour after his birth, he was transported to Children's

Hospital of Philadelphia. He remained there in the neonatal intensive care unit under the care of their doctors.

The hospital discharged Lisette a week after the baby's birth. She needed to stay after her emergency C-section and complications due to her illness. Ruthie didn't say, but Tracey assumed she was fine since the hospital released her.

*Let it go. Let it go. Let it go,* Tracey chanted to herself. Now she knew the full story. In no way could they demand paternity testing now. To even think about it seemed cruel.

*Let it go and pray.*

Which she would certainly do, but one thing continued to trouble her.

BACK IN THE beige cocoon of Dr. Zhang's office, Tracey dropped onto the comfy sofa next to Brian. It was their regular Wednesday evening meeting and she had more on her mind than handing in the homework.

"Let's pray, shall we?" Dr. Zhang bowed his head. "Father in heaven, we come before You right now. We lift You up. You've given us life. You've cared for us. You've blessed us. Father, Brian, Tracey and I are here, and we ask your Holy Spirit to help in healing broken hearts and broken lives. Holy Spirit, lead us during this time. In this moment and always, we rely totally on you. Thank you. In Jesus's name, amen."

"Doctor, can we start with something else tonight instead of what we read in the book?" Tracey asked, not looking at Brian.

He laced his hands in his lap. "We can talk about whatever you want." Talk came out sounding like "tawlk."

"Thank you," Tracey said, clearing her throat. "I'm not happy with how my husband is treating the baby situation."

Dr. Zhang interrupted Tracey, saying, "I'm going to say this before you finish your comments: Don't talk to me. Look Dr.

Jones in the eye. Use "I" language, and calmly tell him how you feel."

She shifted in her seat, directing her eyes to meet Brian's. He sat slightly slumped on the other end of the sofa, looking uncomfortable.

"I hate how you're behaving concerning the birth of Lisette's baby. She's not my favorite person in the world, but if this could be your child, I think you should do more than just sit and wait around while the baby's in intensive care." She looked back to Dr. Zhang. He gave a slight nod.

"Dr. Jones, you can respond to Mrs. Jones comment, but you don't have to. If you need more time, you can ask for it."

Brian sat up straight. "No, I'll respond."

Dr. Zhang nodded again. "Take your time. And remember, "I" language."

"Got it." Brian turned to Tracey, and their eyes met. "I don't understand why you want me to intervene into the life of someone you also want me to avoid. Our marriage will be better off if we don't discuss either of them until the DNA test is done."

He had a point. They got along great as long as they ignored the past. Still. It made her skin crawl to know a woman and her baby needed support—they were in the midst of a medical crisis —and her was husband deliberately giving them the cold shoulder.

"Brian, Elijah is in intensive care!"

"I understand, and CHOP is number one in the nation for handling premature infant issues. What can I do when he's already receiving care?" His eyes narrowed and he moved to the edge of his seat. "Wait a minute, how'd you know his name was Elijah?"

She glared at him. "I asked!"

Now they both glanced over to Dr. Zhang. He opened his hands. "Go on. Remember, if you can keep your voices down, you're talking with opposing views, not fighting."

"I didn't say you should be Elijah's doctor," Tracey sighed.

"Then don't be upset with me," he crossed his arms and leaned back.

She shook her head. "You can't just leave her!"

"Leave her? What—"

"Alone with a baby in the hospital!"

"Tracey, I am ninety-nine percent sure I am not Elijah's father."

"You know what, you probably aren't, but that's not the point."

"Then what . . ." he stopped speaking, took a breath, and continued speaking in a lower tone. "Help me understand what you think I should do."

Tracey stood up out of frustration. "Brian, you will not just drop her as if you had nothing to do with her. You cannot turn your back on the baby and his mother as if they're trash!"

Dr. Zhang put his hands up. "The talking is good, but please keep your seat, Mrs. Jones. Let's stay calm. This is not anger management class."

She eased back down on the sofa.

Brian turned to Dr. Zhang. "Wait! I just figured this out. This isn't even about me!" He shifted towards Tracey again. "This is about you and Kyle. You don't want me to treat Lisette like Kyle treated you!"

She crossed her arms. "I wouldn't want any woman to be treated that way."

Brian shook his head. "It's not the same."

"How is it not the same?"

"Because you and Kyle were at the end of a three-year relationship when he left you. You were in love with him. Lisette and I weren't in love. If she cares for me at all, it's only because we were friends."

Dr. Zhang leaned in, his voice gentle but firm. "Brian and Tracey, I'm going to redirect you now. Brian, you know how Tracey feels. Tracey, Brian knows how you feel. You can't change

the past. Now you must agree on where to go from here together."

They sat in silence for a moment, backs straight, breathing deep.

Tracey sighed. "We're Christians. It's time we act like it."

Brian rubbed his chin. "So let me get this straight. You need me to be kind to the woman I committed adultery with less than a year ago?"

"Do you plan on doing it again?" Tracey raised an eyebrow.

"No."

"Then this is a new day and we need to be there for her if she'll allow it."

# CHAPTER
## *Thirty~Nine*

PRAY.

Have faith.

Stay the course.

The last rule Tracey would hold tight to as she and Brian moved into their future.

It could have been a regular Tuesday morning with the kids in school and Tracey taking care of the day's tasks and preparing to check in on her father. Instead, she rested in the passenger seat of the Lexus, staring out the window at the passing city scenery as Brian drove. She reviewed the first two rules repeatedly during the fifteen-minute drive from their Chestnut Hill home to the underground parking lot for Children's Hospital of Philadelphia.

"I have a strange feeling about this," Brian said as he guided the car around tight parking lanes, looking for a spot close to the elevators. "I don't even know if Lisette will be here this morning."

Tracey turned around and pulled her red trench coat from the back seat. "She's a mother with a newborn baby in intensive care. Trust me, she'll be here."

On the ride up to the NICU, they remained a few feet apart in

the elevator. Awkward. When the ding sounded signaling the floor, Tracey followed as Brian walked out in front of her. Though she may have been the one who pushed the issue of following up on Lisette and baby Elijah, she couldn't force him to do it. In the end, he'd been the one who rearranged his schedule and told Tracey he wanted her with him.

Tracey wouldn't have had it any other way.

He leaned over to her once they were outside of the NICU. "You'll have to wait here."

She nodded. "I understand."

He handed her his keys and trench coat. "If big-mouthed Janette was correct, Lisette is either in the unit or somewhere in the hospital."

"You asked her?"

"I didn't have to ask; I overheard her talking about it," Brian said. He took a deep breath. "I'll go in and ask for Lisette Santana. I can't walk into the unit directly because this area is strictly for the patients, their families, and the doctors and nurses caring for the babies."

Tracey backed away. "You made a good decision," she said, affirming Brian.

"I hope so."

Tracey watched as he disappeared through the double-doors. What could she do except hold their coats, find a bench and wait? If Lisette wasn't there with her baby, Brian would come back and they'd leave.

Tracey seated herself on a bench in the hallway. For a hospital, the place was vibrant and cheery. Sunshine streamed through the glass-topped atrium. Colorful artwork and murals adorned the walls. She silently thanked God for blessing her children with excellent health. Tyler and Brianna were both born full-term, strong, healthy, and bright. Not once did she have to bring either of them to CHOP for a test, surgery, recovery, or diagnosis.

She closed her eyes. *Lord, please keep baby Elijah close to you, bless his growth and health, and provide all he needs at this time.*

She opened her eyes in time to see Brian and Lisette heading toward her, talking furiously. Tracey's arms dropped and their coats slid to the floor as she scrambled to her feet.

"We didn't come up here to alarm you," Brian said to Lisette as they stopped next to Tracey.

Lisette pushed a lock of wavy hair away from her face. "Why are you two here? I don't get it. All I want is to be with my son. He's all I care about now."

Boldness rose inside Tracey. "We heard about your illness and the baby coming early. We came to offer our support."

Lisette squinted at Tracey. "But why? Why now?" She turned her gaze back to Brian. "I called you and asked you to check on me when I was sick. You told me to call 911. You brushed me off! Are you up here trying to make yourself feel better?"

Brian said, "We didn't ignore you. All I said was I had to bring my wife with me if I drove over to check on you. You hung up on us!"

Lisette stopped talking. Her eyes moved slowly from Brian's face, to Tracey's, then back to Brian's. She must have been taking a moment to digest the truth in those words.

Tracey spoke, keeping her voice low. "If you want to be angry at us for us being here, you need to be mad at me. I'm the one who pushed him to check on you and the baby."

Lisette crossed her arms. "Again, why? We aren't friends. We aren't anything to each other."

Tracey stepped closer. "Are there any other people in your life right now, giving you unconditional moral support and praying for your health and for your son's survival? Anyone at all?"

Lisette glanced at the floor.

Tracey raised her voice a notch. "Sixteen years ago when I gave birth to my son Tyler, his daddy didn't show up. Do you know who showed up to see the baby the next day besides my friends and family? Tyler's grandparents! My ex-boyfriend's

mother and father. They hardly knew me, but they were there for me and Ty when I needed people to be there for me."

Lisette's eyes floated everywhere, never resting on Tracey's face.

Tracey kept talking. "My husband likes to help people. He tried to mentor you this winter. He thought he could assist you when you applied to med school. What happened afterward is hard for me, but you know in your heart he doesn't mean you any harm. None. Despite everything, this month we've been on our knees praying for you! For you and your baby!"

Tracey had no clue where her speech had come from. No idea she would even have the opportunity to say those words.

Lisette turned her gaze away. Brian moved and stood behind Tracey, his hands warm on her shoulders. They all remained still for a minute. Tracey shifted her weight from foot to foot. There she was, face to face with Lisette. The Lord was guiding her, showing her how to love in the middle of a hard situation.

"How are you feeling now? How is the baby doing?" Tracey asked.

Lisette answered without looking at them. "My blood pressure is back to normal, and my pain disappeared when Elijah was born. I'll have follow-up tests for liver functioning, so . . ." She shrugged. "Elijah's pretty small, but he's a fighter. His lungs are fine. The doctors told me about some concerns they have about his prematurity," she said before finally glancing up. "Thanks for asking."

"You're welcome," Tracey said. Her eyes met Lisette's gaze.

"Would you like us to leave?" Brian asked, his hands sliding down Tracey's arms.

Yellow sunshine beamed through the atrium making the brightly-colored hallway more dazzling. Lisette ran a hand through her thick brown hair. She motioned her head toward the NICU.

"No. I'm going back in though," Lisette said with a raspy tone. "I was about to sit and hold him when the staff told me

you were here. Brian, if you want, you can come and see Elijah. You'll have to put on a gown and scrub in."

Brian gripped Tracey's hand gently, then released it. She turned and held his glance until he broke away. His eyes held a look of love mixed with sadness. She watched him once again disappear beyond the double doors, this time with the woman with whom he'd been intimate.

Tracey eased back down on the bench.

More prayer time.

# CHAPTER
## *Forty*

TRACEY AND BRIAN SET A GUIDELINE. Brian would never visit the hospital on his own. Together, they made the trip to CHOP three more times before baby Elijah went home in early November.

Baby Elijah was tiny, but by the time October rolled around he'd gained weight steadily and was up to five pounds before Thanksgiving. Since birth he'd suffered a brain bleed and two blood infections. The doctors also mentioned hypotonia, something Brian explained as low muscle tone. The baby felt relaxed and floppy when he was held. As Brian predicted, Elijah had a challenging journey ahead.

"Will all his issues clear up?" Tracey asked Brian one Sunday afternoon after church.

"We need to keep praying. Brain bleeds can sometimes mean brain damage. High or low muscle tone issues can be an early indicator of cerebral palsy, muscular dystrophy, and a number of other disorders."

"And Lisette?"

"She's aware of all that. He's still her son. Elijah is at CHOP and he'll receive the best care in the country for a premature baby."

NEVER IN HER life had Tracey been so grateful to see the return of the routine. Each morning, when she woke with Brian, Tyler, and Brianna upstairs with her, she didn't put a foot on the floor before thanking the Lord for the blessing of her family's presence.

Brianna started first grade and discovered a whole new group of friends at school. She begged to visit a different person several afternoons each week, and spent less and less time by Tracey's side. Now the girl wanted to be a Brownie, and she'd abandoned her Barbie dolls in favor of anything pink and white with a Hello Kitty face emblazoned on it.

Tyler's booming voice and rapidly broadening shoulders reminded Tracey a young gentleman lived in the house now. He kept his word to his father, and once a month he visited New York. Tracey didn't have the heart to tell Kyle that Ty had additional incentive to visit because Eva—the Zendaya look-a-like—had moved to Long Island permanently. As long as Tyler kept up his grades and respected his parents and their home, Tracey and Brian gave him the grace to come and go. No word on the BMW from Kyle. Tyler rode the regional rail and the Amtrak Keystone into New York.

TRACEY AND BRIAN continued their visits with Dr. Zhang every week. During each session, they worked through their emotions about the affair and the aftermath. Nothing was easy, but the more they submitted to the teaching and completed the homework assignments, they continued to build a better relationship.

They also kept up the new way of dating one another they'd started in the late summer. Each week they took turns choosing a

date for the week. Dinner. Concerts. Theatre. Art shows. Movies. The good times brought them closer.

On the last Saturday night in October, they returned from a late movie date. After Tracey thanked Chablis for babysitting, paid her and said goodnight, she set the house alarm, and climbed the stairs to the second floor. Brian sat at the top of the landing waiting for her. He had to be cold, sitting there without a shirt. His taut muscular frame proved the extent of his daily workouts. The rock solid muscles in his legs were hidden by his silk pajama pants.

"What's up?" Tracey climbed the stairs to reach him and rested her forearms on his legs, her elbows touching his knees. "Is everything okay and why are you out here half-naked?"

Brian shook his head. "First, I was getting undressed, and then I missed you and came out here to wait for you. Second, no, everything is not okay."

"No?" she asked, studying his face.

He rested his hands around her waist. "I know I've told you I'm sorry." His looked into her eyes. "But, I want you know, really know, how deeply sorry I am. I was a fool." He reached to touch her hair by her neck and his other hand slipped to her back, gently pulling her closer.

Tracey rested her head on his chest, her arms encircled him. A small gasp of breath escaped from him and she quickly pulled back to see the reason. Her husband struggled to hold back his emotion with tears in his eyes.

"Brian?"

"I love you Tracey." He brought her closer once again. His warm breath fell softly against her lips before he kissed her slowly. Resting his forehead against hers, he stopped briefly, "I promise, I won't ever break our relationship again."

"I love you too," she whispered as he pulled her closer for an embrace.

"I haven't said this enough," he whispered back. "You look

amazing. I love your makeup and your hair is incredible! So sexy. Nice!"

Two days earlier, she'd let Charla sew 20-inch long hair virgin hair bundles onto her head, and style them in beachy waves. Charla also taught her a few makeup tricks with contouring and highlighter. Something different. Flirty and fun.

"Thanks," Tracey blushed and took in a sharp breath. Her midsection felt hot. She glanced down to see his hand covering her in a gentle caress. The desire in his eyes made her feel like she was melting.

"Beautiful," he said, pulling her even closer. "I wanted to beat up all the men staring at you tonight."

She laughed. "That would have been interesting. I can see the headline. *Local Doctor Assaults Men in Movie Theatre.*"

He kissed her cheek, touching her face lightly. "I'd only have done that to show them you're mine."

Brian's skin felt warm against hers. He smelled delicious. She kissed him deeply then whispered, "Yes, I am yours."

Tracey stood up then, stepped up to the landing and slipped off her heels to keep from clicking down the wood hallway. She walked into their bedroom, beckoning him inside with her eyes, her hands, her walk.

He followed her, closing the door behind them.

THANKSGIVING EVE. Tracey paced the dining room with a notepad in her hand, trying to figure out if they had enough chairs for everyone coming to dinner the next day. But more important than that, Tracey wondered which relative would be able to crash at their home overnight so she and Brian could manage to sneak out and have a quick interlude somewhere that evening.

That morning Tracey called Lisette to pray with her for Elijah. Even though Elijah had been released from CHOP in early

November, he had a heart monitor and was still susceptible to infections, so Lisette had to keep him home, away from crowds. Tracey offered to keep praying with Lisette each week. Lisette accepted the offer.

Tracey checked her watch. Two-o'clock. Good. If she rushed, she could make it to the craft store to get a few more decorations for the tables. Thank goodness she hadn't broken the platters or china back in June or she'd have to shop for those as well.

Her phone buzzed on her hip. She slid it out of the holder. "Hi."

"Hey." It was Brian.

She sauntered into the kitchen, dropping her notepad on the kitchen island. "You could have called me on the house phone, you know."

"You're always on the go, so I tried your cell first. You're probably on your way out now, huh?"

She grinned. "Of course."

"I need you to sit down for a second. Something happened at the office today."

She frowned, sliding onto a kitchen stool. "Brian. That is *not* funny."

"I know. Sorry about the intro, but you need to know this. I got a call I was waiting for."

Butterflies started kickboxing in her stomach. She swallowed. "Go on."

"Last week, Lisette had Elijah's cheek swabbed. Then I had mine done at a lab."

"Swabbed?"

"A buccal swab. It's for DNA testing."

Tracey stopped breathing. "Go ahead. I'm ready."

"There's not much for you to be ready for," he said, pausing. "As I pointed out earlier and now the test proves it; I am not the father of Elijah Santana."

She blinked. *Really?* "Wait. Those tests are accurate, correct?"

"More accurate than you can imagine."

*Not. The. Father.*

Tracey gripped the edge of the counter with her hand, breathing out slow. *Not the father.* She felt grateful, but far from joyous. This was no time to celebrate. Elijah and Lisette still needed support.

"Thanks for letting me know. We're still going to be there for Elijah though, right?"

"Trace, I don't think God would let us have it any other way," Brian said. "Listen, I have to go now."

"Yeah, we'll talk later."

She stood up, looking around the clean kitchen—not sure how to feel or what to do first. Her mind wandered over the events of the past year. She and Brian had been through so much since last winter. And everything had started right here in the kitchen. The confession, the lies, the hurt, the fear. The recommitment, the decision to begin again, the hard work of rebuilding their relationship.

Their lives would never be the same.

They'd grown all right. In a new direction.

Not an ending.

A new beginning.

# Book Club Discussion Guide

1. Tracey and Brian's marriage struggles begin when they've been married for less than ten years. Do you think that happiness in marriage declines naturally after three or seven years? Why or why not?

2. Pastors and Christian counselors are a part of the fabric of our lives as people of faith. What did you think about Tracey meeting with Pastor Downes regarding her concerns about her husband? Should she have asked for help from leadership without telling Brian? Why or why not?

3. Tracey's son Tyler, and her daughter, Brianna, are used to experiencing peace in their home. Trouble in their parent's relationship directly affects them. Early in the story, Tracey shares with Ruthie that she doesn't want to leave Brian, mostly because of the kids. What do you think of that statement?

4. When a couple experiences marriage trouble, life doesn't stop. Children grow up. Bills must be paid. Other problems still occur. In the story, Tracey's concerns multiply with both her father's health issues, and her mother's foreclosure notice. Imagine these

issues were happening in your life. Which do you think should take top priority?

5. When a man has an affair, sometimes people hold the opinion that the husband is the only person to confront, and that the "other woman" isn't the real problem. Do you feel that way? Why or why not?

6. Brian broke his wife's heart and altered their relationship permanently with his transgressions. Was he apologetic enough afterward? Should Tracey have forgiven him or pursued a divorce immediately?

7. Tracey's anger after confronting Lisette in the medical office pushed her to nearly hit her with her car. Any woman could see red in that type of situation, but those actions aren't in keeping with what her God would have wanted. Think about changing the scene. What would it have looked like if Tracey had stopped longer to consider her walk with the Lord? How would things have ended differently?

8. Brian mentioned that he felt Tracey used him to pay her family's bills and make sure the children were taken care of properly. He also said she spent so much time doing these things that he felt alone. Think about what he believed. How do you think those beliefs affected his behavior in the relationship?

9. When Brian married Tracey, she entered the marriage with her young son, Tyler. Through their years as a family, Tyler's loyalty remained with his biological father, Kyle. Should Tracey have allowed Tyler and Kyle's father/son relationship give her an opening to drive to Long Island?

10. People are phenomenally complex. Infidelity is an incredibly complex issue. Tracey and Brian's counselor talks with them about honesty and establishing relationship rules. How do you think Brian would

have behaved if he and his wife had created boundaries about friendships and work relationships?

11. Should Tracey have pushed to find out more about Lisette's baby or should she have minded her own business? Do you think Tracey's walk with God influenced her to care more about someone's well-being than the pain she experienced after being cheated on? If you were in Tracey's shoes, what would you have done differently?

12. If you could write one more chapter after the ending, what would you write?

# Leave a Review

Dear Reader,

I hope you enjoy this story. Book reviews are a wonderful way for readers to connect with authors, and they also play a crucial role in helping us spread the word about our stories.

Whether you love the book or even like it a little bit, a quick review on the platform where you purchased it would be incredibly helpful. Even if you received a complimentary copy, your honest feedback is valuable.

Of course, I'd also love to hear your thoughts directly. Feel free to reach out at kl@klgilchrist.com!

Warmly,
K.L. Gilchrist

# Acknowledgments

My journey from initial story idea to finished book was a long one. About ten years, from tip to tail. I could not have completed *Broken Together* without help.

Thank you, Lord, for reminding me daily to use my talents to glorify you.

Thanks to my family, of course, for their love, support and humor. I especially remember those hilarious rejected book titles (ahem... *No Side Chick Formed Against Me Shall Prosper*) .

Writing fiction in the midst of community was an amazing experience. Thank you to the authors, teachers, and students I learned from during the novelist workshops at the *Greater Philly Christian Writer's Conference*. I would also like to thank the Scribes critique group from *American Christian Fiction Writers (ACFW)* for every chapter critique.

Many blessings to the women who served in my very first beta reading group: Chrishante Dandy, Helena Carey, Maxayn Lundy-Cheeks, Stacey Strickler, Theresa Mason-White, and TashaJuanna Muhammad.

Thank you to Karen Engle, whose editing skills and attention to detail made sure this book would make it to publication.

Last but never least, to my spiritual family from Christian Stronghold Baptist Church of Philadelphia, PA. Thank you for the love and support as I wrote and launched this book. I will never forget you!

# Subscribe To My Newsletter

How will you find out about my latest releases, read reviews for recommended books by other Christian fiction authors, and more? By becoming an author newsletter subscriber! You can sign up on my website at klgilchrist.com.

As a gift, all newsletter subscribers receive the free short story collection *Five For The Journey: Stories*

Sign up today! ☺
~K.L. Gilchrist

# About the Author

K.L. Gilchrist crafts true-to-life contemporary stories for women of faith. The author of *Engaged* and other novels enjoys bringing order to chaos and dancing whenever and wherever she can. She and her family call the suburbs of Philadelphia, PA home. Visit her online at www.klgilchrist.com.

# table of contents

# The Story So Far...

## Riyati Rebirth

During a routine visit to the local city park with her childhood friend Jordan, Kylie encounters a life-threatening situation, causing her to have Activation (Act), which grants her the ability to use magic. Soon after, she discovers that she is the reincarnation of Kisate Riyati, crown princess of the now-destroyed magic kingdom of Riyati. Even stranger, her past incarnations and future self (Siani, often called "Sia") now share a body with her, each a distinct consciousness only she can hear. While every mage — an individual that has experienced Act — has a unique ability, Kylie is an exception: she possesses two abilities. The first is empathy, where she feels and senses the emotions of individuals around her; the second is sensory precognition, a type of clairvoyance that allows her to experience the future through non-vision-based senses.

The next few months of Kylie's life pass peacefully as she adjusts to magic in her life. That peace doesn't last, however, as multiple individuals attempt to kidnap her and bring her to a man named Asuza. Asuza was Kisate's — her original incarnation — primary servant and the man who murdered Kylie's previous two incarnations. During one of these kidnapping attempts, Jordan walks in and witnesses the attempted kidnapping. This causes his own Act to occur, and soon after, he's revealed to be affected by the same reincarnation spell as Kylie; his original incarnation is Takite Tanoti, Kisate's fiancé. Similar to Kylie, he shares a body with his prior incarnations (Takite, John, and Dmitri) and future self (Rotanu, often called "Rota"); unlike Kylie, he has the standard one ability — hypermnesia, the perfect recall of his memories since his Act. While Kylie is impartial to magic itself, only disliking how it has changed her life, Jordan despises it. Stemming from long-term low self-esteem caused by a lifetime of being bullied because of his family's low socioeconomic status and abuse from his alcoholic father, he views magic as another sign of being an outcast. This disdain is only increased as he frequently clashes with Rotanu, who he refuses to believe is himself from the future — in part because Rotanu is engaged to Siani, a reality Jordan refuses to believe he could possibly be worthy of.

Come late June, Asuza finally succeeds in kidnapping Kylie. Once Jordan realizes she's missing, he confronts Rotanu, who admits that she has been kidnapped by Asuza and that he even knows where Kylie is held. Jordan decides to attempt rescuing her and enters the run-down building Rotanu directs him to. Within the dimly-lit building, he sees a girl, similar in appearance to Kylie, dead on an altar. Many visions flash across his eyes of additional women that look like Kylie, all dead, and extreme pain manifests in his chest before further hallucinations play out in front of him — one of a reality in which Kylie never had Act. Jordan realizes what he sees is nothing more than an illusion. He breaks out of the spell and reaches Kylie before she dies. Together, they work to cast a spell forcing both Asuza and their previous incarnations to rest, triggering their wings — a form of "magic exhaust" for high-powered spells — during the process. Finally freed, Kylie heads back home and is greeted by her frantic mother and childhood friend Dani.

## Riyati Rivals

The new school year opens with Kylie and Jordan sharing no classes, limiting the time they see each other to after school most days. Even that becomes difficult, however, because Kylie's mother keeps Kylie under constant watch due to her fear of Kylie being kidnapped again. Jordan's friend Richard —

a wealthy, pompous, misogynistic womanizer — quickly decides that he needs to "assist" Jordan by separating him from Kylie. Meanwhile, Kylie is assigned a single biology lab partner for the entire year: Lianne Payne, a haughty woman who shares Kylie's birthday. Unlike Kylie, Lianne changed from non-honors to honors courses over break yet has no regard for her studies.

As a way of escaping from her mother's grip while gaining additional skills to feel safer, Kylie trains in martial arts with Dani weekly. Here, Kylie meets Amalia, a cheery young woman that specializes in healing magic. Siani warns Amalia to be reserved with her healing spells, but Amalia ignores Siani's warning. The relative peace doesn't last long, however, as Kylie and Jordan are soon after attacked by Nimaka, Asuza's right-hand woman, along with two other women associated with Asuza. Siani and Rotanu both effortlessly defeat all three, intentionally not killing them. Rotanu's lack of warning about further incidents despite his hypermnesia furthers Jordan's disillusionment with both Rotanu and magic, seeing them both as ruining his and Kylie's lives.

Attempting to empower herself through martial arts, Kylie continues practicing with Dani and soon defeats her in their mock spars. Kylie sees Dani as unable to teach her further and begs for her to lie, asking her to say Kylie gets to Dani's house earlier than she actually does; this would allow Kylie time to practice magic with Jordan. Dani reluctantly agrees. Nimaka and her allies continue their attacks on Kylie, one of which Richard is present for. Enthralled by magic yet infuriated by Siani, Kylie, and Rotanu, Richard convinces Jordan to "move on" from Kylie and get a "starter girlfriend" to spite Rotanu. Jordan accepts, determined to demonstrate that Rotanu and he are not connected, and begins dating a woman named Emily. Jordan goes on dates with his new girlfriend, but anytime she touches him or initiates an intimate gesture, he has visions of women that look like Kylie.

Kylie continues practicing magic with Siani, and it is during one of these routine practice sessions Siani tells Kylie about an individual that exists to counter-match mages with max magipoten of ninety and above — such as Kylie — calling this individual an "Anti-Existence." While Kylie is initially annoyed that someone else reaps the rewards of her labor, that envy and annoyance quickly shifts to horror once she learns her life is tied to theirs — if she dies, her Anti-Existence will die from a lack of mana, though the reverse does not hold true. While Kylie struggles to process this information, Dani rushes to Kylie's house, panicked after she saw Amalia kidnapped. Siani explains that Amalia was taken by a group that captures mages and experiments on them and that she has never seen her since.

At the next training session between Kylie and Jordan, Kylie tells Jordan about this group. Jordan lashes out at Kylie, overwhelmed by fear, and accuses her of ruining his life. Rotanu attempts to prevent Jordan's outburst, but Siani has recently used blood magic without his knowledge, preventing either of them from gaining control over their younger selves' bodies. Kylie comes home, heartbroken and distressed. Her mother scolds her that evening, having found out about Kylie sneaking out Friday afternoons and the poor grades Kylie has been receiving. Her mother threatens to transfer Kylie to a new school for her senior year if she doesn't improve her academics. The weight of these events pushes Kylie into considering suicide, but the fear of being locked into her next incarnation as her previous incarnations are prevents her from going through with it. She instead blacks out on her bed as she triggers NEO.

The next day, Jordan goes to Kylie's house to apologize for the previous day, finding Kylie in NEO, her consciousness severed from her body. Jordan becomes NEO-Kylie's Arbiter with Rotanu's guidance, which allows him to reestablish Kylie's consciousness. Once Kylie awakens, Siani explains that Jordan has become her NEO state's Arbiter, giving him "control" over her, and that her NEO-state accepted Jordan as Arbiter due to blood magic alterations Kisate and Takite made to Kylie and Jordan, intertwining them at a subconscious level. As proof of his status as Arbiter of her NEO-state, Jordan's aura colors are branded around Kylie's symbol as a thin outline. Jordan and Kylie begin avoiding each other, neither sure what to say.

Richard continues dragging Jordan to the training house, one time arriving as Nimaka attacks Kylie. Once Richard processes that Jordan cannot save him and his life is in danger, Richard triggers his own Act — another individual part of the original reincarnation spell. Richard has a future incarnation named Saite (called "Sai" by Siani and Rotanu), but no past incarnations are present. Jordan brings Richard back to his family's apartment as Saite collapses for the initial cycle. Richard wakes up confused and disgusted with the condition of the apartment Jordan's family lives in. Saite prevents Richard from ignoring Jordan's pleas to not involve others in Jordan's home life, invoking Richard's suggestion ability to calm Jordan's alcoholic, abusive father. Furthering Jordan's disdain of magic, Richard begins avoiding women after one touched his absorption device. In Jordan's mind, magic "takes things away" even from Richard.

Dani asks Kylie for information about Amalia once more, admitting she told her mother about Kylie sneaking out and magic. This destroys the trust Kylie has in Dani, leading to Kylie lashing out as she reminds Dani that they're both at risk of capture by the group that captured Amalia. Dani storms out, and Kylie attempts to refocus on school. As Kylie works with Lianne on their final project for their biology class, Lianne asks why Jordan's and Kylie's auras are so vivid, implying she's a mage. After Lianne presses Kylie a few times, she angrily leaves, only to go missing before arriving home that day.

Nimaka and her two accomplices attack once more, using a spell to separate the older selves from Kylie, Jordan, and Richard. Unknown to Nimaka, this is why Siani and Rotanu allowed them to escape times past. Soon after, Siani pierces Nimaka's symbol, severing her mana connection and killing her while the other two women teleport away. As the creator of the false bodies separating the older selves from their younger hosts, once Nimaka dies, their connection to the past severs. The older selves completely fade from view, leaving Kylie devastated. Jordan interprets their exit as a sign that things are "finally over." Kylie remains in the training house, believing herself to truly be alone. Two months later, a runaway named Maya arrives in Opal Pines, unsure of what awaits her.

# Chapter One

## fresh start

Maya | August 13
Matthews High

I just needed the damn piece of paper. That's all that mattered. I could do this, *would* do this. Yet despite telling myself that more than once in the past few weeks, I still wondered if this had been nothing but a massive mistake. I pulled my jacket tighter around myself. Outside was like a humid swamp hell, but they must've had the AC running full blast inside. It worked for the best since I preferred long sleeves, but outside of work, I hadn't been in an AC'ed environment in weeks now — nearing a month. It brought me back to the question I'd asked myself so many times now: how *was* I going to do this?

Just as predictably, there was only one answer as well: it didn't matter; I had no other option.

More people filed in, all laughing and talking to each other. Likely, I was the only one here that didn't know anyone, but that made sense. They'd probably been together for the past three years, maybe more. Even at my old high school, so much larger than this one, I still was aware of the people in my grade level. Really, I wasn't sure why there were so many high schools in this town to begin with. Three felt like overkill if this one's size was anything to go by.

More students — my classmates, I assumed — shuffled in, wearing short sleeves and shorts, not at all phased by the difference between outside and inside temperatures.

"Why's it so hot out there?" I heard one girl say. Others voiced agreement. I pulled my eyes away, reminding myself that I wasn't here to make friends. Friends only caused problems, so it was better I didn't have them in the first place. Hell knew I'd learned that lesson my fair share already.

Someone finally sat to my right, interrupting the mindless sketch of the classroom I'd been working on. Turning my head, I saw her take in a deep breath. Why'd she sit beside *me*? There were still *plenty* of other open seats literally anywhere else in the classroom. I was in the second row, off to the side, near the window. Most of the students wanted to be near the door so they could rush in and out later, which was why I'd picked the exact opposite.

From the corner of my eye, I saw her pull out a planner, running her eyes over a piece of paper I couldn't read because it was too far away. She wore a t-shirt and jean shorts and had some type of markings around her wrists. Not a tattoo, closer to a scar. Old though, nothing new.

Guess if she's leaving me alone, at least the seat was taken so no one more talkative could occupy it.

I turned my attention back to the sketch. The perspective on it was off; it bothered me, but I didn't want to put the effort into actually fixing it. I hadn't tried to draw anything complex, just what I saw in front of me — the desks, the board, the entrance to the room. Something in my line-art was off though. It was too flat with no depth. Maybe I could hide it with shading. This was yet another thing to pass time until the school day was over and I went back to work.

"Are you new here?" my now-talkative neighbor asked. I nodded, hoping that'd satisfy her curiosity. "I thought so. It's kind of obvious we both are, isn't it?" Her voice softened at the end, so I pretended to not have heard the question. It sounded like she was a talker after all, which was not what I wanted to deal with. Instead, I kept sketching, my eyes on the paper instead of anywhere that might invite further discussion. "My name's Kylie. Nice to meet you."

I glanced at her from the corner of my eyes; if I directed my whole attention at her, she might take that as an invitation for more conversation. "Maya. Same, I guess."

Her head tilted, catching a glimpse of the sketch I'd been working on. "Oh wow, that's amazing. You drew that?" Apparently she wasn't an artist either. Other artists knew better than to snoop on people's sketches. I again nodded. Homeroom hadn't even started yet, and I wanted it over like I wanted this whole year over already. Her voice was contemplative as she glanced around at others in the classroom. "I kind of envy them right now, to be honest. They're with people they know, have known for years, probably."

"Mm." People just got in the way. But I wasn't wasting time arguing with her on this; it wasn't worth either of our times.

An adult walked in, a woman with blonde hair tied in a bun. She went to the teacher's desk in the corner by the entrance door. The student conversations hushed, their attention half focusing on her. This had to be her classroom then. I glanced at the clock above the board: eight thirty-five in the morning. She was late. Hopefully this was just a first day problem and not something that'd be a recurring trend. I wanted her to talk more so that everyone else talked to me less. She calmly walked to the front of the room, saying something to the two students closest to the middle of the room in the front row. A brown-haired girl with gray eyes and thin-rimmed glasses — likely another student since she looked similar in age to the rest of us in here — walked in right as the teacher closed the door, sliding into the seat behind me. I saw my talkative neighbor's posture suddenly stiffen as she turned around to look at her. To her credit, they looked like twins — maybe they were sisters? She turned back around to face the front of the classroom a moment later, her eyes staring at her planner with a perplexed expression. Weird, but whatever. Maybe she'd be distracted with that person instead of talking to me now.

The teacher introduced herself: Mrs. Carslie, who was one

3

of two history teachers in the school. Of note to me, she was the one that taught AP World History, which was my first class after homeroom. I could just keep this seat and didn't need to worry about moving to another. There weren't any morning announcements today, she said, but they would start tomorrow. She said to use the time to check our schedules among ourselves and get to know those around us, so I was stuck with more socializing, the last thing I wanted to deal with.

"Hey," the girl behind me said. "I'm Ashley, new here."

Great, *another* talkative one. Maybe I'd get lucky and they'd entertain each other so I'd be left out of this small talk social dance thing. Kylie turned around and nodded to Ashley. "Wow, I didn't know so many people would transfer senior year. I'm new too. My name's Kylie."

Three people were *not* that many. It really was a small town here, wasn't it?

"What's your story?" Ashley asked, and I unfortunately could tell it was directed at me.

"Maya. Just here because I have to be." I didn't turn around; maybe she'd get the hint. Besides, things would be better once I was out of high school hell. College had to be different. People would leave me alone there.

Ashley snorted. "Aren't we all?"

I thought as social and peppy as both of them were at this hour of the morning, she'd be thrilled to be in high school.

"Anything has to be better than last year," Kylie said, but I wasn't sure she meant for us to hear it since the comment had almost but not quite been under her breath. Her left hand moved to a pendant — no, a ring on a necklace, weird fashion choice — that had been tucked under her t-shirt. Her eyes shifted over to me. "Oh, you're left-handed — me too. I'm excited to have a seat neighbor that doesn't bump into me every two minutes."

"Really?" Ashley said, her foot kicking the back of my chair as she leaned closer. Could they both go somewhere else? "I'm left-handed as well — what a coincidence." Good, they had something to bond over now, and we could all move on with our mornings.

Kylie dropped the ring back under her t-shirt as she turned around to see Ashley better. "Wait, seriously? That's funny."

The bell finally rang, and almost everyone in the class stood up, including Ashley. Unfortunately, that meant only one of my problems left the classroom. Kylie didn't move. I saw her schedule sitting on the corner of her desk and glanced over as subtly as I could.

Great. I shared like half my day with her somehow. So it seemed she was academically intelligent but couldn't take a hint, particularly about how much I wanted to be left alone. She pulled the schedule from the edge of her desk as she wrote something down in her planner before reaching down to her backpack and grabbing a notebook that she flipped open to a blank page. She glanced around, eyes stopping on me. "You're still stuck in here too, huh?"

That was one way to put it. "Yeah."

Her head turned back to the seat where Ashley had been, not yet filled with the students coming into the room now that Ashley had left. "That's so..." she mumbled. I almost asked her what she meant, just because she obviously hadn't intended for me to hear it so maybe she'd understand how it felt to be stuck in conversations she didn't want. With my luck, she'd take that as an invitation to talk *more* though, so I decided against it. Everyone was so damn *talkative* down here. I missed being somewhere where we all ignored each other. She shook her head, as if trying to remove thoughts by doing so. "No. It's a fresh start for the final year."

# *Chapter Two*

## schedules

Something's weird as hell 'bout this, but I ain't sure what it meant. We always met to check schedules the night b'fore a new year started, but Kylie wasn't even home last night. Then today, hadn't seen her in the hall all day. Like how'd we *completely* miss each other *all day*?

I glanced around as I made my way out of the hall. Still no sight of her. Saw Emily talking to Stephanie, someone that'd been here forever like me and Kylie, but I never'd interacted with her much since she's usually in Kylie's classes, not mine. Emily's taking her sweet-ass time talking 'bout whatever, too. Dammit, I couldn't wait around forever today. Had work an hour from now 'til basically closing, and there's no way in hell it wasn't already gonna suck. I'd always been a morning person, but couldn't work the damn early-ass morning shifts 'cause've school starting back. Last time I got stuck closing, was there past ten, and I didn't have hope tonight'd be better. Felt like a goddamn labor mule there: carry this, stock that.

But whatever. It got Jewel off my ass finally, even if the apartment'd gone to hell in a handbasket since I ain't been

7

around to clean it as much as normal. And of course, Thomas ain't picking up any fuckin' slack in that department, and if I tripped over his motherfuckin' goddamn piles of clothes while trying to get dressed in the morning again—

Emily ran to me, latching onto my arm. "There you are!"

Whatever perfume she had on, she'd used like half the damn bottle. Did my best not to gag but also was suddenly glad I didn't have any classes or lunch with her. I'm used to being alone, but I still ain't used to suffocating from her damn perfume fumes. "H-hey. Good first day?"

She traced a pattern onto my neck, which had me nervous as fuck as her fingers got 'bout half an inch away from my absorption device. It's tucked under my t-shirt, but still, didn't want anyone near the damn thing with the conversations it'd invite if they touched it. She kissed my jaw, missing my cheek. Might've been 'cause I'd hit another growth spurt the past month or so, lucky me. "It was *terrible*, not you or Richard around anywhere. Was *so* boring."

"Ah, uh, yeah." Richard's at college in Atlanta, bitching the whole way there and back too while he's at it. Ain't even said where he's going, just that we're still meeting up for "training" regardless. Atlanta had to have been — shit, five hours? Seven hours? I didn't know how far away. Just that I'd never been, prob'bly never would. Even Savannah I'd only been to like once.

A sigh came from her lips as she leaned her head on my shoulder, us walking toward the exit. I tensed, not expecting *quite this much* on school grounds where people'd see us and fuck, would we get written up for PDA over this? I didn't need damn detention the first week; it'd happen soon enough without her help. "I hope we'll get to see him again soon." Couldn't tell her I'd seen him three days ago and he hadn't once asked 'bout her — or anyone here, for that matter. He didn't give a damn 'bout any woman I've seen with him, her included. Hell, since his Act, hadn't even acknowledged they existed basically after whatever the hell happened that one time with his absorption device. It's yet another reminder 'bout how we're just mimicries of normal teenagers. Her finger reached higher, to the nape of my neck, as she twisted some of my hair around her finger. "Oh, your hair's getting longer. Are you growing it out like Richard's?"

"Ah, uh, just ain't had time to get it cut." I rubbed the back of my neck, glancing away as I started walking faster, away from where others'd see us together. Work'd been damn killing me since I'd started it up, and ain't looking forward to doing that *and* school now that we're back. Guess it's only for this year, and I could always drop out if it got too much. Ain't like it mattered if I dropped out or got the diploma now that I had a job. I'd hit my societal expectation cap: not in prison, actually contributing to society in a dead-end job.

Her finger traced down my neck once more as she latched back onto my arm. "Hmm." As if she had the best idea, she added, "I think you shouldn't. Looks better."

Yeah, except then I'd look more like *him,* and that's the last thing I wanted, bangs entirely too in my face as it was. Not like it mattered though. Ain't sure when I'd be finding time to get a haircut anytime soon. "You think?"

"Totally. Also, I need to get some fall outfits... You wanna come with?" For the first time, was actually fuckin' happy 'bout this damn job. I *hated* clothes shopping with her. Still didn't get the point of me being there.

I shook my head. "Oh, uh, sorry. Got work tonight 'til close. Heading over there as soon as I drop shit off, basically."

She pouted as she let go of my arm, breaking all contact between us. Great, now she's pissed. Ain't a lie though, had the fuckin' schedule for the week more than memorized as usual now thanks to damn hypermnesia. "Fine. I'll just see you later then." Without another word, she left my side.

Ain't like I wanted to be stuck working. Ain't like I wanted a lot of the shit in my life, actually, but what else am I s'posed to do? Do one thing, get bitched at. Don't do it, get bitched at by someone else. Thought it'd get better with them gone, but really, just gave more time for everyone else to bitch at me.

Increasing my pace, I trudged to the apartment so I could get changed for work — that just left more time for my thoughts though, drifting back to the one person I'd expected to see today and hadn't. No way in hell she's missing the first day of school, and yet... it's like she completely vanished. Was something I'd never experienced since we met in elementary. Maybe the gap felt even wider now 'cause I'd gotten used to Richard there too, and he's graduated now.

It's just me here, with the same people that'd always hated me and prob'bly always would. Guess it didn't matter anymore. Was the last year of this hellhole anyways.

# *Chapter Three*

## all mixed in

Maya | August 31
Opal Pines Streets

It's always the damn group projects. I should've expected it, but I didn't think it'd happen so *soon*. Why did we have a group project two weeks into the year? What fresh hell was this class? And it's not like I had people racing to work with me, so I couldn't turn Kylie down when she offered to be my partner for the stupid English Lit assignment. I was basically with her all day as it was, so what was *more* time together?

I had the bag I'd brought with me months back, filled with the English novel we're supposed to be reviewing, my notes, sketchbook, and overnight clothes. We had to get this done tonight since I needed to work tomorrow night and thus needed to be back at my apartment before tomorrow's evening shift started. I'd managed to buy a few sets of night clothes and about four days' of day clothes outside of what I wore for work, so I visited the local laundromat rather often. I kept seeing the same faces there when I went, and even worse, they took my frequent visits as an invitation to *talk* to me; I'd never been in such a *small town* before where everyone seemed to care about everyone's business, gossiping to literal strangers.

If anything, I was lucky with how things had played so far. She could've asked to come over to my apartment. No doubt, she'd ask questions — like where were my parents, why was I alone — and there were no answers I felt inclined to share. Instead, I followed the directions from school to her house — well, her parents' house, more like — that I'd printed out from the school library's printers. I was almost there, walking past rows of admittedly quaint townhomes, most well maintained. The specific building address — unit, townhome, whatever it was — that she provided didn't particularly stand out compared to the others. It didn't have much of a front yard, almost all concrete leading into the one-car garage, same as many of the other townhomes here. A few people nearby waved to me, and I waved back, having learned that's a *thing* they do down here.

More quickly than before — I didn't want further attention from anyone that hadn't noticed me yet because then they'd want *more* waves and maybe even to talk or something — I walked up the steps. Without meaning to, I paused before my finger reached the doorbell. Why was I hesitating? Why did my heart race? I was here because of the project, not because we were friends or she wanted me around. No one wanted me around. I knew that. And that was fine, because I didn't need anyone else. Moreover, this was stupid. It was a doorbell, not some big monster waiting to attack me. I pushed the button and heard steps from the other side. An older woman with almost black hair and dark blue eyes greeted me. I shifted my eyes away from her. "Um. Hello, I'm Maya. Is this the Rae household?"

"Oh, come in, come in," she said, opening the door further and stepping to the side. "For the group project?" Nodding, I came inside, feeling the rush of AC greet my face, my cheeks flushing from the contrast of the outside's humid heat compared to the crisp indoor air. "Kylie! She's here!"

A door above us opened, and I saw Kylie up on the steps, dressed not much different from what she normally wore to school outside of missing her socks and shoes. "Oh, perfect timing. You want to head on up?" I wasn't sure where *up* led. I glanced around, not sure if I should leave my shoes by the door or not. I didn't see their shoes there, but I'd never gotten when it was and wasn't fine to be in a house with shoes on. She stared at me, almost through me, as she came down the stairs before I had a chance to reach down to take my shoes off. She gently grabbed my wrist as she pulled, guiding me up the stairs. I guess she didn't care I still had my shoes on?

Not having much choice, I followed her up the staircase. She released my wrist as I trailed behind her. She was faster than I realized, and I wasn't able to keep pace with her. It suddenly made sense why her elective was PE. She had to be the athletic type, even if she seemed more lean than outright muscular. That felt off though with how often I saw her studying, prepping with one book or another. I wasn't even sure exactly *what* she studied so intently when, despite us sharing multiple classes, it rarely related to homework I could recognize. Whatever it was kept her from trying to make small talk, so I took the win and never asked. "Thanks, Mom!" she called as she led me to a room on the left, closing the door behind me. The sound startled me more than I cared to admit and caused me to jump, but her back was to me so she didn't notice.

Glancing around, her room was remarkably... normal. I wasn't sure what I'd expected, but she had photos on her walls of people I'd never seen, mostly a red-haired girl and a brown-haired guy, a few of what looked to be her and her mother over the years. She looked so happy in all of the pictures with people that she must've been close with.

I knew why I'd moved so far away and went to a new school my senior year, but I didn't understand why she had. It wasn't my business to ask, but it hadn't been a question I'd ever considered at school before seeing these pictures and people she was so close to.

She had a thin, black laptop on her desk, half-inch binders of various colors lined up beside it. A clouded-blue book unlike the others was sandwiched between the binders, looking more like a hardback but with no lettering or decoration on the spine. She grabbed a green binder and flipped through it, her planner on the left side of her desk.

13

Not knowing what else to do, I stood where I'd been when she'd closed the door and continued glancing around, bag in my hand. There was something so... tender almost... about her house. Something I'd only really seen in tv shows or movies. I shifted my weight as I watched her be absorbed in whatever page was open in the binder.

"Is that for English?" I asked.

She nodded. "Yeah, sorry. Got distracted." Moving to the bed, she made a waving gesture toward me. "Get comfortable. Doubt this will be polite and end quickly." I glanced around, unsure how to be "comfortable" in someone else's house. "Oh right, you don't know. Been a second since someone slept over, sorry." She walked from her bed, passing behind me to a denim couch on the other side of her room. "It's a pullout, so you can sleep here." She removed the cushions, showing a frame under it. "Already has a fresh sheet, and I'll get blankets down in a bit. But yeah, you can put your stuff over here if you'd like." She tossed the cushions back on, afterward sitting back on her bed.

I did as she'd said, laying my bag on the couch, my shoes on the carpet against the frame. I hated the texture of carpet, so I left my socks on. Not knowing what else to do, I sat on the bed beside her. For the first time, I saw her ankles up close, scarred similarly to what she had on her wrists. They weren't cuts, not like the scars on my right arm or across my stomach, not like the bruises that had finally begun to fade. These had come from something different entirely.

Her eyes did that thing that felt as if she saw through me, her lips pushing into a frown after. It'd happened at school numerous times, but there was something intense about it here at her house compared to at school, as if she knew things she had no way to know.

I didn't want her to know me, didn't want anyone to know me.

For a brief moment, I watched her eyes drift to my right arm before darting away. I had my jacket on, so there's no way she could've seen anything. I didn't like the attention though, so I said, "Are all those binders on your desk for class? Don't think I've seen some of them at school." More like, not all of those could've fit in her backpack.

"Oh, um, not quite. Some other extracurricular stuff I was working on before you got here. Just forgot to put it up so it's all mixed in, but nothing important to getting things done." For nothing important, she spoke faster than normal. So those binders had something she didn't want me to know about. Fair enough.

"All right."

Her hand grasped that ring on a necklace she always wore, usually tucked under her shirt. I half wondered why she didn't wear it as a ring, but I didn't want curiosity to open the door for her to ask me questions. "So, have you finished the book?" she asked.

It hadn't been a fun read, but school reading never was. "Last week."

A sigh of relief came from her. "Great, me too. So I don't mind doing the speaking for the presentation, but would you mind looking up the quotes tonight while I work on the slides?"

Was she *actually* a decent group partner? I just expected I'd end up doing it all. It'd always been that way. Maybe I'd somehow survive until the end of the year after all.

# *Chapter Four*

## missing

Jordan | September 1
Training House

Yet another entirely too goddamn hot Saturday while I'd rather be somewhere else, yet I'm stuck here in the damn training house again. Thought I'd be done once *they'd* all left, but no. Kylie hadn't tried to drag my ass here, but Richard had no problems doing so. At least I got paid to suffer at work, labor slave or no.

Guess for all my bitching and how much I hated this damn house and everything it represented, I'm looking forward to talking to someone besides Emily. I still ain't seen Kylie, and I hadn't had time to try to stop by her house again. It's all weird as fuck, so I didn't know if I should visit in the first place. There's no way I'd just missed her at school this many days now. She ain't there anymore. With all the years I'd known her, she'd never just disappeared like this. But that one bitch'd been killed by Siani, and *he'd* said that things'd be over once they left, so like... she's fine, right? But then why wasn't she at school?

Things'd been so damn hectic trying to balance work and school and shit, I ain't really sure what to do, what to think.

The door creaked open, pulling me from my thoughts.

Richard brushed dirt or some other shit off'a himself. "Yo," he said as he shut the door behind him.

"'Sup?" Even with him here, I still would've preferred being in the library to get outta this damn heat. Fuckin' hated South Georgian summers or falls or whatever the hell this time of the year qualified as. One of the only benefits to the damn store I worked in's that at least it's got the damn AC running, even if I froze my ass off at the beginning of my shift 'til I got moving around.

He scoffed, crossing his arms over his chest. "These freshmen classes they signed me up for are utterly useless. Just busywork, and David kept bitching about how I *had* to pass college. As if it matters."

Wasn't that what most parents expected when they sent their kid off to college? Though, hearing him carry on bitching 'bout his classes just reminded me how *soon* that was now. Most people our age're getting ready for or going to college, ain't they? Knew I'd always be sorted away, separated out, but guess it hadn't clicked that now's when it'd happen. No way in hell Kylie'd not go to college next fall too — Ms. Rae wouldn't let her, and she'd be right to make Kylie go. As smart as Kylie was, she should go wherever smart people went to college. Had always been the top of her class. Meanwhile, I'd be in this same town I'd never left, doing the same shit I always had. "Y-yeah."

Richard let out a bitchy huff. "I haven't had time to practice the actually important shit." Really, that's what happened when we met here on Saturdays: he showed me whatever *trick* he'd learned, and I told him how impressive it was. Ain't like I wanted to know more 'bout or be more involved in this shit than I had to be, so I didn't *practice* a damn thing and preferred it that way. Luckily, he never noticed I had nothing to show. Or maybe he noticed and just didn't give a fuck. That's more likely. "Too much 'initiation' this and 'tour' that, like I *want* to be there or some shit. It's a massive pain in the ass, having to fly back and forth."

So if he hadn't *practiced* anything, why were we in this damn house still? I mean, he had no way to cancel on me, I guess, since we didn't even have a landline and I'd never had a cell phone. But that just meant we could leave *now* and not be stuck in this damn place I thought I'd escaped from whenever *they'd* left. "So should we go somewhere else?" Emily'd be happy as ever if she knew he's in town, so I could make her day at least. And as long as we went somewhere with AC, I didn't really give a damn past that.

He glanced away, as if something caught his attention. Not sure what could've since this ain't near a damn thing. "Yeah. No reason to burn in this sauna." One of the few consistencies with Richard's that he's confident as fuck, and I wish I had even half of his confidence. That made it all the stranger when he avoided eye contact with me, something I did all the time and never seen from him b'fore. "Think it's going to be this way for a month easily, which sucks like hell. Bunch of babysitters up there." He brushed hair off his shoulder b'fore crossing his arms across his chest. "Might be easier to just invite you over to my house."

Was he uncomfortable 'bout his house? He'd never mentioned it as a possibility, but I didn't think he'd ever experienced embarrassment. I knew he ain't exactly rushing back to the apartment I'm at as well, and I couldn't exactly blame him given I didn't wanna go back either but needed to sleep and shower eventually. "Uh, like today?"

He snorted, as if I'd just forced him into a decision he ain't comfortable with — as if I *could* force him to do a damn thing. "Next Saturday, meet at 100 Azalea Way on far North-East block."

Dammit, I hated when he did that — knew my hypermnesia'd catch it, so just threw out whatever shit he wanted and expected me to catch it. I mean, I did, but still felt awkward as fuck, given I didn't *want* my hypermnesia. Just another fuckin' thing I didn't have a damn choice over, like all the goddamn magic shit. "Oh, uh, sure."

"And plan on spending the night. It'll be one night away from that hell-hovel you pretend is a living space."

Rubbing the back of my neck, I glanced away; ain't sure how to take the irritation in his tone. He'd never tried his suggestion ability shit on me, never tried it again on anyone in my family as far as I knew. Even though he definitely could've, he'd never tried to "fix things" again. Maybe I shouldn't've stopped him back then; I ain't completely sure why I had. Maybe it'd just been nerves that it'd piss Father off even more than normal, really get the shit beat outta not just me but Jewel, Elaine, and Thomas, maybe even Richard too.

This town's all I'd ever known, and the idea of being somewhere else's terrifying as hell all on its own. I couldn't imagine never seeing Elaine, Jewel, or Thomas again, leaving them to fend for themselves.

Likely, change just scared me shitless. Nothing more than that.

# Chapter Five

## sunset

Maya | September 8
Grand Cinema Movie Theater

Considering how small this town was, I was fortunate that I'd found a job willing to hire me for almost full-time hours despite being a high school student. Even better, I likely wasn't affording cable anytime soon, so working at this theater let me see whatever movies were out, even if it took multiple partial viewings to piece together something resembling a plot. I appreciated the discounted junk food I often bought with my employee discount, too. Fifteen percent off wasn't much, but all my apartment kitchen had was a stove-top, small fridge, and sink, so it wasn't like I'd be cooking that much to begin with nor did I honestly have the energy to cook between school and work. I'd never been especially averse to eating the same thing either, so I didn't mind five days straight of hot dogs here and there.

I stood at the back of the showing room as the credits rolled. It was the last show of the night before we closed, so the rest of the staff here was *subtly* cleaning and preparing things to close so that we could all get home earlier. To get me out of any last-minute concession station assignments, I'd volunteered to sweep up this showing room along with throwing out trash.

This and setting up rooms were among my favorite tasks — if they could be called that — at work, mainly because the ticket stand and concession counter involved entirely too many people. I wasn't supposed to handle cash to begin with until I turned eighteen, but I'd unfortunately learned that certain managers didn't care about that technicality if a few people called out, even when I pointed out that it was illegal. In fact, that manager had doubled down on me working positions that handled cash after that, and it was one of the few joys of being in school now, given that said manager was part-time and worked weekend morning shifts where I didn't see him as much.

The lights turned on, the movie finally finished, and the last few people left, talking to each other as they exited the room. Most of the latest showings — this one included — finished between nine and nine thirty at night on weekdays. I'd expected to find more high school and college students making out during the late-night showings, but it'd only happened a few times so far. Not that I was complaining, but I wasn't sure why else they'd be watching some of these comically terrible movies in a town that generally shut down at sunset. To their credit, the dating location scene was likely rather sparse here, given everyone — Kylie included — just talked about how much they went to a *park* for fun.

After I finished sweeping up a mostly clean screening room thanks to only a few people being in here to begin with, I wiped down the counter where the trash was and emptied that bag before I took it to the back to the dumpster. "Hey, Maya, right?" I heard a woman call. I looked up, seeing a woman a few years older than me — likely a college student — with freckles and dyed bright pink hair. "Great job on cleanup. We're about to head to the bar. Wanna join?" I stared at her, wondering if she was serious or not, both because I wasn't actually sure if the bars were still open, given nothing else was in this town at this hour, and because I obviously wasn't of age to be invited in the first place. "C'mon, it'll be fun!"

Was this some type of trap? I couldn't get caught doing anything unnecessarily illegal, not until I was at least eighteen. Preferably not at all, actually. She had this awkward laugh that

22

rose in pitch the longer it went on. So it *was* a joke? But she kept staring at me, as if waiting for my answer. "I'm underage."

Her eyes widened at me as her posture leaned away from me. "Wait, *really*? But you go to Jenn, right?"

Within just a few weeks here, I'd learned of "Jenn" — Jenn Community College — where almost all the high school students went after graduating. I happily intended to follow that pattern, given the so-called cheap tuition and ability to at least get started on college and maybe get into a work-study position with better pay than here. Even better, Jenn accepted basically everyone, so as long as I kept a decent GPA this year, I'd be accepted and could try for scholarships to help pay for tuition and some living expenses. "I'm a senior in high school."

I wasn't particularly amused as her eyes drifted below my chin to my breasts. As unflattering as the work t-shirt was, I still apparently looked *mature for my age,* as I'd heard others say numerous times. "O-oh. I just — Jake, why are you laughing?!" The woman's cheeks burned bright red as I heard a few of the other employees laugh behind her as they watched our exchange. I guess this was some type of prank on her. It wasn't the first time I'd been involuntarily involved in a joke, but it left a bitter taste, nonetheless. I walked off. I needed to finish this shift so I could get home and shower. As I'd explained to Kylie and Ashley many times now, I didn't have time for friends; I barely had time for homework and did as much during the school day as I could.

Yet again, I just needed to get the damn piece of paper. That's all I needed, not anything else.

# Chapter Six

## failure

Kylie | September 26
Matthews High

I didn't know what it was about this year, but I felt exhausted all the time lately; it didn't matter if it was first thing in the morning or the end of the day. By the end of the week, I took hours-long naps after school on Fridays, and I still slept extra on Saturdays and Sundays. Maya sharing so many classes with me had become a blessing both because she was reliable and because I had someone to talk to, which helped keep me awake. Even though I'd never been a morning person, I was usually mentally awake by third period. Even that wasn't the case this year, though. Gym being midday was another savior. Between it and lunch, I managed to get something resembling a second wind to finish out the school day.

This morning was even worse than normal though. I'd had a premonition after school yesterday, this sharp stabbing in my lower back like no premonition I'd ever experienced. All the other premonitions had been punches, and even calling them "premonitions" was generous, considering they'd never actually happened, at least that I'd seen; I still wasn't sure why Sia had referred to them as such, really. Either way, the one yesterday had been different, more painful and overwhelming in a way that'd left me in bed the rest of the day.

Taking a deep breath, I forced air through my lungs. The premonition didn't matter. Right then, all I needed to do was focus on running laps. We were stuck in the gym because it was raining out, which meant no fresh breeze to help wake me up. At least we got to avoid the humidity and heat for once. Sure, this wasn't an actual workout compared to the routines I did at home, but I appreciated the mindlessness of this class. My brain took a fifty-minute nap, just one lap after another, around the rectangle line in the gym with all the other students.

Yet another time I realized how reliant on Sia I'd become: I wanted to ask her to take over, let me nap for just an hour or two. But I couldn't. It's just me now, no other consciousnesses sharing a body with me. No one was here to help me or take over if I stumbled. There were no reassurances I'd be safe. She wasn't here, and she couldn't save me if something happened. I couldn't rely on anyone else now. Sia wouldn't have faltered, and I couldn't either: it was my turn to be "Sia" now, strong and smart enough to handle anything. And I wasn't there, not by a long shot.

My empathy yet again made life more difficult: I wasn't out of breath from just jogging, but my classmates were, so my cheeks flushed and heart raced from the empathic reads. At least *he* wasn't here, making things even worse. No especially loud emotions forcing themselves through my lungs. It was better this way. I wouldn't get in his way, and he didn't want me around if it meant he'd be *mixed up* in magic. This way, he had his normal life, one I couldn't even imagine anymore.

He'd never stopped by this summer. Not once. I'd gone with Mom to help her at Jenn the night before school had started back since I'd known it'd sting to wait all evening for him to not show up again. It was better to just avoid the disappointment and move on. That was the point of Matthews: a new start. I was done crying. Sia wouldn't have wallowed in pity, and I couldn't afford to either. She said it was my turn to take charge, and that's exactly what I'd been doing.

Still... I'd kill for a nap right then. This was my third — or

**26**

wait, was it fifth? — lap. It had to have been fifth actually, since I saw Mr. Clark walking toward me, a faint excitement clashing against the overwhelming hive of boredom and dismay from the students in the gym. "Rae," he said. "Were you in track at your last school?"

"Oh, um, no. This is my first PE since middle school." Only reason Mom let me take this class was that I couldn't graduate without a PE credit. It was useless, she'd said, and didn't contribute to my education. The principal didn't care and wouldn't make an exception, so here I was. While it wasn't something I thought I'd ever say, I was glad for state regulations because I was already in basically all AP outside of this one class. I was the only one with so many AP classes at this school, so I was pretty sure Mom had already done some fussing about my classes in the name of *furthering my education* — education I'd frankly stopped caring about because when people wanted me dead, what was the point? But I couldn't say that to Mom. I couldn't get her involved, and I had to keep magic under wraps. Who knew what would happen if the people that hated mages found out about me? Amalia had never come back, and I'd never heard from Lianne after she'd left that day and gone missing.

I wished I didn't feel Mr. Clark's enthusiasm as he said, "You should apply. We have one spot left this year."

"I'm a senior, so I wouldn't want to take the spot from someone who could work with the team longer." I didn't have time to waste at this school beyond what I was already stuck here for. Thankfully, even if he mentioned this to Mom, unless he attached a full scholarship somehow, she would back me up since she'd never cared about physical health if it got in the way of academic pursuits. As it was, she'd already been *hinting* I should look at what university to attend next year.

I just didn't care anymore.

Mr. Clark was exasperated. I braced for the on-coming argument. Why couldn't I just run eight more laps and be left alone? I didn't have the energy for this back-and-forth. "If you went to state level, there's some scholarship opportunities."

"Some scholarship opportunities" wasn't enough bait to force me into dealing with track, but I still didn't want that info

**27**

passed on to Mom. "Can I think about it and get back to you? I'm still adjusting to my classes right now."

Maybe that was the giveaway I wasn't biting. Even without empathy, his sigh was rather dejected. "Of course."

Squeezing my eyes shut then opening them, I stumbled as I felt lightheaded — like I'd cast an intense spell or been past exhaustion. But I'd slept the same as normal, and I hadn't cast anything intense in literal months now. That was its own problem, actually, but especially since school had started, I'd been concentrating on surviving each day. I barely practiced magic during the weekends lately. Even my exercise time had been cut by homework and naps last week, something I didn't want to make a habit of.

What was wrong with me?

Maybe I was just dehydrated. I mean, that could still happen despite mana, right? I actually wasn't sure, but if I wasn't dehydrated, maybe cold — or even lukewarm — water would wake me up enough to make it to lunch. I stumbled over to the water fountain tucked in the corner of the gym. Leaning down, I drank some of the water. My throat had been drier than expected, but the water did nothing to wake me up, that grogginess still weighing on me.

An aura appeared right behind me, positioned between me and the rest of my class. The fuchsia color was familiar, though I couldn't place how, and, even more concerning, extremely vivid compared to anyone in this class that I'd seen so far. I straightened my posture, turning around to see who was behind me that hadn't been anywhere in the gym mere seconds prior. No one was immediately behind me, so I scanned the gym, looking for someone I didn't recognize.

The only other person that had a bright aura in this school was Ashley, but she wasn't in this class, and even then, her aura was gray, almost matching her eyes. When we'd first met, I'd been confused with how similar her aura was to Lianne's, but Lianne was gone. I knew that.

Intense emotions slammed into me, a hate that was raw and barely contained, heart racing and blood pumping. But from where? It certainly wasn't me. I was exhausted but not particularly angry at anything or anyone. For one, that'd require entirely too much energy from me right then. Materializing in front of me was one of the women that'd been with Nimaka. "Look who's here." I didn't remember her name, but her eyes — that lime green outline — were the same as Nimaka's had been, as Asuza's irises had been.

"Y-you — but why?" They'd never attacked in the open. I'd assumed, just like myself, they could get the attention of the people that hated mages. Somewhere public — like this gym, this whole school — attracted too much attention, risked the wrong person seeing and them going missing and being experimented on like Amalia and Lianne.

She slugged me across the jaw, and I staggered back, not anticipating the blow or remotely having the reaction speed to adjust for it in my worn-out state. Everything moved in slow motion as I saw her fist slam into my other cheek, but I just *couldn't move*, too slow with every attempted dodge or shift I made. I wasn't awake enough to fight back even after my heart raced from the endorphins and pain from her punch still vibrated through my cheek. The third punch shifted from my face to my skull, my vision doubling from the impact. Panic ate through me, throat dry and fingers trembling. I gripped the cool concrete wall in an attempt to steady myself. "Feeling a little drowsy, are we?" Why was she so smug? How'd she even know that I felt tired? Something was wrong, was...

I felt her fingers on my throat, ripping me from the wall as she grabbed my hands, smashing them together. A wince slipped from my lips. I was unable to keep up with what was going on as everything ached, my vision still unsteady and breaths disheveled. Something sharp poked through my gym shirt into my lower back, liquid I suspected was blood dripping down my skin. I tried to free my hands but as I did so, she pressed that sharp point further, a black haze momentarily filling my vision. "How...?" I sharply inhaled as she pushed whatever blade she had through more of my back— a pain I recognized, what I'd experienced last night during the premonition.

"Anti-magic sure is effective." Anti-magic? "And now, you're going to suffer, feel the pain you forced on us."

What did she mean by that? My vision finally steadied just in time to see the second woman that had been with Nimaka was here too, holding one of my classmates — Gabriella — by her hair as Gabriella screamed. My eyes met this second woman's and she smiled like she'd been waiting for me to notice her. Her sword stabbed through Gabriella's throat; I felt as if I'd been the one stabbed, coughing but no blood coming, air escaping from my throat as if it couldn't reach my lungs. She tossed Gabriella as if she was a discarded doll, this time grabbing another classmate — Timothy — by the neck. She threw him so hard I felt like his spine — my spine — shattered. Alexa's arm disconnected from her no longer breathing chest, Drew's thumb from his hand, a line of red liquid connecting the two. Next was Sammy, then James, then Alexis, and even Mr. Clark that I'd been talking to about track club mere minutes ago. Why hadn't they run? I saw — felt — each stab, each of my classmates and Mr. Clark and they all—

I couldn't help them, still held down by this first woman, no fight in me as each scream echoed through my ears, each stab as if it was my body instead of theirs.

The track outline was coated in bodies, the rubber on the gym floor a deep red instead of light yellowish-brown. Crimson everywhere, even from me, whatever blade my captor had still lodged into me. They had nothing to do with any of this. "Why?"

"Why?" she snapped, pushing the blade fully through my stomach, making it poke out through my shirt as more blood dripped down both sides of me. My eyes watered. The pain wasn't even the worst part anymore, the sight and screams of my dead and dying classmates echoing over and over in my ears, shrill screams fading to consuming silence. "You took Lord Asuza, our sister Nimaka. And you dare ask *why*?" She withdrew the blade, kicking me to the rubber coated red from my own puddle of blood. "Listen to their pathetic pleas." I couldn't *not* hear them, begging, crying, puking, all of it pushing in as my vision blurred and everything smeared and I only *felt*. "And know it's all your fault. If only you'd let Lord Asuza have his way, none of this would've ever happened."

Her boot stepped on my spine while her other foot kicked my cheek like a ball, my consciousness fading out.

# Chapter Seven

## quiet little town

Maya | September 26
Matthews High

We'd been under lockdown for over an hour. This was just some small town — people *knew* each other. How could anything dangerous be happening *here*? I thought it'd been one of the dumb drills at first, but this lockdown hadn't ended after ten minutes of being confined together with all the lights off. We'd been huddled in the art supply closet, and it was too many people for this tiny closet, everyone pressing into me and me pressing into them. No one dared to whisper, and we were too cramped to even check our phones — not that mine had data to burn in the first place, but people around me probably did and would've been looking things up.

There were steps, someone opening the classroom door. A person to the right of me gripped my arm, and I bit my tongue to prevent making a sound as their fingers ran across a still healing scar on my forearm, covered by my jacket. I knew better than to snap at them for touching me, knew better than to speak at all. Their tight grip wasn't that different from my own racing heart. I didn't know why I cared. Better to die here than be taken back. At least it'd be quick here.

"This is the police! Area secured!"

Was it a lie? A trap?

We were about to find out either way because the art teacher yelled something I couldn't process and then opened the door. I didn't know if I could move. Others around me were the same, the light in the classroom so bright after an hour in a pitch-black room. I heard statements I vaguely processed about how we needed to get out, leave, don't worry about our things. I always kept my apartment keys and cell on me — regardless of rules — so I snuck my sketchbook from where it'd been on the table before the lock-down had started and acted like I'd had it the whole time as I followed a line of students and teachers escorted to the exit. We were being evacuated. There was a reason *to* evacuate.

Hushed whispers started all around me as we moved through the main hallway toward the building entrance. "It's fourth period PE. My mom texted me — it's all over the news."

Something *had* happened. In this quiet little town, this unremarkable school.

Another woman from my art class whispered back, "Gabbi's in that class! She's not picking up her phone."

The doors were held open by people in black uniforms, armed police escorting us to the building exit where even more emergency personnel waited outside. The sight in front of me was surreal: stretchers and ambulances and white sheets over what had to be students underneath, sirens blazing as emergency vehicles both entered and exited. Someone that looked like an authority figure but who I didn't know was yelling that school was cancelled and we needed to vacate the premise, over and over. All around me, people sobbed — to their parents, in front of stretchers.

I had no parent waiting for me. Searching around, I looked for faces I'd tried not to learn — not Samantha, not Charles, not Ashley, not—

Kylie had fourth period PE. That was one of the two classes we didn't share. Was Kylie under one of the sheets like so many bodies now were? Was she hospitalized? Was she past hospitalization, eyes never again opening? Her mother would be here, but I didn't see her anywhere around. The few times I'd met her, she'd been warmer than I'd ever seen my own parents be.

Why did I care? It would have been better if she wasn't around. This demonstrated she was just a vulnerability that would mess me up.

They kept yelling to leave the school grounds, all the commotion overwhelming me. Where would I even go? I was always at school, work, or my apartment. Even though I desperately needed the money, I didn't want to go into work earlier than my already-scheduled evening shift.

Ambulances rushed past me, one after another — a line of them, sirens blaring so much I covered my ears without realizing. More ahead, more behind. I didn't know where the hospital was. I hadn't been and definitely couldn't afford to go even if I needed the care. My feet followed the trail of ambulances; I wasn't sure why, just like I wasn't sure why my heart raced now that I was no longer even at school. I was fine. Whatever had happened, the culprits had to have been caught with as much police presence as was around.

Yet... I kept walking, kept following these vehicles down roads I'd not yet explored. My actions made no sense. This was why I couldn't get attached to people: I'd just end up hurt again.

But why had *she* been in that class, out of anyone at school?

I saw the hospital down the hill I'd been walking down, a dark gray building that had been around for decades, judging by the chipped paint. Even with the ambulances driving in, the atmosphere outside the hospital was completely different to the school ground; the hospital maintained the serene tranquility I'd seen from the town so far despite what had just happened. As I moved through the parking lot, I saw the ambulances at a separate entry from the sign indicating the hospital's lobby entrance. I approached the lobby's glass entrance doors and they slid open automatically. The rush of sterile smells and AC filled my senses, the lobby eerily empty with only a handful of people around, including a woman behind the front desk.

Why was I here? I wasn't even family, hadn't known Kylie for two months — *if* she was even here to begin with.

"Are you hurt, Sweetie?" the lady behind the front desk asked someone. She had to be a receptionist.

After a second passed, I realized she stared straight at me. I shook my head. Kylie's mom wasn't out in the lobby. That was good, right? Maybe Kylie had gone home early and missed all this. Yet I didn't want to approach the counter regardless. My heart raced so fast it hurt; I felt winded despite standing still. "Is —" I swallowed, glancing down to the cream-colored plastic tiles that covered the flooring. "Was Kylie — Kylie Rae?" I didn't know how to ask or why I was even asking in the first place.

"Oh, Sweetie." She tapped a few keys on the keyboard. I wasn't the first or last to ask about a classmate, I had the time to now notice: others had filled in behind me or sat in the lobby as they cried. Why had I taken time from people here who actually needed attention? What was she even able to tell me — wasn't patient information private? Another second passed before the receptionist nodded at me. Kylie *was* here, had been hospitalized from what had happened at school. But she wasn't dead, not yet. "She's in room 118. Go on, Dear."

I nodded, stepping away from the counter. Before I'd left earshot, I heard hiccups and cries from others behind me who hadn't been as lucky. "Lucky" wasn't right. Just because Kylie was in a room didn't mean she was fine. She could be in a coma or on life support.

112. 115. 116. 117.

My feet stopped, turning to my right. Each hospital room had a window to see the patient's bed and 118 was no exception: Kylie's mom sat on a chair, eyes red. Kylie was in the patient bed, her face purple and red, hospital gown on as machines were connected to her. But the machine's lines steadily fluctuated up and down, no flatline anywhere on the graph I could make out.

She was alive.

My hand accidentally rested on the handle, pressing the door open. What was I doing? What right did I have to interrupt this moment between Kylie and her mom? Yet despite seeing her hooked up in a hospital bed with her lip busted and bruises along her right arm, despite hearing the soft beeps from the machine wired to her vitals, *she was still breathing*. I brought my hand over my mouth as I clinched my eyes shut, water rising to my eyes as I quickly inhaled and exhaled. Why did I care? We'd barely known each other for a month. I'd let myself get too attached. I should've known better but... but...

A girl with short red hair ran past me into the room. She went to Kylie's side and grabbed her arm. Kylie didn't move, likely wasn't conscious at all. Kylie's mom stood, saying something to the redhead I couldn't hear. She then stepped away, the door fully opening before I could hide. I couldn't move away quickly from right in front of the door — an uninvited guest peering into a vulnerable moment for this family I wasn't part of. I didn't know what to say, so I looked down at my old sneakers.

"It's all right, Dear. You can go in, especially if you came all this way." She didn't yell at me to mind my own business, didn't tell me I wasn't part of their family and how the receptionist shouldn't have given me the information on where Kylie was in the first place. I brought my hands to my chest, eyes still watering.

It just hurt. Why had *Kylie* been in that class?

Her hand rested on my shoulder, startling me as I glanced up. She nodded once more to encourage me, but I didn't want to go into the room with the redhead. All of this would be real if I touched Kylie, if she didn't respond to me. That was stupid. Of course all of this was real. I saw it, knew it. Many others hadn't even made it to the hospital, fewer still seemed to be in an actual room. I took in a deep breath as I nodded to her before peeking into the room. The redhead said something quiet and the word "again." I wasn't sure what she meant, and she stopped talking as I came into the room, regardless.

"Who're you?" she snapped. "Why're you here?"

I didn't know how to respond, her someone important and me obviously not. "I'm a classmate, just—"

"Dani, can you help me?" Kylie's mom asked as she poked her head in from the door out to the hallway.

The redhead responded to the name, turning away from me. "Oh, sure, Ms. Sarah." They both left the room, however

**37**

momentarily. Yet now that I was alone with Kylie, I knew what to do even less. I stepped closer, seeing her almost-peaceful breaths, the even fall and rise of her chest. How could she be at peace with what had just happened? It had to be morphine or some other painkiller.

How could all of this have happened here, in this quiet little town?

# *Chapter Eight*

## miracle

Kylie | September 26
Crestia Regional Hospital

The first thing I noticed was that my torso felt sore, like I'd done too many sit-ups multiple workout sessions in a row after having not worked out in a while. Next, I noticed I wasn't in my bed — this mattress was firmer, the sheet this scratchy texture instead of the familiar cotton sheets I'd had most of my life. Finally, there were wires connected to me, clipped onto my left pointer finger and in my left forearm. A sterile smell stung my nose, though I couldn't identify where it came from. I opened my eyes to see off-white walls, a window to my left. The sun was setting, wherever I was. A wince escaped from me as I woke up more, emotions and auras overwhelmingly present. Wherever I was, it was *crowded* and entirely *too much* for how drained I felt. Closing my eyes back, I first worked on blocking the auras off — at least I could do something about those until I better gained my bearings. That left me to deal with the emotions — so much worry and anger and this deep sadness I didn't understand but that caused my lower lip to tremble.

"It's a miracle," I heard someone say. "She's the only one so far." Only one for what? "No one else from the attack has—"

All too quickly, smells of blood and sounds of screams and the sight of that woman pinning me down, the other woman killing my classmates in front of me, came back. Of that blade piercing Gabriella's throat or Drew's thumb disconnected from his hand. Terror filled my chest, pushed down into my stomach where I felt nauseous and wanted to throw up. I wasn't sure if I was overwhelmed from the emotions here or if it was the memories being so vivid, screams in my ears despite the only noise in the room being periodic beeps.

Somehow I'd lived, and I was in a hospital room, safe. But what had even happened? They'd wanted to kill me because Sia had killed Nimaka and Asuza, but why now? Why had they involved others?

I stopped blocking auras, trying to search for anyone familiar — I couldn't have actually been the only one, right? It had been a full class, over thirty students. The auras I saw first were extremely familiar — Mom, Mrs. Alana, and Dani, their emotions all some muddled mix of worry and relief and terror and disbelief mushed together and undecipherable.

The door opened, and I closed my eyes back. I didn't want Mrs. Alana questioning me again. I didn't want to go back down to the station, no Sia to lie and cover for me when I wasn't thinking straight enough to know what had happened, let alone cognitive enough to lie about what I'd seen.

I soon realized it wasn't Mrs. Alana's or even Mom's aura that had entered the room, though; it was Dani's. She shuffled close to me, her warm hands on my arm, her worry suffocating my lungs. I refused to open my eyes, pretending to still be asleep. Anything I told her, she'd just tell Mrs. Alana or Mom. That would get me in trouble somehow and endanger them all. Dani wasn't the one at risk of being kidnapped and tortured, of going missing if the wrong thing was said. She didn't understand the gravity of being a mage, wasn't trustworthy as I'd had the *pleasure* of learning last spring.

I bit my tongue as her fingers brushed against my cheek. "What happened to you?" she whispered. Maybe she knew I was awake, but I wasn't acknowledging the question regardless. "First that weird stuff, then Amalia, and now..."

Even though I felt how powerless, how frustrated, she was, I refused to answer. I hadn't been able to trust her, not when I'd actually needed her. I was fine alone. Less people were hurt that way — maybe even Dani herself. This wasn't like years ago where I'd thought she'd protect me, let alone herself, from everything. She was even more helpless than me when it came to matters involving magic, something I'd seen every time she'd struggled to use even the most basic spell.

The door creaked again. This time Mom asked, "Is she...?" The fatigue in Mom's voice didn't remotely convey the extent of the exhaustion she felt, how close to collapsing she was.

"I thought she was up, but... must've been imagining it." Dani's hand shifted from my cheek as she moved away from me and toward Mom. "They said that's normal, right, that she'd be asleep this long?"

They both walked out of the room, the door closing behind them. I couldn't make out Mom's response to her. The relief from Dani's and Mom's emotions moving further away was momentary, my thoughts racing with memories of red and iron-smells and screams when nothing else demanded my attention.

Not only was I not safe, but I'd caused the deaths of so many others. This was yet another indicator that I shouldn't have made it out that June, that living hadn't been a miracle but a curse.

# *Chapter Nine*

# misunderstandings

Jordan | September 27
FamilyCart Grocery Store

When I'd started back in May, I'd been happy that I didn't have to learn the damn registers and talk to people like Elaine did when she worked checkout. I'd since realized maybe that'd have been better 'cause being stuck unloading the damn trucks and then stocking shelves's boring as hell. But 'cause I ain't eighteen, couldn't touch the cash, they said. So I got to do every damn *other* thing instead — like right then, was stuck breaking down yet another damn box after filling that shelf with canned beans. Didn't get why there's seriously nine different flavors of the same brand. Did anyone even buy all this goddamn shit? They must've, since I was restocking multiple hours a day, near every damn day of the week for weeks now.

Out of the corner of my eye, I saw Elaine brush past me. We never spoke here. Hell, barely spoke at home either, in all fairness. She went behind the back desk counter, but I couldn't see what else she did; likely's going on break since she loved those.

"They're still not caught either," I heard one of the middle-aged female customers say to Celia, who worked the register in produce.

Celia gasped, and I couldn't tell if she's truly surprised or being fuckin' melodramatic again. Talking to customers's *good business* and she loved to not have to actually stock, so she chatted entirely too damn much most of the time. Managers let her too, which I guess ain't my problem since she wasn't going to unload the shit I was anyways, but still felt like a damn scam she just gossiped while I'm stuck shelving all damn night. "Still? How does someone do *that* in a high school and be missing? Was it one of the students?"

High school?

I paused, attention gravitating to their conversation. It ain't any of my business, but I couldn't help listening in regardless.

"Not that they've said. There's a reward for any information that helps them track down a culprit right now. At Westly, you'd expect it." Westly's the high school on West Side, one I should've been reassigned to years ago. Was goddamn annoying hearing them bitch 'bout that school every day, as if they ain't shopping in a West Side store. It just pissed me off when people acted like they're better than the rest of us while they're stuck here in this shitty-ass place too, but it ain't worth the fight. Just kept my head down and didn't bother. "But not Matthews. They won't release names, but there's been twenty-six confirmed deaths so far — my niece works as a janitor at Crestia Regional an' I've been hearing things from her. They can't get the students still there stabilized."

Grip slipping, the can in my hand dropped onto the waxed tile floor. Matthews? Hospital?

It couldn't've been — motherfuckin' hell, what if it *had* though? Kylie had to have transferred, even though it made no goddamn sense why, and Matthews would be where she went. She couldn't be one of those twenty-six. She couldn't be.

I barely managed to swallow, my hand still frozen where I'd dropped the damn thing. A few people turned toward me after the echo of the can dropping. I knelt down and picked it up, checking it b'fore putting it back on the shelf.

If she'd been in the attack, she wouldn't have gone down easily. Couldn't have, with her mana. Would've been one of the hospitalized ones, unless something hit her symbol. But fuck, who would've even known 'bout that?

I shook my head. Most likely, she ain't involved at all; it'd just been a big fuck-up, misunderstanding, some type of shit like that. Wasn't real. She ain't dead, ain't hospitalized. She hadn't even gotten hospitalized after that bastard had kidnapped and almost killed her. There's no way this'd been more serious than that. But... but yet...

There's no harm in checking this Saturday, stopping by her house. Hadn't seen her all year, so's a completely valid thing to do. And if nothing else, I'd get called paranoid or some shit, but I'd rather be called paranoid than—

Things felt removed, my heart racing as a violence I'd never craved hit me like a wave. The fuck? I squeezed my eyes shut, shaking my head once more. There's no reason to get this upset: if Siani'd made it here, then that meant Kylie's fine, right?

Was likely worrying over dumb shit, but still. I wished Saturday'd be here sooner.

# Chapter Ten

## intersections

Kylie | September 29
Rae Residence

I wished I was back at the hospital, back where they'd kept drugging me for pain I didn't have because the injury that should've lasted weeks, if not months, had already healed. The drugs should have made me loopy but at best had just been a sleep aid. As I'd found out, the prescription pain meds didn't even do that for me, effectively useless. Mom was cautious but not complaining that I didn't bother to take them, her paranoid about me becoming addicted to painkillers yet confused why I wasn't in more pain, given the injury she thought I still had but no longer did.

A miracle, they'd called me; I was the only one that'd been discharged. They wouldn't tell me who had died, who still was in the hospital, but that had said enough. The emotions running through the hospital had been of fear and grief; only the people near my hospital room had felt anything resembling relief and hope during the entire visit.

Mom didn't know, but the scar on my abdomen was all that remained of the entire attack, and even that was fainter than the scars around my ankles and wrists. I suspected it had to do with

47

either not having the injury as long or because I had more mana now, maybe even a combination of both. It wasn't right that I felt fine. Even the recurring nightmares were tame compared to how Mr. Clark had actually died, how terrified any of my still-living classmates must have felt. None of them knew the truth, and anyone dead never would: it was all my fault. I really had been meant to die that June, and living past that point had only caused others to suffer and die instead.

I squeezed my eyes closed. Their screams were still so fresh. I'd heard the doctors warn Mom I might have *survivor's guilt* or something, that I might need *counseling*, something Mom had thankfully brushed off. They didn't understand: "survivor's guilt" implied I wasn't at fault when my classmates had very literally been killed because of me. I was too much of a coward to say that, but it didn't stop me from knowing I shouldn't be awake and *fine* when others had died. Mom had been an anxious wreck, as bad as when I'd come back from being kidnapped by Asuza. But unlike then, there was no Sia to block emotions; I knew how terrified and exhausted she felt, how she cried when she didn't think I was awake to hear.

If I'd just died back then, she could've moved on, not be put through this again and again.

Instead, all I could do was lie in bed, barely able to go to the bathroom without her trying to help me. Really, it was worse than after I'd been kidnapped because I couldn't even sit at my desk to work on stuff and had no Sia to talk to, only my thoughts that never stopped anymore. Exercising was definitely off the table with my actually non-existent injuries, something further destroying any sense of normalcy I might've had. Mom had requested emergency leave, had groceries delivered in, never left. How much stress had I put on her? How many lives had been destroyed because of me? I'd finally managed to sneak my spell book into bed with me, hidden it to my right, underneath my comforter. But after having it beside me, I lost any drive to actually skim through it despite knowing I needed to figure out what that "anti-magic" thing was. Another sign of disrespect to those that'd died and suffered because of me.

Unable to help myself, I stared at my ceiling fan and sighed:

today would be another long day followed by a long night, I could already tell. Soon after, a dim neon purple aura emerged into my aura scanning range. That was Maya, or at least I was fairly certain it was. But why would she come here? She'd been warming up to me; I could finally get a smile out of her. But...

I heard the doorbell chime, Mom answering it. While I couldn't make out what she said — Maya was typically very soft-spoken — her aura came closer to Mom's. She had to have come inside, wasn't just passing through the neighborhood on the way to visit someone else. Mom walked up the steps, each one creaking under her feet, while Maya's aura remained near the door entrance. Mom knocked on my bedroom door before opening it, not waiting for me to say anything. "Can Maya say hi?" Even though she phrased it like I had a choice, I didn't: Mom liked Maya, and for *appearances*, she wouldn't let Maya walk all the way here and not be allowed in. Knowing my choices were yes and yes, I agreed, even if I wasn't sure what to say to Maya right then. She could've been one of the ones dead if they'd picked another period instead of PE. It would be better for her to be as distant as possible instead of visiting me without any prompting.

The closer she came, the more Maya's anxiousness made me want to fidget; most times I'd been around her, she hadn't been the best at expressing herself, but this was another level entirely. She poked her head into my bedroom, her eyes wide as she searched for me without a word, overwhelming worry and concern radiating as her light green eyes rested on me.

"Hey," I said as I forced a smile.

Mom yelled, "I need to pick up some documents in my office — be back in a bit!" from the ground floor. I heard the door to the garage open then close a minute later, Mom's aura moving away from what I could detect. Had she been waiting for some type of opportunity to get out of the house? Maybe that's where some of her anxiousness had even been coming from, needing things outside the house while feeling uncomfortable leaving me alone. Another person I troubled without meaning to.

"Are you... How...?" Maya's eyes ran over me. There was a

stillness to her body, no movements that betrayed the panic and anxiety she felt.

I pulled my eyes away from her to my white comforter as I nodded. "I'm fine enough. Probably could go back to school, but they want me to rest another week." I needed it for recovery, they'd said. I couldn't argue that I was perfectly fine now, unlike everyone else in my PE class. If I did, I'd be asked questions I couldn't answer, not safely.

She sat down on the edge of my bed, beside my left calf. There were so many emotions coursing through her right then, I struggled to decipher them, to separate hers from mine. To my credit, proximity *really* didn't help. "You can't be fine, not that soon." That might've been the most stubborn I'd heard her, a resolve not normally present in her voice.

Yet another person suffering because of me. I couldn't start jumping up and down in front of her — physically, it would be fine, but the fact that I was fine would raise too much suspicion. I could try to ease some of her concern, though, and even better, it was a great opportunity to finally move more than Mom had been letting me. Mom knew the doctor's orders for bed rest, but Maya didn't. "I need to get up anyways, stretch a bit." As she went to argue, I added, "Doctor's orders: I'm supposed to move around every two hours during the day." Okay, so maybe it was every six hours, with support and supervision and assistance. She didn't need to know any of the specifics.

That said, she didn't believe me but at least didn't argue with me as she scooted off my bed and stepped away, giving me space to get up. Despite her concern, she didn't offer me any assistance getting up, which was comical considering her worry. It was a chance to demonstrate I was *fine*, standing with little challenge. I wasn't even sore anymore, hadn't been for days now. Once I'd woken up this morning, I'd changed out of my pj's before being pushed back to bed rest by Mom. It was minor, but wearing shorts and a t-shirt helped me feel a little less like I was wasting my life away. As I stood and glanced back at the bed, I saw my spell book where I'd left it beside me; I threw the comforter over it, covering the book from her view.

Maya's eyes ran over me, distrust and suspicion blending with her still-present anxiety. I stretched my arms, noticing that whatever muscle was near my injured rib actually *was* still a little sore when stretched. "Don't push yourself," she said.

"I'm thirsty anyways. Need some water." I picked my actually still fairly full water bottle up and walked down the steps, hearing her cautiously follow behind me. I hadn't been able to use this excuse while Mom was home because Mom kept checking on me and refilling the bottle what felt like hourly. Time had been a dull blur the past however many days, so I wasn't sure exactly how often she had refilled it, just that I never got the chance to do so myself.

But as I opened the fridge to grab the water pitcher, I felt a more intense anxiety flood my brain. It couldn't be from Maya. Even if she stood closer to me instead of lingering half across the kitchen, even if she was touching me, her emotions were never this intense. My heart raced, and I wasn't sure if it was anxiety from empathy or from myself, even more so as a bright aura of dark blue and deep red entered my scanning range. I stumbled, my head spinning as my breathing became shallow, unsure what to do or say. Why now? I didn't — couldn't — deal with him, not right then. I hadn't seen him since that day in May, when he'd left, they'd left. He'd wanted out and I'd given it and why was he knocking on the door?

Maya glanced between me and the entrance of the house before she shuffled over to the door. I think she thought I was fatigued and she was doing me a favor; I couldn't think straight enough to tell her otherwise — that I didn't want the door opened, didn't want to see the person on the other side. My heart raced, hearing his voice for the first time since April as he asked if I was home. I didn't hear her say anything in response, but I saw her step aside so he could come in.

Why didn't she stop him?

Why hadn't I said something before she'd opened the door?

I opened the back porch door quickly and ran outside. We never came out here. Unmowed grass brushed against my toes and ankles. Our backyard was at most six yards long, a rectangle enclosed by a brown wooden fence potentially older than I was.

The fresh air invaded my lungs, attempting to lull my mind even with so many emotions blending into and against my own.

"Kylie?" Maya asked, stepping out behind me. He was near her but hadn't said anything. I hated I could distinguish between their confusion, his blaring into me compared to Maya's more subdued emotions. What was he confused over?

I didn't want Maya to see this and be caught up in anything from last year. I didn't want the past to intersect the present. That was the whole point of changing schools in the first place. And I'd made my new home where no one minded me. He had what he wanted, and I—

What was there to say? I didn't know. Why did he just stand there, silent? I kept my back to them both, not trusting myself to turn around and face either. His emotions amplified even further as he took another step closer, but I didn't understand what he felt, only that it stung and I didn't know why.

No matter how much I tried, I still wasn't at Sia's level: I couldn't lie well enough, fast enough.

"Kylie?" Maya called me again. But wait... something was wrong. There was another bright aura coming into view, but it was too close to be someone casually walking or driving into the neighborhood — my aura scanning range was roughly two houses on either side of my own house. This brown aura was vivid, had to be within yards; worse, I knew it, this aura one of the two that visited my nightmares, burned into the thoughts and memories I saw near every waking moment.

Instincts taking over before I fully comprehended anything, I yelled, "Get back!" Turning around, I searched for the source of the aura.

"Ooh, you are getting better." I knew that voice: she wasn't the woman that had stabbed me at school, but the accomplice, the one that had murdered my classmates. She was perched on Mr. Schid's roof, peering down at us. "But it's not enough, you know?" She jumped down off the roof, landing in my yard.

I swallowed. How could I do anything? I couldn't beat her on the best of terms, let alone right then when—

Maya was still here, silent, with her left foot positioned behind her, closer to inside. If she went back inside, then maybe

I could... but what if she called the police? I didn't need more attention on me, on Mom.

Why had they changed from just attacking at the training house or waiting until I passed by the forest to ambushing me in broad daylight with others around? Why weren't they scared of being captured?

I couldn't fight back. Another normal person was here in a mages' fight, just like there had been at the gym. But even if I *could* save Maya somehow, she'd tell people, say too much, like Dani had. I'd been fortunate that Mrs. Alana had blown Dani off, but what if Maya said the same thing? The more people that reported the same things, the more attention I'd receive. Worse yet, *his* heart raced with bewilderment and betrayal, and what *right* did he even have to feel betrayed? He had what he wanted. They hadn't murdered an entire class to get at him.

"Is this someone else you know?" Maya asked, her eyes cutting between me and our attacker.

"Aww, you haven't introduced me to everyone? I'm Sase. Zimihe wanted to come too, but our new boss said we gotta take turns for now. Kinda sad, considering it'd be great to just do you in once and for all — for Lord Asuza's memory *and* what you did to Nimaka."

Both of those names were Riyatian, or at least followed Riyatian character sets. Had Asuza renamed them? Nimaka had been alive, able to bleed, unlike Asuza. Was that the case with these two as well? Regardless, I had nothing I could say in response. If I acknowledged who she was, I'd admit I was involved. But if I didn't, then... then what?

Sase's attention shifted away from me to Maya. Too quickly, I remembered her stabbing through my classmates in the gym, remembered feeling a throat be impaled, a spine shattering. My heart raced, but I couldn't...

I just couldn't let her harm someone else not involved in all this; I couldn't let her harm Maya — no one else was going to be hospitalized because of me. "Why are you here?"

She licked her lower lip before clapping her hands together. "To have some fun, of course!" Even though he'd said nothing, she turned to Jordan. "And that hurt last time, you know."

Unless something had happened to him directly, she had to be referring to Rota stabbing her, back when they'd still been here. The tremble of Jordan's lower lip aligned with his emotions — fear and anger, that betrayal even stronger than before.

Maya hadn't left like I'd hoped she would, but she wasn't drawing attention to herself either. Maybe if Sase kept her attention on me... then what? I didn't know what I could do, should do.

Sase short-cast her weapon — that sword that had murdered so many of my classmates. My whole body tensed, muscles tight as I bit back a whimper. She would kill Maya, and I couldn't do a thing about it. Nothing came to mind, nothing that could save Maya or me from the gym happening all over again.

Yet at the last second, Sase turned away from Maya, instead stabbing Jordan through the right shoulder. His eyes clenched shut as he grumbled a curse; I whimpered, biting back the urge to touch my own right shoulder to check for blood — my shoulder was fine, this was just from empathy and *I knew it*, but his emotions were *so loud* and I was disoriented without any blood dripping down my skin regardless. She withdrew the sword, kicking him down into the grass with her boot heel. A smirk pulled at her lips as she hovered her sword's tip right above his hip. Despite the sharp, throbbing pain from his shoulder, he held his breath as much as possible, preventing any sort of moment from his body. My eyes widened as I realized why: Sase's sword was right above his symbol. She lowered the blade further, metal brushing across his skin yet not slicing through, not yet. Jordan shrieked, water pushing out of his eyes. I struggled to breathe, like it punctured my heart despite Sase not touching me. That pain overwhelmed me; all I could process was that if she cut into his symbol, he'd die as Nimaka had back in May.

All my panic vanished in that moment, a singular peace consuming every thought. The danger to myself or even Maya didn't really matter. Really, the answer was easy, instinctive even, as my eyes honed in on Sase's hand: her hand held the sword; if that hand no longer pointed toward Jordan's symbol, he would be safe. I could turn a lock tumbler with telekinetics, so there was no reason I couldn't turn her arm away. My eyes trained on her wrist, I threw my left arm out to my side. The arm controlling her sword followed suit, mimicking my action. I barely registered the glyph I opened under me, beams of water rushing toward her torso. Before the spell finished, she was gone — teleported away instead of trying to shield against the spell.

The haze lessened, my chest heaving as I dropped to my knees. If she was nearby somehow, it wasn't in a way I could detect. The house just looked like one spot had been randomly pressure washed, and it'd likely take months for Mom to notice, if she ever did. It'd been months since I'd cast anything that intense, first time I ever used telekinetics like that—

Cast.

Spell.

I'd just used magic openly. There was no way Maya hadn't seen, and Mr. Schid was home. Jordan's pain blotted out any emotion reads I could have otherwise had to let me know if he saw anything.

"W-what just happened?" Maya's eyes locked onto me and she maintained her distance from me. "Who was that? How'd she—How'd you—"

I didn't know what to say or if there even was anything to be said. That calm haze had completely vanished, leaving me drained and aching, Jordan's shoulder injury still throbbing like it was my own. All I knew was that I'd been attacked at home; they knew where I lived. School, home, training house... nowhere was safe from them.

No words came to my lips as I stumbled over to Jordan. I knelt down, laying my hand against where he'd been stabbed. As far as I could tell, she hadn't damaged his symbol at all, so this was the only injury he had. If this pain stopped, maybe I could get some degree of mental capacity back.

How *had* I even moved her hand from his symbol through telekinetics? I needed a pin to focus off of for the tumbler movement; even a rock was normally too heavy for me to telekinetically lift. I pushed a healing spell, watching as the blood flow slowed then stopped, the incision healing itself closed. He nodded as his eyes clenched shut momentarily, something involving "fuck" mumbled under his breath.

Yet another instance of someone hurt because of me.

"What's going on?" Maya asked, her voice more forceful this time, clearly directed toward me. "Who was that?"

I lowered my head as I withdrew my hand from its contact with Jordan. How long would it be before she'd betray me like Dani had? Would I end up where Amalia was after all?

"I don't..." The words just didn't come, no matter how much I wanted to lie that it'd all been an optical illusion or something likewise not believable. I felt her attention on me, Jordan's eyes on me.

She took a deep breath, glancing at Jordan and me. "I need a minute." My stomach tied itself into more knots as she stepped back into my house, leaving the backdoor open.

Was she calling someone? Was this how it would happen? There was no more Sia or Rota to help assure that the people who found out were ones that were safe. Even then, Dani had been the one to tell Mom I'd been sneaking out, even when she'd known why.

Before I could chase after her, I heard Jordan ask, "The hell's even going on?"

I didn't have time for this. For him. "It was never 'over.' It's just not your head they're after."

# Chapter Eleven

## beneficial relationships

Maya | September 29
Rae Residence

What had I just seen? Kylie wouldn't say anything, just kept mumbling to herself as if she heard nothing I said. I'd thought she was friends with or dating the guy that stopped by since she had pictures of them together all over her bedroom walls — I think he'd said his name was Jordan, but he'd been stammering so much I'd barely made out anything he'd said. While they definitely did know each other, she hadn't looked particularly thrilled to see him. And after that...

A light had shone under Kylie, turquoise in color; that same color had appeared again from her hand as she'd touched that guy. A woman had come from basically nowhere and tried to kill him, knew Kylie well. I didn't understand anything that'd happened once he'd arrived here; the entire half hour had felt like live fiction playing out before my eyes. I sat on the edge of her couch, a rather pathetic attempt to back-process everything I'd just seen. It already felt like something I'd dreamed up, disconnected from before he'd arrived and even right then. I heard a noise, causing me to turn toward the direction of the click, only to see Kylie timidly stepping back inside. It was like she was a different person than the girl who'd sat next to me in class or even the calmness she'd had when I'd arrived and she'd still been in bed. Her lips opened then closed back as she stared at me, her shoulders slumped as if to make her smaller than she already was. "Just..." She gripped that ring she always wore as a necklace. "Just pretend you didn't see anything, okay? It's better that way."

She said that like that was even possible. I wasn't a stranger to lies, but there were limits to what I could ignore. "Is — was that what happened at school?" Normally I wouldn't have considered asking something like that, given she'd been hospitalized too. But... it all lined up. Answers to questions I didn't even know to ask.

I watched as she moved to the other side of the couch, sitting down and keeping her eyes from me. Her hand gripped that ring even tighter as she nodded. "I didn't know. They'd never done anything like that before — never involved other people."

When I'd wondered why it had to be the class she'd been in, I hadn't known it could've *only* been that class, that she'd been the cause of the incident. Did that mean there's a chance I could've died less than a half hour ago? That woman named Sase seemed intent on harming the guy for sure. There was another shuffle behind us, so I turned around to glance at the back porch door. That guy stepped inside, timidly staring at us, at Kylie. His stride was completely normal, like when he'd first walked into Kylie's townhome. The only indication of his injury at all was the slice through his shirt, crusted dried and drying blood mixing into the dark green fabric. His sudden recovery was another thing that made no sense.

Yet it'd happened, a truth among whatever other lies she'd said. "Will it happen again?"

Kylie nodded, her eyes still away from me; it was somehow completely different to how I felt she saw through me times past. She was intentionally avoiding looking at me, was timid for whatever reason. "They want me dead — their boss or master or whatever he was... He tried to kill me the June before last." Her eyes became glassy as liquid dripped down her left cheek. She had moved her focus from her lap to the ornate dark brown and beige rug covering most of the living room's carpet. "None of this would've happened if I had just died then like the others. I shouldn't have made it out." Her back was to the guy, so I saw what she didn't: his eyes opened wide, his hand reaching out toward her before withdrawing. Who was he? He seemed to know what was going on with that woman, and *something* had definitely happened between him and Kylie, given the stark contrast between how happy they were in the photos compared to right then when she wouldn't even acknowledge him. Their relationship wasn't any of my business, but it still was such a strange reaction for her with how friendly she'd been at school.

He said nothing, instead balling his fists as he jerked his eyes away from Kylie.

I guess Kylie hadn't noticed him since she didn't turn around at all, only sniffling on the couch as her shoulders shook from crying. What did people do in these kinds of situations? I reached out, my fingertips brushing against her shoulder. I wasn't much for physical contact, but hopefully I wasn't overstepping any boundaries of hers by touching her. She glanced up at me, startled. I wasn't sure if I should apologize or ask for an apology or something else. "I don't..." I didn't know what to say to make her feel better then, just like I didn't know why it'd hurt so much seeing her in the hospital. "I'm glad that you're okay."

She reached out, her arms wrapping around my shoulders as her forehead leaned on my collarbone. "Don't tell anyone. Please. Don't tell anyone." So much for my concern over too much contact.

I wasn't sure what she thought I'd tell to begin with. "S-sure..." There was no one else in this town I knew, no one else that had invited me over to their home. Besides, I had the rest of the year with her, and that was a *lot* of group projects, given how things had gone so far. If nothing else, a reliable group partner to get me through high school was worth staying quiet about whatever this all was. As I'd reminded myself so often, my only goal was to get the piece of paper so I could start the next part of my life. As far as I could tell, it was well within my interest to stay silent if that was all she asked in return for not making this last school year hellish, as so many others had been.

The guy's lips pushed to a thin line as he walked to the front door, closing it quietly as he left. The only indication Kylie even noticed him leaving was a hiccup as she gripped me tighter. She kept like that for another few minutes before wiping her eyes. "S-sorry. This wasn't at all what you signed up for."

That was an understatement. "Are you okay?" That was what people asked in situations like these, wasn't it? Well, in movies at least, and that's the closest context I had for whatever happened those few minutes outside.

Kylie shook her head no. "I-I don't even know how to begin." Her head shot up suddenly. "Mom'll be home soon. I need to get back upstairs." So whatever this was, even her mother didn't know. She dashed up the stairs, leaving me to trail behind. As I approached the staircase, I heard a motor rumbling for what I guessed was the garage door opening. Hadn't it just been a guess? How had she been so spot on? Maybe she had something on her phone that had alerted her. I followed her to her room, where she already tucked herself under her bed comforter as if she'd never left — only this time, a box of tissues sat on her nightstand that had been on her desk originally.

I didn't sit on her bed, instead stepping near but staying standing. Kylie took in deep breaths, her nose pink and eyes bloodshot but no longer crying as she had been. "Whatever that was... she doesn't know?" I asked.

Her eyes widened as if I'd told a horror story, her head shaking back and forth rapidly. "No. She can't. Please." Who was I to argue with keeping things from parents? Mine didn't even know where I lived anymore. At least, I hoped they didn't, had to believe they didn't.

It wasn't a problem to mention nothing to her mom, but I was curious and wanted *some* explanation for whatever had happened. "I won't. But could *I* know at least?"

Kylie's lips pressed together, and I thought she was about to deny me entirely. If she did, she did. Either way she was a reliable group partner, so it was in my interest to keep my mouth shut. Instead, she took another deep breath. "Can you give me some time? Just... a week... or until next weekend. I need to collect my thoughts, so I can figure out how to even..."

Was she stalling or blowing me off? What would be the point, though, when I knew where she lived and we shared so many classes? "Next Friday then." If she lied, she lied; it wasn't like I had much to lose either way.

She bit down on her lip as she nodded. "Next Friday, after school." How would she be back at school next week when it wasn't even opened back up yet? Last update I'd gotten was mid-next week, and even then, wasn't that too soon for her to return, considering she had been hospitalized?

"You're going back to school when it opens next week?"

Her eyes lowered, so I guessed it was a question she hadn't anticipated. "No. But I can tell Mom I asked for your notes and you're going to spend the night next Friday to help me catch up." A rather quick yet effective lie that I had no complaints with. Though even ignoring the false premise, she'd still miss a handful of days in class and *would* have to make those up. It wasn't my business how that happened though so I didn't bring it up. Instead, I planned on returning next Friday because as I'd quickly started to realize, a shaky beneficial relationship built on a handful of well-meaning lies was better than being alone in this town that I didn't understand.

# *Chapter Twelve*

## accident

Jordan | September 29
Opal Pines Streets

I still couldn't shake the look she'd had when she'd seen me or hearing her say she should be dead right then. I thought it'd just been she got redistricted, or Ms. Rae had made her, or... something outta her control. But with how she'd refused to look at me, her only words telling me she'd gotten targeted and I ain't...

She'd transferred, and if I wasn't the cause, it's a bonus she hadn't minded. And my fears 'bout that Matthews attack... she'd been involved. I felt like a dumbass now more than ever: he'd lied 'bout everything else, why *wouldn't* he have lied 'bout us being safe after they left? Why'd I believe that shit?

I had my backpack packed with clothes since Richard'd invited me to stay over but honestly wished I could've cancelled. Had no way to contact him, and late's one thing, but I couldn't just stand him up. Ain't exactly in the mood to hang out, though. Hell, didn't wanna be around anyone, except maybe Kylie. Wasn't sure what to even say to her now: I had somehow dug myself into the motherfuckin' ditch of hell, given she'd never ignored or yelled at me b'fore, not like that.

Her words from earlier replayed in my ears entirely too damn easy thanks to hypermnesia. Saw her crying on whoever'd opened the door. Guessed it's someone from Matthews since I'd never met her b'fore. Kylie'd known her less than two months but went to her instead of me. Ain't even sure if the only reason she'd healed me's 'cause of her empathy and not 'cause she gave a damn.

I lowered my eyes as I walked past a group of people I'd never seen b'fore, at least not that I could remember — maybe sometime b'fore my hypermnesia. A few of them whispered as they walked past me, and more than one rolled their eyes, as if I ain't allowed on the street near them. Given how well paved the sidewalk was, not broken like the rest of the town, let alone the barely together ancient slabs on West Side, they likely ain't completely wrong either. I knew Richard lived in a *nice* area, but this's past even that. It must've been in like the highest value neighborhood in the whole damn city. Had checked a map at the library earlier in the week and was thankful I did 'cause him just giving me the address had told me jackshit when I'd never been on this side, 'specially not this far on this side.

Wished I could ask him what the hell to do with the shit I'd seen earlier, but he'd never been 'specially fond of Kylie. I did everything I could to keep the two of them apart, and it's awkward as fuck when they weren't.

I turned another corner, seeing this one huge-ass lot take up as far as I could see, a pristine and polished steel gate around the perimeter. The fuck's something like this doing in Opal Pines? We're in the middle of goddamn nowhere. Yet as I scanned the address on the gate, it's the same number — same road — as what Richard'd given me. Must've been a damn joke, and it pissed the hell outta me, today 'specially.

Hell was I s'posed to do now? Either accidentally or purposefully — and I'd bet purposefully — he'd given the wrong goddamn address to me. Hoped he's at least on this street, otherwise I'm fuckin' going to the library and avoiding every damn other person. Had entirely too fuckin' much on my mind for this shit.

After pressing the intercom button, I heard an older man say, "State your business."

Biting back a jump from the voice, I kept holding the button down, not sure if I should or shouldn't do so. Maybe should've asked, but I felt awkward as hell as it was. "I, uh..." I hated this, goddamn. Felt like an ant compared to a giant, completely insignificant — well, even more than normal. "I'm wondering if you knew Richard — Richard Richelieu. I'm looking for his house."

Almost immediately, the man replied with a snap, "What business do you have with Master Richard?" My mouth opened and not even a cuss slipped out. The only response I managed was blinking a few times as I replayed his response in my head — that *wasn't* the answer I'd prepared for. Richard hadn't been bullshitting me? He actually *lived* in this mansion-like shit? "Excuse me, what business do you have with Master Richard?"

I'd only *thought* I'd felt small b'fore. "I, uh... He invited me over. Said to come by?" I hadn't meant to squeak toward the end, but even I ain't sure why I'm there, honestly. He'd invited me but couldn't have *meant* to. Some type of fuck-up'd happened, and I hadn't realized the scale 'til right fuckin' then.

With an annoyed sigh, the man replied, "One moment." I resisted the urge to run away while he was gone, instead releasing my finger from the button I'd been pressing. Within a minute, the man returned to the mic, his tone entirely different — the boredom and irritation replaced with a frantic tone. "I'm sorry, Master Jordan, I was unaware of the *plans* for this evening. Please, come on through."

*Master* Jordan? What kind of hilarious fuckin' joke's that?

Yet the gates opened, and I didn't dare linger. As soon as I'd stepped through, said gates slammed shut. I bit back a cuss as I suddenly felt trapped. Once I reached the front door, it opened from the inside, a woman in a suit right at the door, holding it open for *me*. "Welcome, Master Jordan. Master Richard's expecting you in the far left wing, in his loft." In his what?

I nodded, not sure what else to say. Took in how *clean* everything was — the chandelier reflected on the waxed cream floor tiles, as if a mirage. This foyer alone's bigger than any apartment I'd ever lived in. Almost felt dizzy, but ain't sure if it's the size of the house or the panic attack at what the fuck I'd just found myself in.

A much older woman in a long blue dress came out, graying hair tied back in a bun. "Welcome, dear, welcome." She patted me on the shoulder. "Right this way." I heard the click of heels, something I otherwise only heard at school from a few teachers. Most didn't bother. Not sure what else to do, I followed her. "I'm so excited Master Richard *finally* found a friend." Had she ever *seen* Richard? Man's swarmed every time he's anywhere, and I doubted it's different at college as quickly as he'd gotten the whole damn school's attention last year. "You're the first person he's ever brought over. We thought he'd never get any friends beyond what Master David and Lady Michelle set up for him." Maybe the first guy, but prior to his Act, Richard'd been fuckin' covered in women. Hell, even the straight guys'd been trying to hang out with him at first; he'd just shot them down even quicker than the women that'd hung around him. Still didn't get why I'm the weird-ass exception outta the whole damn town, or how someone like this's even *in* this town.

She led me down a hallway that's like something outta a ritzy-ass hotel, dozens of rooms with closed doors on both sides. Finally, the hallway ended with a door in the middle, framed in gold. She knocked on it twice b'fore opening it and strolling inside. "Master Richard, your *friend*'s here!" Damn, she made me even more paranoid saying it like *that*. Nonetheless, I followed her since it's either that or hauling ass outta here — the latter's entirely too damn tempting, but I didn't wanna hear Richard bitch either.

"Yo," I heard him say as he glanced up from this large black leather couch that wrapped around in a u-shape, himself sprawled out and half lying down on it. The goddamn biggest tv I'd ever seen's mounted to the wall, silent, though likely wasn't b'fore we came in, given it looked like Richard'd been watching it.

"Uh, 'sup." I awkwardly waved back. Felt so goddamn stiff but hell was I s'posed to do?

The older woman giggled b'fore saying, "I'll leave you two to it." She then closed the door, just me and Richard left in this wide, open room. I glanced around at decor I'd only seen in movies at best.

Richard scoffed, standing up. "SuzyAnne's acting like a damn school girl." Guess her name's SuzyAnne then. "Could've at least showed you where you're sleeping." He brushed past me, dressed 'bout the same as always, but it *fit* here, unlike in town or school or the fuckin' training house. There're three doors on the backside of the wall, two more across from those doors. He pointed to the far left one, against a wall. "That's my room." He moved to the door directly right of his. "This'll be yours tonight." He opened said door, walking into the room.

I followed, blinking once I'd stepped in. Damn room's basically same size as the apartments I'd always lived in. Bed's twice if not three times the size of mine. "Goddamn," I mumbled. I jumped as I heard the door close behind me.

Richard crossed his arms over his chest as he leaned against the door, his eyebrow raised. Guess he'd been the one who closed it, which made the most sense but like hell I knew what's going on — maybe the damn doors shut themselves here? "You good?"

"Ah, uh..." I rubbed the back of my neck as I glanced away. Couldn't say it to him, but ain't really sure *how* I felt right then. Hell's someone like *me* doing in a place like *this*?

"Shower's over here." He walked to that cracked dark-wood door, flipping a light on. I stepped over a few feet, not quite to him but where I could see in. It's a bathroom larger than any I'd ever had — a full shower *and* bathtub, towel already hung. A toilet closed off, and two sinks for some reason. He walked back out, pointing by the door we'd entered from. "Beside the switch, there's a red button. That calls staff if you need something." The fuck? Really *was* like a goddamn hotel.

No wonder he'd flipped the fuck out when he'd first seen my apartment. Didn't know it's possible, but I felt even more mortified.

Those thoughts — how I'm in a place I didn't belong, how I didn't deserve to even see something like this — brought the sting of earlier back to the forefront of my mind, of Kylie crying, of being damn near murdered 'cause've my fuckin' symbol by that bitch that'd called herself Sase. It'd seemed so far away when I'd gotten to his house, yet it all rushed back to the forefront of my attention so quickly. "Mm."

"Sup?" he asked. "Something happen?"

How could I even approach this? I turned around, sitting on the bed — it's the plushest I'd ever sat on, like feathers're under me. Maybe it's even made of feathers, fuck if I knew. I set my bag on the soft green rug. "Kylie ain't been at school."

"Maybe she caught a clue."

My lips pressed into a firm line. It ain't his fault. He didn't know. Hell, likely wouldn't't've cared even if he did know. "She transferred to Matthews."

"Saves you the trouble of dealing with her. Shitty luck though, since that school just got fucked up." He didn't connect the two, not at all. His reaction's different from how mine'd been — part of me'd known that incident'd involved her when I'd heard 'bout it. Ain't sure why or how. Think I'd figured out she had to be at Matthews, and for that specific school to have shit like that happen... it couldn't have been random. I just didn't wanna believe it, wanted it all over and'd been a year-long nightmare that we'd moved on from. I needed to talk to her but first had to figure out what the hell to even say.

I stared at my palm. If I wanted, I could make a small ice shard, a baby candle's worth of flame. Neither'd hurt me unless I got careless, and I didn't even get tired from minor shit like that anymore. Yet... I didn't want anything to do with magic, didn't want my mana. Hell, it was the reason I'd almost died earlier. And how many times'd I fuckin' burned myself when I'd lost too much focus while I got pissed or sad or fuckin' any emotion really? Hell, the pendant under my shirt'd burn the shit outta anyone who touched it, simultaneous frost and fire burns from what *he'd* said. "It's not..."

Richard's bitchy as fuck as he asked, "Not what?"

I'm breaking the peace he had: he ain't involved, prob'bly wouldn't ever know if we avoided the training house from now on. But... even still, the fact that she'd refused to even look at me stung like fuckin' hell.

"It ain't an accident." I balled the fist I'd been staring at. "Those two other bitches came after her — tried to kill her that day, and again today. I went to go see her and one almost fuckin' killed me through my symbol."

His eyes widened as he stepped closer. So he'd been told 'bout symbols then; didn't need to explain the significance of that, thankfully. "The fuck? You all right?"

The heal'd been the only contact she'd had with me. She'd had this wild energy in her eyes that'd never been there b'fore while she'd done so. I didn't know what'd happened to cause that, and it ain't like I got a chance to ask. "Kylie healed me, so I'm fine. But... I don't understand what's going on."

"404-312-1988." I glanced up at him. "My cell. If something happens, have someone text me." Taking damn advantage of my memory again. Nonetheless, I nodded, appreciating the gesture even if I ain't sure he'd make a difference, even assuming he got wherever shit went down in time. Also like, I ain't got a phone to call from and didn't exactly think one'd be around if shit happened again.

Even more than worry 'bout the attackers, my actual concern still ate through my chest, words I couldn't explain to him: I missed her so damn much.

# *Chapter Thirteen*

## distractions

Today was the first day school opened back up. I knew I'd not been affected by the tragedy, all things considered, but I'd still enjoyed the time school had been closed; it'd allowed me to sneak a few extra hours in at work and generally sleep more than six hours a night. But here I was, back in these halls, almost half of the first day down as I made my way to the lunch line.

Homeroom had been quiet, and Ashley must have only been sitting behind me so she could talk to Kylie. This morning, she had sat on the other side of the classroom, leaving both the desk beside me and behind me vacant unless she started sitting there again when Kylie returned. More than once, I saw her laughing with the people beside her now, them whispering back and forth after the announcements.

There'd been rumors around the halls that even past the still-injured and deceased, some parents either had their child stay home a few more days or had transferred them somewhere else entirely while the school had been closed.

Of course, I didn't wish harm on anyone here, but I wasn't

71

complaining about smaller crowds in the halls and lines or fewer people around overall.

As I continued moving through the lunch line, I heard a blonde-haired girl and a carrot-haired guy talking. Both were in my art class, like many of the students ahead and behind me in line right then. The girl said, "Matt's in a coma." I hadn't learned their names since we thankfully didn't have to work with others — one class of freedom from the damned group projects. "Mom and Dad've been taking turns staying with him, but they just don't..."

"He'll be okay. Just give him time," the guy said back, his hand on her shoulder.

Time, huh? That'd been what Kylie'd asked for too.

Finally up to the food selection, I pointed to what I wanted. The lunch people couldn't ever hear me anyway, so there was no reason to yell when pointing worked better. One said, "Here you go, Sweetie," and I barely managed to restrain myself from raising my eyebrow. What was it with people down here and "sweetie"? It made no sense.

After what felt like half the lunch period, I could finally sit down and eat. Yet as I glanced around at the tables, I noticed easily half the cafeteria was missing compared to a week ago. I sat at the table I'd been sitting at for lunch this whole year with Kylie and Ashley, but this time, I had the table to myself. Ashley sat with some other seniors I didn't know, smiling. Her eyes met mine, and there was something terrifying in how she licked her lower lip even though it couldn't actually be directed toward me. It had to be something about the conversation at that table.

It didn't really matter. It was better to be alone. Pulling my sketchbook from my backpack, I opened it to the last sketch I'd been working on, a clock tower study from a movie showing at work currently.

With Kylie gone, I didn't have to worry about anyone taking uninvited peeks while I sketched. She'd always been too nosy, not at all considerate about the fact that I didn't want people watching me draw. Ashley was a lot better about that, but I think it's just because she and Kylie usually talked, distracting each other so I was free to be alone. There was no need for Ashley to distract Kylie since she wasn't here, so she'd moved on to another group as if she'd always been there.

Really, that summed up everything: they were distractions. My goal was to graduate this hell and move on to college. That's why I worked as many hours as I could, why I lived alone, knew better than to get attached to others.

Yet when I looked at the clock tower, each stone I'd attempted to shade so far, all I saw was Kylie in the hospital or that event with so-called magic no one knew about. None of it involved me, so I wasn't sure why I kept thinking about it. It was curious, to be sure, but ultimately not necessary for my goals.

Even so... I couldn't pick up my pen, head filled with entirely too many distractions.

# Chapter Fourteen

## not fair

Mom finally had to go back to teaching class at Jenn, which meant I could finally get back to practice without her knowing. Sitting in a bed wouldn't help me or save anyone. Sase knew where I lived, so it was safe to assume Zimihe and whoever their new leader was knew as well. Even if I could sleep more than I'd been able to since coming home from the hospital, sleep just meant more nightmares. It was better to stay awake and be productive instead.

It'd taken entirely too long, but last night I'd finally found the info I'd been searching for in my spell book: "anti-magic barrier," close enough to what Zimihe had mentioned that day. Since then, I'd read over the entry at least ten times, maybe a couple more, but I still didn't actually understand how it functioned. Even though I disliked the realization, I knew the eleventh time wouldn't suddenly unearth an additional passage or something else on the page. I put the book back into my backpack that I'd brought with me to the training house.

It'd been weeks since I'd last worked out, and I needed to change that right then. I lowered myself to the concrete, preparing for my sets of pushups to get me back into the groove of things. Fingers on the concrete, I positioned the balls of my feet to support me as I raised up and down.

That "barrier" wasn't some type of spell at all, but a machine with up to a two-mile radius of effect that sapped mana from mages, particularly with active consumption. But *how*? My mana was intertwined into my blood as far as I understood things. Yet this machine pulled mana from me without drawing blood and I didn't understand *how*.

As if evading that specific information, the entry hadn't given any technical specifications, only clarifying that *any* mana consumed — including passive mana usage — would have a fraction siphoned. Proximity mattered too, as the closer I got to the physical location of the anti-magic barrier machine-thing, the higher the percent of mana siphoned. I furrowed my brows, a huff coming from my lungs. Every breath caused passive mana consumption. Even my heart beating used mana to some degree. That's how it worked for all mages, part of what signified the transition from a human without Act to a mage.

But if that was the case, then every breath used more mana — potentially *significantly* more mana — than what it otherwise would. And that ignored the strain any physical exercise would cause, which explained why I'd been so fatigued in PE. I couldn't imagine what an actual spell — even the mildest one — would take compared to normal. The passage clarified that the barrier could increase its siphoning to up to three hundred percent more mana consumption right at its physical location. Literally every breath could take three times the mana it otherwise would, a horrifying concept in and of itself.

Finishing the fifty pushups, I sat up, wiping sweat from my forehead. It was so humid that even though the temperature was fine enough, I felt miserable in the AC-less training house. Maybe I was just out of shape from the weeks of missed exercising, but even if I was, it didn't matter. I needed to keep pushing, make use of this time I had. I positioned myself against the back wall, bits of foundation cement cracking off as I applied pressure while moving into a handstand. My legs rested against the wall while I adjusted for balance.

How'd something like an anti-magic barrier even get created? And for what? How'd Zimihe and Sase and their "new leader" gotten their hands on it at all? Had it been in Riyati and passed down? What use would something like that have been in a magic kingdom? Who even *was* this new leader? Was it someone from Riyati like Asuza had been? Whoever they were, they were confident enough to have Sase and Zimihe attacking in broad daylight, in public places — like they weren't at all fearful of being kidnapped and tortured and experimented on as Amalia and Lianne were if they still lived. It made no sense, went against how every other mage attack — even those from Nimaka — had been.

Yet again, I had no idea how to actually handle going back to school, dealing with the anti-magic barrier. Maybe the only option was transferring back to North Pines. Would it save people if I did? But Sase and Zimihe would follow me and kill even more people then, wouldn't they?

I didn't know. I wanted to ask Sia what to do, what she would've done if she had been in my place. Even if she said nothing, that would give me confidence that it'd happened under her eye. I wanted some type of safety-net, some type of assurance and backup. Even if Maya kept her promise, the huge and terrifying *if* that was, it wasn't like she could help me survive.

Really, I was still as alone as I'd ever been since Sia had left.

No, Sia wouldn't have moped. If I ever wanted to be as strong as Sia, I needed to do better than this; I *had* to do better.

Taking in a deep breath, I lowered myself from the handstand and then rubbed my eyes. Anytime my eyes closed, auras instinctively gained my attention now. It normally wasn't much of a problem out here since no one was around. Right then, however, I saw a familiar aura, concern and worry filling my lungs more by the second. Why? Why was he here? There was nowhere for me to hide or leave — not easily, subtly. I'd been distracted, something else I couldn't afford, and I had suppressed auras to concentrate on exercising.

It was the middle of a Tuesday. He should be in school, should—

The door creaked open, his head timidly searching around

before his eyes rested on me. "Thought so," I heard him mutter. He stepped inside, closing the door behind him.

"I can leave." I stood up. If he wanted this house for something, I could just exercise in my room as I had so many times before. I'd come out here with the hope of doing actual magic or Isare practice, but I wasn't sure how without Sia to guide me on starting.

I hated how gentle his eyes were as they rested on me; it made me bite back tears he in no way deserved to see. He wanted nothing to do with me, and I'd given it to him. What more did he want?

He sat down beside me, not meeting my eyes. "Went to your house first but figured you'd be here when you weren't there."

Meager defiance it was, I shifted my eyes away from him, bringing my knees to my chest and wrapping my arms around my legs. "School?"

"No way in hell'd they let you back so soon. Most people'd still be hospitalized right now."

Most people wouldn't have had a class slaughtered to get to them. Most people wouldn't be the only one walking around right then, free to live like nothing had happened. "I'm not most people."

He chuckled, adjusting his posture. I didn't look over to see how he had shifted, making sure to keep my eyes away from him. Empathy was bad enough. "Never have been."

It didn't seem like he was there to practice. No surprise there, given how he'd always hated magic and realistically could ignore magic entirely if he wanted with no one after his life.

I snapped, "What do you want? You'll just get attacked again if you stay around me." If he left, I could try to regroup, do *something* productive here.

There was silence, no response from him. His emotions further ensnared me, baffled me: anger and sorrow and something else I couldn't discern. I didn't understand — no one else was remotely around, so these were all clearly from him. He'd intentionally wanted to talk to me, even came *here* to do so. I finally turned my head to see him just staring at his right palm. He wasn't in pain, wasn't injured, just staring as if Rota was still there, talking to him. But that wasn't the case, wasn't possible. "I fucked up. I'm sorry."

I jerked my head away from him. The words meant more than I wanted them to. I didn't want to forgive him, but my resolve wavered at his tone, his emotion, his words. I hated it. Was this part of the modifications to me from Kisate, like how his emotions were the loudest to me? I hated he genuinely meant the apology, hated this deep drop in my stomach, ball in my throat, all reactions from my empathy, from him. "Your girlfriend would be upset if she knew you were with me. You should go back to her." He needed to go back to where he'd be safe. That was one of the benefits of not being at North Pines: they wanted me, so if he wasn't near me, his life would be peaceful. He wouldn't be roped in any longer. Unlike when all this had started, he had the chance to leave.

Yet... that grip around my heart, my lungs, tightened like the air was choked out of them. My words had hurt him, made him even more frustrated and remorseful. I didn't want to know how he felt; it just weakened my resolve further.

"I just..." His voice weakened. "It terrified the shit outta me when I realized that you might've been one of the ones hurt, and fuck, it ain't even that you're *one* of the ones, you're *the one* they wanted. Why can't you ever be allowed to be just a high schooler again? Why's that so goddamn *wrong*?"

No amount of wishing would make me "just a high schooler" again. It wasn't even worth wasting time on the notion. And why should I have been happy when so many people had died because of me? I didn't have the right to be "just a high schooler." "Because..." Because I'd lived, so many others had died. "I made the choice. I'm a mage. No amount of hiding will change that." Sia had told me when I'd had Act that death would be easier than living through what happened after. I'd said I didn't care.

I wished that was still the truth.

"We didn't even know or understand. Not really."

Neither had my classmates as I'd watched them be stabbed in front of me, losing their limbs and their heads as blood seeped further and further into the rubber gym floor. "Is that what you wanted to say?"

Another response that hurt him; his emotions further filled my body, clouding my mind, weakening my resolve. I bit my tongue to prevent apologizing. I hated memories of our childhood coming to mind, of when we'd been eight and I'd scraped my knee, him finding a band-aid and patching it up while I'd cried. Or how he'd listened to me complain about Mom and Dani so many times, problems so mundane and stupid now, but he'd always just smiled. He'd only ever yelled at me once, and he hadn't been wrong: I'd ruined his life.

His aura was still engraved around my symbol, and I didn't even know how to ask why or how. If I upset him too much, would he just get rid of me? I didn't understand NEO beyond him having some amount of control over me. Until he'd come to my house that day Sase had attacked me, him, and Maya, he hadn't even glanced at me since I'd gained the branding. I didn't know what'd changed for him, and I wasn't sure I could afford to ask.

I'd missed the softness of his eyes so much, missed having someone who understood things like no one else could. It was a warmth I hadn't felt in months, one I couldn't afford to get used to again.

His fist balled and I felt his nails pushing against skin. I felt anger — a temper that scared me in its intensity, like I'd never felt from him before. "I really fucked up, didn't I?" That rage remained despite his grip releasing.

"It's not fair."

"That's what I'm *saying*: it's not fair we're dragged into this bullshit, and—"

I lowered my head, squeezing my eyes shut. "It's not fair Kisate made those changes to me but Takite left you alone. It's not fair I feel that you're genuinely sorry and I want to forgive you despite everything. It's not fair your emotions are *so damn loud* and I don't get a choice about it. But nothing's fair so *here we are.*"

He paused, his anger replaced by genuine confusion.

"What're you talking 'bout?" He really was free then, just like I'd suspected.

I refused to cry in front of him. But my lip quivered regardless, so *tired* of everything. "Kisate modified me somehow, something to do with you, right before Chloé died. And it's what made your emotions so *loud* and why... why when I had NEO, you got..." I couldn't even say it, not knowing how to verbalize the emotions I felt and unable to mentally separate what was mine or his or even emotions we were both experiencing right now. "Something to do with berserk and forcing us together and I don't know. But Takite must've had more of a conscience because it's obvious he didn't follow through."

Jordan said nothing, his emotions calm, removed, and even confused for a brief moment. I finally turned my attention to him, hearing him mumble, "The fuck's...?" He shook his head. "Sorry. That's just..." He took in a deep breath before releasing the air through his lips. "It's okay to be pissed at me. I deserve it. I just... I thought 'cause they're gone, it meant things'd be over. That they wouldn't have left 'til things were. And summer got hectic's fuck, and..." His voice quieted, the rapidness of his words slowing closer to their normal speed. "Guess none of that matters though, huh? You're right. I left you, like you said." His eyes turned to me, a determination in them I'd never seen before from him. "But I can promise you this, on whatever you want — my life, if that's worth a damn. I don't want you ever scared of me 'cause of Arbiter. Only reason I got it at all's 'cause he said you'd be in NEO forever without it."

He'd always been a poor liar, even more so with his emotions blaring through me. There was no way he lied, not knowingly. That tremble finally snuck into my own voice, my resolve shattered by his words, his emotions. "Why didn't you ever say anything to him about how he acted around me? Why was magic okay with him but not me?" I hated how childish my voice was right then, that tremble that refused to leave. "Why wasn't I enough?"

His arm reached to my shoulder, hugging me from the side; his fingers pressed into my side as his forehead brushed against my neck. "Goddammit..." Another deep breath from him, warm exhales onto my collarbone. "It's not you. I was... I *am* scared — scared shitless, really. And it felt like Richard's the only one who just saw me for me instead of for the damn magic shit, but... you've never been the problem. And I'm sorry I made it seem like you ever were."

I wouldn't cry. But... it was the first in a long time that I wanted to cry because of other than how alone I felt. It likely was nothing more than his emotions clouding my judgment. "You're just going to ignore me the second he's around. And you have a girlfriend. You should be with her, and..."

There was no hesitation as he said, "I'll do better, listen better. If I don't, yell 'til I get it. You deserve better."

I didn't cry, but when I finally hugged him back, I didn't want to let go. None of it was fair.

# Chapter Fifteen

## apologies

Apartment's silent for once, and I wished it ain't.

I hadn't ever meant to hurt her. Only time I knew I had's the day I snapped at her, and I apologized the next day 'cause I knew I'd been outta line. All I'd thought 'bout's how I wanted my friend back, the way she used to smile and no longer did; thought if I just waited 'til things're over, everything'd go back to normal and she'd smile like she used to.

Now, it's so obvious what a hell'va selfish stance that'd been. I'd assumed she had the same choice I did: as long as I didn't use magic publicly and didn't get caught by whatever fuckfaces those people were, I could just ignore it all. That'd never been the case for her though — eyes always drawn to her, now more than ever. Just 'cause I had time to stall shit out didn't mean she did.

Her words played back in my mind: how she'd pushed me away in ways she'd never done b'fore, how many times I'd almost gotten up, given up. Ain't sure if I'd inadvertently guilted her, but goddammit, I just wanted to make shit up to her even though I knew the past's done. Over. And I couldn't *make* her believe I'd meant it when I said I'd fucked up and was sorry. If nothing else, I hoped I got through to her 'bout NEO 'cause I didn't want that power, didn't want Arbiter — would prefer to pretend it'd never happened, throw away the key, forget the whole fucked up thing. If our positions'd been swapped though, how would've I handled this shit? I couldn't begin to imagine and couldn't blame her for not trusting me.

Not helping my case's that I'd gotten distracted by these random-ass images — no, like a movie, almost — when she'd talked 'bout Kisate and Takite. It'd been so goddamn weird, like this choppy-ass, blurry movie with missing chunks played out b'fore me. Reminded me of how I'd experienced memories from b'fore my Act now that I had hypermnesia. Pretty sure I hadn't made it up 'cause I'd never been 'specially creative. Even worse, I'd barely heard her the first few seconds it'd happened, my attention on whatever that'd been — a woman that'd looked like Kylie had when this'd all started, short hair to her chin, eyes a little more green than Kylie's'd ever been. But that woman could've been her twin, would've easily passed for Kylie without my hypermnesia comparing the two. And the voice that'd spoken to her'd sounded so close to my own in pitch and even tone — vulnerable and unsure. But I'd never had that conversation with Kylie. Hell, didn't even know what it's 'bout or meant. I'd tried to figure it out a few times since I'd come home, but despite replaying it in my mind — it having the same clarity as when I'd experienced it while with Kylie, gaps and all — I'd only gotten brief flashes of emotion, of hesitance and sorrow.

There's something so unsettling 'bout it, and it freaked the fuck outta me — so familiar, yet so distant. It *had* to be something with my hypermnesia, but *what*? And it wasn't like I could talk 'bout it with Kylie. Sure, I'd managed to walk her back to her townhome and we'd caught up a little, but I'm far from being able to call in favors to her anytime soon, not to mention she had enough shit going on anyways, didn't need this too. Speaking of failing people, had kinda bailed on Emily today when I'd decided to cut class to check on Kylie. Was off today, so should be holding the damn shopping bags as she bitched and gossiped 'bout whatever, but Kylie'd worried the hell outta me when I saw her Saturday, and testament to how shitty I was, I didn't even regret ditching Emily.

I heard the front door open, the same creak that'd been there the past four months.

Shit. Not that anyone cared I cut class, but I ain't in the mood to deal with whatever bullshit's coming through the front door. Had enough on my mind without my family's extra *assistance*. I stayed quiet, hearing Elaine grumble some cusses b'fore she slammed the bathroom door shut. That's my cue for escape, and I fully intended to use it. Waiting 'til I heard the shower cut on, I got up, throwing my tennis shoes and a jacket on as I grabbed my keys and slid them into my pocket. Softly closing then locking the door, I managed to escape outta the apartment without additional bullshit. But where to now?

Could go to the park or library; weather's a bit cold but not shitty enough that outside's outta the question. Then again, didn't wanna be around my family, but as hard as it'd been keeping up with Kylie while dealing with the damn thing, randomly out in public's prob'bly a shitty idea too. I'd been lying on my bed the past hour, staring up at the peeling white popcorn ceiling. If I did that while randomly standing around, prob'bly'd end up mugged or worse. Even the library's not gonna work 'cause they'd get pissy if I just sat in a chair, staring at a wall, which's what I needed to concentrate on this shit. Those're the only two "alone" places I got, though. Guess that damn training house too, but it ain't safer than the other two, really. Where *was* safe, though?

Just a few days prior, I'd spent the night at Richard's. He'd said I could come over any time — that the room I'd slept in'd be held for me. Hadn't exactly been his subtlest moment, clearly referencing if Father's in a shitty mood and not random-ass visits but... something 'bout that vision-memory-video-whatever-the-hell-it-was bothered the fuck outta me, and I needed to figure it out. Guess that meant I'm burning even more favors today, but I also knew that Richard ain't the type to offer for the sake of courtesy; ain't sure he even knew how to be polite in the first place. He'd said "any time" and that's something I'm taking him up on today as my feet too easily retraced the path I'd taken to his house on Saturday. Most of the town's empty right now 'cause everyone's at school or work, so made it painless enough getting to his house. But all too soon, I was back at that intercom, pressing the button — at least I'd learned when to hold and let go of the damn thing this time around.

"How may I help you?" The older man that'd answered last time wasn't the one on the intercom today, a middle-aged woman speaking instead.

Unfortunately, I'd been counting on the same guy there that I'd met last time, and I couldn't say I'm here for Richard today — he's still at college in Atlanta. "I, uh, I'm Jordan, and Richard said to stop by any time so, uh..." Fuck, I hadn't thought this through either and only now realized what a shitty-ass idea it was.

"One moment." The woman sounded less pissy than the man the other day, but that ain't a high bar. A few minutes passed, leaving me awkwardly rubbing the back of my neck as I stared at the trimmed grass, perfect lines across the lush green lawn despite the rest of the town's grass dying from it getting colder out. Any other place, and I'd wonder if it's Richard's doing with his earth alignment but doubted that's the case here. "My apologies for the wait, Master Jordan. I confirmed with Master Richard and have made a note so this won't be a... recurring concern." How many fuckin' people worked here where they had *notes* on people?

The gates opened. "T-thanks." Still felt uncomfortable's fuck being addressed as "master" too. Pretty sure they all made more than my family's combined income. Would likely be a promotion to work here, but that felt awkward's fuck too 'cause Richard's my friend, and well. Yeah.

I stepped inside, gates clanking shut behind me. As before, the front door opened from the inside as I approached, but I didn't see SuzyAnne waiting for me, instead a much younger woman in a suit was at the door. "I'm happy to escort you to Master Richard's loft if you'd like."

Shaking my head, I said, "I, uh, I remember, thanks."

She nodded to me as she turned away, walking out of the foyer. I walked as polite as I could without making it obvious I hauled ass to the far left corridor — "Richard's loft," as they'd called it. Opening the door at the end of the hallway, I saw dimmed lights and the tv turned off, unlike last time. They kept the lights on even if no one's around? Ain't that expensive?

...then again, I think expense's the last thing this "house" was concerned with.

Richard'd said the room beside his's reserved for me so hopefully it's fine just to crash in for a few hours. I knocked on the door to be safe, but no one replied, only a ringing silence that unnerved the shit outta me. After waiting a few more seconds just to be sure, I cracked the door slowly, peeking inside to see much the same as this living room area with some dimmed lights but otherwise vacant. A relieved sigh slipped out as I stepped inside and closed the door before turning the bedside lamp on. Sitting on the edge of the bed b'fore lying back with my feet still on the ground, I stared at the intricate bronze trim around the walls, the similarly bronze ceiling fan still. Was surreal to have a place like this — somewhere private, to myself, a thing people like me never got. Really, privacy itself'd become all but nonexistent after my Act, making it that much more disorienting to have a damn mini-apartment all to myself.

That ain't why I'm here though. Needed to get my ass focused 'cause I couldn't spend the night — needed to get back to the apartment this evening so I could get ready for school and work tomorrow.

Really wished I knew what the hell I'm even trying to focus *on* — like an itch I couldn't reach, a thread unraveling an ocean wave hitting the shore, but I couldn't explain *why* it felt like that. That girl that's similar to Kylie... she looked like the girl I'd seen back at that castle too, actually. *He'd* said that'd been Chloé, but fuck knew if it'd been a lie or not. Even more so, actually, that girl's one of the ones I saw whenever Emily touched me, latched onto my arm, or tried other PDA-shit.

Hypermnesia only worked after Act, *he'd* said, and I actually could confirm that one since I'm barely able to recall even the day b'fore my Act or 'specially like Kylie's Act compared to the day my Act's on, those b'fore Act memories so faint and faded. These memories of the Kylie-lookalikes're all like that, but I remembered those brief flashes like all my memories after that first time. Like snapshots of memory, a movie with only seconds to it.

A loud single knock yanked me from my thoughts. I jumped to my feet, ready to get cussed out by whoever's room this actually was. Rushing to the door, I opened it, saying, "Ah, so sorry, I—" What I hadn't expected was Richard there, raised eyebrow and arms crossed against his chest.

"Something up?" he asked.

Lowering my eyes away from him and onto the expensive carpet, I ain't sure what to say. It was, it wasn't, some middle "I don't know hell's up, but I guess I'm fine physically, kinda" option I didn't know how the hell I'd begin to explain. "I don't know."

He pushed past me as his arms lowered and walked into the room, moving to the left wall, near the connected bathroom as he regained his posture of leaning against the wall while crossing his arms over his chest. "When I said any time, didn't think that'd be three days later in the middle of the day."

After closing the door, I walked back to the bed, sitting on the edge as I stared at the freshly vacuumed beige carpet. "S-sorry. Just didn't know where else to—"

"No." He huffed. "I'm not saying it's a problem you're here. I'm saying the hell's happened to need it in the first place?"

How'd he even gotten back here so damn quick? On second thought, I prob'bly'd look even more like a dumbass if I asked him that. I flipped my hand over, staring at my palm. I think it's 'cause that's how I'd learned how to generate small fires and ice shards, so it'd become the instinctual connection when thinking 'bout magic shit. "I talked to Kylie."

"Mistake number one."

I wanted to snap that ain't the point, to leave her alone for one goddamn minute now that I'd seen how affected she'd been by him. Didn't know how to say that to *him* though, least of all when I'd barged into his house uninvited to begin with. "She'd been telling me 'bout something, and like... some weird shit happened during it. I just wanted to try figuring it out but didn't know where else to go. Sorry, didn't mean to cause problems."

He walked over to the wall switch, holding the metallic button that he'd said worked as an intercom to the staff. "Bring a chair in here. Breakfast set."

As he released the button, I heard a voice from the switch reply, "Of course, Master Richard."

His eyes refocused back on me as he said, "Mic's only live when the button's held. Can tell this's going to be a second, and I'm not standing here this whole time."

"Oh, uh, right." It really *was* like room service, and he seemed to think that's perfectly normal, expected even. Ain't sure I'd ever understand the difference of worlds we lived in even with seeing it first-hand. "Sorry."

I heard him scoff, moving back over to that left wall. "Quit apologizing. Do what you want with the room. If you want to cut and crash here, I don't give a damn. But it's not something you'd do for the hell of it either."

While I'd never taken school seriously and hadn't ever exactly showed up on time consistently, he ain't wrong that I'd never really just outright cut just 'cause I'd felt like it. At least I got free meals at school, and being home's just another chance to get my ass beat or someone bitching at me. "Y-yeah."

Someone knocked at the door. Richard answered it without even glancing at me. Three different staff members brought in a small circular table and two chairs. Richard directed them to place it against the back wall, snapping at them to hurry and being rather bitchy the entire time. All three weren't remotely phased, rolling their eyes when their backs were to him. After this entire furniture set'd been dropped into the room, he wasted no time kicking them out, afterward moving one of the two chairs across from the bed. After sitting down on said chair, he crossed his ankle over his thigh as he brushed hair off his shoulder. "*Finally.* Took them long enough. Now back to what you were saying."

He acted like they took forever when really, it'd been fast as hell. The fact that the staff's used to it's even worse the more I thought 'bout it, and I still didn't get *why* Richard's randomly nice to me but admittedly an ass to everyone else. "I, uh, she's telling me 'bout something." Even replaying her words back more than once — something 'bout Kisate altering her but Takite not doing the same to me — I couldn't make sense of what she'd meant and hadn't dared to ask once the conversation'd moved on. But that'd been when that vision, memory, whatever the hell it was, suddenly hit me. "But I got this, like... flashback thing. But it ain't of me, and there's this girl that *looked* like Kylie, but it ain't her either. And the person I saw through, that's talking with her, *sounded* like me, and it's just..."

"Just?" he prodded, surprisingly patient in tone, but I could tell it ain't gonna last long and he's already annoyed I ain't being *direct*.

But like... how could I describe whatever the hell it was when I wasn't sure myself? "I saw *something*, like the actual event she's talking 'bout, I think, but like, neither of us — hell, any of us— would've been alive for it. Would've been back hundreds of years ago, definitely not within the past couple years. I don't... Did I just make it up? Why's it feel just like a *memory* then? I don't..."

He'd been quiet long enough that I got the courage to glance up at him. Saw him sitting in the chair, hands folded in his lap as he blankly stared in the direction of his feet. As I'm 'bout to apologize, he stood b'fore leaving the room, door still open. I waited, not sure what else to do, and he returned a few minutes later with his spell book. Guess it's hidden somewhere in his room so none of the staff saw it. He closed the door back with his foot, flipping through pages so aggressively I'm surprised none ripped. His fingers traced a line on the page as he mumbled, "Damn," under his breath as he sat back down on the chair.

Richard annoyed or dismayed rarely worked out for *anyone*, and I didn't wanna be in the middle of whatever he ain't happy 'bout. "Uh? What's wrong?"

"Thought I'd read something similar to this, but not quite."

Did I really wanna push this? If I just said I must've been tired or gotten overly creative, he'd drop it. Could call it a normal memory problem, something I hadn't had in years now. Something I knew ain't right, deep in me. I pushed my lips together.

Whole thing'd been a mistake.

"Sorry, didn't mean to interrupt shit," I said. I'm chasing literal illusions, wasting everyone's time. Hell, even my own, not that it's particularly valuable.

He stopped skimming the page he's on, his attention now centered on me. I shifted uncomfortably, rubbing the back of my neck. "One of the first things you told me — have shown me more times than I can count — is that your memory's damn near perfect. If you say it's a memory, it's a memory."

For not the first time, I wished I had his confidence in anything, but 'specially in myself right then. "What if I just made it up, like some over-active imagination shit?"

He snorted, raising an eyebrow at me. "Never mentioned confusing shit like memories and imagination before."

That's 'cause it'd never happened, but that didn't help me right then — not in the way I wanted it to. "I-I mean, haven't really, but..." Shit like whatever I saw ain't really happened b'fore either — closest'd been like when Emily'd touched me or even those hallucinations in Asuza's castle that June. "I mean, unless, but like..."

I heard the chair creak as he adjusted. "Unless what?"

My mouth dried. I'd never mentioned the kidnapping to him. He didn't wanna hear 'bout Kylie, and I didn't wanna remember that event more than I already did every time I saw her wrists. But... "Something that happened b'fore your Act. It's the closest thing to this... whatever it is, but still different."

"Tell me then."

Memories rushed over me, every moment since my Act, since this hell show'd made my life worse than it already'd been. "Not sure if it reached you, but Kylie went missing the June b'fore last — June 29th. The bastard that'd killed her last two, uhm..." I knew the word to use. Couldn't even argue it, really: incarnations. But it felt wrong. Felt like admitting defeat and submission and that *he'd* been right. "The two b'fore her."

"Shame he fucked up this time." That's too far. My heart raced as I wanted to snap at him more than I'd ever wanted b'fore. The memories of how Chloé'd been dangled in front of me like a trophy so vivid, or when Kylie and Leah and Chloé'd all blended together, barely conscious and bleeding and she'd really almost not made it. Of Kylie just days prior saying she wished he would've succeeded, words that'd knocked the breath outta me when I'd heard them.

My voice strained, lower than I almost ever spoke, as I said, "He killed them by draining them of mana, of blood." I saw Chloé, her lips purple and skin cold as I touched her cheek and saw no breaths from her chest. Shook my head, water pushing to my eyes and—

"Jordan?"

I let out a breath I didn't know I'd been holding. The fuck'd I just seen? That'd felt so real, but it hadn't been what I'd seen in that damn castle, for sure. Squeezing my eyes shut and then reopening them, I wiped liquid from where my eyes had watered. "The fuck...?"

"You okay?" He'd leaned forward, might've been bracing for me to black out, given his posture.

I pushed air through my lungs, trying to steady my now shaky breathing. "There's another one, just now. Something I've never experienced but felt so damn real."

Richard paused before asking, "Guessing Rotanu saved her and she came back, ever as much of a bitch. What's that got to do with this shit you're seeing?"

The hallucinations're the first time I'd seen shit like this, but I'd thought it's 'cause of Asuza fuckin' with me and maybe John and Dmitri. But... that couldn't've been right, I realized. How would've *he* or me known what Chloé or 'specially Leah looked like? Chloé's body'd been mostly preserved on the altar, but Leah's hadn't been there at all, yet I'd still seen her briefly too. "The first time," I mumbled, these pieces tying together but still making no goddamn sense. "I just... I thought it's part of that bastard's hallucination shit, but..."

"What hallucinations?" I'd not mentioned anything 'bout what it'd taken to get *to* Kylie that day, just the result — just as little as I could get away with talking 'bout.

All this time, I'd thought those visions had been part of that mind fuck spell Siani had pulled me out of. But what if it hadn't been? What if it'd actually been a real memory I somehow had, triggered from something I'd experienced, like how it'd happened over and over with Emily? "He'd a body laid out on an altar — it'd been the one b'fore Kylie, still there, dead. But that somehow triggered this like... mind fuck where I saw her and the one b'fore her and Kylie and a ton of other shit. But... what if... what if the other ones I saw, what if... that's from Dmitri's and John's memories somehow? And then that one earlier today, that's from Takite's memory? And what if what I just saw's from Dmitri's memories again? Then what... how...?"

If hypermnesia only worked after Act, then how the mother goddamn fuckin' hell did I have memories from *other incarnations*? They didn't have the clarity of my post-Act memories, but I shouldn't've had them at all.

"What about Riyati itself? Are they all around that bitch?"

*Were* they all of Kylie? I focused on trying to remember something from the damn place that'd started it all. I saw this room, stone all around, dimly lit by a torch in a man's hand. Something tense's going on, this deep stomach-turning terror eating through my body. Screams from somewhere, but not the room I'm in. My eyes rested on a man with long blonde hair, tanned skin — Richard, but older, decades older than he was now. I felt warm hands on my arm. My free hand went to rest over those holding me, cold sweat against her cold skin. Her?

Even though I couldn't see, I knew the one touching me's Kisate, which'd make this from Takite.

"Woah, Jordan—"

Everything felt removed, disoriented, and spun all around somehow. I took shallow breaths as my lungs gasped for air I ain't sure why I suddenly needed. Richard'd grabbed me from falling forward onto the carpet, but why the fuck was I so winded and light-headed? Like that time I'd mana transferred at Asuza's—

Like mana drain.

Richard pushed me back onto the edge of the bed as I prioritized shoving air into my lungs and steadying my doubled vision. My head throbbed like fuck. Yet whatever I'd seen, I recalled it like a normal hypermnesia memory. I mumbled, "Fuck," as I brought my palm against my right temple.

Releasing my shoulders where he'd kept me from falling, Richard stepped back. "The hell just happened?"

They *were* memories — memories of those b'fore me, of lives and events I'd never led yet somehow could remember if I focused or saw something that triggered them. Trying to force it burned a fuckton of mana if this time's any indication, leading to this damn splitting headache, weak legs, blurred vision, and uneven breaths. But the fact they *could* be recalled — fact that I remembered them...

It meant what I'd seen that day's real: Takite and Kisate had cast a spell, but it didn't match what Kylie'd been saying. I didn't understand much else from the bit I'd seen, but something to do with berserk and alignment adjustments and... fuck, I didn't even know these words, not with how they'd been using them. "Trying to force memories's an outright bitch," I said between a few coughs of air to my lungs.

"Wait, so you actually...?"

I nodded, squeezing my eyes shut. I finally caught my breath, but that only reminded me how much everything *else* hurt like fuck. "I think... yeah. I'm somehow remembering those b'fore me, their memories." No idea how the fuck I'd managed it, though hypermnesia's at play somehow, given I seemed to be the only one.

"Well? What'd you remember? This is fascinating."

My mouth opened, but my heart still raced, words not coming. I struggled to vocalize the brief memory I'd seen. Took a deep breath as I replayed the memory, more prepared. It acted like a damn regular memory for me now, just like the one with Kylie in the training house or the ones at Asuza's or the ones with Emily. "It's, uh, it's somewhere dark, lots of stone. I think... it's somewhere on that damn island though—"

"Island?" Richard raised his eyebrow once more, a distance in his eyes despite him staring straight at me.

"Y-yeah, it's on an island. I mean, I *think* it is." I didn't think. I *knew*. But... *how* did I know that? I'd never been there. Kylie hadn't been there. Richard hadn't been there.

"How long's this been going on? You're getting a lot more of them recently, it sounds?"

If this, the hallucinations at Asuza's, and what I experienced so much any time Emily touched me're really all the same, then... "Oh my god." I thought Rotanu'd been fuckin' with me, kept implanting memories or some shit. What if he *hadn't*, though? 'Cause from what I'd seen... it ain't just him and Siani that'd been together: Takite'd loved Kisate. John'd loved Leah. Dmitri'd fallen for Chloé, much like I wanted Kylie but had never dared to even dream'd happen.

Richard'd said more than once I'm just "stuck" on Kylie, and I knew he ain't necessarily wrong 'bout that, but now... Why? Something ain't making sense; this all *meant something*. Ain't sure *what*, but, like, how'd I fall for the same damn woman every single incarnation? Worse yet, how'd I fuck up so bad that, unlike Chloé or Leah or Kisate, not only's Kylie uninterested, but she didn't even wanna look at me anymore?

"Care to share? Seems an exciting time over there." That bitchiness's fully in his tone now, concern replaced by impatience.

I nodded, moving my eyes back to the carpet. "These memories've gotten more detailed. That one's just the one that really got my attention, but it's been happening since that day she was kidnapped. I hadn't..."

He sat back in the chair, that answer appeasing him enough. "Your hypermnesia's getting stronger then, like my suggestion potency is from more mana."

The lessons I hadn't wanted that Siani'd given anyways, 'bout magipoten and mana and Kylie's empathy getting stronger the higher her magipoten became due to an increase in mana sustaining her body. That wasn't just Kylie. It wasn't just Richard.

It's me as well.

All our abilities continued strengthening regardless of if we wanted them to or not, just like mana itself.

My eyes watered, body still weak from trying to force that one memory and mind racing at answers I didn't want and realizations that wouldn't leave my damn brain. God fuckin' damn Rotanu'd been right: I loved her, wanted Kylie and not

**95**

Emily, and like a damn ass had been using Emily as a substitute for Kylie. I'd wronged both of them. I couldn't make Kylie return my feelings, but I sure as hell wouldn't lead Emily on anymore, not more than I already had.

"I'm sorry," I said.

Richard grimaced. "What're you even apologizing for *this time*?"

Balling my fist, I didn't know how to say I'd been wrong. Had wronged Kylie. Had wronged Emily. Fuck, had wronged goddamn Rotanu even. Felt my mouth move, unsure what to even say since I knew my realization'd just piss off Richard.

"I-I noticed a pattern in those memories. The bits I've had..." My eyes watered; it ain't that I felt sad, but just felt *too much* somehow, like chaos swirled around in a bottle with fear and acceptance and anger and affection mingling together in ways I didn't know's possible. Maybe Kylie had those feelings and memories of Kisate, Leah, and Chloé somewhere deep in her, but my hypermnesia brought them into my consciousness while hers and Richard's weren't. Maybe that's even why she'd accepted me as Arbiter despite clearly not trusting me like she once had. Or maybe I'm fuckin' grasping to have not completely fucked up everything with her, wishing for some second chance and latching onto any half-not-even-possible theory I thought of. Yet...

"I..." I'd never said it out loud. My family'd never been the affectionate type, us stuck together for pragmatism in coping with Father more than any strong affectionate feelings. "I don't think I'm moving on from her. I..." I swallowed, head still throbbing and I wanted to cry without even knowing why, but goddammit, couldn't the damn tears wait 'til I'm alone? Always been such a fuckin' crybaby. "The past incarnations, I... All of them, I..." *I*? They weren't me. But I had their memories, their feelings, their thoughts for those brief glimpses.

Richard stepped closer, kneeling in front of me. "Uh, you okay?"

Even more so than the last time he'd asked, I wished I had an answer. "John and Dmitri — the two b'fore me — they..." Why hadn't it clicked? Why'd it taken 'til now? Siani'd said it, clear as day: incarnations only persisted past incarnation cycles if they'd died unclean deaths. I knew Kisate and Takite, knew Leah and

Chloé. But John and Dmitri shouldn't've been here during my life. "They committed suicide, seeing Leah and Chloé's dead bodies. They all... they loved her. And I..."

He huffed, rolling his eyes. "She's just another bitch."

I squeezed my eyes shut as I shook my head. "I-I fucked up b'fore, not saying shit, but she..." I loved seeing her smile, something that never happened now, loved seeing her entranced when something caught her interest. "I want her around. I was being a damn immature idiot trying to prove Rotanu wrong, but..." He'd been right. Maybe not 'bout everything, but this... this I couldn't deny any longer. "I love her."

"You *what*? Love? That's the *grand realization* you had?"

It ain't a surprise he didn't get it but didn't matter. I knew. They were words I couldn't take back, and more so... knowledge I wouldn't hide from any longer.

# Chapter Sixteen

## secret-logic-defying-thing

Maya | October 5
Opal Pines Streets

I walked faster than I strictly needed to. It was Friday, the day Kylie had said to come back. In hindsight, I probably should've checked with her that she still meant it, but my phone was for emergencies only. Refills required money I really needed to use elsewhere. If she said she still had no answers, I wouldn't "tell" — whatever she meant by that — because there wasn't anyone for me to tell. It didn't change the fact that I'd still like to know more though, however surreal it felt now that it was over.

This past week, I'd tried to take better notes than normal, and I'd brought them with me for the classes I shared with her. Regardless of anything else, she'd been hospitalized and kept on bed rest while getting behind on homework. She had more than enough going on outside of catching up on school, so maybe my notes would help her with the very unpleasant makeup work waiting for her.

I rang the doorbell, as I had times past. Kylie's mom greeted me, welcoming me in. As I saw Kylie at the top of the staircase, she didn't run down to greet me like she'd done previously. She had bags under her eyes that I didn't remember her having when we'd talked last week, her hair only partially brushed. Was she stressed over whatever she planned to tell me?

Pointing to the backpack on my back, I said, "I brought my notes, in case they'd help with catching up."

"That's so sweet of you!" Kylie's mom looked far more excited than Kylie herself. "It'll really help since she's starting back on Monday."

For her going back to school so soon, why did she look worse than last weekend?

I barely heard Kylie softly say, "Yeah..." Her eyes stared through me, maybe not even at me at all, as far apart as we were.

"I'll leave you girls to it." Kylie's mom walked off into another room. Kylie still hadn't come down the stairs, and I wasn't sure if I was welcome up with how exhausted she looked.

Her lips pressed together as she nodded, lacking the energy that'd so annoyed me the first day we'd met. "It's okay. Come on up."

Doing as she'd said, I walked up the stairs, following her into her room and shutting the door behind me. As she'd told me to do past times, I sat on the pullout couch, taking my shoes off and setting them to the side, my backpack on the carpet beside my shoes.

"Thank you." She stared out of the window near her desk, her head turned away from me. "For not saying anything in front of her."

Why would I have? "You said not to talk about it, didn't you? Why would I then?"

She chuckled, moving from standing between her bed and chair to sitting on her desk chair with her legs crossed as she faced me. But she still wouldn't look at me, her eyes glazed over. "You'd be surprised. That doesn't stop some people."

Exactly how common was whatever this was? "So a lot of people know?"

Her hand moved to her necklace ring yet again. She shook her head. "Every person is a risk. And I... I don't want Mom caught up in this. It's already been hard on her." So whatever this secret-logic-defying-thing was, Kylie's mom truly had no idea. I guess that's why her mom seemed so happy in comparison, like Kylie had the first couple of weeks of school.

"Risk? Like when that woman appeared?"

She still wouldn't face me, something unsettling about how she went out of her way to avoid doing so. "There's that, yeah, but at least that's just for me." Her grip around the ring tightened. "I guess... to start more at the basics, the woman who attacked us... her group wants to kill me. That's why they attacked the school, and I'm not sure why they didn't finish the job when they had the chance."

So the school attack really was tied to whatever all this was, whatever had happened last time I was here. I knew it, but I still wasn't sure what to say in response. Why was someone who had seemed so sheltered involved in something deadly? "Was that why they followed up last week? Has it happened again since?"

She shook her head once more. "I don't know what they're trying to do, or even what their end goal is outside of killing me. I haven't slept much because I've been anticipating the next attack, but nothing's happened so far." So that's why she had such dark bags. I guess it made sense: if they knew where she lived, where else could she hide?

The why had been confirmed, but not the how or what. At least I had some answers, a start to figuring this all out. "What happened last week anyway?"

Kylie's lips pulled into a slight smile. What was funny about my question? For the first time since I'd arrived today, she gained more of her usual demeanor. "You're not at all worried?"

What would I have been worried about? None of this involved me. "About what?"

"I mean, you're just..." Her eyes lowered once more. "Very calm, I guess. Detached might be a better way to explain it." I'd had a week to process the bit of information I had. "And you're not... I guess, like, when Dani found out, she didn't believe anything I said. Still doesn't for parts."

"Danny? Was that the guy that was over here that day?" She'd said a lot of words, but barely any of them had answered the questions I'd asked; it didn't seem an intentional attempt to

**101**

evade anything though. Right then, she somewhat resembled the person to my right in class, social and rambly. There was still this removed distance compared to when we'd talked at school or even in this room times past, though, a level of tension deep in her breaths.

"Huh? Oh." She shook her head, a light flush to her cheeks. "That's not... Dani's not really involved in things. Lacks the, I guess you'd call it 'aptitude,' but tries to force her way in regardless. She's someone I've known since my childhood. I don't think you've met her." That must've been the red-haired girl I'd seen in pictures. She was likely the same red-haired girl I'd seen at the hospital as well, then. I didn't bother to correct that we'd sort of met, only nodded. "She's, um, I guess it's easiest to say every person has the ability to use magic to some degree."

"Are you still on the painkillers?" Was she drugged? Or high, for that matter? The hospital probably had administered some fairly strong drugs, but she hadn't seemed to be on anything last week. Maybe it was sleep deprivation getting to her.

She softly laughed that time. "Not since I left the hospital, sorry." I watched as she glanced around, and I raised my eyebrow at her in response. "I guess that'd be the easiest." She held out her left hand, a soft orb of light resting above her skin as the immediate few inches around the orb increased in brightness.

I focused my gaze, trying to see how the orb functioned. "An optical illusion?"

Chuckling, she moved to directly in front of me. "No illusion." Her eyes lowered to the orb. It steadied as her hand dropped to her side while the orb hovered midair. "Well, guess that's actually technically not true. It's shifting some air currents with refraction from the light within those air currents. Though actually, it works in the dark too, so maybe there *is* more to it than that." For that brief second, she was the same person I sat beside in class. "Oh, um... That wouldn't matter for what you care about though. For that, it's easiest to just say it's magic, yeah." Her left hand flicked, and the light disappeared.

Something like that couldn't exist. But it'd been clearly in front of me and now wasn't, much like how her hand had glowed when touching that guy and the woman had held a sword of some type with no sheath that had appeared from nowhere.

Magic wasn't real, but it was somehow in front of me, nonetheless. "You said all humans have it, this 'magic'?"

Kylie nodded. "To varying degrees, and even then, there's like an 'on' switch for using it. We call it 'Activation,' or 'Act.' Mine was near two years ago now."

"But mine hasn't been flipped on or whatever?" I'd never seen any of this, heard of this. How could it apply to every human, yet no one knew? That made no sense. Yet if she was lying, she was doing an exceptional job — even more so with the trick she'd just shown.

Her head tilted to the side as she stared at me. "I don't know, honestly. I can see your aura, sure, but I don't know of a way to verify if Act has or hasn't happened. Interesting question though." She turned around, pulling a hardbound book from her desk as she ripped a sticky note off and wrote something on it, sticking it in the book. "I'll try to look into that, but I probably can't get you an answer today because it takes a while to find things in my spell book. I'm still trying to better memorize how it's organized, let alone everything in it and the spells themselves." She turned back around to face me. "I doubt you've had Act though. Even at a low magipoten... um, like, low mana, which is like, um, the amount of magic in your blood or body, or something like that. But if it's low, you should still see some auras probably and have an ability of some type, so you'd probably know. Though I guess Dani can't really see auras despite Act, but that's another problem entirely."

I didn't even know where to begin asking — so many words and not great explanations just thrown at me as if they made perfect sense. "So it's 'probably no' because I don't see... something and I... don't have the ability to... see that something?"

"Oh, auras and an ability. So mages — that's a person that's experienced Act — can see auras, they're like... each person has a color that represents them, and the brightness is relative to their mana. So like mine's a lot brighter than yours. You can generally see some resemblance between people who share blood too, like siblings or parents and children. Won't be exactly the same, and there's always exceptions, and—"

I realized I'd only *thought* she rambled at school. That had been nothing compared to these drawn-out explanations. "So you see auras with an ability."

She shook her head. "They're separate, though some people can have an ability that affects aura reading. Abilities are like... unique traits or talents. There's two branches of them: passive and active. I have two for some reason, but people should only have one. Both of mine are in the passive branch, but they both kind of suck, honestly."

More than once, I'd noticed how she out sped most people I'd ever seen. "Is it how fast you are?"

She bit her lip. "Oh, I thought... I need to work on that. No, that's from the air alignment, but I guess I don't notice as much as I used to. I didn't think it was that obvious."

Air alignment? I wasn't asking anything else; one poorly explained topic at a time.

"The first is empathy. It's like... feeling emotions of people around me."

What? My heart raced, vulnerable in a way I'd never remotely imagined. "Of other 'mages' like you? Like the auras you mentioned?"

Her eyes wouldn't meet mine again as she shook her head. "Everyone." Her voice was softer. "Like right now — I can feel it scares you, which is... reasonable."

I didn't want anyone to know me; my emotions were mine to know, my secrets to hide. "How long?" How long had she been in my head in a way I hadn't known was possible? How long had she been—

"Since my Act. It's not— I don't *want* to, it's just... like a sense. Like hearing nearby sounds."

I couldn't get far enough away. Even if I left her house, we still had school together, still spent most of the day together. I had to make this work, at least until I got the damn piece of paper and could move on to college. She winced, eyes clenching shut as her left hand went to her temple. "Okay. It's easier on both of us if you just talk instead of clamming up. I'm not going to go around, shouting your emotions to people. You usually get washed out by half the class anyways."

"Wait, how many people can you...?"

She took a deep breath, releasing air through her mouth. "No limit really. It's more of a proximity thing, with one exception that's louder than others. But outside of that person, it's just how close people are and how intense they're feeling things, which is why..." She whimpered, her left hand moving from her temple to her right forearm. "Not now," she mumbled.

I did have a cut along my right forearm, but it didn't hurt, not to the extent she seemed to feel pain from right now. "Kylie?"

When her eyes opened back this time, they were weak. "It's... it's not you. Sorry, you shouldn't see this." She stood, stumbling away from her chair, almost falling to her knees. I stood up as well but didn't move since I wasn't sure if I should support her or if she'd reopened a wound and I should call for help somehow. Her eyes clenched back shut as she shakily stumbled step by step to her bed before collapsing onto it. "I'll be fine in like twenty minutes. Sorry." She gasped, and I stepped closer. Should I get her mom? Should— "My second ability's a type..." Another wince. "A type of precognition. I don't see the future, but I feel it." Feel the future?

My left hand shifted to my right arm. Did I hurt her just by being around? "Are you sure it's the future?"

She gave a weak nod. "This is just the phantom one though. Nothing ever happens. It never lasts more than half an hour so just... give me a few. Sorry. You can get on my laptop or whatever."

Not sure what else to do, I sat down at her desk. Beside her laptop was that book she'd pulled out earlier, sitting closed. Not sure what else to do, I flipped it open to a random page. There was English on one side, these weird characters on the other. I ran my fingers across the foreign characters — a type of braille? But there was no indent in the page itself. It looked like the English was a translation of the foreign language words, but even the English made no sense. A few of the words Kylie had used earlier stood out, but otherwise it might as well have been in another language too.

"What language is this?" I asked. She didn't answer. Turning around, I saw that her eyes were closed, steady breaths moving her chest. Had she fallen asleep?

Assuming she wasn't lying about anything she'd said, I needed to leave and never speak with her again. People wanted her dead, and they'd already demonstrated they'd kill others to get to her. She claimed to feel my emotions, would unearth a past I never wanted to come out.

But even then, I couldn't leave, caught between fascination with this text and the fact that even though we were practically strangers... she trusted me. It made no sense, but after how timid she'd been when I'd gotten here, I'd seen her smile. For once, I wasn't ruining the lives of people around me.

I guess I just really wasn't used to that.

# *Chapter Seventeen*

## too far

Kylie | October 8
Matthews High

I wasn't ready, but I wasn't sure if I ever could be. The school day had always been safe because there were just too many people around for any type of attack, those eight hours during five days a week where I pretended I was just a normal girl. Well, as normal of a girl as I could be between empathy and auras and precognition attacks and everything else. Really, Maya noticing my speed showed no matter how hard I tried, I just wasn't a normal girl in any sense now.

Thus far, I'd made it through the first three class periods, but now was when I should be going to PE. There was no fourth period PE anymore: I was the only one back at school. The halls themselves felt empty, faces missing. Always would be missing — they were dead because of me. Emma and Cassie were in a coma. Liam was hospitalized still, permanently paralyzed.

I was a *miracle,* they said.

Yeah, right. If only they knew I was the *curse*, not some miracle at all. Maya had been hesitant around me — more withdrawn than normal, even for her — since I'd explained my empathy, but she hadn't ignored me. She'd genuinely stayed quiet about magic as far as I knew. Ashley had been the polar opposite; she hadn't said a word to me, glaring from the other side of the classroom this morning during homeroom.

Yet Maya and Ashley were the only two friends I had here, if I could even count Ashley as a friend still. She'd never had the friendliest emotions — at least if I'd been correct in matching emotions to the person — but I'd just assumed she wasn't a morning person. Ashley had reminded me of Lianne when I'd first seen her — they both had a similar shade of gray eyes and even gray auras. They weren't the same though. Lianne had been missing since she'd left my house that day, and I doubted she'd ever be found; she'd very likely been taken to the same place as Amalia, the same place I'd go if the wrong person saw, found out. There was no Sia to protect me anymore.

Switching out books in my locker, I took a deep breath in through my nose and released it through my mouth. Even more people whispered around me: they felt sorry for me or were curious about the *miracle* that'd lived. But none of them approached me, same as they hadn't the rest of this morning. More than one person had been resentful: why was I all right and their friend or sibling or partner wasn't? I wish I had an answer I could give. Really, I wished I wasn't around to give it in the first place.

A soft warmth approached me — neon purple: Maya. "Are you...?" She was genuinely concerned, timid and withdrawn but caring in her own way.

Pushing a smile, I nodded. "Yeah, it's fine. They reassigned me to the computers by the library for some type of programming class." I'd never looked into programming, but the bit I'd seen reminded me of the strict syntax I'd been getting used to with spells. My choices were programming, band, or art, and I *certainly* wasn't going into art or band. My brain had never worked for those "creative" classes; it'd been a blessing to ditch them mid-middle school, and I wasn't going back now.

Her eyes lingered on me. She didn't believe me. No matter how subtle her emotions were even in this hallway, I knew the hesitance came from her, so distinct from everyone else's emotions around me. "All right. I'll meet you for lunch." That

**108**

was the great thing with Maya: while she didn't believe me, she didn't push either.

I nodded, us parting ways as she went toward her art class and I headed in the opposite direction to the computer lab right beside the library. My heart raced. I'd never been new to a class *mid-year*. Everyone had been wary of me in my classes today, but at least they'd known me from before the attack. Here, I really was the focal point of the class, someone new almost a quarter in. I'd started on the makeup work I needed to have done before the end of the quarter, but I'd yet to finish it. I'd likely have no idea what I was doing in this class this week and wasn't looking forward to it. I'd struggled doing even the bits of homework I'd done, but it all felt more meaningless than ever.

Sitting down in a front-row seat behind a computer, I took another deep breath. I hoped I hadn't taken someone's spot. More than almost ever before, I just didn't want to be perceived — not special, not noticeable. With me being "the miracle girl," though, that likelihood was near nonexistent.

My head pounded so much, my lungs felt like lead. There's no way I was this nervous, and this wasn't one of those fake premonitions either. Why was *breathing* hard? Tiring even — like my body struggled to function.

Really, I knew exactly what that meant, didn't I? This classroom was closer to the anti-magic barrier than my other ones or the gym had been. I was already behind in this class, and catching up wasn't going to be easier when I struggled to breathe. But I didn't have a choice. This was just how things were. As Mom had told me many times growing up, complaining changed nothing. That was truer than ever right then since I had it the easiest: I was alive, back at school as if nothing had happened. I was the "fortunate one."

The teacher walked in. I hadn't caught her name yet, but she had graying hair and wore a long skirt and blazer. I felt under-dressed for this class suddenly, but it wasn't like I was the only student dressed in normal student clothes in a t-shirt and jeans. She didn't draw attention to me as she walked to the tall podium at the front of the classroom. I watched her head move between a piece of paper on her desk and the classroom. She must be taking roll without calling anyone's name, silently noting my presence without drawing attention to me. I wished that mattered. I heard murmurs all around me and felt so much *pity* in the room, as if I had a reason to be pitied.

My head pounded even more. Between empathy and the barrier, I wasn't sure how I'd make it to lunch today, let alone how I'd do this all week. I knew I needed to be on guard. What if they attacked this class next? They didn't seem affected by the barrier, so that likely meant they controlled it somehow, and that only put me at a further disadvantage. And—

Oh. The teacher had started lecturing, something now on her screen that broadcast to the class. I wasn't sure when she'd started and quickly navigated to the program she had open, watching the syntax on the screen as I typed it in on my computer. This was mindless enough: just mimic what she typed. I could figure out what it all meant at home later when breathing wasn't difficult. Compared to Sia, my current magipoten wasn't even that high. Why'd this hurt so much when I had so much less mana than Sia? When less of my lungs and heart and whatever else depended on mana to survive? I mean, I hadn't tried alt form here, but I certainly didn't want to either. For that matter, I wasn't sure I *could* push enough mana to finish the spell. And if I was in alt form, every breath would only be harder so it wasn't exactly something I wanted to race off and test.

Even in the hospital, I hadn't been so focused on just *breathing*. It felt so weird to struggle with such a basic, automatic bodily function, like my lungs were made of iron, heavy, like I'd run marathons and not slept — well, I hadn't really slept last night so that might not have been the barrier.

The minutes passed and the bell finally rang. I couldn't tell if I would or wouldn't like programming or the teacher or anything with how little I'd focused. But for a first day back with the *pleasant* surprise of being even closer to the barrier, I'd survived. That meant *something*, didn't it?

I packed my things back into my backpack, heading to lunch as I tried not to stumble in the hallway or bump into the other students. I'd swap my books out after lunch, but for now, I just

**110**

wanted to get in line and put as much distance as possible between me and that classroom. I hoped and prayed for a second wind to kick in, but I knew it wouldn't. Those never happened until I power-napped when I got home, which I had to do before even attempting any homework. I heard students behind me in line talking, gossiping. They'd likely known each other their whole lives, much like everyone at my old high school did, much like I had.

It wasn't like I could go back now. There's no way Mom would approve of me going back. Besides, it would put them in danger too. I didn't need to be around anyone really, and this way Jordan wasn't involved in things.

They just wanted me; the further I stayed away from others, the safer they were.

Finally through the line, I sat at the table Ashley, Maya, and me had claimed at the beginning of the year; Maya was already here, the art classroom near to the cafeteria. Matthews was smaller than North Pines. Lunch periods were designated by grade level, not randomly around classes. All the juniors and seniors had lunch fifth period, which was nice. The last time my whole grade had done lunch at the same time was elementary school, years and years back.

"You look more exhausted than normal," she noted, half glancing up from the textbook in front of her.

I snickered without meaning to. "Yeah, I feel it too."

She bit into her sandwich, continuing to skim said textbook, not at all interested in my fatigue. At least, I *thought* mild amusement came from her. I was by far physically closest to her, but Maya's emotions were often overshadowed by emotions physically further away. I appreciated the subtleness of hers compared to others — especially Jordan, as I'd had the *joy* of remembering recently.

She shifted uncomfortably at the word "feel." "Because of...?"

Shaking my head, I stabbed the pea. It was too mushy. "Just didn't sleep well." I didn't know how to explain the barrier, and I really hadn't slept either so it wasn't a lie.

Ashley's aura edged closer. Was she going to sit with us after all? But this smug emotion came from her, anger and jealousy and… was it someone else? I thought it was her, seemed right on proximity, but… Maybe I was more exhausted than I realized.

"How can you just sit there like that?" she asked, a snap to her tone. She didn't even have a lunch tray, arms crossed over her chest.

She stared straight at me, so the statement was clearly intended for me. "I, um, like what?" Surely she wasn't pro-peas in this cafeteria. They were already bad enough in the best of circumstances, but they might as well have been a disgusting liquid for how mushy they were when this cafeteria cooked them.

Her brow furrowed further, irritation even more visible. "Happy. Everyone else is basically dead, yet you're here laughing like nothing ever happened."

My lips opened, but no words came. She wasn't wrong. I just…

"Hey," a guy said. I faintly recognized him from the programming class I'd just been in. "That's going too far."

She spun around to face him. "Well, how *else* do you describe her being the only one here? How many were in that class? Twenty? Thirty? No one else is back — most aren't *ever* coming back. Don't *you* think that's suspicious?"

That same guy spoke back up. I didn't even know his name. "She was in the hospital too, wasn't she?"

I stared at my plate. She wasn't wrong: it was my fault. "I think I forgot something in the lab, but it might take me a minute to find it. Don't wait on me for heading to sixth." I picked my tray up, trashing the food before Maya had a chance to respond. I wasn't hungry anyways.

My feet took me to the computer lab, the tightness in my chest overwhelming me once more.

At least I understood that.

# Chapter Eighteen

## deserved better

I'd swapped work shifts, this afternoon now free in exchange for losing my normal Saturday off. Sucked ass, but this's something I needed to do — should've done this a hell'va long time ago, and I guess really, shouldn't've ever happened to begin with. I'd done the bullshit needed to swap work shifts without much hesitation, but now that the school day's over, I just...

I'm nervous as fuck. Never done this b'fore. Never thought I'd be in a relationship to begin with, and ain't gonna lie, there's a part of me scared shitless it'd never happen again — that I'm throwing away the only normal thing I'd ever had and maybe ever would. Yet...

Since I'd put shit together, I'd been going through memories — from when I'd started dating Emily, from that damn castle's hallucinations, even my own interactions with Siani and Kylie. It'd been goddamn obvious, hadn't it? I'd just not wanted to know.

No. It'd been even worse than that, honestly: I'd known for years, but'd been a damn ass that'd wanted to prove Rotanu wrong even if it meant no one ended up happy. It'd been the most fuckin' pathetic thing. Emily deserved better.

I waited by the school exit, as I had since we'd started dating; ain't like there's really anyone else to talk to, 'specially now that Richard and Kylie weren't here anymore. Once I went through with this, I'd really be alone at school. In the past, at least Kylie'd been around, but...

It's fine. Maybe this'd help make amends, in some weird-ass way.

I felt hands around my right arm, holding tightly and pressing my arm into her, uh... My cheeks flared, eyes dashing over to the dead grass that'd broken through the concrete off to the side. Ain't the first time she'd done this — far from it. I'd always found it kinda hot if anything, but that just made shit even worse, the moment more awkward and entirely too easy to pretend nothing's up when I knew we *could* finish out the year, then never see each other again, just let things—

No. Fuck, I needed to do this sooner than later 'cause all my resolve's running away shitless. "H-hey, how's your day?"

She huffed warm air into my ear that caused me to bite back a shudder. "Bo-ring. It sucked. Nothing exciting happens this year."

Nothing exciting, huh? Guess that's a change I'm gonna give her. Almost wished I'd heard that complaint from Kylie instead, her never *bored* now. Ain't even sure she smiled anymore, and yet—

That's why I had to do this: literally was thinking 'bout Kylie again when I'm with Emily, ain't treating either of 'em right. "Uh, I, uh, I-I see. Sorry 'bout that."

One of her fingers drifted up, running along my cheekbone. I jerked back, but she didn't seem to care. I always recoiled like that. Never been fond of unexpected touch, and now I realized so many of these past incarnations' memories're tied to intimate gestures. Memories of Leah or Chloé or even Kisate instead of Emily there.

It's so goddamn *obvious* now.

"I miss Richard. Any word from him?"

Didn't dare mention that I'd seen him just a few days ago when he'd *flown in* on a private jet 'cause I'd stopped by unannounced. She had no a damn idea 'bout him, and it ain't my secret to tell. But all the rumors'd actually been more modest than what I'd seen so far, and I'm pretty sure I ain't seen jackshit still — luxuries and choices I couldn't possibly imagine're his everyday life. Fuck knew the strings he pulled last year to go here his senior year and *graduate* from a public high school instead of the elite prep whatever he'd been at, but it definitely ain't carried over since he went to some elite college now.

"I, uh, I think he's in Atlanta right now." Should be, at least; was s'posed to be there weekdays for class, but that didn't mean he ain't able to come back the same day regardless as I'd recently found out. I pulled myself away from her grip and walked forward, away from the school. She followed, huffing as she struggled to keep up in those heels she always wore. I slowed my speed, letting her catch up.

"You need to tell me next time he's back. We all need to go out together." I guessed she'd never noticed he'd stopped dating after his Act. Had better things to do now, he said. She straightened her skirt as she continued walking with me, and I made a conscious effort to walk slower so she didn't have to struggle keeping up.

I rubbed the back of my neck, nodding as I glanced away. "Sure. Though, uh—"

"I wanna get more clothes today. You said you're off, right?" This's one thing I ain't gonna miss at all. Being her clothing-cart-bitch's better than the lessons Siani and Rotanu'd put us through, but it still sucked ass — made me feel even less than I was, not able to imagine what it'd be like to spend that much that often on clothes, or anything, really.

I nodded, pushing those thoughts aside for now. Had more important matters to deal with, no matter how much said matters caused my heart to race right then. "I, uh... Could we talk a sec first, b'fore that?" I paused my steps, us alone on the sidewalk.

She'd stepped ahead of me, rolling her eyes as she turned around to face me. "I guess. Why did you stop though? I wanna get there before the rush. The summer sales're already going on."

Man, I felt like such an ass; I couldn't meet her eyes, felt so damn guilty she hadn't noticed a damn thing's off. "I, uh..." My throat's dry, like I hadn't drank anything all day. I reached up, rubbing the back of my neck again, feeling the pulse from my neck on my palm 'cause've how fast my heart raced. What if she ran off crying? She'd tried so damn hard to make this work. Deserved better than me. Honestly, deserved better than Richard'd treat her too, but damn near every woman deserved better than the way he acted if I'm honest — still ain't sure why he gave a damn 'bout me when he basically despised everyone else. A morbid part of me wondered if he also had memories of his original incarnation, just tucked away out of reach, and that'd influenced shit. Maybe I just wanted to feel less alone though, not be the only one with the weird-ass memory recollection of prior incarnations.

"What?" Her tone had a snap to it, yanking me from thoughts I'd accidentally distracted myself with.

It's now or never. "I, uh, I-I think you deserve better. Someone better than me."

She did that thing where she ran her finger across my bicep, a tease that just made me uncomfortable as hell. "If you're good enough for Richard, you're good enough for me." While normally, I'd say that logic's sound — Richard had damn near impossibly high standards I passed as either a fluke or 'cause've said potential memories — this time it ain't.

"I mean it. A-and it ain't right for me to waste your time. You've been amazing. I mean it. Just like..." She's attractive, obviously wanted me worked up, and fuck, did it work sometimes. But I didn't actually enjoy spending time with her. Didn't really care to hear what she had to say, didn't make me laugh or, hell, ain't even sure I'm gonna cry over things ending. If I did, it's more 'cause this meant I'd likely never get another chance like it.

It meant acknowledging magic ain't going anywhere. Was part of me — my life — now.

"Are... are you breaking up with *me*? After all the shit you've pulled, you're... whatever. Just don't tell Richard so I can still go out with him. All you're good for anyway."

I guess I deserved that. Hurt like hell, but she ain't exactly wrong. "I'm sorry. I just—"

"Save it. Only reason I put up with your pathetic ass's 'cause I wanted to be with Richard. You're not even good for that now." She walked off, leaving me standing there alone.

I kinda deserved that, but damn if it didn't sting like fuck.

# Chapter Nineteen

## good options

Kylie | October 24
Matthews High

Another day without sleep, which *really* was not ideal with this barrier. At least it hadn't been from nightmares this time, but that would've been more justified. I'd had a sensory precognition attack all last night instead, and while I would love to assume it had been one of the fake ones, there had been some type of stabbing involved around my stomach. The fake premonitions had punches and blunt impact, never stabbing.

I wished I knew how far out I could pick things up. Who was at risk this time? Just me, or would they involve others again? Should I have avoided school? But what if they attacked and I wasn't here? What if they came to my house because I avoided school and hurt Mom because we were both home?

What if it actually *was* one of those fake attacks and I just misinterpreted the premonition entirely?

For not the first time, I wished I didn't have sensory precognition at all. It only made me anxious, never actually helped.

Even though I tried, I couldn't focus on this English lecture. She said something about an upcoming essay, prep for the lit test we were having in a week. I couldn't concentrate on it despite knowing I really needed to pay attention — I'd already made a B Mom didn't know about and would *not* be happy about. Multiple people in the classroom being tired was not helping *my* fatigue at all, either. I saw Maya doodling on the side of her notebook, a plant — maybe a venus flytrap? Never been the artistic type myself, so it was impressive to watch her sketch, especially when she didn't notice. I didn't mean to make her self-conscious; it was just really cool to watch, even more so because of how steady her emotions were while drawing. They were peaceful compared to everything else around me. I usually used this class to either take notes or review spell charts, but I just didn't have it in me today, or in general lately, really. No sleep, a sensory precognition, and the intensity of the barrier had really done a number on me.

Interrupting my exhaustion-daydream was a new emotion I picked up — a faint smugness, hunger and hatred swirling around it somehow. I thought it was from just one person, but the intensity made me second-guess even that. Sure, Ashley hadn't exactly been friendly since I'd come back, but we only shared homeroom, nothing else. I shouldn't be able to pick her up from whatever classroom she was in right then — not to this degree.

I sat up, straightening my posture and fidgeting as I attempted to hone in on the source of the emotions. It was stronger to my right — toward the outside of the building — than inside. I normally minimized auras as much as I could in school since it functioned as just another sense to overload me near the barrier, but I needed more perspective, if for nothing else than to calm my fears about another massacre like the gym had been. Bracing for even more sensory information, I quit suppressing the reads; auras illuminated beyond what my eyes could actually see. Maya's vibrant purple, my own multi-blue hue, Pete's faint light green... I needed further than this classroom, though, so I expanded the range. Immediately, I was both thankful I had and wished I hadn't since there was an aura I knew too well, one that I never wanted around this school again: Zimihe's. That fuchsia aura made my throat feel as if it closed in, tighter and tighter.

So many simultaneous thoughts and instincts threatened to

overwhelm me. I wanted to shout for everyone to run and had to actively remind myself not to do so, not to warn them to get as far away from me as they could. I knew that'd only cause more chaos, get me attention from my classmates and maybe even from Zimihe that I wasn't prepared to deal with. But... I couldn't let her hurt anyone else, couldn't let her ruin any more lives.

The easiest entrance was through the window on the side, but they'd somehow known the school enough to teleport into the gym. I hadn't learned anything about teleporting to know the exact specifications there, but knowing she *could* teleport meant that I wasn't even sure where her entrance point would be. I didn't see Sase's brownish aura with her, so for some reason, Zimihe was here alone. My eyes shifted back to Maya's notebook, seeing her sketch water drops onto the plant. Water... I couldn't make enough water to do anything helpful even outside the barrier, let alone in it. Yet Zimihe's aura edged closer and closer, her apprehension and elation and exasperation like sirens through my body now that I'd matched said emotions to her. My time was limited. I needed a solution, *somehow*, to save my classmates.

That premonition had been for me: I would be stabbed by Zimihe. I wouldn't let anyone else get hurt in my place. They were just high school students. They didn't deserve to live in fear, not like I'd experienced so often since my Act.

As I glanced back to the board, I saw a sprinkler at the very top of the ceiling. I couldn't make water, but could I telekinetically rip the sprinkler? Just one of the sprinklers... all I needed was for the little red glass thing to break: it'd trip the sprinkler in this classroom, and everyone would have to evacuate. I glanced at Maya, pretending to elbow her as I gestured to close the notebook with my hands. She raised her eyebrows but did so. I then moved my attention back to the sprinkler, honing in on that red glass thing as I used my fingers as a mental anchor, concentrating on piercing that little red dot. It shattered, water busting into the classroom from the sprinkler.

"Everyone, calm down!" Ms. Nelson yelled, but my classmates were already shoving each other out of the room as they yanked up their backpacks. Ms. Nelson followed while raising her voice even louder as she repeated to calm down.

But I wasn't alone, Maya still beside me as our hair stuck to our faces, her bangs almost covering her eyes. I felt her confusion as I heard her ask, "You...?"

Zimihe's aura had moved closer, but not from the direction of the window. How? I couldn't tell if she was in the school building or not, but there were no screams, no terror from my classmates. "Get out of here," I said to Maya, voice hushed. Even if it was a pitiful attempt, I tried to sound more confident than I was. This was likely it: I hadn't even scratched Zimihe in the gym, and I'd only injured Sase's arm, nothing remotely systemic.

"Are you thinking that..." She wasn't scared, just confused. I didn't have time to explain — she needed to leave, flee while she could. I was their target: if I was dead, they wouldn't go after anyone else.

Wait, I'd lost track of Zimihe's aura, focusing more on Maya for that brief moment. "Get out of here!" I hoped yelling at her would cause her to stop questioning and *go*.

"But it could be such a fun time, the three of us." I didn't want to turn around; Zimihe's voice was behind me, closer to the door. I knew Maya was between us; she hadn't escaped in time.

I balled my fist, wanted to hide and ignore the tremors that threatened my hands and legs. Maybe I'd come to terms with myself dying, but I didn't want Maya getting hurt because she'd been concerned about me. What could I even do? This barrier prevented most magic, and we likely only had minutes before they'd get the water turned off and make it back into the classroom. My instinct was to never turn around, refuse to acknowledge her, but that'd do nothing and I knew it.

Even if it killed me, if I kept Maya alive, that would mean something, right? Would it make amends to my classmates that had died?

"No!" I yelled, manipulating the water on the tile into a light stream as I turned, the water slicing out a few feet in front of me.

She scoffed. My control of the water didn't even make it to her, splattering against the desks and chairs and tile with all the other water. "Best you got? Little barrier has you down, I see." I did my best to charge her, but I couldn't build speed. I was simply too tired and weak from the premonitions and lack of sleep and the barrier. I couldn't stop her as she grabbed Maya from behind, holding her by her neck as she used her as a shield. "You like this one, do you?" Her lance went through Maya's stomach, from the back to front. Maya whimpered through the sharp exhale of pain that shot through her — that I felt right then, that I'd felt during the premonition. "Too bad you're too helpless to do anything. She'll die, and it'll be all your fault *yet again.*" I felt Maya's consciousness fading, edging closer and closer to blacking out.

No. I couldn't, she couldn't...

Zimihe withdrew her lance, letting Maya fall to the wet tile. "And if you somehow save her this time, we'll just do this again and again until you have no one left." Zimihe was gone, teleporting off once more.

I ran to Maya, yanking her hoodie off of her. The hoodie was black, so nothing showed on it, but her dark brown t-shirt under it was a different story, blood leaking out easily through a four-inch stab wound. She chuckled. "Should've listened, I guess..." Her voice was softer than normal, weak yet amused.

Every day, I struggled to breathe in this barrier, yet... yet... I couldn't let her die because of me — couldn't let another person suffer because I'd lived that June. Pressing my left hand against her stomach where blood poured, I pushed mana for a heal spell. It wasn't enough, couldn't finish mending with the siphon from the barrier. I forced air into my lungs, focusing even more mana to use the strongest heal I could manage. It finally went through, but she needed more. I cast another one, chain casting three more at that potency. My lungs burned, chest heaved. But her pain was gone, eyes opening fully.

"We need... to get out," I mumbled, vision blurry. I stood, swaying as I stumbled to my drenched notebook and backpack, hair sticking to my face and arms and clothes clinging to my body.

She stood, glancing over herself and then nodding, gathering her things as well as sliding her hoodie back on. As we walked out, there was no one in the halls. I guessed the whole school'd gotten evacuated again, though from what they saw as a

**123**

mechanical defect instead of tragedy at least. Spots filled more and more of my vision, each breath strained.

I might've burned too much mana, but at least she was alive.

# Chapter Twenty

## long shot

Kylie had mumbled she didn't feel well but couldn't go home as we'd snuck out the back entrance of the school. I wasn't sure why she couldn't go home, but she definitely looked exhausted so I didn't argue and called a taxi I'd needed to use a few times since moving here. Thankfully, they'd been nearby because as soon as we got in the cab and closed the door, she blacked out. Not sure what else to do, I'd had the driver drop us off at my apartment, me carrying her and our bags up the stairs in multiple trips. I still just had a futon on the fake brown laminate flooring. I'd been saving up to eventually get a secondhand mattress, but I hadn't had the funds to do so yet.

As it was, I had my usual work shift this evening, but I felt uneasy leaving her here alone. Even if I left a message on her phone or wrote out a note, I wasn't sure she'd know where she was, given this was the opposite side of town from school and her mom's townhome. Even if she could figure out where she was, her face was much paler than normal. Was it just the lack of lighting? This apartment didn't have overhead lights outside of the kitchen area and bathroom, and I just had a single lamp I used for everything else.

She'd been fine until she'd done whatever it was to make my injury vanish. Right after that, she'd started stumbling and swaying so much, mumbling as she'd struggled to hold her eyes open. But I wasn't involved in any of this; I didn't know if something was wrong, and if it was, how to help.

Something about her unconscious face dug deep into me. I guess I owed her my life — or at the very least, she helped me avoid a hospital bill I couldn't pay. Maybe that was why I felt like I had to help her. But it wasn't like I could take her to a doctor. It would have to be someone who knew about this magic stuff, and Kylie hid magic from everyone but me at school. She'd mentioned that Dani knew about magic but was all but useless, so there was no reason to try to find out about her. That left that guy as the only other person who might've known, the one that'd been stabbed that day I'd found out but had walked out fine a few minutes later after Kylie had done to him what she'd done to me earlier.

What was his name? I saw his face so clearly, always having been better with faces than names. Kylie had transferred from North Opal Pines High School, she'd said, so that was where she had to have known him from, given the school project picture I'd seen of them in her bedroom. It was a long shot that he'd be able to do anything; maybe he was like myself, just someone that had accidentally found out.

Realistically, though, it's all I had to go off of. And while it was stupid to bring someone I didn't even know the last name of to my apartment, I couldn't ignore Kylie. She wasn't bleeding, but something wasn't right. He was the best and only shot I really had, and least this town was small. North Opal Pines High implied it was in the north section of the town, so I made my way there. It was predictably easy to find. I still wasn't sure why they needed three high schools here. Even two felt like overkill, but whatever.

The front office was to the right of the school entrance, but by the time I made it there, classes must have already dismissed since students were exiting the building. Hopefully, he hadn't left before I'd gotten there, because if so, I was completely out of options and had wasted time on this whole little adventure. There were so many people — more than Matthews High, for sure. It wasn't as big as my former high school, but it again made me question why Matthews High and North Opal Pines High weren't, like... combined somehow. Matthews High looked newer, so maybe that had something to do with it.

So many people talked to each other, close groups and inside jokes. I briefly wondered if Kylie had been like them when she'd been here. I didn't know why she'd transferred because while Matthews High was a bit closer to her house, it wasn't by much, not for senior year of all years. Ultimately, it wasn't my place to pry, but... just was strange. I kept my eyes on the different groups of people walking out the best I could; most likely, I'd need to interrupt some type of conversation *and* figure out a way to separate this guy from whoever he talked to. More people passed by, none of them even noticing I wasn't supposed to be here. But then...

I saw him, or at least I was pretty sure it was him. Opposite of my expectations and better for the current situation, he was alone with his eyes to his feet as he walked out, away from the crowd. No one around him noticed him, or they were so used to him that he didn't flag their attention at all. He had what I'd wanted at Matthews High and Kylie had never given me.

I still wanted that, didn't I?

Then why was I here?

He didn't notice me, so I followed him out from the crowd of students as he walked across the grass at an apparent shortcut. Even better, he headed in the direction of my apartment. I sped up my steps — he had a fast gait, but thankfully he was nowhere near as fast as Kylie. Comparatively, it was easy to catch up with him. "Hey," I said. He kept walking. Did he have headphones in? I didn't see any, but his hair covered most of his ears. "Hey!" I still couldn't remember his name, but I knew that was him, the guy that'd been in those photos, the one that'd showed up that day.

Turning around, he said, "Huh? Are you—" His eyes

focused on me, lips parted. "You're the girl that's... Matthews, right? Why're you here?"

I released a breath, some measure of progress. At least he remembered me because that helped simplify things. I came closer, only a foot away from him. Normally I wasn't a fan of being this close to anyone, let alone a stranger, but Kylie wanted this stuff a secret for reasons I still didn't completely get. "Something happened. You know about that other stuff, don't you?" He hesitantly nodded, a cautious nature to him that hadn't been there a second prior. "Kylie — there was an attack — I don't..." My mouth moved faster than my brain; I couldn't articulate everything that had happened. "She's at my apartment, but... I don't know what's wrong with her. She's out cold and pale."

"Shit," he mumbled. "Fuck knows what I can do, but..."

He'd come to check on her after she'd been released from the hospital. I didn't know what went on between them, but it was him or no one. Even if she hadn't spoken to him in front of me, she obviously trusted him, given how he knew despite how secretive she was about all this stuff. "We need to get going."

Hopefully he could help Kylie, and if nothing else, he could keep an eye on her once I went to work at five; especially after that taxi fare earlier, I needed every hour I got and then some.

He followed me, easily matching my pace. Even better, he seemed to know this area. I guess for a local, that made sense. I might've underestimated Kylie as well, in hindsight. "So, uh, what's your name?" he asked.

"Maya."

"I know I mentioned it b'fore, but I'm Jordan, uh, nice to meet you." This wasn't the time for pleasantries. I just nodded — I wasn't here to be his new best friend or whatever; I just wanted to make sure Kylie was fine. She'd saved me, and I had to return the favor. That's all it was. He glanced around before interrupting the blissful silence with another question. "You live on West Side?"

"Is that a problem?" Everyone in this damn town acted like they had to know everything about everyone. All I wanted to do was graduate so I could go to college. Then I'd work through college, get a desk job, and never go back.

He rubbed the back of his neck, glancing away. "N-no. Just clear across town from Matthews so didn't expect it."

My transcript had gotten me moved to Matthews High, supposedly. It would've been easier to go to school at either of the other two, but this town was small enough to be walkable so I tolerated it for the one year it'd be a problem.

I turned into the complex, faded sign only half-attached to the post. He paused as he glanced around — if he judged me, fuck him. I made it work, all by myself. But he said nothing, just increased his pace to catch up from where he'd fallen behind me, staying close as we approached my apartment door. As I opened the front door, I noticed Kylie still asleep where I'd left her. She didn't look like she'd stirred at all the entire time I'd been gone. He stepped in, almost entranced as he timidly stepped closer to her, kneeling down by where she was lying. Her hair was damp, but she wasn't soaked anymore. Her left fingers still had blood from where she'd touched my former wound. That reminded me. I probably needed a shower before I went to work on top of everything else. I closed the door, afterward standing close to her. "How is she?"

He brought the back of his hand to her cheek. "None of this's my specialty, honestly." Great, so was this just a big waste of time, after all? If he didn't know what he was doing, couldn't he have said that before making me chat with him the whole way here? "But..." His fingers moved to her neck, checked her pulse as his eyebrows pushed together. "Doesn't look like she got hurt even?"

Wasn't she, though? Why else would she have collapsed? "She... I was the one stabbed." His attention moved back to me. I took my hoodie off, raising my t-shirt up to show where I'd been stabbed in the stomach. All that was there now was a faint scar, like it'd happened years ago. "Here. But it's gone now somehow — like she did for you that day. After she finished was when she started acting weird, stumbling and swaying, then passed out a few minutes later."

His gaze shifted back to her. "A heal shouldn't've taken her out, but..." His cheeks flushed as he leaned down. His lips rested on her cheek. Was he taking advantage of her? He wasn't seriously dumb enough to do that in front of me, was he?

I noticed a dark red and blue emanate from his lips, shades of blue starting from Kylie's cheek before echoing out. I didn't know how much he was or wasn't taking advantage of things, but he certainly did *something* for those colors Kylie had described as an aura to show from them both despite her being unconscious. As he pulled away, he coughed and wheezed. How had kissing her cheek knocked the breath out of him?

"Are you... all right?" I didn't care about him specifically, but it wasn't like I wished him ill. Plus, I didn't want him also passing out in my apartment. Three people were already too crowded for this one-room apartment as it was.

He nodded, falling back as his palms caught him. "She's just... just..." He took a deep breath. "Hell'va low on mana. Had to've used a fuckton of mana on that heal for some reason."

She really had almost died saving me. She'd said she needed mana to live, yet she'd used so much to save me, she had blacked out. "So she'll be all right?"

He gave rapid nods, still struggling for breath. "Yeah. Will be fine now, I think."

# *Chapter Twenty-One*

## the last time

Jordan | October 24
Maya's Apartment

It'd been a struggle not to fall asleep once the immediate relief'd passed. Had to've been around six now, judging from light shining through the one window by the front door. Maya'd left us here. She'd used Kylie's phone to text and say a group project had gotten changed and Kylie needed to stay over tonight. Between the two of us, we'd somehow made a convincing enough lie that Ms. Rae'd even believed it — mostly Maya on that one after I'd mentioned Ms. Rae'd do damn near anything if Kylie attached grades to something.

Never'd been a night person, but today'd been 'specially bad with the mana transfer I'd done earlier. Even worse, I didn't turn any lights on 'cause I didn't wanna wake Kylie up. She'd been out this whole time. Even with the mana transfer, she'd still been exhausted.

Hell'd happened to cause this? Nothing ever happened at—

Guess that ain't completely true. Someone trying to kidnap her at school'd been what'd tripped my own Act. But not when the school'd been crowded, during the normal school day. My Act'd been after school, when most people'd already left.

Heard her turn, so I opened my eyes to check on her. She sat up slowly, glancing around. "You okay?" I asked. It's either that or "good morning"; both felt inappropriate as fuck.

"Mm." She'd never been a morning person, but that response's off even for her just waking up. Was she still pissed at me? Guess that'd be understandable, but not sure Maya'd had much other choice. "I, uh, I can leave if I'm the problem. Maya got me 'cause she was scared. Transferred some mana, but not sure if that's even the problem, just all I could do."

Her head lowered, tone faint yet monotone. "It's fine."

She sounded anything but fine — would've rather her cussed my ass out than how this conversation's going. Wasn't sure what else to do, so I moved closer, from against the wall where I'd been watching her to only a foot or so away. I made sure not to touch her though, not to force anything on her, as much as I could at least. "Hell even happened?"

I watched as she squeezed her eyes shut tightly, the rest of her body language obscured by the darkness of the apartment. The moon shone in, and I really needed to close the blinds since people could see in now, but I didn't wanna move even those few feet away to do that with how she was right then. "I need a favor. It'll be the last time."

The last time? She wanted to cut all contact with me? A knot formed in my throat as tears pushed to my eyes. I wouldn't cry in front of her, though; didn't want her to feel guilty for — fuck. Empathy. I couldn't stop myself from feeling goddamn terrified, but I didn't want that pressure on her. Ain't right, but I just... "'S-sup?"

Her eyes opened, gazing aimlessly at the cheap laminate wood under us. She didn't seem phased by how different this apartment's from her own townhome; she hadn't even asked where we were.

"Kill me."

I couldn't have heard that right, but replaying the memory, I couldn't find another way to hear what she'd said. "I tried last year. I just... I'm too much of a coward to go through with it." Her voice gained a tremble, no longer as steeled as it'd been a moment prior. "I'm scared of how Kisate was... Does it mean

I'd be stuck forever like they were? And how painful *is* dying? But I shouldn't have made it back then. It was all a mistake, one that has to be corrected."

Too easily, I saw those memories that weren't even mine: of Chloé dead on the altar. Of her killed minutes b'fore I — Dmitri — had gotten there. Of it happening with Leah and me — John. Even if the memories weren't mine, the grief might as well be. Couldn't bear the idea of her gone, would rather her just cut me from her life if it at least meant she'd be happy, live a better life. I shook my head, words not coming, nothing good or coherent enough.

"It's not just me being selfish." She still wouldn't look at me. But her arguments showed her empathy's as strong as ever, knew her words sliced into my heart, but dammit, I didn't know how to *stop* that, how to pretend to just be *fine* with her wanting to die, wanting me to *murder* her. "They — Zimihe — outright said it: they're going to kill everyone around me. Even you're at risk if you're around me."

She wanted to protect us. Worse yet, she saw it as the *only* way she could protect us, as if it's an acceptable cost that she died. "It's not..." It ain't right. She shouldn't have to choose between the people around her and herself. Magic'd fucked our lives, but she'd been fucked the most. She deserved better, to live.

"I've already ruined your life the past couple years. It'll be over if I'm gone. You won't have to worry about things anymore."

Had I done this — pushed her into this corner? Siani wasn't here. Rotanu ain't here. Just us, and she's the target, and I'd just...

I had no right, but I hugged her, held on as I bit back tears. "You didn't ruin my life." Often, she'd been the only light in it at all. Only one that'd seen *something* worth a damn in me. "I'm the one that failed you. I'm so sorry. So goddamn sorry."

She's strong, always had been. Had put up a brave face all this time. I'd been bitching 'bout how she'd never smiled anymore without trying to motherfuckin' help at all, understand at all. Maybe I *was* everything they'd ever called me. Deserved every name.

It's as if she didn't feel a damn thing from my hug. She didn't

**133**

lean into my touch, didn't pull away, didn't acknowledge my presence at all. "It's not something you should have to worry about or will have to worry about once I'm gone."

I wouldn't burden her with my feelings, even if it had to be goddamn obvious with her empathy. Wasn't sure if she's truly that dense or it's her polite rejection, and it didn't matter. I wouldn't force things on her; if I'd fucked up what Rotanu'd had — if I'd fucked up enough that she didn't have the feelings for me that Siani'd had for Rotanu — then that's my fault, something I'd live with. But that fuck-up ain't gonna kill her: she deserved to smile, even if it'd never be like b'fore that day in March years ago.

Pulling her into an even tighter hug, I didn't wanna let go. "You're not a coward. You want to live, and you *deserve* that. It ain't a mistake." One fuckin' time, she deserved to live a normal life, not die young. "I fucked up. But I wanna do better, 'cause you're not alone in this. Not anymore."

She shook her head, a sniffle from her nose. "It's fine. I-it's fine."

It wasn't fine at all. But it's all I could do now. "We'll get through this. Together."

I hated magic. Hated the weird-ass ways it'd changed my body, hated how my damn memory worked — even more so that I remembered bits and pieces from past incarnations, could so easily confirm said past incarnations existed 'cause've the memories I'd seen. Hated how fuckin' weird it was I could make fires and ice outta thin air, how often I burned shit, 'specially myself. But... I'd be — maybe've been — everything I'd ever been called if I ain't there for the one person that'd believed in me all these years. "That's the last time you're gonna be alone. I promise."

The rigidity in her posture finally lessened as she leaned against me; I felt tears seep through the thin fabric of my t-shirt. "Why..." she mumbled between sobs. "Why's it so wrong that I wanted to live?" I'd used her strength as an excuse to run, avoid shit I didn't wanna acknowledge.

"It's not. It's not wrong at all."

Her breaths're no longer steady, sharp inhales through her lungs. "I'm so scared. And tired. Everything always hurts and I just... I just..." She hiccuped, and I kept her close to me. Didn't really know what else to do. Couldn't tell her to calm down — she had every right to be as pissed and angry as she wanted. But I'd been part of the problem. How could I argue when she's crying 'cause've me? It's not even arguing really, it's trying to convince her that she deserved to goddamn live too.

"It'll have to be week to week scheduling, and ain't gonna be that long, but I'll start coming to training again." I didn't wanna learn jack shit, but she shouldn't have to feel alone, and she valued those hellish hours; it's something I could help with, something I could do instead of focusing on what I hadn't, and it'd be a damn better use of my time than holding clothes for Emily'd ever been. Didn't know how the hell I'd pull it off between work and school, but I'd make it work somehow, sleep be damned.

She shook her head. "You hate training, everything associated with..."

Training's goddamn annoying as shit and shoved every weird-ass thing 'bout all this in front of my face. But if this's what it took, then I'm fuckin' going back in that goddamn house as often as I could: I never wanted her to feel her only option's sacrificing herself, for anyone, but 'specially myself.

"With your empathy, you said my emotions're louder than most people's, right?" She hesitantly nodded. Made me paranoid as hell all over again seeing the confirmation but worked for this moment. "Then you already know."

Yet another timid nod came from her, her forehead against my collarbone. "I just... I wish I was strong like Sia."

Siani had survived, made it past this. Guess to Kylie, Siani's the picture of success 'cause've that. Yet the parts of Siani she likely most valued, I already saw so much of from Kylie — a steeled resolve so different than she'd been b'fore all this shit'd started. Maybe I'd fucked my own future, but she's closer to Siani than she knew. "You've made it this far."

Her head violently shook. "Sia never got injured and didn't let Dani get a scratch, let alone..."

I guess it's natural she didn't see how much she'd changed — all she could afford to focus on's making it day to day. But I saw

**135**

it, that connection between who she'd been and who she wanted to be. Maybe I even saw it in a way only someone that'd been around for all this shit could've.

When I'd first learned Rotanu called Siani "Kyle," I'd bitched it made no goddamn sense — was a masculine nickname and her name's short as it was, why have a nickname at all? Part of me'd hated the implication he's closer to Siani than I was to Kylie, and it'd been goddamn accurate in ways I'm only beginning to understand. He'd snapped that I'd "get it" one day, and right then, it pissed me off he'd once again been right despite all the damned lies.

"I'm proud of you." "I love you." "I'm with you." I couldn't say any shit like that to her, not now, maybe not ever. But it'd be a connection to show her she's made progress in a way only I could have known. "I, uh, I think..." My cheeks burned regardless of how serious the moment was. "I think I get why he called her 'Kyle,' a-a-and, uh, if it's okay with you, could I do that too?"

"But I'm not..."

Maybe one day, she'd see it too, how far she'd come. "I think, it's just... uh, I'm not sure how to..." I had no idea how to convey the importance to her.

She nodded, laying her forehead on my collarbone. "If it's that important, then it's okay. Also, I think I might need a bit more..." She trailed off, her eyes closed. Ain't asleep, but not far from it either. Didn't know what else to do, so I stayed, let her lay her head on me.

Maybe it'd go some way to fixing the times I hadn't been there.

# *Chapter Twenty-Two*

## used to be

"You know," Zimihe said, her voice low, danger and joy intertwined. "If you weren't around, they'd still be here." Of course I knew that. It was something I lived with daily. I saw her holding Tiffany's head, severed from the rest of her body. Tiffany's eyes were on me, scrunched into a glare, as her disconnected body crawled toward me.

Her lips parted, screeching sounds coming from her as she said, "I had a life! Why are you so important that you get to live and I don't?!"

I wished I could answer her.

I wished I'd died instead.

Shaking my head, I tried to back away, but I tripped over Alex's fingers, hand dismembered from his arm. His fingers gripped onto my ankle, skin frigid, nails purple with red bloodstains. My eyes watered. There weren't enough words to apologize. No matter how many times I said I would have taken their place if I could've, they didn't listen because I still lived and they didn't.

My body jolted, hearing the doorbell. I didn't immediately

get up, my chest heaving as I struggled to force air through my lungs. It was just a dream — a nightmare, better said. I glanced over at the clock, seeing it was almost six o'clock in the evening. I squeezed my eyes shut, taking an intentionally deep breath. I deserved the nightmares; they weren't wrong: people had died because of me. Nightmares were nothing to what my classmates had dealt with — losing their lives, their futures.

The doorbell rang again. I didn't want to answer it once I noticed it was Dani's aura. Why was she here? What did she want this time?

Rolling my eyes, I steadied my breathing as I walked down the steps to the front door. I didn't bother to wipe the sweat from my forehead before opening the door to her standing on the worn-out welcome mat.

"Hey, how's it going?" she asked.

I didn't move to welcome her in. "I'm busy. Did you need something?"

She tried to casually push her way inside. I didn't budge. After she left, I needed to work out — a hundred sit-ups and pushups, maybe practice some minor levitation after. "I mean, it's just been *forever* since we hung out, y'know? We used to do this all the time on Fridays."

Even now, she didn't seem to get that the girl that'd hung out with her all those Fridays wasn't me, not anymore. Once she'd gone into the forest that day, she'd died. And I certainly didn't need people around that couldn't keep their mouth shut. *Maya* had kept secrets better than Dani so far, despite all of Dani's so-called friendship. "I'm busy, so I can't." There wasn't any time to waste on "hanging out." Sase and Zimihe didn't just want me dead; they wanted everyone *associated* with me dead as well. I had to get better; there was no other option.

"C'mon, for old time's sake!" Dani moved closer to the entrance, tone playful, trying to hide the hesitation and irritation my empathy picked up on from her. I raised my eyebrow. Even then, she didn't believe my empathy was real, no matter how many times I'd explained it. It didn't matter; there was nothing to say. "Kylie? This isn't like you."

Rather, it wasn't like the Kylie she wanted me to be. "You should head home. Your mom will get worried."

I felt her heart race, her cheeks flush in frustration and embarrassment at my rejection. "I'll tell your mom — about *everything*. You need help."

When she'd told Mrs. Alana back in the spring, I'd felt angry, betrayed. Now though? Now she just further justified the distance, demonstrated again why she wasn't trustworthy. "Go ahead. I'm sure whoever took Amalia would love to chat with you too."

I knew the words tore into her, the fears she had that I wasn't supposed to know about. She'd seen Amalia taken, been closer to the incident than I'd ever been. Her palm slapped across my cheek, eyes watering. "I'm just worried about you, but forget it!"

I used to be a girl who would've cried at being slapped, used to be a girl who would've stepped aside for Dani to enter, used to think Dani knew everything. I also used to think I deserved to live, but I'd learned a lot these past few years.

# Chapter Twenty-Three

## irreplaceable

Jordan | October 27
Richelieu Residence

Here I was, back at Richard's house. I needed a favor and was scared shitless of asking. But the look in her eyes's too damn vivid — it wouldn't fade, like all my memories didn't, even when I wanted them to.

She felt the only option left to her's death. I'd never felt that way, and it's largely 'cause she'd always been there, oblivious to all the shit everyone else saw when they looked at me. All I'd done so far's proved them right, proved her wrong.

As I pressed on the intercom, I heard a man answer, the one that'd been here the first time I'd come. "Welcome back, Master Jordan. I'll open the gate for you now." It'd been a lie to say I'd gotten used to being called *Master Jordan* or having a huge-ass iron gate open and close to allow *me* access — pretty sure I'm the type of person the gate's s'posed to stop, not let in — but I did my best to ignore those feelings. As I approached the front door, it opened for me, the same man nodding as I entered. "Master Richard's in his living room. I've already alerted him that you're on your way."

"T-thanks." If Richard's here, he's almost always in his

"living room," so I ain't sure why they acted like it's such a surprise. No reason to take it out on them though, likely're just doing their job.

Down I went through this long-ass hallway again. I lowered my eyes, not sure if I should wave or say hi or what to the staff that walked past me. Richard acted like they weren't there unless he needed shit from what I'd seen, but I didn't feel comfortable enough to even ignore 'em.

Instead, I kept walking, unsure how to ask or what to ask or any goddamn thing 'bout all this 'sides I'm in over my head and needed help. Opening the door to Richard's loft — and, therefore, living room — I heard the tv blaring. How fuckin' loud did he need this shit?

Yet his eyes immediately directed at me as I stepped in, lowering the volume. "Another sudden visit."

I nodded, sitting down on the armchair across from the couch Richard sat on, sprawled out with his laptop on his lap. "Sorry."

He huffed, already sounding pissed. "It's fine. Why do you apologize over every damn thing?"

"Sorry — or, uh..." I rubbed the back of my neck with my right hand. "Yeah..."

Not sure what else to say — had I already fucked this up? — we sat in silence for 'bout a minute b'fore Richard sighed. "I assume you didn't walk all this way for the hell of it."

I hated I felt like I'm just using him. That ain't what I meant either, just didn't know who else to turn to considering, well, it involved magic shit, but also, ain't like I had a blossoming social network. I had *Kyle*, and I had Richard. And it's involving Kyle, so couldn't go to her 'bout this. "I'm not sure what to do, but, uh..." I glanced toward the area the bedrooms're at b'fore moving my eyes back to him.

He moved hair off his ear, pointing to his earring — more specifically, the earring that's his absorption device. I nodded, and he sighed as he stood, walking to his bedroom. I followed, him leaving the door open for me to walk in behind him; I closed it once we were both in the room. "Hell happened? You get caught up in shit again?"

Not able to meet his eyes, I shook my head. "Not me. They attacked her school again."

Hearing movement, I glanced up to see him roughly drop into his office chair, rolling his eyes. "So those bitches went after another bitch. Just let them fuck each other up."

Her eyes're so vivid in my sight once more, still yet terrified as she asked me to kill her. As she thought it'd have been a mercy, the only way to keep people around her safe. He didn't understand. "It's not..."

"I'm telling you: that one's more trouble than she's worth. Tons more waiting that'd be a hell of a lot easier. Sure, she's a mage, but that's about all she has going for her."

Why'd I think Richard'd help with something involving Kyle? I knew he hated her. But still, I didn't know who else to ask. He thought he's doing me a favor, but he didn't understand a goddamn thing. I just didn't know how to get it through his motherfuckin' head. Swallowing, I kept my eyes from him, stared at the intricate carving on the side of his wooden desk. "She almost died again. Those bitches attacked the one friend she'd made, and she almost killed herself trying to save that friend. She needs help, but I don't..."

He snorted. "To say the least."

I heard her ask me to kill her, as if she's in the room, asking right then. "You don't fuckin' get it." My eyes watered despite attempting to calm myself. He didn't know. Though hell, even if he did, likely wouldn't give a fuck.

"You knew her in another incarnation or whatever, right? It's not *that* big of a deal. We had to have known each other as well, given how this whole reincarnation thing seems to have worked."

Kisate's the oldest she'd ever been: twenty-two. Leah and Chloé both died long b'fore then. Hell, was a goddamn miracle Kyle hadn't, and that made it all the worse that she felt like it's a mistake. Her being alive ain't a mistake. There wasn't much I knew, but that I'm sure of.

I shook my head, not knowing how to express this tightness in my chest, how breathing hurt like fuck every time I thought 'bout her not being here. "I talked 'bout b'fore, how I remembered some shit from those previous incarnations?"

"Yeah?" Richard shifted in his chair. "Mostly involved said bitch, you said."

There's a reason for that, one I hadn't wanted to admit for a long time. I sat in a side chair Richard had in his room, by a table. Still unable to meet his eyes, I stared down at the palms of my hands. "Yeah." I wasn't sure if I should thank my hypermnesia or not for the realization those brief glimpses'd given me. "If we die unclean deaths, our consciousness's trapped in the reborn incarnations 'til something dismisses the consciousness entirely."

I knew why John and Dmitri'd died, had experienced their deaths when I'd seen Chloé's body that moment at Asuza's, even if it hadn't make sense 'til much later: suicide. I'd only had the brief second of pain, of overwhelming grief; the glimpses're too vague to give greater context than that bit I'd pieced together. But it'd been enough: the sight of Leah's death drove John to suicide. When Asuza repeated the scene with Chloé and left a weapon nearby, Dmitri did the same.

Even back that June, I wasn't sure I'd been different. Now... the more memories I had, the more bitter her words became: she felt death's her only option. Finally, we'd done it. Finally, she ain't weighed down by that damn bastard.

Finally, she'd get to *live*. With me, without me, fuck, it didn't matter as long as she's happy and not being tortured to death.

"Yo, you can't drop something like that then go on a daydreaming spree. The hell you mean?"

I nodded but didn't move my eyes back to him. "I don't know the full hows or whys. Something to do with the original reincarnation spell: 'unclean deaths' lead our consciousnesses to get trapped in the next incarnation. All of mine and Kyle's previous incarnations shared a body with us after our Acts 'til that June." I knew the exact date — June 26, 2017 — but it's awkward as fuck to be so *specific* in conversations where it ain't needed, an unwanted quirk of hypermnesia. "They're not with us now, got 'dismissed' through a spell. Guessing it never happened with your incarnations outside of the first one since it's not a problem for you."

He huffed. "I don't give a damn about *them*. I care about us, *me*. Are you sure it wasn't just something in the technicalities of former incarnations or something else we don't know about?"

Of course I ain't. I shook my head. How'd I know if he lied or Siani'd lied or any fuckin' thing like that? All I *could* do's take their word, even knowing how often they'd both hid and lied 'bout shit. "As sure as I am 'bout everything else, basically. Just going off the explanation I got."

That ain't the response he wanted, but I'd given the best answer I could and he seemed to get that. "Sudden new nightmare fuel aside, why bring it up? Something they said years back?"

He'd never been subtle in that he viewed women as objects, entertainment 'til he got bored. Even if I did my damnest to explain, ain't sure he'd really get it. "I said it b'fore, that the other incarnations... they'd fallen for her incarnations each time, right?" Out of the corner of my eye, I saw him roll his eyes once more, though he did nod. "The last two, they, I..." Those moments're surreal, me but not me. I'd sometimes remember what they'd been thinking or feeling or seeing or whatever, but not consistently. Just little bursts of memories, of these past moments I'd never lived yet were me.

"After seeing her die, it'd just..." My eyes watered, this sadness I couldn't control swallowing me. I knew what happened, yet it felt wrong to say — like I'd be admonished for something I ain't even done, in this life at least. Yet I saw her asking to die, Leah dead in the chair, Chloé on the altar, as if they're all happening that second. A tear slipped down my cheek. "John and Dmitri, the two b'fore me... it hurt them so much they killed themselves when they realized she'd... And she'd been the only person to give half a damn 'bout me my whole fuckin' life — 'til I met you basically. She's just..." It surprised the hell outta me he ain't interrupted or snapped at me yet. But he hadn't. "She's irreplaceable."

"*Nothing* is irreplaceable," he retorted, scoffing. But he's wrong: people were. Once they're gone, that's it. I didn't know how to explain it, that fragility I'd seen through their eyes so many times now. Yet as another second passed, me still unsure

**145**

of what to say or do or shit, he sighed. "Fine. If that bitch's *that* important to you for whatever god forsaken reason, then I'll fix things. What do you want?"

He said that as if I had a damn clue myself. "Uh? Just for her to be safe, but hell knows I ain't got an idea of how to achieve that."

As he leaned back in his chair, he tilted his head back. "It'd be so fucking easy if it wasn't around magic. Just detail a guard, problem solved." I wasn't sure how to take designating guards as an "easy" solution; this's yet another indication of exactly how different the worlds we lived in were. But he's right that, assuming what Siani'd told Kyle's true and what Saite'd indicated to Richard that day, it's a whole goddamn ordeal that's way above our heads the second magic's involved. Yet he stopped rocking in his office chair as his eyes steadied on me. "Best option, likely."

What was? "Uh?"

Tapping on his phone and then turning on the large computer placed on his desk, I saw him slide the reading glasses he wore at his desk on. His head turned back toward me. "I'll ask once more: you really think that bitch's worth the headache, let alone whatever the hell she's involved in?"

I didn't know what he's thinking, but he had some type of plan. As much as I'd like to say I had no hesitations, it'd be a lie. And yet... I nodded. Little that it mattered, I just wanted her to live.

# Chapter Twenty-Four

belief

Since Kylie's fourth period was on the opposite side of the school from the cafeteria, I'd become rather accustomed to having the first ten minutes of my lunch blissfully alone even though the table could easily fit around eight people. The senior class was the smallest so there were plenty of extra tables. I liked it because it meant I wasn't crowded around other people; she'd said she liked it for similar reasons, but I suspected she really meant something to do with her empathy instead of introversion.

Unfortunately, I had a feeling that my regularly scheduled alone time wasn't happening today, and it might be gone for the rest of the year, given I saw him searching around the cafeteria, walking in my direction after he noticed me.

"Is, uh, is it all right if I sit here too?" he asked, wearing the same faded brown — maybe once even red — hoodie he'd had on the other day with a faded pair of older jeans. I thought people had talked in a small town like this when I'd transferred here. Maybe I'd just missed it, or it would've been a bigger deal had Kylie and Ashley not been new seniors as well. All of our

147

transfers were normal, however, compared to moving not just senior year, but in the middle of the week near the start of the second quarter.

There was plenty of open seating at other tables. Under other circumstances, I would've said no, but I wanted answers so I'd make this work for today. "Kylie sits there." I motioned across from me. "Otherwise, the table's empty."

"Thanks." He sat down to the right of the seat Kylie regularly sat at. "Fuck..." he mumbled under his breath.

Despite it only being midway through the day, he looked more exhausted than he had at the end of the day at North Opal Pines High when I'd seen him. "Are you visiting?" All the gossip I'd overheard suggested otherwise, but I wanted to hear from the source himself.

Rubbing his neck, he glanced away. "Ah, not quite. Guess... power in numbers or some shit, not that I'd be much help really, but, uh, yeah..."

The lunch line must've been shorter than normal or Kylie had gotten into said line faster than most days as she slid into her spot sooner than expected. Jordan scooted over a few inches to increase the space between them even though he wasn't actually in Kylie's seat. "They're pretending to serve food again." She stabbed a carrot, clearly intent on not eating it. "Why don't we get, like, pizza more often? At least then when it's cheap, it's tolerable."

For not the first time, I wondered if she was allergic to vegetables with how much she whined and bitched every time they were on her plate. "So what exactly is going on?" I asked, attention directed at her. Her routine vegetable tangent could wait until I got my answers.

Her cheeks flushed, standard vegetable protest pausing as she set her fork down to grip the ring she wore as a necklace that was usually hidden under clothes. "The hope is, if it's not just me here, then maybe..." He certainly wouldn't stop the attacks from happening since he'd been there when I'd found out. Putting together both of their responses, it sounded like the plan was that with him in the school, he'd assist if there was an emergency. But the only periods his schedule had overlapped with ours so far were AP History and lunch. She glanced over to him suddenly, her attention completely redirected. "Actually, how'd you end up in *AP History* of all things?"

His own cheeks flushed as he glanced away. "Ain't used to actually knowing the answers. Fucked up."

Kylie's lips pushed together a brief moment before her eyes widened. "Wait, your hypermnesia?" He nodded, hesitant and still avoiding eye contact with her. "Oh, that is *not* fair."

"Hyper...?" I asked. Maybe he'd be useful after all, distracting her so I'd get to sketch during lunches without her constantly trying to watch. But not yet. I wanted to know more about what was going on, both for pragmatic reasons and admitted curiosity about these things I'd never known existed until recently.

Jordan had yet to look back at Kylie, but that hadn't stopped Kylie from glaring at him nonetheless — I assumed in jest, but maybe she did so seriously; it was often hard to tell with her. She turned her attention back to me. "So like I have empathy and sensory clairvoyance." So the ability things, meaning whatever this was involved magic, as I'd suspected. "His is with his memory — hypermnesia, where he has like a perfect memory."

"That's not..." he mumbled.

She ignored whatever protest he attempted, an energy in her eyes I hadn't seen from her lately — enthusiasm closer to how she'd been the first day of school. "So if he already read — or even *skimmed* — the book for class, he doesn't have to study. An actual *useful* ability compared to what I got."

He rolled his eyes, so I was pretty sure he didn't agree with that assessment. Maybe he'd be a welcome guest here after all, both entertaining her *and* being entertaining in his own right.

"Damn... feel like shit." While he'd said the comment under his breath, it'd been easy enough to hear regardless.

Kylie's eyes turned to him, almost as if she saw through him. Her lips pushed together, playfulness of moments prior vanished. "That's the barrier, the one I mentioned."

Another thing I hadn't heard about. "Barrier?"

Kylie nodded, that distance not leaving her eyes as she continued to have a pensive expression. "Mm. It's like... I guess

**149**

you'd say a poison of sorts, with roughly a range of the school grounds. But it only really affects those of us that've had Act, since otherwise the mana siphon isn't really noticeable. It is for us, though, since mana's used basically every second, if not intentionally then from just basic body functions like breathing."

This whole time, she'd been dealing with some type of magic-siphon? Jordan had mentioned he was confused why the healing spell she'd used on me had caused her to black out; that might've just been the answer, one I'd never noticed from her all year. "Why don't you transfer out instead of...?" Why would he come here instead of her transferring back?

Kylie's grip on her fork tightened. "I don't... I don't ever want to go back there." That hadn't been the response I'd expected, her knuckles white from how tightly she gripped the fork. "And even if I did, I'm pretty sure the people who want me dead purposefully put it here. They'd just move it since they control it somehow."

"You know where it's at, then?" Jordan asked. I wasn't sure how he made the connection between those women controlling this thing and Kylie knowing its actual location, but he likely knew pieces I didn't.

She smushed the carrot into her plate with her fork. "On the other side of the school. I've tried getting as close as I could a few times to see if I could shut it down somehow, but I've never been able to find it without having to back off from getting too close to passing out. This's about as weak as it gets while staying on premise."

"Dammit," he mumbled, rubbing his eyes.

Other side of the school... that'd be around the library or computer lab then. I guessed that explained her constant lunch exhaustion, but it didn't make up for all the bitching she did about vegetables during said lunch. "It's still surreal," I said.

Kylie's posture stiffened, though I wasn't sure what about my statement caused her to tense up like that. "Oh no."

I turned as I traced Kylie's line of sight. Oh, that explained it more. Ashley strode near us, her eyes locked onto Kylie with her regular glare. I wasn't sure if the glare was meant for Kylie specifically or all three of us, but I wished she'd do like she did in homeroom and avoid us. I wasn't sure what had happened from her being friendly at the beginning of the year to this behavior after the gym attack, but she wasn't worth the drama she caused.

"Word of advice," she said as she stared straight at Jordan. "You picked the wrong crowd. Everyone around *her*" — she gestured to Kylie — "has *unfortunate things* happen to them. Better leave while you can before you end up in the hospital or dead like everyone else around her."

Kylie's eyes lowered to her plate.

As Jordan moved his attention away from Ashley's face, his gaze rested on Kylie. "I'm fine here."

Ashley rolled her eyes and huffed. "Your death." She stomped off to the other side of the lunch room to the people she usually sat with now.

Before Jordan said anything, Kylie released her fork, pads of her fingers indented by the fork's metal from how firm her grip had been. "I forgot something in the lab and need to check the library for something after. I'll meet back up in English." She forgot things there all the time. For someone so otherwise put together, it was rather confusing; maybe that barrier thing caused her to space out on that side of the building.

Kylie stood up, gathering her things. "It's not your fault," he said as she walked behind him to head to the tray drop-off. She didn't reply, just kept walking. His fists tightened, but he didn't turn toward her. "Library's beside the computer lab, right?" Given we were the only two around now, I assumed the question was directed to me so I nodded. "Knew it. She didn't forget a damn thing."

So she just wanted to be alone? What was wrong with that? "Maybe she just needs some time."

He chuckled, shaking his head. There was something gentle yet hurt from him, an expression I didn't know how to interpret. "I don't think so. Not if she's heading there."

"How so?"

Swallowing, he finally turned his head to the exit she'd left through. "This barrier's like a lead vest on my lungs: hard to even fuckin' breathe, let alone anything else. If this's as weak as it gets, then like..."

It was a form of self-punishment, self-harm even: she'd effectively been suffocating herself, over and over, only able to process survival and the endorphins from pain. There'd be no time to focus on the words that still echoed through her head no matter how much she tried to silence them. Her library trips were no different than the scars along my right arm, across my stomach, still not faded. "Maybe she really did forget something."

"Not a shot in hell." He chuckled again, a soft smile contrasting with the bitterness of his tone. "I've known her since elementary. She's got school shit together. No way she forgot a damn thing, 'specially not as often as it's seemed to happen. And she kept looking at her wrists..."

So he even knew about those scars she had around her wrists then. I'd never asked — it wasn't my business, after all — but I'd wondered nonetheless. "Those scars?"

It was like he spaced out, staring ahead. I didn't interrupt, not sure if I should repeat the question. If he didn't want to share, I was hardly in a position to force answers.

"Two years ago, this bastard kidnapped her. Tied her up, which's where the marks on her wrists and ankles came from." His eyes clenched shut as he swallowed before quietly adding, "Almost killed her. Did, every other time he tried."

How did this kidnapping guy *kill* Kylie? She was right here, wasn't she? Well, within the school and no longer in front of us, but still. I didn't interrupt, but I made a mental note to ask one of them about it later.

"Then this shit starts up again. I get whoever that was doesn't know jackshit 'bout what's actually going on... but she's no less a victim 'cause she made it out than the ones that didn't."

# Chapter Twenty-Five

## fake attack

Kylie | November 9
Training House

We had one hour: Jordan needed to be somewhere afterward, and I had a backlog of homework — let alone spell work — to look into. It was the first training I had with him since last March — the first time with just us, no Sia or Rota as guides. I'd said this would be helpful, but...

"You okay?" he asked, yet again worried about me. He cared too much, always concerned about me lately.

I shifted my weight. We weren't even in alt forms. That was mistake one, wasn't it? Any practice should be in alt form, if only because he had somewhere he needed to be and neither of us needed to get scuffed up while trying to squeeze this bit of training in. "I guess... I've always had someone tell me what to practice."

He sat down, patting the concrete beside him. Was it really all right to waste this much time just talking about what to do instead of doing anything?

Then again, it wasn't like I had a better plan. I sat down beside him. Light shone in through the busted windows, but that was basically all the light coming in since we hadn't turned the lamps on. "Haven't you been practicing since they've been gone?"

It felt like an insult to what Sia and Rota had organized, to call what I'd done since they'd left "training." "I have. But it's... different, and it honestly hasn't been successful. I've learned some spells and tried practicing with Isare, but it's just..." It felt empty. Directionless. How did I decide what to practice? What was the best choice for what I'd be dealing with next?

The uncertainty paralyzed me.

Jordan said nothing for a moment before asking, "What've you been working on when you come here?"

"Trying for telekinetics but..." I picked up a pebble through telekinetics; it was around the weight limit for what I could telekinetically move, which was useless if I was attacked. That day Maya had found out, I'd momentarily controlled Sase's limb, but I'd never been able to repeat anything close to that since. As it was, I still wasn't sure how I'd broken the trigger on the fire alarm during the last attack; it might've just been luck.

His attention directed to the pebble as I continued the eye contact needed to maintain levitation. "Still's fuckin' impressive." Even then, he was uneasy with magic, his voice timid compared to seconds ago. Besides, *impressive* was useless, just a trick for a talent show.

"Won't save me next time they attack."

I felt his eyes shift to me, and it was one of the few times I'd ever been uncomfortable under his gaze; his emotions were warm and sad, with a sudden distance. I'd assume I just picked up on multiple peoples' emotions if not for the fact that it had to be him. As usual for the training house, no one else was remotely nearby. "Guess that's true." Another moment passed, us sitting in silence before he spoke up once more. "Something I'd like to learn, if it's all right, is that damn healing spell."

I nodded, not sure how to behave. I knew it was purely pragmatism he'd asked to learn, especially if we ever actually did any training. But it was the first time he'd ever expressed interest in a spell, at least since his Act. Suddenly, I realized I'd never taught him anything either. Sia and Rota had taught him everything so far, and I'd only instructed Dani. It wasn't a stretch to think they'd learn differently, given their near polar opposite temperaments. "Oh, um, sure. That should be easy."

As I reached for his hand, a fake premonition started as soon as I felt his cooler skin against my fingertips; a wince escaped from me as I felt a punch to my torso.

"H-hey, you okay?" His hands moved to my shoulders to support me. This shouldn't be a problem. At least with these fake premonitions, no one was hurt. The only reason it affected me so much right then was because I'd already been worn down from the barrier at school.

I nodded, squeezing my eyes shut as I felt another punch, this one against my collarbone. "I-it's fine, just one of the fake attacks. It'll pass in a few minutes."

His hands remained on my shoulders, the firmness something I latched on to ground me away from the premonition. "Fake attack? This's your precognition, right? How the hell'd something like that be fake?"

What else could I call them, though? It definitely was a premonition, but I'd never seen them play out. "Yeah. It's just a bunch of punches, but they never happen. They've just gotten more frequent the higher my magipoten's become." His posture — mood — froze, hands withdrawing from me as if I'd stung him. I caught myself, a wince escaping; I'd relied on his support more than I'd realized, something I shouldn't have let happen. "Jordan?"

"I'm sorry." He sounded — felt — so defeated.

While I hadn't expected him to pull away, I didn't think it was that big of a deal. I also wasn't sure why me having a fake premonition upset him so much in the first place, but I didn't want to ask, given how instant his reaction had been. "I think it's starting to calm down now. Though, um, for me to show you how to heal, something needs to be injured in the first place."

His eyes ran over me. It was one of the rare times I felt self-conscious about my appearance since he so intently focused on me. "Yeah. Prob'bly better for me to learn it sooner than later. Just show me what to do."

Why was he so resigned? He'd only had this look when Sia'd forced him to do something he didn't want, and even then, that had been different from how he felt right then. Maybe he didn't think I'd be a good teacher. It *was* the first time I was teaching him. I didn't see a way he'd be more difficult than Dani, but I also knew there was no way I could measure up to how good Sia had been and he might've expected that from me.

"Is, um..." I didn't know how to ask about his emotions. While I couldn't *not* know, should I pretend I was unaware? Was he trying to hide how he felt? His emotions were so loud, I wasn't ever sure. "Are you sure this is something you wanna still do? I know I'm probably not the best."

More guilt flashed through him instantly. "Ah, oh, fuck. It's not you. You'd think years in, I'd be used to this shit a lot more." He shook his head. "So how do I do this..." A gentle smile pushed to his lips; it didn't erase the guilt and timidness he felt, but there was a peace that hadn't been there a second before. "Kyle?"

My cheeks flushed. He thought we were still heading in the right direction, that I hadn't screwed up what Sia had set up for me. He trusted my judgment, something I couldn't pretend to do right then.

Maybe we would get through this, one day at a time.

# Chapter Twenty-Six

## for her

Jordan | November 10
Richelieu Residence

I'm so goddamn tired and my lower back hurt like fuck despite healing every damn thing I could reach. This time'd been different than others though 'cause now I knew I ain't the only one who felt pain from the damn beatings. But what could I do? Felt fuckin' helpless, and it's even worse 'cause she didn't have the vaguest idea.

Dammit, just thinking 'bout it pissed me off again.

I increased my pace to Richard's. We met up every other Saturday, but I didn't get my schedule 'til Mondays or Tuesdays so I never knew how much I'd hate myself on the scheduled day. Today'd been hellishly busy as the holiday rush'd started picking up and I'd worked from open through a late shift. I'd always felt like ass in the evenings and now it's worse than normal 'cause've fuckin' work. Still drug myself over. Might've been late getting there, but promise's a promise. Also, I didn't have a way to cancel 'cause I prob'bly would've if I did.

People at the gate and even inside knew me now, called me *Master Jordan*, which's as ironic as ever.

As I made it to Richard's living room, I saw him on the

couch like always, this time his glasses on. His laptop's to the side while he had some rectangle device on his lap, phone and remote in the built-in drink holder on the couch arm. How many damn electronic device things did he even have?

"Later than normal," he said without looking up, tone dry. Couldn't tell if he's amused or pissed, and ain't sure I got the energy to care either way.

"Yeah, sorry. Things ran over."

That got his attention, him glancing up from the corner of his eyes to me despite still facing toward the rectangle thing he hovered a pen over. "Things or *things*?"

"Uh." I had no damn clue what he meant. "Work things?"

His attention turned more toward me as he clicked the pen into the rectangle thing b'fore tossing it on top of his laptop, both making a clanking sound. "Why're you even working? You're not out of high school, let alone college."

I sat down on the black leather armchair, dropping my bag to the plush rug. I snorted, not sure how else to respond. We needed the money, and he'd been to the apartment, had to have known that'd be the case. Besides, me going to college's a hilarious joke. Sure, the past two years're decent enough, but the first two ain't. And with what money? He kept staring at me, so guess he actually expected an answer. Shit. I averted my gaze. "Need the money. Why else'd anyone work?" Between the four of us, we seemed to actually make enough to *not* get evicted every few months, and I hated I understood why Jewel'd ridden my ass 'bout working so much, given the impact just my paycheck made.

"That's where you've been so much then."

Hell he mean by that? "Uh?" Actually, I ain't sure I cared enough to ask. This armchair's comfy enough to pass out on, and it's entirely too fuckin' tempting right then. His house's warm enough that with my hoodie on, I'm actually hell'va comfortable. Wonder how pissed he'd get if I just slept here? Didn't have work 'til closing tomorrow, so there's time enough to catch up tomorrow morning if his ass actually got outta bed b'fore noon.

He stood b'fore walking to the door for the room I normally slept in when visiting. "Over here."

Oh fuck, now he wanted me to *move*? Hell. But I'd rather move than deal with a bitchy Richard, 'specially since this's something he didn't want others to overhear. I stood, grabbed my bag, and followed him over to the room, biting back my own bitching while doing so. He closed the door behind us, flipping on lamps from a wall switch.

"'Sup?" I asked as I yawned, dropping my bag on the carpet beside the bed. It ain't that I didn't care, just goddamn, sitting showed me how exhausted my ass's after work *and* that motherfuckin' barrier.

Richard's arms crossed over his chest as he leaned against the door. "This isn't sustainable."

My lack of sleep? Yeah, for fuckin' sure and that's why I wanted to pass the fuck out, the sooner the better. I somehow doubted that's what he meant though. "Uh?"

He rolled his eyes. "I thought you've been with that bitch and that's why you've been so busy lately."

That'd been the case somewhat during the school day — even though it's annoying as fuck that I had to walk *even further* to class every day and back now. And we'd gone to the damn training house an hour here and there, but I hadn't spent more time there than I'd done holding shit for Emily earlier in the school year and at least it'd actually been productive. "Not really. Ain't got time, between work and pretending to give a shit at school." Dunno why I did the latter, actually. Wasn't like there'd be a "next year" once this one finished.

"Have you even applied yet?" I blankly stared at him. Hell he meant? Applied to *what*? He huffed, further agitated with me. "University. Wherever you're attending."

Jewel'd managed to get into Jenn, but she had state scholarships and however else she worked it. I ain't got any of that — hadn't ever had the chance to put homework first, and even if I had, never would've.

"Uh, I ain't? That'd take money I don't got and my grades're shit. Not exactly college type. Just wanna graduate so I'm not stuck doing both, like now." Even I wasn't completely sure why

**159**

I felt I *had* to graduate, just did. Guess it's a milestone I wanted to complete after getting all the way up here, little the act actually meant.

Richard's eyes honed in on me; I fidgeted from the intensity of his scrutiny as I rubbed the back of my neck with my hand. "Won't work. Isn't acceptable," he said, as if it's the most obvious shit out there.

"Uh?" Did we *really* need to have this conversation right this damn minute? Couldn't we bitch and him cuss my ass out tomorrow once I'd slept instead?

Richard shifted his weight against the door. "When're you even getting practice in with magic? Not for her, for *you*."

When I accidentally gave myself more damn burns, which still happened too damn much. "I'm not. I just try to support her 'cause they don't give a damn 'bout us." He kept glaring at me. Why'd he even care? Normally he just "forgot" to ever ask 'bout her since he'd realized she ain't leaving and's still pissed 'bout that. The hell changed, and could it've waited 'til after I'd slept?

His fist clenched as he turned his eyes away from me. He mumbled something under his breath, but I couldn't catch what he'd said. His gaze refocused on me a second later. "You're going to college, even if it's the damn community one."

"I, uh..." Was half tempted to ask if he's paying for it if he cared 'bout me going so damn much. "Don't think I've got the grades. Ain't had time to keep up." Given it's him, I ain't arguing money. He couldn't get how it felt to have jack shit just like I couldn't get how it felt to not have to worry 'bout getting kicked out every other day. Easier to blame it on my piss-poor grades than argue 'bout something that ain't gonna happen.

He scoffed. "Doesn't matter. You're going."

I just wanted to go to goddamn bed. Didn't wanna fuckin' argue, 'specially not over something I'd always known'd happen. I'm a *success story* for having any employment and looking like I'd finish high school instead of dropping out. I knew where I'm at on the social status hierarchy, and him being bitchy 'bout it ain't gonna change a damn thing. I'm exhausted, worked stocking shit all fuckin' day, and didn't wanna come here just to get bitched at by him.

"With *what*? You've seen our apartment, and we barely manage that. Even b'fore this magic shit, I didn't have a shot in hell. It's only made things that much more complicated." It'd taken my oldest friend from me; it'd taken her and broken her and I couldn't even say I'd been there for her 'cause I'd been a damn coward.

"You're going," he repeated. A light green circled his outer irises, the color reflective of his aura. I'd seen it b'fore, just once: his ability.

Wait, was he trying to use the damn thing on *me*? "Uh, you, uh, you know that ain't gonna work, right?"

The intensity of the hue increased as his stare honed in on me. Glad to know he'd 'parently been practicing on people, ain't at all morally questionable or terrifying. "You're going."

I rubbed the back of my neck as I glanced away. His tone made me wanna agree, just let it go. But... I'm tired and kinda pissed he's trying to literally force me to do something I just *couldn't*. How'd he think it felt to hear everyone around me talking 'bout future plans and knowing I ain't got a future, how right then's as good as it's getting? Hell, better than it ever should've been, really.

I felt an anger that'd been reserved mostly for Rotanu and absent with him blissfully gone. "With what money? With what time? You act like doors open for me when all they've ever done's slam shut in my goddamn face." I felt my heart race, cheeks flush. That damn hue's still in his eyes and it pissed me off even more. "And drop the fuckin' suggestion already — ain't gonna work 'cause it's an active and I got..." I hated he made me say this, but I hated it's true even more. "I got a higher magipoten. Won't ever work on me." Even on the days I wished it would, where I wanted him to make me believe I'm more than I was.

Passive abilities — like empathy, like hypermnesia, things that modified the senses or extended natural abilities — had no mana scaling as far as those perceived. Active abilities, like Richard's suggestion, did though. Didn't get the categorization or the reason, just's how Siani'd said it worked and it obviously's true, given all he'd done's piss me off.

**161**

I shifted my eyes away from him, every second seeing the hue just making me even bitchier at this point. "It's because you deserve better, and if you're not going to fight for yourself, I'll do it," he said.

I didn't know what I'd expected to hear, but that wasn't it. "What?" I replayed his words back in my mind but still couldn't process them, didn't understand what he meant or why he's so goddamn pissed 'bout what I'd known's coming forever now.

He didn't immediately reply, and that caused me to glance up. His aura color'd faded from his eyes, which'd changed focus from me to the back wall of the room. "You deserve better than that hellhole."

It's the first time anyone'd said that to me. Water rushed to my eyes, so I rubbed them to clear it out. What's *more*? I didn't deserve it, had always been told I'm nothing, and how'd *Richard* of all people see me as worth a damn? "I-it's fine. Just been a shitty day."

"You're a dense idiot." There's a fondness in his tone, amusement even, despite him actively insulting me. "First person I'd ever met that didn't see me for my parents or their corp." I remembered what Mrs. SuzyAnne had said to me when I'd met her: I'm the first person Richard'd ever invited over; she'd called me his "first friend" even. I'd thought she just didn't know how he acted outside this house, that she didn't know he's always the center of attention, all the girls he'd had on his arms wearing the gifts he'd given them b'fore inevitably dropping them once he lost interest.

"Everyone's better off than me, so just never..." It's obvious *now* that he's *someone* with how he dressed and acted and hell, all the shit he owned. I'd known he's richer than Kyle, but nothing else besides that.

"That's why it isn't fair." Life wasn't fair. "This's really all you want? This, for the rest of your life?"

Of course it ain't. But what other choice was there? I held back more water in my eyes; it'd just been a long day, and he's dragging the fuck outta it. That's all it was. "I'm just a waste of taxpayer dollars. I got that memo years ago, trust me."

"No, you fucking aren't." That anger's back, one different from the usual bitchy annoyance he had with women he dated or the staff here. There's a growl to it, a danger that I would've buckled from normally, but I couldn't fuckin' think straight enough to even do that right then. "They're all wrong. And I'll drag your ass myself if I have to show you that."

Now I had goddamn sniffles and couldn't even blame it on a damn cold 'cause he knew we couldn't get 'em anymore 'cause've mana. "Even if you're right, it doesn't matter. I can't just bail on my family." We needed the money. They depended on me now, and I couldn't bail on them like Father did, like I had for Kyle last year when she'd needed me. I wasn't like him, just able to do whatever the hell I wanted without affecting anyone else.

"How much do you need?" he asked, a neutral nonchalance replacing any irritation or fury he'd had.

I shook my head, not meaning *that* either. "I, uh, you don't—"

He rolled his eyes. "Fine then. How much do you make?"

Any number I gave him'd be pitiful and fuckin' embarrassing. I knew what he actually asked but didn't wanna answer the damn question. "I get enough handouts as it is, okay?" Whole damn life'd been a handout. I didn't want more.

Richard just nodded, as if *that* made sense to him outta all the shit I'd said. "A trade then."

What'd *I* possibly have that he wanted? He could buy the whole damn town out prob'ly. "Uh..."

His eyes centered on me, and while he didn't have his suggestion ability active, I wondered if it'd be less intimidating if he did. "I'm not asking that bitch for help, but I didn't get the training you both had. Teach me what you were taught then and Riyatian. Benefits us all, doesn't it?"

A damn trap's what it felt like. "I mean, I can do that now though — well, tomorrow. Not *now* now." He'd been roping me into that shit since b'fore they'd even left; ain't sure why he's acting like it'd be a sudden new thing.

"Saturdays from now on. Late afternoon until Sunday. Shouldn't be a problem, should it?" How the hell's he so

**163**

confident and also deciding this shit b'fore I'd remotely agreed to a damn thing?

Besides, I wasn't a dumbass — not enough of one where I didn't get what he's actually doing, trying to spare my pride and shit. It's still a favor; he didn't actually need me. "This isn't something you gotta worry 'bout, really."

He scoffed, no longer looking at me. "You seriously think you'll forever avoid conflict with any of the numerous groups that seem to want us dead?" It ain't *us*. It's Kyle. Just her. "If you're at the end of your wits now, imagine when something actually happens? What then?"

What'd happen next time they attacked her? The spells I knew're hilariously limited: mana transfer, Nateka's summon incantation, healing, and I guess aura blocking, if that counted. She seemed to know dozens of spells, and even that hadn't been enough.

I swallowed, throat suddenly dry. I didn't know if he seriously thought we all were in danger instead of just Kyle or if it's his way of saying that without getting better, I'd just be a liability when she's next attacked. Maybe in a way, he's even looking out for her, knew with the few hours a week we snuck, I'd never be able to have her back.

Siani ain't here anymore. Saite and Rotanu're gone as well. We're the only ones left. What's the point of the strings Richard had pulled to get me into Matthews if I did jackshit when the time came? I barely managed to not sleep through class each day, constantly exhausted between the damn barrier and work. I'd failed her last year, and god fuckin' damn Rotanu'd tried to warn me, to tell me I'd crossed lines and not listened.

*Jordan* wasn't enough for her, not to keep her alive. The memories of her crying and holding on to me, of when she'd activated NEO, hurt so damn much. I ain't enough, not to stop any of this shit going on. But *Rotanu* had been.

If it meant she didn't have to live in fear, I'd do this for her.

# Chapter Twenty-Seven

## a bit selfish

Kylie | November 12
Matthews High

I bit back a yawn as I made my way to the lunch table. While I wasn't sure exactly what it said about this year so far, I'd somehow adjusted to feeling run over after finishing fourth period. The barrier's effect now reminded me more of when I'd had math class at like eight thirty in the morning in seventh grade instead of a never-ending gym final exam. It helped that I enjoyed programming itself too, the rigid structure and rules reminding me of magic theory. The unfortunate news was that as my mana increased, so did the siphon, and I'd really rather not deal with the stupid thing at all.

As usual, Maya and Jordan had made it to the table before me, the art lab and whatever Jordan had fourth period both closer to the cafeteria. Maya had a book from the school library open, half through the book as she read while eating. I wasn't sure if she'd completely ignored Jordan or if they'd been talking before I got there, but he sat to the right of where I sat for lunch as he'd done every day since transferring here.

Moving into this comfortable routine, I huffed as I took my seat at our table. "It's Monday and I already want to go back to bed."

"You say that every day during lunch," Maya replied, not looking up from the book.

For the record, I *meant* it each time too. "You deal with the stupid barrier and feel fine."

She took a bite of her sandwich, completely unfazed. "By all accounts, I do."

It wasn't the same, and she knew it. Well, she knew it as much as she could from Jordan and me always being exhausted and complaining about the barrier since she couldn't detect it herself, but still.

Jordan was rather frazzled, had been all day but especially right then. He hadn't said anything, but just like earlier in second period, the intensity confirmed the anxiousness originated from him. He uncharacteristically poked at his food, ears and cheeks red. I turned to him, my head tilting to the side as I did so. "Everything okay?" I'd ask if he had a fever, but unless mana drain caused it somehow, he couldn't get those anymore, from what we knew.

"Ah, uh, y-yeah." He wore what I was pretty sure were new jeans and a quarter length button-up shirt I'd never seen him wear under the brown unzipped hoodie he'd had for years. He was embarrassed, my own heart racing despite being entirely too half asleep for a racing heart. Also, weren't those supposed to wake me up? Yet again, I never got an actual perk from empathy.

That said, I wasn't sure why he felt so embarrassed, so I wasn't sure if it was something I should pretend not to notice. "Something happen in class?"

He shook his head, rubbing the back of his neck with his right hand. "Nah, same old shit." Maybe he didn't want to talk about it? "B-but, I, uh, I got a cell phone this weekend if you want the number. In case shit happens and I'm not around."

Mom had gotten me a cell phone in elementary school since I was alone from a young age because of her work schedule. Jordan hadn't ever had one before, nor had he really ever expressed an interest in having one; him and technology usually ended up with one-sided, rather colorful arguments in general so I'd never thought much about it. He'd never really had a home computer either from what he'd said, and I wasn't sure why he'd get a cell phone now of all times. He wasn't wrong though that it'd be easier to keep in contact instead of always trying to coordinate ahead of time.

"Oh, sure! Do you remem—" Of all the questions I could ask, asking if he remembered something was around the most useless. "Or, um, it might be easier to give you my cell and you just text me later." I'd seen too many classmates have their phones taken up here; no one cared at North Pines, but they certainly did here.

His cheeks turned even redder as he nodded. Maybe he'd not slept well or something so he felt the barrier's effects more than normal today. "Yeah, that works."

As I gave him my cell, I realized I instinctively slowed down and repeated the last four digits; it was something Mom had taught me to do growing up, but it wasn't like he needed me to repeat anything since he could just recall it as needed. He didn't complain or tell me to hurry up though, just nodded after I'd finished.

"You're not going to put it in your phone?" Maya asked, looking up from her book.

Jordan rubbed the back of his neck once more as he glanced away. "Nah, I'll remember it."

I couldn't get a read on anyone else's emotions with Jordan so close. His emotions were intense enough that I effectively perceived two groups: Jordan and Not-Jordan, with Not-Jordan expanding out to basically the whole school's emotions from what I could tell. I remembered when my immediate proximity empathy reads used to overwhelm me to the point of blacking out, yet here I was handling the whole school *and* Jordan without it really being a problem. Even without Sia, I was managing, somehow. Even in this barrier, as tired as I was, I managed to deal with empathy instead of wanting to throw up like I used to when I had Sia's help and far less mana.

That said, my empathic range's cap *had* to be close, right? I hoped so because the alternative was the range increasing for basically the rest of my life.

Maya nodded. "Oh right, you have the memory thing. Sorry."

He nodded, that flash of embarrassment spiking once more. There was a peace to our lunchtime, just Maya, him, and me here. They got along well enough, far better than Dani ever had with Jordan, and well... I didn't ask about Richard. I didn't want to know; if I didn't know, I could somewhat pretend last year had been some long nightmare and not something that'd actually happened. That was a bit selfish of me, wasn't it? No one innocent had died because of me last year, but yet this year hurt less. It was disrespecting their deaths, wasn't it?

"Kyle?"

I glanced up at Jordan, not sure what I'd missed. While it'd become more instinctual to answer to my new nickname from him, I still wasn't as used to it as my actual name. He was happy each time he said it though, and I didn't feel embarrassed as much as I used to — even if I was nowhere to Sia's level, regardless of what he said. "Hm?"

His concern crowded into my mind; he had turned to face me instead of the table, closely observing me. "You okay? Zoned out pretty hard there."

If I said what had been on my mind, he'd get upset again. I shook my head and replied, "Oh, just a bit more tired than normal. I got a little too close to dozing off there, sorry."

Closing her book, Maya glanced up at me. "Isn't that worse than the beginning of the year?"

"Oh, um, it's because mana isn't stagnant. So like, even if I'm getting used to it, I'm still increasing mana too, which makes the siphon strengthen too." It was another lie, but at least this one had a foundation in truth: everything I'd said theory-wise was correct, I just adjusted faster than the mana increase happened. That said, I knew better than to use any active mana, anything besides the passive mana consumption, to live. I still wasn't even sure if I'd be able to get into alt form without blacking out or, if by some miracle I got into alt form, how I'd tolerate the even more potent siphon.

From the corner of my eye, I saw Ashley peer at us. I couldn't pick up her emotions. Too much distance with other emotions, *Jordan's emotions*, between us. But she definitely didn't look pleased, rolling her eyes as she turned away once she saw I'd noticed her. How long had she been staring at us? She'd always been irritable, even if she hadn't expressed it, but... I guess she couldn't forgive me.

That was all right.

I couldn't forgive myself either.

# Chapter Twenty-Eight

## it's a start

Jordan | November 17
Richelieu Residence

Last Sunday, Richard'd basically reorganized my whole fuckin' life. I thought he'd gotten me transferred to Matthews fast, but holy fuck, that'd been nothing compared to him writing my resignation letter, dragging my ass to get new clothes for the first time in my life, and somehow getting a fuckin' bank account opened *on a Sunday*. He'd put himself as primary and me as secondary on the account for something to do with tax shit or something I still didn't completely understand, but he'd been rather *clear* that I ain't allowed to have the rest of my family on the account. That's how it'd always worked for us, us all sharing one account with Father's name and depositing everything into it. He'd said that'd been the most dumbass idea he'd heard, 'specially with how Father was. Wasn't like I really had a good argument either since Father stealing money for more beer'd been a recurring problem for basically my whole life. Now Richard had money auto-forwarded from this new account into my family's so they wouldn't notice a difference in pay. He said the rest in the account's mine to fuck around with,

**171**

and it's hilarious he thought I knew what "fuck around with" money was in the first place.

Now's the first real day of providing my side of our deal, and it'd be a poor lie to say I ain't intimidated and still uncomfortable as fuck with all this. I knew he didn't need me, regardless of what he'd said. He's doing me a hell'va favor, and I hoped I wouldn't fuck shit up too bad. I wasn't able to get that much time with Kyle this week on practicing shit, but we'd already set up more days I'd train with her next week. It wasn't the time to be prideful; I needed to take advantage of this one break I got so I'd actually *be there* this time for her.

They yet again greeted me as *Master Jordan* at the gate; I guess Richard'd never told them he'd technically "hired" me so I'm the same as them, except they actually earned their keep instead of getting handouts 'cause of pity. When I opened the door into Richard's living room, I saw him sprawled out on the couch, flipping through tv channels. "Yo," he said.

"Uh, 'sup?" I ain't sure how to even greet him. Hopefully that wouldn't piss him off? Sitting in the armchair I usually sat in while over, I didn't lean back this time. I stayed right at the edge, my feet firmly on the rug. I had the duffel bag I'd gotten last week, meant for training shit, but worked for spare clothes here too.

He said nothing in response as he stood up and strode to one of the rooms on the opposite wall from his own room. He opened the closed door. I followed him in, not sure what else to do. I'd assumed all the rooms in his *loft*'re bedrooms, but I found out otherwise with this room that's painted bright white, vivid lights overhead shining down on all manner of workout equipment I'd never seen b'fore. There're no windows, just some mirrors and waxed tile flooring. Richard motioned for me to enter further b'fore closing the door back once I was in the middle of the room. Fuck, of course the room he wanted me in's the one where they skipped out on the damn heat too. There had to be a fuckin' fifteen degree drop between his living room and this room. "Can't do actual weapons training here, but other shit, knock yourself out."

"Uh..." I didn't wanna touch a damn thing in this room —

if I didn't break the equipment, prob'bly'd kill myself on it. There's a treadmill. I knew that one. And some type of bike thing but attached to the tile... A punching bag, and a bench with a padded cover... I didn't know any of the shit in here, and every new machine I noticed only further confirmed that.

Richard crossed his arms over his chest. "What's the problem?"

"I, uh, I've never seen like half of these b'fore, so, uh, prob'bly best I don't..."

What I didn't expect's him dragging me over to one of them that had a bench and a bar with weights over it. "Then you'll learn."

This's *really* what he wanted me to do during my so-called "working" hours? What happened to me teaching him Riyatian and shit? Yet I already knew I ain't winning against that tone he had. Even worse, he wasn't wrong that I'd never been particularly in shape, always scrawny and underweight. My alt form's stronger, but I'd assumed it'd been 'cause fuckin' mana, like everything else. I had a sudden reason to doubt that assumption, I unfortunately realized. "I, uh, i-if you're sure..." I'd yet to see Richard ever *not* be sure of something, but there's always first times.

He sat on the bench, lying down on it before gripping the bar with weights. He lifted it up and down with no sign of struggle. He put the bar back in the holder. "You try."

Fuck. He really wanted my ass doing this shit. I'd always hated having an audience for anything, and that's 'specially the case when I had no goddamn idea what I was doing, like right then. "Uh, sure."

He moved off the bench, motioning for me to repeat what he'd done. What he didn't seem to understand's me having the damn memory didn't necessarily mean I got what I'm s'posed to do. More self-conscious than ever, I lay on the seat and reached up to the bar, biting down on my tongue; even lifting the damn thing's hard as hell. How'd he make this look so fuckin' *easy*? An exhale squeaked outta my lungs as I *finally* managed to get the damn thing off the holder, only to feel the bar slam into my stomach and knock the fuckin' breath outta me. "Fuck!"

**173**

Richard grabbed the bar off me, raising an eyebrow. Wait, so he *hadn't* planned for that to happen? I ain't sure if that's better. "Worse than I thought. Try it in alt. I'm curious."

He wanted me to do *what*? *Here*, where staff could walk in and there're fuck knew how many cameras? "But, ain't..."

Unconcerned, he walked back over to the entrance, flipping a lock. "No cams. Now stop being such a bitch."

I'm more interested in getting a damn heal spell off on what felt like a broken rib, but whatever. Wincing as I sat up, I mumbled the damn transformation phrase. The pain instantly disappeared while my clothes shifted and hair's longer, tied back. I didn't bother asking what to do next and got ready to repeat the same damn thing that'd just kicked my ass less than two minutes ago. Lying down, I once more grabbed the bar, noticing it's easier to get off the rack. Even more surprising, my arms didn't let out this time — still strained, but nothing compared to what'd happened.

But what now? "Uh?" Did I just hold this thing? 'Cause that sounded fuckin' miserable.

He sounded far more satisfied this time when he spoke, his normal confident tone present. "Thought so. My alt form can add another hundred to hundred fifty on. Figured yours would be similar."

So that meant I could put the damn thing up, right? I set the bar back onto the rack, sitting up after. I stared at my gloved hands. Sure, I knew my alt form's stronger, but *a hundred pounds of lifting* stronger? Even worse, there's no practical point in exercising in said alt form. More important to build myself up, and I suddenly ain't at all looking forward to that. "Damn..."

I still hated this form, and it's even worse that every day made it more obvious I needed to be *more* like Rotanu, the differences now goddamn goals.

"We'll go to the training house tomorrow." He had a whole damn agenda lined up, and I ain't sure why I'm so surprised. "For now, we'll stay in here and you can teach me something with magic. No one'll expect a thing."

He'd really thought every damn thing through, hadn't he?

Unfortunately, I still knew basically jack shit 'bout magic that wasn't *how not to burn myself*. "Uh... The heal spell work?"

He shrugged. "It's a start."

# Chapter Twenty-Nine

## deviation

I really hated how my apartment had become the assumed sleepover spot. Kylie said it was closer to where she and Jordan had been going after school, training-something, and that it was easier to work around her mom this way. She usually paid for takeout, so I shouldn't complain, but her bedroom at least had actual beds. I just had my pallet on the floor still. Kylie never complained about that though, or that I kept the heat as low as I could; she just wore a jacket and never took it off.

"I hate math," she grumbled, poking her notebook page with her pencil.

Raising my eyebrow at her, I replied, "No one made you come over." I was perfectly fine studying on my own. I'd always done so, and I could continue doing so perfectly contently.

She blew air from her lips. "I need to focus so I get a good grade. Mom's already going to hit the roof when she sees I got a C on the last quiz."

I didn't see why her grade problems were being made into *my* study problems. I rolled my eyes. "Don't show her?"

She snickered. "Hilarious."

While I didn't see what was so funny, it also wasn't going to be a question on the upcoming test. I resumed reviewing the equations we'd covered since the last test. She moved around, so I glanced up in time to see her grab her spell book. "Thought you needed to study math?"

"I do. But I want a break." Her lips pursed together, staring at the two books open in front of her. "It's..." She nodded as if she agreed with me despite the fact I'd said nothing. "Mm. I know I'm avoiding it."

Great, so she's doing the emotion-thing again. Jordan had been around often enough that I usually got left alone on that now, but he wasn't with us for sleepovers for obvious reasons.

"But school just... it's not teaching me how to live or what to do if another fight happens. It just feels like a waste of time compared to what I should be focused on, and that makes it hard to care. Why learn all this when I could be learning some theory or a spell or *something* that might make the difference if I die next time or not? Mom keeps pressuring me for college applications, but I just... they're a waste of time when I'm not even sure I'll be alive for college, and it's all I can think about every time I click on an admissions page."

We were apparently having *feeling time*. Wonderful. Though even as annoyed as I felt at my limited study time being wasted, I understood. I seemed to be the only one besides Jordan who knew, or at least the only other one she talked to about things. It likely was a compliment, something I wasn't used to since people never really depended on me, least of all for emotional support. Others had always been better at that type of stuff. "That's why he's at school too now, isn't it?"

Kylie nodded. "Yeah. But..." She didn't exactly sound confident that he'd make a difference, and he hadn't the day I'd found out about all this, so I understood why. "I just think about how much better Sia was, and I'm not sure I'm ever getting there. Or at least, I'm not getting there *fast enough* to make it matter."

"Sia?" She'd mentioned the name a few times, but I'd never asked. If she was going to distract me anyway though, I might as well hear stories I actually was interested in.

Her hand moved to the necklace ring again, holding on to it. "Mm. How do I...? It sounds really out there." Basically everything around magic did, so I wasn't sure why this needed the special disclaimer. "Me and Jordan, and I guess one other person..." Her tone soured on the last person's mention, but if there was someone else involved in all this, why hadn't that been brought up before now? Seemed like a third person would've helped the rather desperate odds. "Or, well, I guess... how do I?"

What had I just gotten myself into? She'd never stumbled this much on rambling about magic before. "It's complicated?" Maybe she'd just say yes, and we'd drop it. I regretted asking already and she hadn't even started the inevitable monologue.

She nodded. "I guess. There's more to it than what I've said, because at least, like... I can tangibly show magic. It's basically the same as gravity theorems, just less well known." *Lesser known* was putting things mildly, but she wasn't wrong in that this fantastical-whatever actually somehow aligned with the world instead of against it.

"Back a long time ago, I don't really know how much, there was a country that was primarily composed of mages. There was a coup, and the ruling line was overthrown. The country fell into anarchy soon after." It wasn't like any of that was particularly revolutionary — it'd been the course for countless civilizations over the centuries. "But the crown princess and a few others were able to escape to a degree because they used otherwise forbidden magic — a reincarnation spell that killed all involved as soon as it finished."

When she hesitated, I knew the implication, but that had to be wrong. "But then..."

"That's why me and Jordan, and the other person to a far lesser degree, have so much mana compared to most people now."

I didn't know if I wanted to ask more. The sheer idea overwhelmed me, like multiple layers of thoughts all colliding into each other. "What's that have to do with this Sia though?"

She still wouldn't look at me as she stared down at our textbooks. "When I had Act — Activation, which started active mana generation, so basically the event when the magic 'seal'

**179**

gets broken and someone can actively use magic, um... So when I had Act years ago, I found out that if an incarnation died uncleanly — including from that original cast, which all counted as unclean deaths — that incarnation's consciousness carries on to the next incarnation. There were only supposed to be three other consciousnesses, but a fourth was there for me and Jordan both. They were ourselves from the future somehow, or at least that's what they said. That 'future me' went by Sia, well, Siani. Jordan's 'future self' went by Rota, Rotanu."

If she didn't look so serious, I'd assume she took me for an idiot. And maybe it was a lie, but it was a damn good one based on how she acted. But what could I even ask or say to something like that? "If they're the 'future you,' then how could you not be... whatever you're expecting then?"

Instead of the quiet tone, her voice changed to a much more frantic tone as she asked, "What if I screwed up? Deviated? Not worked hard enough or should've learned something different or..." Her voice became subdued. "Sia wouldn't have let them die."

I didn't care if I lived or died. Either one was better than going back home. I didn't know what to tell her when she wasn't *wrong* that if she hadn't been there, her classmates likely would be still alive. But I guess... I would like for her to live, and I didn't mind her company as much as I once had.

"Regardless of if you're 'deviating' or not, you can only handle right now, today, not yesterday or tomorrow." I didn't know this Sia, but right then, I wouldn't have minded meeting her and maybe understanding Kylie's clear admiration better.

As she looked at me and chuckled, she nodded. I wasn't sure what was so funny, but I also wasn't asking for fear of another tangent when we had plenty to work on as it was. "You know? Maybe you're right. Thanks. I think I needed to hear that."

# Chapter Thirty

## grateful

Jordan's schedule had opened up a few weeks ago, and we'd settled into something resembling a consistent routine, a few hours after school three days a week and then early Saturday mornings until late afternoon. That blissfully left us both to crash Friday evenings; I wasn't sure about Jordan, but I relished my Friday after-school naps, given how beaten down by the barrier I always felt by then.

A rather irritable emotion swarmed me during my half-asleep daze, and the only aura close enough was from Mom, just now coming home; she had a committee meeting late afternoon on Fridays this year, so she usually got home very late. That worked for me since it meant she wouldn't notice that I napped every Friday. She didn't know to ask questions, and I still went to bed at my normal times on Friday because really, the nap just helped negate some of the mana drain from the barrier all week. My guess was something in the meeting had set her off, which basically never worked out in my favor. Glancing at the clock, I saw her meeting had run later than normal. I'd been napping close to three hours, everything dark already.

Sitting up, I rubbed my eyes. I'd been trying to prep for the end of the quarter finals this week and maybe that'd taken more out of me than I'd realized since I felt like I could've used a longer nap than what I'd already had. Really, I had half a mind to roll back over and let whatever she was upset with be tomorrow's problem.

Exhaustion aside, I knew I should at least see why she was so irritated, though; after all, it likely would become even more of a problem if I didn't and it somehow involved me. Worse yet, I heard her march upstairs, which caused me to grimace. The only reason she'd come up to the second floor was if whatever had her upset *did* involve me. What'd I do *this* time?

She knocked on my door but didn't wait for me to say to come in as typically happened. I was less than appreciative as she snapped my overhead light on, my eyes stinging from adjusting to the rapid increase of light and setting off my own agitation with whatever was going on. "Have you gotten any acceptance letters yet?"

I hadn't even submitted an application. What was the point? College might as well have been a decade away with how removed it felt from my current life. My concerns were when I'd be attacked next, who I'd be attacked with, and with not sleeping too hard if Mom was home. That was part of what made the Friday naps great. I was alone, so if they attacked, only I would die. I didn't need to worry about anyone else.

"Not yet..." I wasn't awake enough to lie right. For that matter, I wasn't even really awake enough to pretend to block out any empathy or auras either; "luckily" for us both, her irritation rapidly cleared the fog of sleep from my brain. She knew nothing about magic-related things, but given that I hadn't fully woken up yet, I struggled to comprehend, let alone distance myself, from Mom's irritation-anxiety swirl of emotions.

She crossed her arms over her chest, which meant that had been exactly as wrong of an answer as I'd braced for. "And how many have you applied to?"

Maybe I wanted to go back to her being overly worried about me; that felt more controllable than her frustration and

**182**

anger, which filled my head and made it difficult to not lash out in turn. "A few."

"Which institutions?"

"Um." I couldn't say Jenn. It didn't matter if it was legal or not, she knew enough people to get someone to verify if I'd submitted an application. And since Jenn didn't really decline anyone to begin with, there was no question of acceptance, just of if I'd applied. There was the state college I guess, but she wanted me to go to a *more prestigious* university so if I didn't get accepted while saying I did, I'd be in a mess when I did apply if they didn't actually accept me. "I don't remember off the top of my head."

Mom huffed as she rolled her eyes. "Fine. Your room will help jog your memory since you're grounded for the next week. Maybe you'll *remember*."

Since I was eighteen now, wasn't it, like, illegal to keep grounding me? Probably not with my luck. "Okay." I didn't know what else to say. Even if I was locked in here *again* — since it'd be far from the first time now — I'd learned plenty of strategies to keep myself busy. More importantly though, being locked in this room wouldn't help me survive or keep the people around me alive.

Mom turned away, sighing. "I thought getting you away from him would help you refocus."

It wasn't Jordan's fault, not this time. Mom didn't know he'd transferred to Matthews, but she'd always blamed him for everything and I was sick of it. "I've just been busy. I'll put some out this week, like you said."

Yet that response made her even more livid somehow. I just said I'd give her what she wanted, so why was she furious about it?

"Busy with *what*? I saw that C and those two B's you got two weeks ago."

She didn't know what I dealt with. I understood that, but her expectations felt like a weight on my chest, suffocating me worse than being in the computer lab. Her expectations weren't reasonable. Even from her perspective, I'd been kidnapped and lived through a school attack within the past two years. Didn't she think that affected me? Why would I walk out unscathed, even ignoring everything she was unaware of?

"You ignored Dani when she came to check on you," she added.

Yet again Dani had tattled, further confirming my suspicions that I couldn't trust her, and really, part of me wondered if we'd ever been friends. It didn't matter. Even if we had once been friends, now she just passed information on to her mom like a *good child*, and that would only put people in danger.

"The only friend you've made at Matthews is Maya, and you never mention just visiting, only working on group projects."

It was hard "catching up" to someone you spent almost all school day with every single week. At least she'd been fond of Maya from day one — teacher's instinct, she'd say if I asked, just like she'd used that phrase against Jordan for years now.

"So where's all your time going if you don't have time to apply to institutions you're going to *in less than a year*?"

I was busy trying to survive, busy trying to figure out if it was even ethical to survive, busy wanting not to live in fear for even a few hours.

What could I say? Nothing. It didn't matter if I wanted to yell back because I didn't know the words to say — didn't know how to explain there was no point applying when I wasn't sure I had a future. "Yes, ma'am."

She huffed. "I can't do this for you. *You* have to do it." Maybe she couldn't legally or ethically, but I wasn't sure why that stopped her; she knew what they wanted to hear better than I did. "If you get three applications in this weekend, I'll consider shortening your grounding."

She left my room, shutting the door behind her. I knew she was anxious and frustrated with me for not applying; I felt her concern like it was my own, stuck in my throat, eating into my chest. I needed to clear my head, and her emotions barging through me made that near impossible. I needed to get away for a few hours, and a few extra hours of training were more beneficial than sulking in my room anyways. How could I escape, though? There was no way to easily leave; I was on the second story, and that definitely wasn't an accident since Mom heard any movement up here on the ground floor, where her bedroom was. Only one potential idea came to mind: I'd been practicing telekinetic control, so just maybe...

I stood, concentrating on placing air between my feet and the carpet — not much, just a fraction of an inch. To my surprise, not only had I done so, but it was easier than expected. For whatever reason, I wasn't struggling to manipulate air around my body compared to how much I struggled telekinetically moving and levitating objects I didn't have direct contact with. I walked to my window and unlatched the lock, maintaining the levitation so each step acted like it was on an invisible and silent surface.

Could I do this? If Mom found out I snuck out from the second story, it would *not* be a great time for me. But I needed fresh air, and I refused to play the "lock Kylie in her room for months on end" game again. It never helped me *or* her, even if she didn't realize that.

I grabbed my tennis shoes I'd barely kicked off at my bed before napping and put them on; next I opened the window as quietly as I could before stepping out, levitating myself just off the carpet, just off the window seat, then just off the roof. But then what? I closed the window back as quietly as I could, thankful it hadn't squeaked. Where next? I needed to be absolutely silent while avoiding any windows on the ground floor. Noting my options, I saw the tree toward the front of the yard; it'd be close, but if I ran and got momentum, I was pretty sure I could make that.

If I left the house, I'd be committed to this. Mom wouldn't know I snuck out onto the roof if I just went back inside right then. But I couldn't make myself turn around. Mom's emotions made my heart race and clouded my mind; the only reason I'd gained any clarity was thanks to the crisp breeze.

Simmering in my room wouldn't keep me alive; it'd just needlessly endanger Mom. All I needed was an hour or two where I practiced in alt form so I wouldn't even need a shower, just something to give me distance from her emotions until my own settled. Taking a deep breath, I ran, free-falling for a moment. I reached my hands out to grip the tree branch but winced as only one caught onto the bark before even that grip slipped and I plummeted to the grass. At least I'd fallen only a few feet from where I'd wanted to land. My wrist throbbed, but I'd check it out later. First, I needed to get out of the neighborhood in case anyone else was also outside.

Once I was out of the neighborhood, the only emotions around me were a passive hum. There wasn't anyone within my field of vision, something I typically only experienced at the training house. But Opal Pines had always been like quiet at night since not much was open past ten; by seven or eight at night, the town had mostly turned in for the evening. I felt more and more crisp air fill my lungs, soothing in its own right because of my elemental alignment, the same comfort water now provided me when nearby.

As the training house came into view, I felt a hum of emotion nearby. But from who? This area was always abandoned. A few steps closer, and I made out a familiar red and blue aura, but why was Jordan here at this hour, or at all really? He didn't fight me on practices, but I wouldn't call them his favorite pastime either. The closer I came, the more intense his emotions became, as usual, but... something was wrong: I felt a throb in my left shoulder blade. That pain had to come from him, but why was he in pain?

I opened the door, seeing him in the training house as expected. He wasn't in alt form, though he did have Nateka out. The lamps were all on, scattering dim light throughout the otherwise dark area. He jumped and turned to face me, lowering Nateka after recognizing me.

"Kyle? What're you...?"

"Sorry. I didn't know you'd be here. Um, I can leave if it's a problem." But *why* was he here? He'd always been a morning person, and this was past when he'd said he went to bed, let alone for a Friday evening where he was as exhausted as I was after school.

He dismissed Nateka, shaking his head. "Oh, uh, nah, it's fine. Was just practicing stances. Not really something worth wasting time on when we're together." He practiced without me around? But he always fussed about coming here. Sure, said complaining was a lot less than when Sia and Rota had been around, but I'd never expected he put in extra effort on top of our sessions. Had he injured himself practicing tonight? But then why hadn't he healed himself?

"You already collapse like fuck on Fridays, and there's no way your mom's fine with you out this late. What's up?" he asked.

I felt so embarrassed, interrupting his private training time because I'd gotten into a fight with Mom. My cheeks flushed as I glanced away. "Yeah. Sorry. I needed to get out of the house for a bit. Mom's mad at me, and I just can't deal with the empathic reads right now."

He sat on the cracked concrete that made up the training house's remaining flooring as he drank from a water bottle he had nearby. "Bad grade?"

Without meaning to, I grumbled — his emotions were so peaceful despite the flicker of pain every few seconds. It was a nice change from the house and Mom, a gentleness that contrasted the intensity of Mom's emotions despite Jordan's being significantly louder to me.

"A bit. But mostly because I haven't put in college apps. Just... it hasn't been my priority lately, with everything else."

"Yeah. She doesn't know, but you've got a hell'va lot going on."

Even if I logically knew that, hearing it from him reassured me. I did my best; it wasn't enough, but I didn't know how to do better. As he moved his arm to set the water bottle down, I felt that same sting from my shoulder blade. "Did you hurt yourself training?"

"Huh? Nah, just stances — oh, uh, empathy?"

I nodded. "Yeah, before I came in especially. It's mostly calmed with you sitting, but I was guessing it's difficult to reach since you haven't healed it."

He shook his head, heart suddenly racing; that tranquility had vanished, replaced by apprehension. "Oh nah... Don't worry 'bout it."

Realistically with our mana, most minor injuries healed in minutes — the sprain I'd gotten leaving the house had likely already healed up despite it happening less than half an hour ago. The fact his left shoulder and lower back ached meant it was something outside of a quick slip-up. Unless...

**187**

"Wait, they didn't attack you, did they?" Had he come here to nurse wounds because Sase and Zimihe had gone for him instead of me when I wasn't around? Did he not feel safe going home?

"Who — oh. Nah."

Then, was it... "The people who try to capture mages, they didn't...?"

That time, he actually chuckled, again shaking his head. "Like I said, don't worry 'bout it." While I was glad his anxiety had subsided into amusement, I still wasn't sure how he'd been injured to begin with.

If he wouldn't say how it'd happened, the least I could do was heal him; he'd been practicing with healing magic, so I assumed he wasn't able to have direct contact with the injury. "Let me heal you at least. No reason for you to go around in pain."

"Like I said, it's fine."

This time, I was the one that stared at him, eyebrow raised. "We both know you're in pain. I've already derailed your practice, so I might as well make myself useful."

His heart raced faster, nervousness shifting into outright fear. But why? Why didn't he want to be healed? Why did he *want* to be in pain? His lower lip trembled as he glanced away.

"A-all right."

He unbuttoned his shirt, sliding it off before turning his back to me, barely illuminated by the lamp closest to us. Despite the poor lighting, I immediately noticed a large purple bruise. Even if he'd somehow dropped Nateka on his back, it wouldn't have bruised like this — the area was too wide, rounded. He had another long purple bruise along his lower hips, right above his pants line.

I rested my hand on the bruise on his shoulder blade. These injuries were familiar. I knew them. There was no way he could've done them to himself, though. He said it hadn't been Sase or Zimihe, and they likely wouldn't have stopped at just bruising, so that checked out. But if not them, then... who?

"You're used to these." His actions and reactions told me, didn't they? He'd downplayed the seriousness; without empathy, I would have no idea something had happened. Even more so, Jordan had always been a poor liar, but he hadn't stumbled at all while trying to convince me he was fine. He knew how to hide this.

"Who did this to you?" Anger flooded me faster than it ever had at Mom. He'd always been timid, and he'd always hated touch, especially when we'd first met.

I pushed healing magic on the first bruise. My aura resonated with the injury as they both faded from my view, the throb from that location vanishing as expected.

"It's, uh, I just fell on the way here."

I wanted to roll my eyes at him. *Really*?

"The injuries aren't consistent with that. You have others that have mostly healed already too, and what's left of those don't support a fall either."

I laid my hand over where his kidney was located, that bruise mostly faded to a dull yellow. It was like that fake premonition yesterday, down to the...

That premonition had felt like punches, and his bruises concurred. He hadn't been scared of the pain though, only of me knowing he'd been hurt.

"I-it's fine. Really."

Who would he protect this much?

"It's not Richard, right? He isn't..."

He had no hesitance as he said, "Oh, fuck no. I mean, we've been sparing and shit lately, sure, but he's, uh... He kinda really sucks ass with Kutari."

The bruises were bigger than my hand, most women's hands, I'd guess. Who else did Jordan hang out with besides me and Richard, though? He hadn't lied about Richard not hurting him, I could tell that for sure, but...

It made perfect sense, actually. I'd just been too self-centered to ever notice. Laying my hand over his lower back, I felt his posture stiffen as his heart raced and the muscles ached from the contact with my hand. "This isn't something new, is it?"

I'd only seen Jordan's dad once or twice at school even though we'd known each other most of our lives. I'd never seen his mom, never heard him even mention her.

"Just a mistake."

The mistake was that I'd found out, not that he'd been hit. I

**189**

repeated yet another healing spell, this one on his rib. He'd already attempted healing this one, but he hadn't mastered the spell to fully mend what would've been a fractured rib.

"I don't get it." I'd whined about Mom just minutes ago. How many times over the years had I grumbled about her to him? He always had this distant look in his eyes whenever I complained about her; I'd assumed I bored him, but... that wasn't right. It'd been envy for what I had and he didn't, what he deserved to have. And how many times had Sia blocked his pain? She had to have known, yet she'd never even implied anything.

"You know how to fight back. But you don't," I said.

His hands trembled so much that I barely restrained my own from mimicking the gesture because of how intense the empathy read was from him. I struggled to breathe, my throat clogged as if rocks had lodged all along my vocal cords.

"Just don't suffer, okay? At least, if you can't heal something, let me do it for you. There's no reason for you to sit in pain. Especially with our mana already siphoned all week at school, you don't need to deal with any additional mana loss from your body trying to mend itself."

His voice was defeated as he said, "You got mana drain worse than I do. Don't even."

Technically, he wasn't wrong, but he made it sound like far more of a difference than it actually was day-to-day. "I napped earlier, so it's fine."

As he lowered his head, his voice stayed quiet. "Aren't you going to lecture me or some shit?"

"About what?" I didn't really know what to say, if I was honest. I'd been tortured and had watched — felt — so many people slaughtered in front of me that I guess this was mild comparatively. Even so, I didn't know how to process the life I'd never known he lived. If I felt anger, it was at myself for being so self-centered that I'd never noticed the fact he'd been hurt at all. How could I have been upset at all at him though? I knew there was no way he had asked to have been hit.

He shifted, the light now illuminating another pink bruise that had yet to fully heal. "Like, that I'm supposed to do shit or something."

I didn't know. Of course, I didn't want him hurt, but I'd be no different from Dani if I ran off telling people. I'd had so many premonitions — so many of those "fake attacks." Sia had once said she had limits to blocking my premonitions, and that completely checked out knowing how many of them came from Jordan. She'd known what emotions to block from me, the secret to hide. Rota had certainly known... I was the only one who hadn't.

"I don't know. Honestly, I feel awful I never noticed. Even though I've had those premonitions for years, I didn't put anything together." He didn't ask what premonitions, so it seemed he'd already figured that one out himself, his emotions further spiking with anger and helplessness. "But I know these couldn't kill you, not now. Even if it's directly to your symbol, blunt trauma can only hurt — not kill — us with the amount of mana we have." He still stayed silent, so I added, "I can't *not* know, but it's not my secret to tell. You could've gone to the police after my Act, or when I was kidnapped... but you didn't." An act — pun unintended — that likely had saved my life, considering what would happen if the group that hated mages found me.

He laughed, more amused than anxious so suddenly. "Guess so."

"What's so funny?" I'd been serious, so I wasn't sure what had him so entertained. It wasn't a bad thing considering, just unexpected.

Sliding his shirt back on, he turned around after he'd buttoned it. His eyes were soft, his mood gentle somehow despite everything. "It happened b'fore my Act so I'd kinda forgotten, but the second time I met Siani, she said something similar. Hearing you say it reminded me and's comforting, in a weird-ass way. But also, thanks... I mean it."

She *had* known then, just like I'd assumed, and had hidden it from me. My empathy would've picked up pain from Jordan a long time ago, so it was the only theory that made sense. "Guess after how Richard handled it, I just..."

Even *he* had known before me. Of all things, that shouldn't be my focus, but it still annoyed me. "I can't imagine going through the past couple years with..." I didn't know how to say

**191**

it. I remembered how strange his reaction had been — how he'd flinched — when we'd first tried sparring. Now it made so much sense, another sign I should've noticed. Even Sia had let up for those few moments, and that should've been a sign on its own. All this time, I'd failed him.

"It's the first time, I think..." From the faint light, I saw him glance over at me, his cheeks burning red. His eyes moved away from me just as quickly, refocusing on the broken window where moonlight shone in. "That I'm actually grateful I had Act."

Was I grateful? I wasn't sure. I guess it didn't really matter right then, all things considered. "Not being in pain is generally preferred to pain, so I can get that."

He snickered as he nodded. "Not wrong." His eyes moved back to me. "And thanks. Thanks for everything, Kyle."

# Chapter Thirty-One

## worth something

Jordan | December 22
Boyle Residence

One thing Richard'd been riding my ass over's punctuality. While he ain't actually done shit 'bout it besides bitch, I didn't wanna test the limits of that either, 'specially since the alternative's staying in this damn frigid-ass apartment.

Each time I packed this bag, I brought less and less shit; Richard'd said to just leave whatever I wanted in the room I used, and at first I'd just left the gym shit I only used there, but I'd been bringing a few more things each week, like a few of the birthday gifts Kyle'd gotten me over the years — felt safer in that room, even if it meant I only saw 'em a few days a week. If we got evicted again, didn't need to worry 'bout whatever's at Richard's, nothing getting lost or broken.

That said, it's still weird as hell even *having* new clothes instead of donation-store purchases I constantly patched up. I'd done my own laundry for years, so no one here'd noticed, or at least hadn't said shit if they had. I preferred it that way since it meant no questions I ain't sure how to answer. I put on the zip-up jacket I'd gotten a few weeks back, then slid my old hoodie over it. Once I'm outta West Side, I'd take it off, but it helped avoid attention and questions in the meantime.

Zipping my bag up, I heard footsteps — heavy but fast — entering my bedroom. Turning, I saw Thomas, a book from the local library he must've checked out in his right hand. "Where're you going? Been gone a lot lately."

Throwing the bag over my shoulder, I shrugged and kept my eyes away from him. "Work."

"With a bag?"

Yeah... Guess that didn't exactly check out. Dammit, this's why I tried to avoid questions.

"Yeah, shit to change into."

I walked out of the room b'fore he could ask another question and fuck me further 'cause if he asked why I needed a change of clothes, I ain't sure *what* I'd say. Testament to my shitty-ass luck, Jewel's at the kitchen counter sorting through mail.

"You need to cover dinner tonight," she said, eyes on me.

"Can't. Got, uh, work. Heading off now, actually."

She huffed, dismissing me with a wave. "Thomas, get in here!"

I ain't waiting around for *that* conversation, given that Thomas's cooking sucked ass: burned every damn thing, sometimes while *also* under-cooking it, even though I had no fuckin' idea *how* he did both at once. I closed the door, not bothering to lock it since Jewel and Thomas're home, and shoved my hands in my jean pockets. Yet again too damn cold out.

In part to limit freezing my ass off, I power walked to Richard's for my so-called *job*. I ended up keeping the extra hoodie on 'til I got within a block of Richard's 'cause it was colder out than I'd realized. Didn't exactly love taking it off even once I got within the extra block 'cause of the extra layers helping to keep me warm, but I'd been trying to be better 'bout looking more *professional*, as Richard'd called it. I didn't exactly care, but as many favors as he'd done for me, I didn't wanna embarrass and let him down by being *me*.

As many times past now, I pressed on the intercom; as usual for Saturday evenings, Jane's on gate guard. She buzzed me in, and I let out a sigh of relief once inside the warm house, making my way to Richard's loft. I opened the door, hearing some

**194**

obnoxious-ass screeching sound boom from the tv stereo set. However they sound-proofed walls, it's a hell'va masterpiece with how fuckin' loud Richard watched shit. I saw him with his tablet, sketching something on it.

"Yo," he said, not glancing up.

"'Sup?"

Tossing the tablet to the side of the couch, he stood. We always worked on magic shit in his room or the gym. He walked over to his room, so guess that's where we're starting tonight. I dropped my bag off in what he'd termed my room — as if I'm a permanent resident instead of a very awkward guest — then moved to his room and closed his bedroom door once I'm inside. He'd already begun pulling his spell book outta the locked cabinet he kept it stashed in.

It's bittersweet how fuckin' easy Riyatian came to me. It's still goddamn magic shit, but also, I ain't used to feeling *capable* in any-fuckin'-thing. For once, I didn't feel like a completely useless dumbass — the memories I'd tried to ignore since all this had started that came to me so easily.

"So, uh, can you write out the character sets?" I asked him.

He handed me a sheet of paper, having put his reading glasses on sometime since he'd come into the room, likely while I'd dropped my bag off. My eyes skimmed across the character sets.

"Ah, you messed up ka. Put ke, and actually, you..." I reached over to his desk for a pen but found none in my reach; he handed me one so I didn't need to look up. Without thinking, I marked through anything incorrect I saw.

"Damn things all look like nonsense."

The first few times I'd written Riyatian, it'd felt weird, stiff. Now it's far less so, as automatic as English.

"You forgot all the spell modifiers too. Dunno actual use case for those, but they are part of the character set so I wouldn't omit them." I handed the sheet back to him.

He sighed, flipping open his spell book to a page he'd bookmarked.

"That makes more sense for this spell. Of all the things to omit, why doesn't the damn thing have the character chart included?" It ain't the first time he'd been on this bitch-topic, and I suspected it wouldn't be the last either.

Working out's one of the most beneficial things I did here, but it'd be a lie to say I *liked* benching shit and doing pull ups and crunches and squats and whatever hell routine Richard signed me up for on Sunday mornings. This though — the translation work, sometimes literally attempting to translate from Richard's spell book, which I couldn't quite pull off yet but'd been slowly decrypting — this I actually liked, somehow. It's a full opposite from working at the grocery store, where it'd felt dead-end and boring as hell. For once, I felt like I'm *worth something*. And that feeling's prob'bly the thing I couldn't ever thank Richard enough for — a place to hide away, not be the weird kid that's only a matter of time b'fore ending up in prison or passed out drunk somewhere.

# Chapter Thirty-Two

## charmed

While Kylie had stopped by this so-called "training house" when on the way to spend the night at my apartment more than once and she'd said I was welcome to stop by when she and Jordan "trained," I'd never taken her up on said offer before. But I didn't work until closing today and there wasn't much homework or housework needing to be done, so I figured why not see what this so-called "training" was. Standing outside now, I wasn't sure why I hesitated knocking on the door. What did I expect to find inside?

Maybe that was the problem: I didn't know what to prepare for.

As I reached for the doorknob, the door swung open from the other side; I saw Kylie there, a slight smile as she looked at me. She wore an outfit that I'd never seen nor looked like anything else she'd worn before — a blue and white jacket vest and shorts, combat boots, arm warmers, and fingerless gloves. Her hair was somehow longer and tied back. Almost as if coordinating outfits, I saw Jordan awkwardly hold a gloved hand up in a half wave. He was in a red and black outfit styled similarly to Kylie's, his hair tied back despite never before being long enough.

"Impressed you found it all by yourself." It wasn't like this town was that big or confusing to navigate — maybe too many of the same trees made landmarks difficult, but otherwise, it was fairly straightforward.

"Mm." I didn't know what she expected me to say. I guess that'd been a good enough answer for her since she went back inside the house and left me to follow. I did, shutting the door behind me since it'd been closed before.

Kylie faced toward the entrance as I glanced around the house, her lips pursed together. "The counter back there should be pretty safe." Given she stared directly at me, she must have meant the comment for me. But why was she suddenly concerned about my safety? What were they even doing here that safety was a concern?

Unfortunately, it was too late for a sudden change of plans, especially with Kylie's *empathy* — which for the record was still the most invasive thing I'd ever dealt with, even if she claimed Jordan's emotions usually overshadowed mine. I walked to where she'd indicated, pushing on the counter to test its sturdiness. It was remarkably stable considering how ruined everything else was here, so I sat on it as if it was a bench.

"So, uh..." Jordan rubbed the back of his neck as he glanced away. "What now?"

Kylie took a deep breath, having turned around so that her back was to me; Jordan awkwardly glanced between me and Kylie. I'd assumed Kylie had checked with him about me visiting but I suddenly had the suspicion she actually hadn't. I wouldn't have come if I'd known it made him self-conscious, but thinking back, I'd never really heard him participate in spell discussion or even use magic as I'd seen Kylie do here and there. The only reason I knew he was a mage was because of that first time he'd given her energy or mana or whatever it was called, and that both of them had confirmed it multiple times. I guess his memory thing wasn't normal either, but that wasn't the same as the spells Kylie cast or how she knew my every emotion. Admittedly, her empathy had been handy a few times when she'd correctly deduced pop quizzes, but even that wasn't consistent. She had to figure out the teacher's emotions separate from the class and then decipher what those emotions meant, all within a few minutes... At least that was the condensed summary of the explanation she'd given.

"Can I practice telekinetics?"

He shrugged. "Sure. I can take a break for a bit."

Kylie shook her head, the braided ponytail swaying back and forth. Kylie's hair was normally around her ribcage, but her hair was longer than that braided right then, let alone however long it would be if not braided. How *had* her appearance shifted so much? I made a mental note to ask later.

"Actually, I kind of need you this time. I'd like to see if I could lift a human that's not myself as a weight check in alt form. I don't think I can do it without alt form, but I'm pretty sure I have the technique itself down."

"Uh." It wasn't hard to see he absolutely didn't want to be involved with this idea of hers. With her empathy, I wasn't sure how Kylie missed the memo. Maybe she just ignored it. "S-sure, I guess."

She nodded, taking a deep breath. "Here goes."

I watched as she turned her left hand so that her palm was facing up, placing her thumb in between her index and middle finger. I couldn't see her face, but her head was directed toward Jordan. Her left hand maintained that same position as she slowly lifted it upward. I watched as Jordan followed, eyes moving to the concrete as he mumbled, "Shit." He had to be two feet off the ground, maybe more.

"Huh?" Kylie's head jerked up; Jordan crashed to the concrete, a string of curses following as he landed wrong on his left foot. "Oh, um, sorry. I broke concentration, and that... didn't go well."

That was certainly a generous way of explaining what had just happened. Jordan bit on his lip as he sat down, removing the boot and liftin his pants so that his ankle was exposed, inflamed and red. His tense posture and the thin line he pressed his lips into indicated he had more complaints and likely curses he wanted to say but bit back on, probably because of Kylie.

From what I'd just seen, she deserved any complaints he had for this one.

"Yeah." The fingers of his right hand, now gloveless, rested over his ankle. "Can see that."

I saw light radiate from his hand — that same deep crimson and dark azure mixture as the day he'd kissed her cheek and nearly passed out — the redness on his ankle gone once the colors around his hand faded. Afterward, he slid the boot back on, glove following right after.

Kylie held her hand out to him. "Got some practice in with the healing spell too, at least?" That might've been the most sheepish I'd ever heard her, her voice squeaking toward the end.

He just raised his eyebrow at her while remaining sitting on the concrete; I didn't blame him at all.

"So you did what you wanted there?" he asked.

"I, um..." She stepped back as he took her hand, her pulling him back to his feet. "Want to try it again, actually."

To Jordan's credit, I was surprised he didn't flat out deny her. Instead, he sighed and nodded.

"Just like... not that high again. At least if you drop me, don't make it breaking shit height." Even with their magic healing or whatever, his ankle had looked more sprained than outright broken from what I'd seen. Either way, him asking to not be dropped again was a rather reasonable request regardless of what his actual injury had been.

She nodded to him before repeating the same set of actions. Just as before, he rose from the concrete, though only about half the height as before. He was completely silent this time and seemed to very intentionally not look down. I didn't much blame him there. Kylie lowered her hand and he slowly lowered back to the broken concrete that served as a floor here. He released a sigh, likely from relief.

Since Jordan seemed safe now, I asked, "How'd you even do that?"

Kylie turned around to face me. "It's a bit complicated." I already regretted asking. "It's something anyone — to a degree — with air alignment can do, at least if I understand right. But the strength of it — telekinetics, how it's referred in magic theory — is dependent both on magipoten and user skill level.

So with my alt form, I'm able to use more mana than what I would normally have access to, making it more of a skill limit. It really helps with proficiency testing, though with some... admitted downsides, especially if I lose focus."

Just as I'd feared and expected, I barely understood a word she'd said and struggled not to zone out halfway through. "I see."

"So like—" I guess the explanation wasn't done. Lovely.

She paused, blinking as her lips pushed together.

Jordan noticed her reaction as well, moving closer to her with a concerned expression.

"Kyle?"

"Maybe I should leave..." she said, her voice far weaker than the hyper rambling from just a second prior. What had changed?

The entrance door opened, and I saw a rather attractive guy with long blonde hair and blue eyes, dressed in a neat suit. Jordan mumbled, "Shit," nowhere near as quietly as he probably thought before pulling Kylie over to the side and whispering something to her I couldn't make out.

The blonde guy slid off his coat, tossing it beside me and crossing his arms over his chest. He peered at me, raising an eyebrow. "Who're you?"

I couldn't decide if his arrogance was hot or obnoxious. "Maya. Yourself?"

"Why are you even here?"

To his credit, I'd wondered that myself the whole time so far, but I hadn't left yet either. Admittedly, I'd enjoyed just watching Kylie and Jordan, their back-and-forth antics entertaining and the more open use of magic enthralling. "Kylie invited me."

He rolled his eyes. "Of course she did."

What did *that* mean?

Jordan jogged over to us. Kylie still faced away, only her back showing as she stood still. I wasn't sure what had her attention so much since she just faced a wall, but she hadn't acknowledged whoever this new guy was.

"Why're you here? You're like three hours early."

"Got bored."

Jordan looked less than amused as he moved even closer, only a few feet between him and me now.

"Yeah, but..." He glanced from this guy to me. "Oh, uh, sorry, Maya. This's Richard. He's... I guess you'd say in a similar boat as me and Kyle. But we usually practice shit later in the day."

So he was Jordan's friend, not Kylie's. Jordan then gestured to me.

"This is Maya. We go to school together. She got caught up in shit, been helping us."

That was a rather generous description, given all I did was listen and I had no one else to talk to.

"Pleasure's all yours," Richard said.

Kylie's reaction made increasing sense with every word this Richard said. Attractive or not, he had an absolute winner's personality, apparently. "Charmed."

"I have at least another half hour with Kyle. You're gonna hafta wait, sorry." With that, Jordan rushed back to Kylie, touching her shoulder as he said more things I couldn't hear.

Richard said nothing in response, instead leaning against the counter I sat on as he observed Jordan and Kylie. There was no reason for me to press conversation, so I didn't. Kylie turned enough that I briefly saw her face, now pale and red; was she crying? Jordan was the most visibly pissed I'd seen him, his posture even more tense than it'd been right after Kylie had dropped him earlier. Normally, he was surprisingly easygoing once past his shyness, and he hadn't really made enemies or friends at school, just went unnoticed by most people.

A sword appeared in Jordan's right hand from thin air. He nodded to Kylie, who shakily returned the gesture. Testing the sword in his grip, he swung once, then again in her direction. I saw, as the sword just about reached her, a long staff blocking his sword; Kylie held the staff, somehow the sword not cutting through. Jordan shifted more weight, Kylie pushing back. Given she was shorter and more petite than me, I was surprised she was able to deflect Jordan's strength, both just using a single hand.

"He's going easy," Richard grumbled. I was pretty sure I wasn't supposed to hear it, so I didn't comment. Maybe Jordan *was* "going easy," but he still had a bead of sweat along his forehead that caused his bangs to stick to his face.

"Swap," Kylie said, her voice still so weak compared to normal.

Jordan immediately backed off, nodding as the sword disappeared. He swallowed. "Ready... I think."

This time it was Kylie who charged, but she didn't establish actual physical contact as a water beam like I'd seen the day I'd found out about all this shot toward Jordan. His eyes clenched shut as a circle of fire around his calves moved up, encasing him in flames. The circle evaporated Kylie's beam where they intersected, but it increased in intensity and split into two beams that focused on different parts of Jordan's circle shield. A pillar of ice blocked the water from reaching Jordan's ankles despite the weather being way too hot out for ice.

"Dammit," he mumbled, his chest heaving as the water from Kylie ceased before he fell backward onto the concrete, water drenching him but otherwise leaving him unharmed.

I didn't expect Richard to shift as if he was uncomfortable. I thought he didn't care about Kylie one way or another, but maybe he did, after all. Kylie knelt down and offered her hand to Jordan, him once more taking it as she helped him stand back up.

"Charmed, huh?" Richard asked. I wasn't sure if he even meant for me to hear the comment and I wasn't going to pry. He wasn't my problem, and I didn't need any additional headaches in my life. After all, I had enough going on. Just watching this was enough — more than I should've ever known or wanted.

# Chapter Thirty-Three

## luxuries

Jordan | January 10
Opal Pines Streets

In a fun bit of irony, I'm almost always the last one out of school this year. At least my last period ain't a stressful class. — Spanish's basically all memory work, and, well, yeah. Foreign languages're actually kinda fun when you're not bullshitting each test 'cause you never studied vocab or charts and shit. Struggled with my accent and couldn't roll a damn r to save my fuckin' life, but listening's easy as hell and written'd not been a problem since it's still Latin-based characters. It'd been a weird as hell revelation, but I ain't gonna complain 'bout a rare perk to shit.

I navigated through the halls since I'd already swapped books at my locker, following the crowd in front of me to the school's front exit. Kyle and me're s'posed to go to the damn training house again today, and while I still ain't a fan, she'd been gaining confidence, which made the hell worth it. I'd been skimming through her spell book for the language sections — both to teach Richard and admittedly just to learn. She refused to acknowledge I sucked ass at the spell bullshit, but the language shit came a lot easier to me.

205

As I left the school building, I saw her sitting on a concrete ledge, her usual place while waiting for me. Maya ain't with her, but she'd mentioned having an early shift today, so prob'bly's off to work already. I hadn't been that different a few months back, and the only reason I wasn't still that way's 'cause of Richard. No one in my family'd figured shit out 'cause I'm gone so often, practicing shit with him and Kyle, and since money kept getting deposited into Father's account, nothing'd flagged as off I guessed. Elaine should've noticed since we'd worked in the same damn store, but she likely didn't give a damn as long as it didn't mean more work for her.

That bitch — Ashley — was cornering Kyle again. Kyle nodded as she lowered her eyes to the dead grass, an avoidance I knew too well. Ashley had her hand on her hip while glaring at Kyle and saying something I couldn't hear. I shifted from casually walking to a jog — bitch must've seen Kyle alone and gone after her. Dammit. I'd never been exactly intimidating, but she usually hauled ass if anyone's with Kyle, even me. Usually Maya and Kyle talked after class for a few minutes since both of the science labs're near each other, even when Maya had work after school, but Maya's schedule must've been too tight for even that today. As I approached them, Ashley turned away. I'm pretty sure her *accidental* bump against me ain't accidental at all.

Kyle's eyes're still downcast as she frowned while holding her absorption device. Honestly wanted to just hug her, tell her it ain't her fault yet again, but I'd already said it shitloads as it was. This's just another reminder why I busted my ass at that damn training house now 'cause I never wanted her to go through shit like that again.

"I-I'm fine." Was a bullshit of a lie, and she had to know it.

"Yeah. Prob'bly's best to get going so we have as much sunlight as possible."

Sun going down earlier'd made training more of a bitch, and I couldn't practice whatever she wanted while generating a flame to act as a lamp in the damn excuse of a house. Both've those damn things took all my concentration on their own, really, and the lamps worked fine at dusk — even when I felt like shit — but weren't enough to practice during the actual night.

She nodded, walking forward. The training house's clear across town from Matthews, so it's always a damn voyage. Wished I knew what to say to cheer her up, but I didn't. Didn't even know who to ask for advice on what to say. Best I had's my memory, observing damn Rotanu's interactions with both Siani and Kyle to decipher cues he'd recognized that I hadn't. It's where I'd learned the distraction tactic I'd just used, 'specially while getting her away from the damn situation.

But now, I didn't know what else to say or do. Instead, there's silence, goddamn painful and ear-shattering loud at once.

Her voice struggled to sound normal as she said, "I did what Mom wanted, put in applications all over the state."

Back b'fore her Act, she'd been kinda excited 'bout college 'cause it's a chance to not have her mom breathing down her neck and seeing every grade. "You don't wanna go?"

"I don't know. Sometimes, I wonder what the point is, if it just means..."

If she's a danger to everyone around her, would going somewhere more crowded be cruel? Ain't the first time she'd implied it.

"You should. Something you've always wanted." I wanted to sound more confident and supportive than I did, my own feelings getting in the damn way since I knew if she left Opal Pines, I wouldn't see her anymore. This's where I was born and likely where I'd die too, same as Father and his parents and fuck knew how many generations back. I couldn't just leave my family, no matter how much they pissed me off.

Her chuckle's strained, but guess it'd been impressive to get one at all outta her right then. "What would I even major in?"

She'd wanted to be a lawyer at one point. A doctor another. A pet walker for like two weeks, but pretty sure Ms. Rae shot that one down. "Don't have to decide day one, d'you?"

"I've been putting down psychology because I guess it'd help with my empathy, but the idea of being stuck with tons of people and their emotions all day doesn't really sound... thrilling either."

I rubbed my neck. "Ah, yeah." Was all made worse by my emotions being damn sirens to her, and every time she brought it up, I felt embarrassed as fuck all over again. "Opposite'd be like... the computer class you're in?"

She paused her stride; had I fucked up suggesting that?

"It's weird — kind of like spell theory, at least in the syntax structure rigidness. It's been kind of a fun puzzle, in that way." Her expression softened. "If I'm honest, that's more of what I'd really like to spend my life doing now. Just... figuring out things before deciding anything. But that won't work for Mom."

"Figuring things out." I knew she meant 'bout magic and spells and all that shit, and I hated I related to her on it. I wanted to better understand these damn snapshots of memories that poked up, like deju vu except *real*. Shit that'd happened to Takite, to John or Dmitri. Flashes of memories or feelings or knowledge that I couldn't connect to anything else. Hypermnesia meant once I had the snapshots or knowledge pop up, recall worked normally, but they're still different from any of my actual memories post-Act.

Maybe... I guess this's the first time I had the luxury to think of something other than just surviving, to reflect on the past and the future. Now that I'd had the chance, I wanted to know more 'bout where I came from. Not just the me now, but of those past incarnations — of Riyati, how shit went down and why, and I dunno. I think I wanted to understand.

"At least there'd be less people?" She'd always been the more extroverted one between us — still was, really — which made her avoiding crowds more than me as ironic as ever.

"Mm." She chuckled. "That'd be nice. Maybe one day I'll even have a chance to work on blocking out empathic reads."

Wait, that's possible? I definitely couldn't block out my memory, no shot in hell there.

"You can block it?" Also, why the fuckin' hell didn't she block emotions all the time?

"Don't get too excited." Another laugh at my expense. At least she'd cheered up. "But eventually, I think so. Sia could block both of our empathic reads, so once I have time, I want to try to learn too. Just... there's so much else to do first that I haven't been able to prioritize it." She had to learn how to survive b'fore *luxuries,* like not being a human emotion pincushion, were on the table. "I tolerate everything fairly well now, unless I'm really worn down. Even by Fridays, I'm not—"

Her steps paused, a wince coming from her. I stopped walking, immediately turning in her direction. Her eyes squeezed shut as her hand went to her chest. She leaned forward, panting.

"Kyle?"

She shook her head.

"It's just..." It's one of the damn sensory precognition attacks. We're out in fuckin' middle of West Side too, not exactly a place to take a random-ass breather. Was it from me again? Father beating my ass for one reason or another, and she took the hits too 'cause she picked up premonitions from the pain I'd feel? There ain't a damn thing I could do 'bout it, which just pissed me off even more. She winced.

"Don't... not right now."

If I got angry, the emotions passed onto her, causing additional stress for her. How could I *choose* what I felt? I ain't that disciplined. But I had to try, so I took a deep breath, focusing on our surroundings to help distract me.

"We're almost there," I said.

Even more than usual, I kept my eyes open, scanning each person near us as the crowds thinned, her stumbling step by step behind me. She winced again, each strained breath making me want to reach out and hug her, try to heal an injury that didn't exist. I helped her down some of the unsteady footing she's normally fine with, momentarily leaving her as I opened the door to the training house b'fore going back and guiding her the rest of the way. I closed the training house door after we'd both entered, her stumbling to the back sheetrock-exposed wall and sliding down to the concrete. I noticed a bead of sweat across her forehead as her eyes clenched shut.

"I might need a minute."

No fuckin' shit. She needed to be in goddamn bed, but we'd been so close by the time the damn thing'd started that walking all the way back to her house'd be even worse than just waiting it out here.

"Is it...? Or can you not tell?" I didn't know how to ask if it's my fault she had a premonition, if it's Father beating my ass and her experiencing it b'fore I did yet again.

Her eyes're unfocused as she shook her head.

"I don't think so. It's..." She looked so weak, panting and sweating from the pain, and I couldn't do a damn thing to help. "A stab. Not the first time with this premonition." The fuck did she mean "not the first time"? Why the hell'd she not mentioned that she'd been getting them? "They started in the evening last night, tend to come in groups of two, so I guess my mana's increased enough to detect stuff earlier than at the beginning of the year."

"Why didn't you say anything? No way in goddamn hell you should've come out today — could've told me at lunch, or like..." She shouldn't've come to school in the first place, really.

Her lips pressed together as she shook her head, voice weak yet so goddamn fuckin' stubborn. "I *need* the practice. This is for someone I know, likely know *well* — maybe even myself. I *need* to be better."

Partially 'cause she *knew* she'd been having these damn things and still tried to train today, partially 'cause I'm pissed her premonitions *could* fuck her up like this at all, I snapped, "You *need* to be in a motherfuckin' bed 'cause your ass's 'bout to pass out."

She wouldn't look at me anymore and a moment of silence passed before she said, "I couldn't say anything. I didn't want to worry Maya, not after..." Last time those bitches'd attacked, they'd honed in on Maya. If anything, Maya had a hell'va reason to know 'cause of that.

Yet again I hated she's so fuckin' goddamn stubborn as fuckin' hell, but it ain't like that's particularly *new*. I sighed — arguing with her on telling Maya'd get us nowhere 'cause I doubted she'd relent and admit it'd been a dumbass decision.

"Next time, 'specially if you *know* us coming out here's a dumbass idea, text me, or write something, or just... some sign 'cause this ain't where you need to be. Your ass needs to be in bed if you want a chance to even be *awake* during the damn thing."

She didn't agree, only squeezed her eyes shut further and winced. This was yet another time I'm at the mercy of a past I didn't know and a future I didn't wanna experience.

# Chapter Thirty-Four

## reactions

Nothing had happened yet. I hated knowing *something* would happen to me or someone I cared about but not *when*. I'd had the premonition enough times now to know there was little to no shot it came from Jordan's home life; this premonition definitely involved stabbing — multiple times. The only reason that made sense outside of a sparring session — which had never prompted a premonition before — was something from Zimihe, Sase, and whoever led them.

"Are you sure we shouldn't just go to your house? Actual internet would be helpful for this one," Maya asked.

I couldn't involve Mom. At least if something happened to Maya — my prime suspect of premonition recipient — I could heal her, use magic openly in front of her. I couldn't get Mom involved, and it would be near impossible to navigate around her if we were attacked.

"Yeah. I can just use my phone — it's easier since I'll already be on that side of town anyways."

She brushed hair off her shoulder. "Oh, you and Jordan again?"

"Mm. It's easier to work through spells with him around."

I didn't like the mischievous glint in her eye as she chuckled. "You two are together more than most couples are."

Oh *great*. She was on that bandwagon now too. I was suddenly glad I'd never mentioned *that* about Sia and Rota. "It's not like that — we've just known each other a long time, and it's easiest because, well..."

She'd never smiled when we'd first met. Back then, getting her even mildly amused had been difficult. "So you say. But you never practice with what's-his-name. Richard."

Unfortunately, Maya's social cue and nuance reading needed some serious work sometimes, and this was definitely one of them.

"Yeah. He's Jordan's friend." Truthfully, I hated Jordan even still talked with Richard, but they met up weekly, he'd said. And Richard hadn't done any of the things he had the previous year — he barely acknowledged me at all if he came while Jordan and me practiced. He just watched us, and I couldn't distinguish between Jordan's emotions and what might've been Richard's to give me an idea why he did so. Jordan said Saturday midday and evenings, they practiced with each other. I knew that meant Jordan intentionally separated us, but it wasn't really enough for me. I couldn't say that though, not when Jordan had literally changed schools to support *me*, to train with me so often despite his life not being in danger — or at least it wouldn't be if he didn't use magic.

"Yeah, sure." She still had that teasing tone, and I guess that was for the best. She hadn't noticed anything was up, so she didn't have the worry me and Jordan had about the premonitions I'd been having.

Speaking of, I saw Jordan rushing out toward us.

"'Sup?" he said as he nodded to us.

"Ready for sparring?" I asked.

He sighed. "I hear you. Don't have to sound so damn giddy 'bout it though." It wasn't that I necessarily loved sparring, but I knew it was the best shot we had to improve. Instead of feeling helpless, I felt empowered, emboldened to believe I'd be able to *do something* if they attacked again.

Maya shifted her weight, backpack adjusting to her left as she did so. "I'd stop by, but I need to prep for this weekend and clean up things since I didn't have a chance earlier in the week. You said you'd be over around seven?"

Nodding, I jumped down from the overhang I'd been sitting on. "Around there, yeah. Jordan's *insists* he doesn't like evening training."

"Look. It gets damn dark and I don't wanna be dealing with this shit when I'd rather be in bed, all right?" He'd always been this way, most awake as classes started, half asleep as the sun set. So often growing up, he'd teased me at how much I hated mornings, but he was just as bad once the sun began to set. And for the record, I *still* hated mornings and wanted classes to start at like ten or noon, not eight fifteen.

With a slight pull of her lips, Maya waved as she said, "Well then, hope you both enjoy your date." She walked away before I could snap back how we were *far* from going on a *date*.

Scoffing, I rolled my eyes. "Not her too." It really didn't help that Jordan's cheeks were red, my heart racing from the empathic reads from him. He must not be any more amused by the accusation than I was. Maya had found a topic she enjoyed jabbing at, and she stubbornly ignored every explanation I gave about her misunderstanding things between me and Jordan.

His eyes shifted to me, a steady concern in them despite the redness still in his cheeks.

"Are you all right?" He asked me that entirely too much now.

"I mean, outside of the barrier, I guess so. I had another premonition before bed last night, but nothing today so far at least." Part of me felt guilty I wanted the stabbing to have been something that happened at his house, with his family, last night. He didn't deserve that pain, all those premonitions I now recognized as punches thrown at him that I'd never noticed. But... I knew he wouldn't die from the things that went on with his family unless his symbol was pierced. Both injuries of this premonition had been in the chest and collarbone areas, far away from his symbol on his hip.

His lips pushed into a frown. "Should you even be practicing today? What if you get an attack while we're heading that way again?"

He was right that I didn't need to be practicing, but not because of the possibility of another attack.

"There's no way I could pick up more than a few days out from that initial premonition. It *has* to be soon." But I didn't know if staying away or being nearby was the best way to protect anyone else involved. I didn't know how to plan around variables I didn't understand. "Maybe light training, but I think nothing serious today. I'd just like to be on that side but not right beside her, just in case." I wanted to hedge, but I wasn't sure how to do so.

"Gotcha. We should start heading over then." Jordan started walking, myself easily catching up and then keeping pace beside him. "Just don't push yourself too much. It's gotta be shitty on you to have so many that close together."

I hated that was objectively and unfortunately not wrong. "Mm." I *had* to push myself. Otherwise the same events that'd nearly killed us earlier in the year might succeed the next time. Like Sia, I couldn't hesitate, couldn't falter. I needed to be *ahead* of things and couldn't even figure out who was directing Sase and Zimihe, couldn't figure out why they were suddenly so brazen or why they had access to that anti-magic barrier that didn't affect them but continuously ate at Jordan and me all week. I felt like such a failure. I had no idea where they hid when not attacking us, no idea how I'd even find something like that out. Outside of my sessions with Jordan, nothing had changed from the beginning of the year, no matter how much effort I put in.

"At least I figured out how to do a few basic modifiers on spells, like the water beam one. If I adjust the potency down by a .45 margin, I should get away with a triple chain cast in alt form, which is a net gain, assuming all three go through."

He sounded exasperated and yet amused as he asked, "Did you even sleep last night?"

That was beside the point. "A few hours. Better to study more theory instead of just staring at my ceiling all night while waiting for the adrenaline from the premonition to wear off."

He grumbled but nodded. "Yet you sound entirely too fuckin' enthusiastic."

Magic theory was fascinating, the patterns and structures, the logic that actually stayed consistent and *made sense*. Maybe one day he'd understand.

"I mean, I've been kind of working on empathy too — mostly with focusing in on who's feeling what. I noticed if I can hone in on that, I can quiet the reads a bit."

That got his attention and he glanced over. "So you can block out other peoples' emotions?"

I snickered at his rapid change in tone, that hope of his emotions not blaring into my head. "Not for a while yet." I wished I could since I had a mild headache from fatigue, and everyone else's emotions — especially his — didn't help with that. "But it's a step, I think. Of those, you're probably going to be the last as well, since... yeah." Since Kisate had modified me. I didn't know if Takite had done the same to Jordan. Originally, I'd thought Takite hadn't, but I wasn't as sure about it now.

"Oh, uh, 'bout that —"

Did he know something? Last time we'd talked about it, he'd completely dazed out. I felt my phone buzz, so I pulled it from my pocket. It was Maya, which was strange. She never called, rather stingy with her pre-paid cell minutes; even texts were *to the point*, as I'd been informed more than once, and I thought those were basically unlimited on most plans now.

"Hey," I said.

"Better be quick." That wasn't Maya.

The line cut, my brain trying to process the voice and—

My eyes widened. "We need to get to her apartment. Now." They weren't even waiting for me anymore, were fine attacking Maya without me present. It'd be my fault if something happened to her. I'd tried to stay away, just not tell her so she didn't have to worry, but—

Jordan put his hand on my shoulder, his touch yanking me from my thoughts. He nodded, and I fought the urge to run as fast as I could. I didn't know the correct choice, the correct balance. If I exhausted myself before we got there, would I be too fatigued to save her? Going at a steady pace was just as terrifying, the possibility of arriving too late so tangible as I thought about Zimihe hurting Maya as she had my gym classmates.

I increased my pace to a light jog, Jordan trailing behind me. Even though we trained together, I was objectively faster from my air alignment and that gap would only continue to widen over time as my magipoten increased. Each alignment had certain common strengths and weaknesses trait-wise; they weren't set in stone, but they happened enough to be established trends.

Water alignment, in comparison, typically excelled at healing magic, and I likely was about to rely on that once more.

The most enclosed area between us and Maya's apartment was the corridor right outside of said apartment, which made it the best chance to get into alt form without others seeing. As I stepped into the poorly lit outdoor hallway, Maya's apartment door on my left, I set my backpack down. I couldn't afford the mana loss from shortcasting, so I used the full alt form spell.

"Riyati, obey your mistress's command, activate withdrawal."

There was a paperclip in the heel of my alt form's boot. It didn't get in the way of combat or maintaining traction, and I hadn't noticed it the first many times I'd practiced in alt form. Its placement was strategic though, another lesson from Sia I hadn't understood the importance of back then but did now. I threw my backpack over my shoulder. On the off-chance we made it out of this, I needed my backpack not stolen, which would certainly happen if I left it out here. Jordan had already swapped to alt form too. He had a confused expression as he glanced at the paperclip but said nothing. I made out Zimihe's aura, and I assumed she saw mine and Jordan's as well. I wasn't sure how far she or Sase could track, but I was able to get around a mile in alt form, so I had to assume they could read out that far as well.

Aura reading gave me two pieces of good news for this otherwise catastrophic situation: only Zimihe was there — no Sase or whoever their leader was — and Maya's aura was faint but present so she should still be alive.

Focusing, I slid the paperclip into the lock, manipulating the surrounding air with basic telekinetic manipulation. The tumbler turned on the first try, those hours I'd spent frustrated at my bathroom lock suddenly more valuable. I opened the door quickly, setting my backpack right at the entrance. Before I could glance around, I smelled iron. I used the auras to orient myself toward the kitchen, where I saw Maya on the counter, her shoulder caked in blood. She was unconscious, though I couldn't tell if she'd blacked out or if Zimihe had put her to sleep somehow. As I'd deduced from her aura, she had strained but present breaths — she was still alive, if only barely.

Jordan came in behind me, closing the door and setting his own backpack down.

I heard clapping, and I turned my head to see Zimihe by the bathroom entrance.

"Oh, you managed to get the door open. Very impressive."

Her voice sent a combination of terror and rage through my entire body, only increasing as I realized the smug confidence in this area came from her. She knew we had no shot. This was all some game to her: no matter how much training I did, how much time Jordan and I put in, we couldn't make up years in hours, couldn't compensate for the decades more experience they must have. I wasn't Sia; he wasn't Rota.

But Maya couldn't die because of me — *wouldn't* die because of me. It was fine if I died, but no one else should suffer.

"I'll keep her distracted," I whispered to Jordan. "You get to Maya, stabilize her."

While he initially looked like he wanted to argue, he nodded after seeing Maya. I would buy him time. I could do that, at least.

I'd give them the best chance to make it out that I could.

"What an inventive strategy," Zimihe said, implying she thought I hadn't wanted her to overhear.

I didn't need the element of surprise when all I cared about was stalling long enough for Jordan to stabilize Maya.

"Isare, heed your mistress's call, summon forth!" The staff in my hands, I swung toward Zimihe. Maya's apartment was only around 400 square feet and had no bedrooms. Isare was taller than me, probably closer to five and a half feet, and I usually gripped at the first third or half, depending on the swing and technique. The ceiling itself couldn't be higher than seven feet. The small environment meant Zimihe had few places to back-peddle to, her lance manifesting mid-swing but unable to retaliate.

"Look at you, thinking you know what you're doing with your little toy," she said.

I kept pressure and ignored her words: just buy Jordan time, that was all I needed to do.

"But you know..." She locked my grip with Isare, closing the distance. I saw but couldn't react fast enough as she kicked my jaw. I felt it pop and didn't want to admit how much it pulsed. "I got clearance to finally kill you today. Boss lady doesn't care anymore, lucky me. Sucks though that Sase wasn't allowed to join us today for even more *fun*. She sends her regards to your corpse."

I tasted blood, but I refused to acknowledge the pain as I threw a punch at her. "And who's your ringleader anyways?" Not that it was particularly important, given the high likelihood we weren't making it out of this fight, but I had to push regardless. Maybe it'd distract her or make her careless or something. Maybe I'd finally get some type of lead about what had caused such a change from them compared to when Nimaka had been in charge.

She sneered, dodging to the right of my punch, where I struggled to maintain my footing.

"Wouldn't you like to know?"

I hated she knew I couldn't figure things out, was mocking me about it. Zimihe yanked on my braid, knocking me off balance as I struggled to regain my footing. She didn't follow up, releasing my hair and withdrawing from my arm's reach, a smirk on her lips.

Fear sank into me, sweat on my neck as I struggled keeping my hands steady. Zimihe was one step ahead of every move I made, toying with me. This was a game, and I was her hunt. I knew that — knew I was just a decoy for Jordan to help Maya, but...

What did it matter when Zimihe could kill us whenever she wanted? My fear and anger were nothing but laughable amusement to her and Sase, no matter how much I practiced.

She didn't even need magic, her spear and punches enough to bruise and batter me.

Something cut through the fear I felt, sudden relief I didn't understand; it had to be Jordan's emotions. He'd done it — he'd saved Maya. Between us both, could we do *something* to Zimihe? Did we actually stand a chance?

I directed my attention back to Zimihe as she resummoned her lance. I blocked another charge with Isare as she struck toward my left arm. She still had a sneer, no weariness at all. At the last second, she shifted her lance's trajectory, pushing it backwards instead of toward me. Despite the lance being further away from me than before, I gasped. It felt like I'd been stabbed through my chest, almost through my heart.

Yet, I hadn't been stabbed at all: Jordan had, his back toward Zimihe while he still faced Maya. He hadn't even summoned Nateka yet.

He shrieked, and I didn't know why neighbors weren't checking on us or why no one had called the police when Maya likely had screamed out much the same. Was no one home in the entire complex? But how?

Why had I been distracted with her actions, her comments? I hadn't reacted to anything fast enough, constantly in fear from how much control she had over the fight — I didn't understand the point of just *toying* with me as she had. Now, it was so obvious: she didn't want to just kill Maya; she wanted Jordan dead too. Why *settle* for me when she could kill all three of us at her leisure? I felt his consciousness fading, his body struggling to mend with how close the attack was. Just an inch to the right, and she would've pierced through his heart.

Maya had been saved, but now Jordan was dying instead. His strained breaths echoed through my chest, each choked breath vibrating through my lungs. He fell backward, his head colliding with the laminate flooring with a loud bang, throbbing and aching as his consciousness further faded.

It felt like someone else controlled my body, like Sia was back, but there wasn't another consciousness in me, not anymore.

"No more." My voice was low, a growl of fury I only partially recognized.

She had taken my classmates, had tried to take Maya... and she'd never touch Jordan again.

"What, did that hurt your little feelings?" She stabbed Jordan through the kidney, but he didn't move — barely winced, no longer lucid.

I'd thought I'd rely on water alignment's affinity toward healing magic, but now I itched to use the opposite — air alignment's affinity toward poisons. While I'd learned many spells invoking ailments and venoms, I never used them in practice — it wasn't worth the risk to Jordan if one of them ended up stronger than intended or if the systemic damage couldn't be easily mended. I had no such hesitations as my eyes steadied on Zimihe, fingers pressing the release for Isare's blades. I prepared a specific poison for Zimihe, one that shut down organs after entering the bloodstream. Even if she ran, she wouldn't hurt him ever again. I'd assure it.

She stabbed through my collarbone, the lance pushing through from the front to out of my back. I barely felt the pain, instead focused on loading the poison. Yanking her spear from me, she stabbed through my left lung. Blood dripped drop by drop, a stream from just below my collarbone and upper shoulder, from both the front and back of my lower torso. Spots — black, fading in and out — consumed my vision, yet it didn't matter. Jordan would survive.

Zimihe charged me once more, and I drew all the mana I could grasp hold of.

"I'm used to a certain amount of pain." I stumbled forward — it wasn't enough. I needed more mana, a stronger potency of this poison. Nothing else mattered, everything else irrelevant. Blood dropped onto the laminate flooring, more spots clouding my vision. Zimihe prepared to stab me once more, but I couldn't even be bothered to tense or attempt to dodge. Instead, I shifted Isare to my right hand, focusing teleknetics anchored to my left hand as I threw my arm out to the side, this distant sting implying I'd used muscles she'd severed. Zimihe's left arm followed the direction of my hand; I felt each creak and crack of her sinews and bones as her arm completely dislocated from the rest of her, only attached by skin. She let out a scream, the burning pulsing through my own shoulder, melding with the stab wounds she'd inflicted on me.

This wasn't enough; she'd hurt Jordan and deserved more pain for such a transgression. I pulled even more mana, wings manifesting on my back as feathers brushed against both the ceiling and flooring.

"W-wings? There's no way." She tried to back away but couldn't since she was already pressed against the back wall. Her right hand struggled with attempts to pop her left shoulder into place.

I sliced into her skin with Isare, red coating us both, our blood mixing into one puddle on the floor — an ever-increasing red ocean of iron. "You will *not* touch him again."

She coughed, poison infecting through the cut I'd made.

"I-I get it. You win. I'll just—" As she moved to teleport — run away again, to hurt him again another day — I telekinetically levitated and then threw her spear through her chest, pinning her heart. She clawed at her neck with her good hand, air not filling her lungs.

A smile pulled at my lips. Her chest no longer moved, eyes open but lifeless.

Jordan was unconscious, same as Maya. The only emotion left was my own pain, blaring through my lungs as the consuming tranquility faded. I stumbled over to Jordan. He still bled from the wounds on his chest and through his upper shoulder. I pushed heal upon heal, sweat dripping from my forehead onto his face, his shoulder and forearm.

Finally, he stabilized, relief all I processed as my lips brushed against his cheek. Too many spots filled my vision so I closed my eyes, feeling clammy and cold at once. It didn't matter though, I needed to keep transferring mana so he'd recover.

Because now she'd never hurt him again.

My lips brushed against his cheek as my vision doubled — he'd heal faster with more mana. That was all that was left now — just transfer more mana to him, and he'd be okay.

And she'd never hurt him again.

# Chapter Thirty-Five

## wasted time

The hell's shaking me? Everything hurt like fuck, and a too fuckin' strong iron smell flooded my nose. I'm under something warm, comforting, firm but soft.

"Jordan! Wake up, damn it." That's Maya, pushing my arm, which's bare despite it being cold as fuck 'cause it's January. I went into alt to heal her so — wait, she's awake? How long'd I been out?

Grimacing, I attempted moving but struggled since whatever covered me's heavier than expected. It ain't Maya since she's to my side, didn't feel like skin at all, actually. But then...

"Fuck time's it?"

"Past eight."

I'd been out like four hours then. Yet again attempting to push whatever's on me off, I woke up enough to process feathers, clouded-blue and gray, covering me. I turned my head away from Maya to see Kyle in alt form, the feathers originating from her — she'd summoned her wings.

"Holy fuck."

"You see that?" Maya pointed away.

225

I'd only had the damn things out once, but they'd been sensitive as hell. Last time Kyle'd had 'em out, she'd felt even slight touches so I assumed it's the same for her now. Knowing it's her damn wings holding me down, I made sure to be a hell'va lot more careful as I guided the one over me upward and slid out from under it. She didn't stir behind me, so guess I succeeded in not putting her in a fuckton of pain. Able to finally examine her better, I saw her face's pale as a puddle of blood surrounded us both. Somehow, she's still breathing, still alive, thank fuckin' god.

"Yeah, I gotta heal her."

"No, *that*." Maya pointed once more, and I saw she hadn't been gesturing to Kyle at all now that I sat up.

I couldn't believe what I saw, what Maya gestured at, though: that goddamn bitch didn't get stalled... She was *dead*, impaled by her own spear. That must've been why Kyle had her wings out, and I still ain't actually sure how she'd pulled it off even *with* her wings.

"Goddamn hell..." I mumbled. Didn't know what else to say. Moving my eyes back to Kyle, I saw her wings dipped in the blood pool I'd been lying in. Now that I'm awake more, I registered I didn't know how much of that's s'posed to have been *in* Kyle and fuck, why hadn't she woken up with us talking and shit? I needed to turn her over, and that's gonna be a bitch of a task 'cause of her wings.

"Can you help me? I need to turn her."

Maya stepped closer, kneeling down. "But how? And what even are...?" Her eyes directed at Kyle's wings.

Kyle could give whatever fuckin' explanation she wanted later; that shit ain't something I'm attempting to explain.

"She had to use a shit ton of magic for 'em to trip — prob'bly only way she pulled off fuckin' that bitch up."

I picked Kyle up around her waist, scared to reach higher where her wings're manifested through her shoulder blades.

"Move her legs with me."

Maya hesitantly nodded, grabbing Kyle's ankles and helping me rotate her. As we laid her back down, I half wished we hadn't turned her 'cause it's hell'va worse than I'd feared, with

Kyle's stomach and collarbone coated in a sticky red that had yet to heal. Without her mana, she would've been long since dead; even with her mana, it just slowed shit down enough for a slow death. She needed external assistance — a hell'va lot of heals. I set her down, her wings lifeless — if not for her strained breaths, I would think we're too late.

"Can look away if you need." I sure wanted to as I unzipped the vest and then ripped the undershirt around her collarbone and stomach.

"It's fine." Woman had a damn stomach of steel — I wished she's the one healing this instead of me if she fine with the sight. There just so much fuckin' blood.

Normally something like a glove wouldn't've interfered that much with healing, but I needed the best potency I could swing and that required direct contact with the wounds. Swallowing as I removed the leather glove from my right hand, I then laid my palm on Kyle's stomach. Some of the blood's caked, squishy like a gel. I couldn't watch, tried to not think 'bout the sticky liquid coating my fingers being Kyle's literal organs and blood, to ignore the sight and smell that made me wanna puke. Squeezing my eyes shut, I focused the strongest healing spell I could manage. I dared to glance at her once it'd finished. Thank fuckin' god, there'd been a large improvement. She still needed more healing spells, but I could tolerate seeing her stomach now, which'd seen a marked improvement. I couldn't stop myself from panting by the third healing spell, light-headed from using so much mana so quickly.

"Are you okay? Don't pass out beside her."

Maybe it's worse than I realized if Maya'd noticed too.

"C-could..." I took a deep breath to recover, but I felt like I'd just run a goddamn marathon. "I get water?"

"Oh. Sure." She stood up, going to the kitchenette and getting a plastic cup with the downtown movie theater's logo, which she filled with water from the tap and brought over to me.

I took the cup with my still gloved hand, chugging the water. I felt the liquid slide down my throat into my chest. The water helped ground me, the light-headedness finally fading. I set the cup away from me so it wouldn't be covered by the mess. Was a hell'va clean up Maya's apartment needed.

"Thanks." Now for round two…

Reaching over Kyle, I laid my blood-caked right hand on her collarbone. I pushed another heal. At least this one ain't as bad as her stomach'd been. Still took two more heals, but the second'd been the lightest of the heals by far.

The color finally began returning to her cheeks, her shifting to her side as her wings enclosed her, as if they're natural to sleep with. She likely's out like fuck 'cause ain't no way that's true.

"What even are these things? They look like bird wings, but Kylie's never had them before — did they come from her?" Maya gestured toward Zimihe.

I remembered Siani's description and instruction regarding wings perfectly; remembered the half-assed commentary from Rotanu 'bout them, too. Even with those memories, I had no fuckin' idea how to describe them. Didn't blame Maya for asking, but for all that I'd tried to get used to this shit, seeing Kyle's wings made me realize magic still freaked the fuckin' shit outta me, and this's one of those things I just ain't comfortable talking 'bout out loud.

"Happens from a lotta magic usage."

"Like a side effect?"

Close enough, so I nodded. "Must've pulled a hell'va spell. Only seen her trigger them once b'fore accidentally." When she'd been kidnapped that June, the last and only time I'd had mine out.

Maya said nothing, not touching Kyle, but her eyes scanned around us. "I don't even know how I'm going to clean everything up."

Following her gaze, I didn't blame her getting overwhelmed at the fuckin' large-ass bloodbath that covered her apartment. She ain't got much stuff, which helped simplify shit — outside of a few blankets that needed hell'va washing and wiping shit down, ain't much else to do but mop. A fuckin' intense mopping, but at least she ain't got carpet. "You got cleaning shit, right?"

"I've got a mop, bucket, broom, and dust pan, but this will

take... more than the bleach I have on hand." That also ain't an incorrect observation. Her shit needed to get to the laundromat sooner than later too, get the blood out b'fore it seeped in more than it already had. I didn't feel comfortable leaving Kyle alone though, not for at least another half hour.

We needed one more person, and I unfortunately knew who'd be up and in town: Richard. He always came back Friday afternoons, constantly bitching 'bout how *inadequate* his dorm room was. As soon as his last Friday class finished, he hauled ass back here.

I stood, going over to the sink and taking my other glove off, washing my hands a hell'va lot to get all the damn blood off me. I then went over to my backpack, digging through the pockets for where I'd stashed the cell phone Richard'd given me. He'd put his contact in, but I never bothered since I remembered the number anyways. I typed said number in and hit send, hoping to hell he didn't have his damn tv on so loud he missed the call. Heard him pick up, finally one fuckin' thing going right.

"Hey, I, uh... I need a hell'va favor." I asked Richard to bring a few more bottles of cleaning shit and gave him directions. He bitched and grumbled, but damn, I owed him for saying he's on his way.

After I hung up, Maya's eyes moved from Kylie to me. "Is this all right? Kylie's less than ecstatic whenever he's around."

We didn't have much of a choice. I knew he'd start whatever the hell he'd been doing with women last year right back up if his absorption device hadn't given him hell over it with whatever'd happened there. And he still didn't like Kyle, I ain't that stupid. He'd backed off from outright bitching 'bout her as much, but I'd hardly call them friends and ain't sure that'd ever be possible.

"He's like her." Kyle's out cold, but steady breaths moved her chest as her left wing laid over her arm. It twitched as she shifted in her sleep. "And..." There ain't a point to deny it, even if I still wanted to. "Me, I guess."

"Mages?"

I nodded, not wanting to verbally agree despite how obvious it was. My phone beeped; I picked it up, seeing Richard's number. He'd gotten lost, not exactly *fluent* in the broken roads and dark streets of West Side. After figuring out where the hell he's at in his damn-ass luxury sports car in fuckin' *West Side*, I stayed on the phone to guide him to the damn unit this time, afterwards going to meet him on the street to carry shit in — knew better than to expect him to do manual labor. He followed me, predictably carrying not a damn thing.

"Now's when you call?" he snapped. "Why not when you knew something's fucking happening to begin with?"

Really, it's past my damn bedtime. I knew I had no right to be agitated with him, but I'm bitchy and exhausted regardless. "Happened too fast." Also, fuck's he s'posed to do? He's damn near useless compared to Kyle.

He rolled his eyes. "Bullshit."

Thankfully, we made it to Maya's door then, unlocked as she kept an eye on Kyle while starting to soak up the remaining blood from where Kyle and me'd been unconscious with all the towels and blankets she had. Maya said she'd head to the laundromat, but I knew this area and didn't feel right having her out this time of night, so I said I'd handle it. Richard lingered at the entrance; I had him keep watch on Kyle while Maya cleaned up and bleached shit.

They'd replaced a few of the washing machines since I'd lived here, so I went for those as I bought the on-site cleaning shit and took up all three washing machines the complex had. An hour later, I had all the bedding and towels cleaned and dried, so I rushed back with them. Maya'd gotten most of the apartment cleaned up while I'd been gone, and Richard'd... not helped, but at least it looked like he'd kinda kept an eye on Kyle and maybe even moved her outta the way for Maya to clean under her at one point. Or maybe Maya'd done that herself, which's actually more likely since I saw no blood on Richard.

The most out of the ordinary thing left's the dead woman impaled on Maya's wall. Compared to Kyle, she'd barely bled at all, so ain't even sure how she'd died. As I stared at her, Richard asked, "So what're you doing with that bitch?"

I blew air from my lips as I set the bedding materials where I'd found them. "Fuck if I know." Prob'bly's almost ten o'clock at night by now, and I just wanted to be in a goddamn bed. After changing into his alt form, Richard yanked the spear from Zimihe. It disintegrated once it no longer touched her. Likely'd something to do with mana and her being dead, but I didn't actually know why it happened.

"I have an idea," he said, and I hated that damn tone he had, too damn awake at this hour. "Set the thing on fire. Turn the bitch to ashes, problem solved."

He wanted me to do fuckin' *what*? And goddamn worse yet, I didn't have a better suggestion. "I can't do that — I'd fry anything else in contact too."

Richard's suddenly the most entertained he'd been all night, and I'm pretty sure that's gonna be a damn problem for me. He threw Zimihe over his shoulder, a smirk on his face.

"Follow me."

Oh fuckin' hell, what's this goddamn idiot wrapping me up in this motherfuckin' late at night?

There's a field toward the back of this complex, nearish to Maya's apartment. He kept that same damn smirk as if we ain't hauling around a fuckin' dead body in plain sight. At least it's dark as hell out since this place never replaced street lights, but *still*. A handful of yards into the field, he dropped Zimihe b'fore kneeling down in the grass. I watched as he grew a patch of grass higher, clearly satisfied with whatever the hell he's doing.

"If you roast her, I can regrow the grass. Ice around the area so it doesn't spread, and then after, cut the fire entirely. Problem solved."

I had so many fuckin' layers of regret at following him out here. I rubbed my eyes as I mumbled, "This's a hell of a dumbass idea." Unfortunately, he still ain't wrong 'bout my lack of better plans so fuckin' here we went. My hands shook. I didn't wanna use magic out in the open like this. Hell, what if someone saw us? Sure, no one's around and it's in the middle of the damn night, but...

Kyle'd kept us all alive somehow. Hell, Richard'd come out to somewhere he'd never been at this goddamn hour just 'cause I'd asked. I needed to at least handle this one thing. A spark from my right pointer finger emerged as I squeezed my eyes shut. I brought the fire to Zimihe's corpse, sweat dripping from my hairline as the fire expanded over her and into the grass. I increased the temperature, biting back every damn hesitation and doubt I had as I watched the fire burn her body yet leave mine alone.

"I wonder..." Richard said, somehow not at all concerned. The earth dropped under her, like a sudden sink hole, fire still burning. I heard an unexpected pant from him as the earth sunk even more, somehow in the outline of Zimihe's body while missing us. How the ever-loving fuck had his control gotten so precise? I couldn't even see her body now, wasn't sure if the flame I'd started still burned or had gone out. Then the dirt shuffled again, hole refilling and fresh grass popping back, more lush than the surrounding existing grass.

She's gone, like she'd never been here.

He stood, dusting his gloved hands as he walked back toward Maya's apartment. I didn't know how he's so *unbothered* by what we'd just done. I knew we didn't have a damn choice, but... it still felt wrong. I staggered behind him as we both went back to Maya's apartment. She'd somewhat tucked covers over Kyle, as best's she could've considering the wings and the dried blood still caked on Kyle.

Not in the mood to deal with getting bitched at for coming home so late, I decided to just go with Richard. At least my actual clothes and body're fine. Alt form's the one that's a goddamn mess that needed cleaning up. Another benefit of Richard's: no one bitching 'bout me taking a late or longer than normal shower.

I sat in the passenger seat. Didn't have a license 'cause I'd likely never get a car. Richard's smugness from earlier'd been replaced with uncharacteristically sharp breaks and turns.

"Did none of it bother you?" I asked. I ain't sure why, likely exhaustion, but the sight of burning a body, burying a body, replayed in my mind and horrified me each time it did.

His grip around the steering wheel tightened. "It's us or them. Had to be done."

He ain't wrong. At least... not if he got involved. Even more so than me, he could've avoided all this shit. I moved my eyes to outside the passenger window.

"You could prob'bly get away not having to deal with this shit, not hafta go through that type of fuckery." I guess I could too — *had* done so too last year. If Richard wanted nothing to do with magic shit, we'd still be friends.

For once, he didn't even have the radio blaring as it'd been turned off. The silence likely would've unnerved me any other time, but I'm so goddamn tired and my nerves'd been thoroughly frayed with everything else that'd happened today.

After he turned onto his street, he finally said, "I'd rather to be known as a 'Riyatian' than a 'Richelieu.' I don't want whatever 'future' David and Michelle have perfectly planned for me. At least whatever choice I make here's *mine*."

Choices... It's ironic: I felt like I had no choices, Kyle felt she had no choices, and somehow, *even Richard* felt like he had no choice in his life. Kyle had the intensity I'd seen so much from Siani now, drive beyond anything I'd ever understand. I *couldn't* leave her alone in all this shit and wanted to be a damn sight better of a man than I'd been last year — never leave her alone like that again after she'd always been there for me.

But she ain't the only one that'd been there for me as tonight'd more than proven. I ain't sure why it came to mind, but it did right then.

"When they were still here, Rotanu called Saite 'Sai.'" I'd thought the nickname'd been just as dumb as him calling Kylie "Kyle" back then. But what Richard'd just said... maybe "Sai" made more sense too, a reminder of the choices Richard made versus what he'd been told to do, to be.

"Really?" he asked, only sounding partially interested as he pulled into the private garage for his loft, letting us avoid both the main gate check and having to walk all the damn way to his loft.

"Mm. Thought it'd been just another dumbass thing he did but... what you just said brought it to mind — like choosing his Riyatian name over his birth one or some shit like that." Really, I'm too fuckin' tired to even be attempting this conversation and wished I hadn't started it.

Richard paused while shifting his car from drive to park. "Call me that from now on."

Another piece'd aligned, another aspect of the "future" that made so much sense now.

He moved the car to park and left me as he went in, myself stumbling out with my backpack not long after. No one's around as I walked to the room I used here, where I'd left some night clothes from another visit. It hadn't been for situations like this, but hell if I ain't thankful right then regardless. I closed the door with me inside the room, air releasing from my lips that I hadn't realized I'd held in.

Wished I could just collapse into bed and put this whole goddamn day to rest, but I couldn't yet — there's no Rotanu to make clean goddamn alt form. I had to do it, and better get that damn joy over with now so I ain't thinking 'bout it when trying to sleep.

Walking into the bathroom, I closed the door and turned the water on, noting the towel hung up to be used. I said the transformation phrase, my form replaced with alt form once more, bloodied yet with clean clothes. Still didn't get how the hell that worked but whatever. I quickly undressed myself, stepping under the scalding water. Half asleep, I'd forgotten to pull the hair tie out and had the joy of doing that mid shower. I put said hair tie on my left wrist. Alt form's longer hair drenched my shoulders and collarbones, freshly wet blood washing off me and going down the shower drain.

While scrubbing myself clean, I noticed scars I didn't actually have yet. I didn't know if they'd come from home or're magic released, just that I ain't there yet — just like how I ain't as muscular as alt form despite me working out every week now. Even then, this body felt like it's a mistake, someone else's — more scars and longer hair and in better shape; I still fuckin' hated it if I'm honest.

Finished scrubbing myself, I'm finally clean of all the blood that'd been in alt form's hair and caked onto the body. I would've lingered longer, but it's gotta be near midnight and I just wanted to be in fuckin' bed.

Stepping outta the shower, I saw the mirrors all fogged.

Almost couldn't tell I'm even in alt form from the vague outline that rapidly began defogging, leaving my eyes on my alt form's upper chest and face.

She'd summoned her wings.

If I had been awake in her place, *could* I've done that? Siani'd tried to teach me how to summon them, and I'd been a damn coward and run away.

Replaying her instructions in my mind as I redressed alt form's body, I noticed the shirt had exposed shoulder blades.

That's intentional, ain't it?

I pressed my lips together. Another time I wanted to hide and ignore, and goddammit I wished I had that luxury still. Wished I didn't remember her asking me to kill her, a mercy kill meant to save everyone around her. Even me.

My lip quivered.

I'm scared shitless — not that I couldn't, but that I *could*. Further proof of exactly how intertwined I was with all this shit that I didn't wanna acknowledge but had no choice but to now if I wanted her alive.

Swallowing, I focused mana, grabbed as much as I could.

Just as I'd expected — just as I'd feared — wings appeared on my back, attached at my shoulder blades as they'd been with Kyle earlier. I saw them in the mirror, the right one shifting closer to my arm as the left rested in a more neutral position.

Last time I'd seen them'd been the day we got rid of Asuza, and that'd only been a glimpse from a few feathers and the sensation of them attached and sending sensory information to my brain.

My heart raced as I panted — summoning the damn things'd gotten me winded. Yet I couldn't pull my eyes away from the mimicry of a human I'd become: giant dark red and deep blue wings naturally attached to my body, a body that still ain't truly *mine,* in clothes I'd never owned.

I'd proven I could summon them, mission success if it could be called that, and now I wanted the damn things gone. I replayed Siani's instructions like some prerecorded tutorial, wondering if it'd been intentional on her part and why she'd never really fought me with shit like she had Kyle. She'd always had this smile I'd never understood — honestly still didn't even now.

The wings faded from view and I released the alt form transformation. I quickly swapped into my night clothes b'fore folding my day clothes and placing them on the night stand to change back into tomorrow.

My mind wouldn't quit racing. I *had* to keep pressing forward. I'd wasted all the spare time we'd had and regretted it like fuck right then. I ain't okay or handling this shit well at all really, but I couldn't bother Richard — *Sai* — or Kyle when they had more than enough going on too.

Richard'd become *Sai* and Kylie'd become *Kyle*, yet I felt nothing at all like Rotanu.

# Chapter Thirty-Six

## middle of the night

Maya | January 12
Maya's Apartment

I awoke with something soft yet firm and warm pressing against my cheek. Sitting up, I heard shuffling as whatever I'd felt shifted to brushing against my fingers as well.

"Oh, sorry. Didn't mean to wake you up." Kylie sounded fine — *normal* — as if she was having a routine middle of the night bathroom visit instead of regaining consciousness after nearly bleeding to death on my apartment floor.

"Are you... Can I get you anything?"

"Mmn. I was just going to dismiss my wings, then revert back." I assumed "revert back" meant to her normal self instead of the form she often used in the training house, with longer hair and strange clothes.

Reaching over, I flicked the lamp I had on; it still didn't have a shade but worked well enough. "You're not injured anymore? Jordan said it took a lot of mana to even have them." I gestured to her wings. "I've never even seen you use them in practice."

She nodded, a tender smile on her lips as she kept her eyes from me. I knew she read my emotions right then; Jordan wasn't around to block me out, as she'd described it more than once. I still hated her feeling my emotions, but it was an invasion of privacy I accepted as part of having her around. As much as I hated to admit it, I'd come to enjoy her companionship.

"It's not really worth practicing with them, not right now at least. They're basically just mana exhaust, but only past certain thresholds and it involves linage and stuff too. A lot of mana's needed, more than I can really access outside of alt form."

Alt form. I guessed that was what these longer-haired and weird clothes versions of her and Jordan were called. "So it's like a stronger mana form?"

"Kind of. It's... complicated." Kylie never said something was complicated, especially not with magic. She wanted to avoid talking about them for some reason. "And I'm sorry that you were hurt, were attacked in your own home because of me. I wish I could promise it's the last time it'd happen. I really do," she said, her voice growing more vulnerable with each word.

I didn't know how to say that her dying scared me more than my own death. I liked studying with her and being her partner on projects, liked that she didn't ask questions about my past. She just smiled and talked about the present. This was the first time I'd ever felt accepted by someone and that frightened me. I was terrified she'd betray me somehow, but even more so, I didn't want to imagine the very real possibility she might not wake up after one of these attacks.

"I'm just... I'm glad that you're okay."

Her left wing twitched as she stood, both she and the wings attached to her stretching out. The right wing brushed against the wall of my apartment.

"Will need a shower, but I'll deal with that later and stop taking up half your apartment in the meantime."

I brought my fingertips against one of the outer feathers of her wings, inspecting the texture. It didn't feel like bird feathers, none I was familiar with at least.

"Are they functional?"

"What's functional?" She turned around to face me, blue-gray feathers slipping from my grasp.

Gesturing to her wings, I added, "Like, for flying. Or do they mimic some other animal's instead?"

"Oh." This was a rare moment her cheeks flushed while Jordan wasn't around. "Um, I've never tried actually. I guess they should be able to glide if not outright fly. It's something I've never really had the space to test."

I wasn't sure if I was more curious than normal because of relief at her being all right or because it was the middle of the night and I wasn't thinking straight. It wasn't hard to see that she was uncomfortable with the subject, but they fascinated me and I wanted to know more. "They're just so strange, I guess."

She chuckled, turning her back to me as she pulled forward her blood-matted braid and sat down, wings adjusting around her posture. "If you wanna look at them closer, go ahead."

While she likely was just being polite, I still took her up on that and moved closer. Both her vest and the shirt under the vest tapered in, leaving her shoulder blades exposed. I ran my thumb across the outer feathers of her left wing, noticing as the wing pressed back against my hand. "You feel from them?"

She nodded timidly. "They're really sensitive — my spell book said they have a high nerve density. They're definitely more sensitive than like either side of my hand, even with the feathers themselves not really having any nerves that I'm aware of."

"They're really beautiful." Majestic was another word that described them well. I noticed her left wing pushed further against my palm and fingertips; how conscious was her control of them? That specific movement almost seemed like it was a subconscious reaction to my words.

She brought her knees to her chest. "I just appreciate you not telling anyone. It's dangerous for mages to use magic, be seen."

She'd mentioned that many times. Even when those women wanted to kill her, she was always more concerned for others, not herself, so what had her so concerned with her own well-being when women trying to actively murder her hadn't caused the same level of concern?

"Why?"

Her posture stiffened, head lowering as her wings slid out of my grasp to adjust around her, enclosing her.

"There's a group out there that experiments on mages, kidnaps them from their families. I've known two mages that've gone missing so far." Her voice weakened further. "It's probably wrong of me after how many people have died *because* of me, but I just... I don't want to be kidnapped and taken wherever for being experimented on or tortured or whatever it is they do to mages."

"It's not wrong." She had a drive to live; that was normal, human even. That same drive had been the reason I'd left home and run away to this small town.

She nodded but said nothing else. I brought my thumb over the section of her left wing that connected to skin. How could something like these wings look to be genuinely part of her body? It was seamless, tissue and muscle and even bone connecting as if she'd been born with them. She squeaked, jerking forward.

"I, um, sorry. That's like the highest of nerve density there, I think, and I hadn't expected, um..." Her postured shifted, a fidget to her normally still movement. "Just be gentle right there."

Hadn't I been? But I noticed her cheeks were flushed, the left wing pressing harder against my fingertips. I wanted to better understand these strange additions to her body but withdrew my hand instead. From what I could make of her explanation, she could summon them another time; I'd ask again when the timing was better.

"Thanks for letting me look at them."

"Oh, um, sure. You don't have to stop. I just, um, it caught me off guard."

She had to be exhausted, regardless of whatever else she said. "It's late, so we should both get some sleep in."

"Mm." First the wings disappeared, then she changed back into her normal self, including the clothes she'd worn to school today, no longer bloodied at all, not even her hair.

I didn't know the words I wanted to say, the emotions I didn't understand. "I appreciate you coming for me, even knowing the danger."

Kylie turned around to face me, lips pursed. "You were only involved in this *because* of me. It's my fault to begin with."

Yet most people would've run when the risk to their own lives was so great. "And I'm just one person, but... I'm glad I met you."

She hugged me, and I didn't know what to do. How was someone so much more powerful than me so small? I sat there with my knees folded under me until she released me. Her eyes were glassy as she looked at me and nodded.

"I'm really glad I met you too." It was the first time anyone had ever said that to me, and I didn't know how to respond. She smiled as she put space between us.

I think... it might've been the first time I'd ever felt valued just for being near someone. It was a rather strange feeling.

# Chapter Thirty-Seven

## split path

Jordan | January 13
Opal Pines Streets

At this rate, gonna be moving even more shit over to Richard's with how much I'm there lately. Wait, no, not Richard's, *Sai's*. Gonna be like it was for Kyle, where I'd be correcting myself for motherfuckin' ever again, but it'd stick. Eventually. Ain't a memory problem as much as a pattern problem, and hypermnesia did jackshit to fix that.

Regardless, problem's still that I'm over there multiple days a week now. Guess it ain't wrong to say if I'd been working, I'd also be home less, but that didn't feel the same since I ain't hating every minute of the time away like I had while stocking shit... 'cept for the time spent in that damn gym. He's fuckin' hellbent on teaching me 'bout every machine in there. Was goddamn miserable with him bitching at me constantly in there.

But it'd paid off: we'd lived. Barely. But fuck, we'd *lived*.

Opening the door to the apartment, I'm hit with the familiar stench of alcohol as soon as I stepped in. Apartment looked shittier than normal, garbage everywhere. I ain't had much time to clean shit here like I used to; even b'fore working so much on magic shit with *Sai* and Kyle, still back at the grocery store, I hadn't bothered cleaning shit when I came home either 'cause've how sore and exhausted I'd been. Jewel ain't said shit to me 'bout it 'cause I brought in more than she'd bitched 'bout wanting from me, so I wasn't the nearest striking victim anymore. Bet Thomas's the one getting bitched at 'bout cleaning shit now, which's actually terrifying as fuck since Thomas burned damn near everything and couldn't even put his damn dirty clothes in the bag to be washed. Was one thing I ain't minded at Sai's: never tripping over goddamn everything when I had to piss in the middle of the night.

Those thoughts immediately slipped from my mind as I saw Elaine with a black eye, heard Father screaming at Thomas in our room. Heard a thud and a wince from Thomas. This surge of emotion slammed into my chest, split between wanting to haul ass out b'fore he noticed me and...

Anger.

It's the first time I dared to be *angry* at Father. I didn't know how to handle it, this desire to slug him back for not keeping his hands to himself.

Elaine kept her eyes away from the room I shared with Thomas where he and Father still were. Hell, she avoided eye contact with me even. I knew I could make her bruise disappear like I had for so many of my own. But I couldn't. It's this line I couldn't cross, this divide between things *Jordan* knew and *Rotanu* knew and was I just afraid? Scared shitless of the idea that Thomas or Elaine or Jewel or, hell, even Father'd run their mouths and I'd end up missing too? Was I just a selfish ass for not taking the risk? It ain't the first time he'd hit them, but he'd always gone for me over them. What happened when I ain't here though?

I knew the answer, and even if I hadn't, I saw it clearly in front of me right then.

Walking to the fridge, I pulled out an ice pack, wrapping it in one of the kitchen towels and then handing it to Elaine. I didn't say anything else, not wanting to draw Father's attention back to her. She took the ice pack, nodding as she pushed it against her swollen eye. I tiptoed into our room, saw Father

**244**

passed out on Thomas's bed. Thomas sniffled, rubbing where his lip was busted.

How'd I feel more powerless *not* being the one getting my ass beat? This sinking pit in my stomach that I didn't want, couldn't tolerate. I gestured to Thomas to come to me, and he did so; I took him into the bathroom and put medicine on his lip.

I needed to be in more than one place: with them, with Kyle, fuck, in school and hell knew with Sai and sometimes even just by my goddamn self. I'd made the choice to be there for Kyle, knew she *needed* me and barely survived even now. She'd barely lived yesterday; not being with her meant leaving her to her motherfuckin' death.

But... why'd helping her come at the cost of my siblings getting their ass beat? Unlike me, they couldn't just use a heal spell to get rid of the pain. What'd happen if they needed to go to the hospital and they ain't gonna know I might actually have money to help them? Why ain't any of this shit *fair*? I felt like a selfish ass, but I didn't know what else to do or who to even talk to 'bout it. Couldn't mention it to Kyle; she'd say to stay here, that she'd be fine, but it'd be a fuckin' lie. Sai'd say to never come back here and to hell with my siblings; he's still pissed I didn't want him involved and lived here at all.

There's a split path, and it goddamn hurt knowing there's no way around suffering, around someone getting hurt. And even if I left Kyle on her own more, didn't practice as much, I couldn't always be here. I'm just a selfish ass to not even try healing them, too much of a coward, too scared of the consequences.

It's strange, like I ain't really part of this family now, no longer really their brother. I had a safe place to run, more than enough money to keep us from getting evicted, and could heal shit as long as my symbol's fine, I didn't die, and I could reach the injury.

I'd become just an impostor with the same last name, hadn't I?

# Chapter Thirty-Eight

## truths

I wiped sweat from my forehead. Thankfully, it was still in the coldest months of the year. I certainly wasn't complaining alt form's hair was braided back, though. Jordan swung Nateka at me as I blocked with Isare, releasing the blades to catch Nateka in a gridlock. Jordan mumbled a curse as he tried to yank Nateka back, but I pushed his wrist grip down from angling, forcing Nateka to drop from his hands.

As soon as Nateka hit the concrete, I withdrew Isare and retracted the blades.

"Damn things're nasty as hell to deal with — blunt and bladed weapon at once."

I stretched, putting extra weight on Isare for balance as I did so. "It's difficult to know when's the best time to use the blades still."

He grabbed his water bottle, drinking a large sip. We both usually brought a few with us to these sessions now. "Could've fooled me."

"I mean, I have advantage of range since Isare is longer than Nateka, at least in their default forms."

He was amused, a roll of his eyes. "Take the damn compliment."

I fidgeted. He wasn't wrong in that I could actually see progress, but not just for me — for him, too. Dismissing Isare, I grabbed my water bottle, sitting against the wall for back support.

This time last year, my life had progressed into a living hell. I guess it wasn't really that much better now: I was far less safe without Sia and Rota. So many people had died because of me, and Maya had frequently almost been added to that count. Even Jordan had been near death more than once this past year because he stayed around me.

I still couldn't fathom graduating high school and going to college like some normal teenager. No matter how much Mom wanted it, I just couldn't bring myself to even pretend to care about my future. Yet... I was happier this year. I'd basically destroyed my years-long friendship with Dani, knew I was hunted, accepted Mom being perpetually disappointed in me. But I didn't feel so alone anymore, not like I had last year.

"Kyle?" Jordan moved near me, sitting down to my right. He had his water bottle in hand, us both still in our alt forms.

It felt like I knew him so much more after these past few months, as if the years of friendship before meant nothing. Was it because of empathy? I'd gotten better at identifying emotions from others, placing them. But it also meant I understood people — emotions — in a way I couldn't have prior to my Act. That still didn't feel like what had changed between us, though. I just wasn't sure what it actually was. For that matter, I still didn't understand the difference between his behavior last year and this year. As I lowered my leg, I saw my thigh, the Arbiter Seal around my symbol. I'd never brought up anything involving it, and I was scared to even think too much about it. Even then, I didn't understand NEO at all. He supposedly had some power over me, and his aura was literally branded around the center of my mana, effectively my life. "Hm?"

"'Sup? Didn't fuck up your arms or shit, right?" His concern filled my chest with warmth.

I shook my head. "Oh. No. Just was thinking, sorry."

That got him even more concerned, the opposite of my intention. "Something happen?"

If I brought it up, would I be taking a hammer to this happy picture we'd created? The past was past, but I still wanted answers. Why was he here now, supportive now, and not then? I didn't know how to respond, nor did I know what I wanted from him if I did ask — an apology wouldn't change what'd happened. Any explanation he gave wouldn't change how alone I'd felt this time last year. I'd never even asked how he had time to train and practice now when before he'd always been busy going on dates with his girlfriend or hanging out with Richard. I knew he and Richard still frequently hung out because of how often Richard came to the training house during our Saturday sessions, but Jordan hadn't mentioned his girlfriend in months.

"Kyle?"

My eyes rested on the red and blue outline of my symbol. "Can I ask something?"

Out of the corner of my eye, I saw him lean forward to get a better view of my face. "'Sup?"

"I guess..." I didn't know how to ask, how to form a question from the concepts and words floating around in my head. I couldn't ask him why he was here now and not then, not point blank — that would make me sound ungrateful when I knew I wouldn't have made it out of the last attack without his support. "You're here so much. You... still get time to go see her, right?"

"Uh, who?"

He was really going to make me spell it out, wasn't he? While his emotions didn't indicate he was intentionally oblivious, that didn't make it any less annoying right then. "Your girlfriend."

"Oh." He moved, and I saw him rub the back of his neck with his right hand, still gloved. "We broke up months ago."

So he only was with me now because they weren't together then. I lowered my head, nodding. "I-I see. I guess that's why you have a lot more time now."

"Huh?" He wasn't dating anyone, so he had time now

compared to last year when he'd been busy and therefore hadn't; it seemed pretty straightforward. "Oh. Uh. I actually broke up with her, months back. It, uh..." His voice softened, that warmth from him filling my chest once more. "It's when you first started talking to me again. When I tried to talk to you and you said why your empathy's louder around me, I realized it just wasn't ever gonna work with her so I broke things off."

He broke up with her... for me? Or maybe because of me? I wasn't sure which, but I hadn't anticipated either. "But I thought you liked her."

Why was he amused? His emotions were tender, encompassing but not overwhelming, like I was surrounded by an electric blanket during a cold snap.

"I mean, she was kinda hot, yeah." I wasn't sure what I'd expected him to say, but that wasn't it. He'd never really said he'd found anyone attractive, and I thought he wasn't really interested in those types of things. "But I don't think I could've done right by her, not really. And it's more important that I be here — just realized that day, this's where I'm s'posed to be."

Where he was supposed to be... He sounded so much more certain of the present — let alone future — than I was right then. "Even though Sia was here, I felt so alone last year." My voice was weaker than I liked, than I truthfully should allow.

"I know. I fucked up."

The question I didn't want to ask or hear the answer to slipped from my mouth anyways: "But why?" I wanted to blame Richard, but he had barely said a word to me this year. It wasn't like last year, where he'd constantly gotten in the way every time I'd tried to talk with Jordan.

"I don't know." He set his water bottle down as he brought one knee up and rested his wrist on it. "I still don't love magic shit. Like us beating the shit outta each other ain't my definition of a fun afternoon, nor's the constantly being in danger of dying from those damn bitches or whatever the hell the people who kidnap mages want. And hypermnesia fuckin' sucks when you have shit you'd rather not remember, or the amount of times I've gotten goddamn burns the past couple years." His resolve strengthened as he glanced over at me, this peace washing over him. "But I'm s'posed to be here right now. And was wrong to ever leave you alone to deal with this shit. Or let Sai — uh, Richard — run his goddamn mouth and never say shit." So he called Richard "Sai" now, as Sia once had called Saite, as Rota'd called Sia "Kyle" and now Jordan called me that. Jordan's voice gained a pensive edge as he added, "I think... I just really wanted to prove that we weren't the same."

"Me and you?" There were more differences than similarities between Jordan and me: he was a guy, and I was a girl. I was in honors, and this year's AP history was the only advance class he'd ever taken. My elemental alignments were water and air, his fire and ice.

He snorted, shaking his head. "Not... quite. Me and Rotanu."

I glanced at the boots I wore. It wasn't like alt form — Sia's form — was any taller than me. Outside of how much longer her hair — *my* hair right then while I was in alt form — was, people might not even have noticed the difference. Yet I felt like I'd never measure up to her. I'd never ever be as good, never be as strong.

"I wish I was worthy of being grouped with Sia. She'd never let the things get as bad as they have this year."

"You're stronger than you think. She'd be proud, I know."

That was another thing I hadn't expected him to say. "Maybe." She'd likely chastise me for anyone getting hurt, for Maya almost dying.

He looked at his right hand, a small cube of ice manifesting a fraction of an inch above the glove's leather. "At points, I hated Rotanu. Just... pissed me off so goddamn much. So I said I ain't nothing like him, looked for every opportunity I could to spite him, and was a motherfuckin' idiot and complete jackass 'cause of it."

It wasn't like he could just say pretty words and lie to me thanks to empathy. I knew he meant it, felt his frustration and even anger as if they were my own.

I knew better than to ask, but I was desperate for last year to have been a nightmare that'd never return, wanted him to say she'd misled me like she had so many other times.

"Sia lied, right — about NEO?" He couldn't *actually*

control me or whatever, right? He hadn't mentioned it once since that day we'd talked back in October, not even the vaguest implication.

Yet his eyes drifted down to my symbol as his heart raced, my cheeks flushing from empathy and his emotions passing on to me. "I don't know what she said or much 'bout it at all, honestly."

But why did I have his aura colors around my symbol? Why did his heart race and cheeks flush right then as he saw my symbol? "She said something about you being 'Arbiter,' could *control me,* and that's why your aura outlines my symbol." That NEO was a fail-safe for strong mages, and someone had to be qualified to be accepted by NEO.

His head jerked away from my symbol, no longer looking in my direction and instead staring away from me entirely. "That's..." His head hung. "It sounds correct, from what you just said and the bit I know, saw."

Sia hadn't lied, not there. "So you could just tell me to do something, and I..." Had *I* even forgiven him, or had he *ordered* me to do it and I just wasn't aware somehow?

His eyes widened, panic rushing through his chest. "Fuck no, I'd never — I'd forget I even *had* Arbiter if I could." His lips pushed together. "If I hadn't claimed Arbiter, you'd never have 'woken up,' at least if Rotanu told the truth. I just wanted you away from... that. It wasn't you at all, like some doll, a machine."

What if he changed his mind? What if he decided he just wanted a "mechanical doll" one day? "I-I see."

What I didn't expect was him hugging me from the side, the bridge of his nose against the top of my shoulder and neck. "I swear. I'll never do that to you."

Would I even know if he did? "Just for a minute, to see what it's like... can you?"

"Huh, but..." It was a science I needed my own confirmation of: evidence that I hadn't just slept late that day, that he wasn't lying and Sia hadn't been lying. I needed to know how it felt if he went back on his word and decided to do whatever it all was.

"Please? Just for thirty seconds even? I just... I need to know something."

He was terrified, repulsed — wanted to refuse. His eyes rested on me as he said, "Okay, one minute. Then I'm bringing you back 'cause it's creepy as hell, and..."

I nodded. Every qualifier and hesitation from him soothed my concern more: he didn't want Arbiter, not at all.

"Activate NEO based on Arbiter's command."

Then he shifted to the right suddenly. Had he been working on teleportation magic? That seemed way more proactive than he ever was with spells.

"Was that good enough?" he asked. But he hadn't done anything.

"No time passed though. I know I said a minute, but, like, an actual minute."

His eyes became glassy as he shook his head. "It was two. I timed it." He felt too much distress for him to be playing a joke or lying. And it made sense, given how he'd shifted so suddenly. I truly had no recollection, time marching on regardless.

Sia hadn't lied: I'd truly have no idea. He could have me kill someone or steal something, and I'd remember nothing. Given how instant it'd been, some part of me literally obeyed *orders* from him, like commands into a terminal. "I..."

His hand rested over mine. "I swear, I don't want it. Please." His voice was frantic, pleading with me. "Don't avoid me 'cause of it. Just forget it's a thing. I won't..."

What choice did I have but to take his word? I nodded, biting back my sudden tears that were not helped by his emotions crowding my mind and body. As I felt his distress, his rage that didn't seem directed at me, I nodded.

"I trust you." Not that I had much say in the matter, but he'd just given me what I'd asked. "So just... please remember that."

# Chapter Thirty-Nine

## fantastical

Maya | March 9
Training House

I hated it when I didn't get assigned Saturday shifts — unlike during the school week, I could work any shift on the weekends and it didn't matter if I stayed up late on Saturday compared to Sunday. Unfortunately, I wasn't alone in my preference for Saturday shifts, so more often than I liked, I got only a partial shift or — like today — nothing at all.

I still needed the money and would've preferred to be at work, but I didn't mind having the weekend free as much now as I had earlier in the year; as I'd learned, Kylie and Jordan practiced here in the training house until midday quite often, and I'd had more than my fill of entertainment watching their antics. After their training, Kylie and I planned to head back to her townhouse for once since her mom was out of town all weekend. In the meantime, I had my sketchbook in my lap as I sat up on the counter, though I never actually sketched that much while here — watching Kylie and Jordan proved too entertaining.

Right then, Jordan and Kylie were in their "alt forms" as she'd called it. I watched as Jordan swung a punch at Kylie, a gritted hesitance to his step. Kylie, for her part, lacked any hesitation as she maneuvered to the side and kicked, landing a blow on his shoulder.

He grimaced as he grumbled "fuck" along with a few other words I didn't make out.

"You okay?" Kylie relaxed her stance, tilting her head as she examined where she'd struck him.

Jordan rubbed his shoulder, nodding. "Yeah, sorry. Didn't expect that to land so you hammered the shit outta me there."

Kylie stepped closer to him, laying her hand over the swelling skin. She used the so-called healing spell, any redness vanishing once she withdrew her hand.

I heard the entrance door open. Turning my head, I saw our rare last guest appear. As soon as he shut the door behind him, he transitioned into what I assumed was his own alt form. I wasn't sure why he bothered since he never joined Jordan and Kylie in these practices, instead just standing over to the side where I sat. Kylie's back was to us, but her posture gained a rigidness it'd lacked a few seconds before.

For his part, Jordan nodded while giving a half wave with his gloved right hand. "'Sup?"

I'd met him as "Richard," but I'd noticed Jordan referred to him as "Sai." I wasn't sure if it was like "Kyle," Jordan's personal nickname for Kylie, or something more general. After I'd heard him refer to her as Kyle a few times, I'd asked her if she wanted me to call her that as well; that'd been my first cue her protests of "just friends" was a lie, given how she'd blushed and stammered about how it was just something he called her and not a typical nickname. I wondered what the story behind said name meant, given how embarrassed she'd been about it, but I hadn't ever asked since it wasn't any of my business.

But because of Kylie's response, I wasn't sure how to handle Richard's name, and really, the best solution was to just ask.

He plopped down to my right. Thankfully, the counter held us both — if this broke, I'd have to bring a chair or sit on the concrete.

Kylie and Jordan resumed their training, this time Kylie practicing her *telekinetics,* as she called them, and I didn't envy Jordan *at all* as she lifted him into the air and then moved him left and right, as if he was held by a large invisible hand. Her left hand sharply jerked to the side, and Jordan went rushing through the air, crashing into the concrete wall with a yelp.

I wished I could have said that was the first time I'd seen the sequence play out, but unfortunately for Jordan's back, it was closer to the third or fourth time this week. Kylie rushed over, yet again concerned and sheepish. She had more power than control, she'd explained, but it was hard to refine said control for larger weight ranges, which was why she needed Jordan's assistance — his weight, in this case.

Better him than me.

"Damn bitch," Richard mumbled.

While Kylie's mistake had clearly not been intentional, I didn't blame him for his irritation with her, given Jordan had been hurt yet again — I'd be surprised if Jordan wasn't agitated as well, really. Jordan gripped his forehead, eyes clenched shut like he had a brain freeze. He stood with her help a few seconds later, any signs of pain vanished from his demeanor.

"Could I ask you something?" I asked.

His eyes shifted to me, but he said nothing. Guess that was a no, so Richard he was.

I directed my attention back to Kylie and Jordan, seeing them with weapons now, the same ones they always used. I watched as Jordan brought his sword above his head and held it with one arm — a posture I hadn't seen before, something aggressive with the stance that contrasted his normally passive demeanor. Yet as he charged forward, Kylie spun her staff, locking Jordan's sword. As if he'd anticipated that, he swung his left fist into her stomach. Kylie stumbled as she coughed, and he let his sword drop before it reappeared in his hand, pointing to her torso.

Kylie gave a strained laugh between breaths. "Okay, that was pretty good. I didn't expect it."

Jordan lowered the sword, right hand moving behind his neck as he rubbed the back of it. "It's a different stance, so I ended up shifting weights, which allowed for... uh, I mean, y-yeah. Are you okay?"

Her voice was so playful, casual even, as she replied, "Better than your back, I'd guess."

Richard huffed, his attention now back on me. "What did you want?"

Oh, guess he wanted to talk now, or at least he wanted to distract himself from what Kylie swore wasn't her and Jordan flirting but I was fairly certain anyone with eyes would've recognized otherwise.

"Your name's Richard, right? Or is it Sai? I've heard Jordan use both, so I just wanted to know what you'd like to be called."

"Sai. But you're not even supposed to be here."

I couldn't really disagree with that: I wasn't part of this fantastical world; I'd only found out through chance — I wasn't sure if it was good chance or bad chance some days, but it was certainly chance, regardless.

"Is it a problem?" I could stop showing up if it bothered him that much. It'd be rather dumb since he just sat here the whole time until Kylie left from what Jordan had mentioned, but it also wasn't worth a fight. I had plenty of other things to do instead. Admittedly though, I'd grown comfortable with Kylie and Jordan, felt safe around them.

His arms crossed over his chest as his attention further shifted toward me. "You're a liability." He wasn't wrong; I had almost died enough this past year to demonstrate that rather objectively.

"I agree." But Kylie had so often stressed how grateful she was to have me around, so I wasn't one that bothered her somehow.

"You're not even from here, are you?" It wasn't any of his business whether I was or wasn't from here, so I didn't answer the question. "Well? Are you? There's no one with your name in this city prior to this past July."

How did he know that?

It didn't matter. He wouldn't have asked if he knew for certain, so I just turned back to Kylie and Jordan. She made some water shield as Jordan threw a few small ice shards at it. His ice shards were pitiful though compared to the water currents she often drenched him with when they reversed defensive and offensive positions.

*Sai* grabbed me by my right wrist, startling me, and my head turned back toward him. "What?"

"I asked you a question."

What was his problem? "Yeah, and I'm not answering it. It's my business, not yours."

A light green hue contrasted with his blue eyes. "Yes, you will. You're a liability, and you owe me information."

It wasn't wrong that I knew far more about them than they knew about me. Kylie had never asked; neither had Jordan, for that matter. Maybe it really was right for me to share things I didn't really want to. Tell them my secrets as they had told me theirs.

"I—"

I hadn't even heard her move, but Kylie's fist collided with Sai's cheek, the impact recoiling his head as his attention immediately redirected from me to her.

"Don't you *ever* do that to her again." There was a growl in Kylie's tone, something dangerous I'd never heard from her before.

"You're the one that got found out to begin with," he snapped. "Putting us *all* at risk with your idiocy."

Despite Kylie and Jordan using literal weapons against each other routinely, I'd never seen her react that violently before.

"You will *not* hurt her. There's no reason she should *ever* have to be on guard here. Not from one of us."

Jordan stepped closer, his lips pressed together as his eyes shifted between Kylie and Sai. He pointed to me and gestured to come near him. I had no idea what was happening so I moved away from the counter and over to Jordan. His tone was almost a whisper as he asked, "You okay?"

Why wouldn't I be? "Yes?"

Kylie's eyes were the hardest I'd seen them as she stared straight at Sai, this look of defiance in them she hadn't had minutes prior. Sai kept arguing with her, words I couldn't quite make out. Whatever he said, Kylie wasn't a fan. Her fists balled tightly as I wondered if she was about to punch him once more.

"Shit, I'm so sorry. I never would've... I'll talk to him later, away from her when he'll listen to damn reason. But I'm so sorry."

My attention shifted back to Jordan. "For what?"

His eyes glazed over a moment before he continued speaking

in that near whisper. I assumed it was so Kylie and Sai wouldn't overhear.

"So like I have hypermnesia." I had no clue what that was. "And Kyle has empathy and sensory precognition." Oh. The ability things. That first word he'd used was the name for however his memory worked. "Sai's got something called 'suggestion' — basically's a mind control to some degree. Kyle noticed his aura flare and I saw his eyes, and just... shit. I'm so goddamn sorry."

Thoughts I thought were mine had been *suggested* to me. If Kylie hadn't interfered, I'd have told him whatever he wanted. My heart raced, a new sense of violation I hadn't known was possible — something as bad, maybe even *worse,* than Kylie's empathy.

"I-I see."

"He won't do that again. Ever. I'll make sure of it. And I'm so sorry." While I believed Jordan's sincerity, how could he stop Sai? They were two separate people.

Yet as I saw Sai's eyes gain that color once more, Kylie leaned on her left hip, glaring at him.

"Is he... to Kylie?"

"I think it's subconscious there. He 'slips' when he's too emotionally invested in an outcome. Won't work on her though. She's too strong a mage, won't get past her defenses so's just adding fuel to the goddamn fire."

While I had no idea what he meant, what I'd learned was that they'd been looking out for me — even here, where I was just a background spectator of their training sessions.

Maybe this was the price for a normal human observing the fantastical that I'd otherwise never see.

# Chapter Forty
## boundaries

Jordan | March 9
Training House

It'd been hard as fuckin' hell getting Kyle to leave; I'm pretty sure the only reason she ain't still here chewing Sai's ass out's 'cause I convinced her getting Maya outta here's a better idea and that I'd deal with Sai instead.

Unfortunately, that meant I *actually* had to deal with him. I'd never been much of a fighter, 'specially with him of all people. Closest I ever came to snapping at him's that night I said I ain't going to college, which'd pissed him off. Still wasn't actually sure *what* I'm doing after I graduated, but at least Sai ain't brought that hellish topic back up. I released alt form since I ain't sure what me and him're doing; if it didn't need alt form, I preferred to not use the damn thing. Luckily, mana's the biggest difference now — all the damn gym work and swordplay practice'd made the gap on physical strength a hell'va lot less than it'd been at the beginning of the year.

Sai rolled his eyes as Kyle closed the door, Maya already ahead of her. Once she's outta hearing range, I needed to ask him what the ever-loving fuck he's thinking on this one, but I feared I knew the ultimate answer: Sai and women had always been a fuckin' landmine of a shit storm, and lucky me, seemed like it's 'bout to be my fuckin' problem again.

"Damn bitch. Don't know why you put up with *that*."

I had to be bitchier or tireder than I'd realized 'cause I had a snap in my tone as I said, "Your ass fucked up on this one." To damn near everyone else, it's obvious he'd been the one that fucked up, but that ain't exactly a concept Sai's familiar with and I knew it.

"Excuse you?" He raised his eyebrows at me.

I fidgeted 'cause I didn't wanna meet his eyes, uncomfortable with his snappy-ass tone. It ain't a lie to say I depended on him for shit now, and I'd seen his temper too goddamn often.

"The hell'd you think you're doing? Maya's been a goddamn saint through this shit." Kyle needed someone that ain't me, someone Ms. Rae didn't hate. Just... someone else away from all the shit we dealt with, much like Sai'd given me so many times.

Guess that's why I couldn't back down: even if it fucked me over and I went back to the damn grocery store from Sai having a bitchfit, I *had* to enforce this boundary for Kyle — for all the times I didn't last year.

He crossed his arms over his chest, still in his own alt form. It ain't 'cause he wanted to train in it; more likely's that he didn't want his actual clothes getting dirty since that's something he bitched 'bout constantly when he's here outside of alt form.

"She's not one of us — could sell us out at any minute. Why *aren't* either of you asking questions? It's not normal."

"So could've you b'fore your Act." I dunno why he acted like he'd been here from the beginning. He'd known for a little over a year, and it'd not even been a year yet since his Act.

"Like I need money." He snorted, brushing dirt off his jacket collar. "I prefer it this way. We've been over that."

Maya'd been loyal, even if I didn't get why; he wasn't wrong that she'd put herself in the middle of all this shit when she didn't need to. She didn't really talk to many people, mostly just read and sketched a lot. I ain't sure why or even how she'd gotten so close to Kyle, but I'm thankful for it — hell, was thankful she tolerated me and I didn't have another fuckin' Dani on my hands.

"Kyle's got the most to lose out of any of us." I wished she didn't, but I'd done everything I could and it still ain't enough. "Maya's been there for Kyle and has had hell'va chances to talk but hasn't. Just... leave it alone. Please."

He scoffed again. "You're willing to put yourself at even more risk for that bitch?"

Maybe one day I'd argue that he shouldn't call Kyle a bitch — I hated it, but it's just not a fight I'm willing to fuck with. Instead, I nodded to him. "I'm not the one living in fuckin' fear every day — or fuck, with those goddamn premonitions she has no control over." There'd only been two types she'd ever mentioned: feeling me getting my ass beat by Father and someone getting severely fucked up. She never had premonitions for joy, only pain. "It's just like... I wanna see her happy, and Maya's been a good friend. She's helping her and makes her smile. That's enough."

Really, I'd underestimated how goddamn dense Kylie'd been all these years; I always knew it'd been bad, but fuckin' hell, I had no damn idea how she ain't figured out how I felt despite her damn empathy blaring every other damn thing at her. Maybe she just ignored it out of kindness. It didn't really matter; just being by her side's enough.

"So we're supposed to leave the gaping vulnerability just *sitting there*? No information or hedging at all?"

I nodded. "If she betrays us, then I'll take whatever hell comes from it." Granted, that assumed I'd even be around to take blame for shit. That's a huge-ass assumption in itself, considering.

Sai shook his head, rolling his eyes as he sighed. "This is *beyond* idiotic, just like your damn insistence to stay in that hell hovel."

Yet he'd learned to respect that boundary, as much as he still hated it. "Thanks for looking out for me." I wondered if we both would've been better people if we'd met earlier in life. Guess there's no real way to know now.

"You're my ticket out of the damn *family legacy*. That's all." Bullshit, and I ain't sure why he bothered pretending otherwise.

Unable to help myself, a slight smirk pulled at my lips as I met his eyes. "For someone wanting outta that life, you fuckin' don't act like it. Dunno how your ass ain't gotten robbed on this side of town so far."

This time when he snorted, it's hell'va amused instead of annoyed. "Oh? Maybe you should tutor me in the art of uncoordinated clothes."

Maybe we had more to learn from each other than I ever would've thought when we'd first met in the damn forest that day.

# Chapter Forty-One

## human lie detector

Kylie | March 9
Rae Residence

Even though we typically went to Maya's apartment for sleepovers since it was on the same side as the training house, we came to my house this time since Mom was out of town at a conference for the weekend. Really, I wished Mom went to *more* conferences: she always came back in a better mood, and it kept her out of my hair for a few days.

Out of danger too, even if I didn't want to admit how much that influenced things.

Another perk to Mom being away was that I didn't have to worry about hiding alt form. I'd already showered in alt form to clean off the bit of blood and a lot of sweat I'd worked up during training; now I got the *joy* of detangling and blow-drying its hair. At least I didn't have to deal with my own after this. My actual body was still clean since I'd been in alt form the entire time we'd practiced today.

Grabbing my hairdryer from under the bathroom cabinet, I huffed as I sat down on the carpet next to a power outlet. Time to waste an hour of my day blow-drying, which was as *riveting* as ever. Maya sat on the futon, sketching in her notebook; as I'd learned at the beginning of the year, she did *not* smile upon my curiosity at what was in said sketchbook.

My brush already beside me, I set the hairdryer down onto the carpet so I could detangle all the knots first. Maya glanced up in my direction, but I couldn't tell what had caught her attention since I had my head lowered while I brushed through the ends of alt form's hair. Empathy assured I knew she was entertained for whatever reason though.

"Why's your hair so long when you're like that? It seems more hassle than it's worth."

I rolled my eyes; Maya's hair was above her shoulders, so she wouldn't understand.

"It's Sia's form, so it's just how long my hair gets."

She moved from the futon, positioning herself behind me as she took the comb from my hand and worked through a knot for me. Especially compared to my own impatient manhandling of knots, she was surprisingly gentle — one hand held hair above the knot to prevent pulling as the other continued dealing with this particularly stubborn knot. As short as her own hair was, I hadn't expected her to know how to handle longer hair.

"Okay? Question still stands: why not cut it off? It's still your decision."

"I've been too busy, and I'm not even sure it'd stick in alt form, given how some things reset and others don't."

"Mmhm." Why was she even more amused? I wasn't lying: alt form logistics were basically a black box as far as I actually understood the spell's composition. Also, the more entertained Maya got, the more trouble for me as of late.

"Jordan likes long hair, then?" she asked.

I shrugged, unsure of the answer. "Maybe? His alt form has longer hair too so it's a possibility. It's just not to the same extent as my alt form's."

She ran the comb through my hair, knots eradicated far more quickly than I would've managed with significantly less pulling. I hated how much time maintaining two bodies took. I'd rather deal with the pain if it meant I wasted less of my already-limited time on this type of stuff.

"Mhmm. Not at all what I meant and you know it."

Rather than replying, I rolled my eyes. She continued running the brush through my hair. It reminded me of being a child, when Mom used to brush my hair out for me in the evenings for school the next morning, a calmness to the moment.

If nothing else, she was relaxed now, wasn't on guard like when we'd left the training house a few hours ago. If he ever tried that again on her, I wasn't sure what I'd do, but I'd do *something*.

"Hand me the hairdryer?" she asked. I did so, feeling the warm air blow through my hair after she turned it on and directed it toward my back. I closed my eyes, emotions and auras filling the sensory void from my current lack of sight. She felt happy, secure. How though? Any second, we could be attacked. She might die. Just a few hours ago, she'd almost had details forced out of her she'd in no way consented to sharing.

I felt her finger trace my right shoulder blade with the hand she'd been using to comb through my hair. "Something wrong?" Had I missed another bruise or cut? It wouldn't have been the first time.

She turned the hairdryer off, still examining my shoulder blade with her finger. "It's fascinating that your shoulder looks completely normal now. It's like the bird wings weren't ever a thing. I thought you'd have a marking or something, but there's really nothing there."

"Oh." My cheeks burned, not at all helping me. I understood wings were just a byproduct of intense mana consumption, but it'd have been a lie to say I wasn't a little self-conscious when they were brought up. Even though I'd only seen them once, it helped knowing Jordan had them as well, that it wasn't just me. "Yeah. From what I've heard, you can't really tell unless they're triggered."

"Can you have them when you're yourself too?"

I assumed she meant when I wasn't in alt form, so I shook my head. "Eventually, but I don't have enough magipoten — well, probably better said enough mana at the moment, technically speaking. I'm not sure what the actual threshold is, though, aside from something rather difficult for most people to reach."

She turned the hairdryer back on, finishing out my hair and then brushing through it once more. For once, all I'd have to do is braid alt form's hair, and then I'd be done with double body maintenance until the next training session. Maya left to take her own shower while I finished said braiding. My house's water heater did fine with hour-long showers, but I'd learned when Dani used to stay over that two showers back to back meant the second person ended up with only half a hot shower at best. After I finished the braid, I released alt form, a sigh escaping from my lips as I changed into my pj's and checked a few things on my laptop.

After ten minutes or so, Maya's mood shifted from peaceful to pensive. I did my best to pay it no mind, but with Mom not here, the closest other emotions came from others in the neighborhood and they were all too far off to mask Maya's emotions, so I also got the pleasure of noticing that whatever had her interest continued once she'd shut off the water. I struggled to keep myself from fidgeting once she opened the bathroom door and looked at me, still uneasy. But she'd mentioned she wasn't a fan of my empathy almost as many times as she'd fussed about me trying to glance at her sketches, so I did my best to pretend I hadn't noticed anything.

We'd already readied the futon for her to sleep on earlier, so she sat at the foot of it, her feet on my carpet as her eyes still rested on me. In part to hide the nervous energy I felt from her, I grabbed the hairdryer and put it back under my bathroom counter. She still hadn't relaxed though, so I sat down to her left at the end of the futon.

"All better now?"

She huffed, rolling her eyes. "Will you always be a human lie detector?"

That implied she'd *lied* about anything, and that wasn't the case as far as I knew. "Well, I mean, yes and no. I know Sia could suppress the 'reads' — like, ignore the stimulus — from empathy, but the ability itself is just kind of... there. It'd be like saying you could ignore your hearing or something touching you. Like yes, with enough practice, but that sense is still there even if you actively attempt to ignore it."

That was not the answer she wanted, regardless of its accuracy. "It's all right to lie and say yes."

I smirked, enjoying the rare moment I got to tease her instead of being teased. "Then you'd yell at me for lying — that's just setting me up."

She rolled her eyes once more, amused rather than the annoyance she pretended to feel. "Just *pretend* for a few minutes then."

Even with the playful gesture and teasing words, the caution hadn't left her. "Mm. Can." I didn't understand what made my empathy different then compared to any other time; I wasn't sure why she asked me to pretend it wasn't there when we both knew it was a point-blank lie.

"What he said earlier."

I really hoped she meant Jordan because I didn't want her stressing out over what Richard had said, what he'd tried to do — I still couldn't believe he'd attempted that. Well. I guess I believed he'd do it, given everything else I'd seen him do, actually. I just didn't want to think I'd put Maya at risk of harm any more than absolutely necessary, that she'd been threatened by a supposed ally.

"Don't. He had no right to try to pry details from you."

Her gaze moved to her sketch pad lying closed on the carpet to the right of her feet. "He had a point though: for all the secrets you've shared with me, even welcoming me into your home despite not being one of you... you've never even asked why I live alone."

She was new, lived alone, had to work to survive. When we'd first met, I'd noticed pain from scars running up her arms and stomach that I wasn't supposed to know about even now. I had theories, but they didn't matter because she'd done what only Jordan and admittedly Richard had accomplished so far: said nothing, given away nothing. The fact I was still here told me she wasn't against me.

"It's your business, not mine to demand," I assured her.

Maya had never been a very touch-prone person, even less

than myself or even Jordan had ever been; that remained the case as she sat with her hands in her lap, staring downward. I felt her nerves, this consuming tightness of her chest. I wanted to comfort her, but since she'd asked me to *pretend* not to know, I said nothing, acknowledged nothing.

"I appreciate that — it means a lot that you didn't ask questions even though you had to have them. But you... should be able to. You've literally saved my life more than once now."

I brought my knees to my chest, laying my forehead on my kneecaps. "You wouldn't be in dangerous situations to begin with if you weren't around me. It's not exactly that generous on my part."

"You could've left me to die. Many would've."

She wasn't wrong: people ran when they were scared, and I wasn't some grand exception to that. When all this had started, I probably wouldn't have gone to her apartment that day if it had given me time to hide. Why *had* I gone? Was it just the only way I could think of to make amends to those that hadn't made it because they'd been in the same class as me?

"Doesn't mean it'd have been the right thing to do."

I nearly jumped as she leaned against me, her damp hair against my shoulder. "The 'right thing,' huh?" That might've been the first time she'd initiated contact with me, ever. Yet right then, her tension faded. Not completely, but noticeably regardless. "I think that's where I'm at as well. This is something I need to do so I don't feel I've wronged you."

Of course, I'd been curious about why she lived alone or anything that'd happened before the start of this year. But secrets weren't things to demand from people.

"Just don't feel pressured to say anything you don't want to or because of whatever he said."

She nodded. "Mm. I won't. This is of my own accord."

I didn't get why now if it wasn't because of what Richard had said, but there was a strength in her resolve — it really was something she needed to do, to say. I nodded back, not sure what else to do besides listen to her.

"I'm not from around here, though you probably already knew that, given how small this town is." She assumed I knew a lot more people than I did. "I ran away." While I guess I hadn't been completely confident about that, I'd been fairly sure since she lived alone and provided for herself despite being months younger than me and a minor still even though we were less than two months from graduating. "I was adopted when I was five, and it just..." She paused, and I struggled to not hug her with how I felt her muscles tense through my empathy. "I can't go back. I'd rather die than ever go back."

I brought my arms around her left arm. "You're mine. No one's taking you away, sorry."

"Yours?" She snorted. "Not my type, sorry."

What was *that* supposed to mean? "Um. What is then?"

That earned me yet another snicker. On one hand, my response had distracted her from her anxiety; on the other, I was pretty sure said entertainment came at my expense. "Not women."

Oh, *that* kind of type. "Um, oh, that's not what I meant. I don't like anyone like *that*. I just meant—"

A slight smirk. "No one, huh?" I didn't care for that coy tint in her tone, and I had no intent on giving her further free ammo. Her tone sobered as she said, "I'm sure you've noticed, with your mom, I have... really mixed feelings. I guess it'd be best described as envy."

I'd identified what she referred to more than once, but it'd never been that consuming toxicity I associated with envy. Instead, it reminded me of Jordan's feelings while talking about Mom — of a longing he had for what he'd been deprived of, just the same as Maya.

I couldn't change their childhoods or the weight they carried. But there was one thing I did know.

"If someone tried to take you somewhere, and you didn't wanna go..." Despite her being in more danger around me than anywhere else, I truly meant my words. I felt a resolve I wouldn't waver with. "They'll have to go through me first. That's what friends are for, right? When we stumble, we're there for each other."

Whatever she'd expected me to say, that wasn't it. She had this internal warmth I couldn't identify as she leaned further against me. "You know, that actually sounds reassuring coming from you of all people. Even if you're rather terrible at hiding your empathy."

"You *said* pretend. *And* you're directly touching me. Not fair."

"Nothing ever is."

# Chapter Forty-Two
## something

Jordan | March 28
Matthews High

My cheeks still burned like hell. Mrs. Hermez'd complimented me on how *adept* at Spanish she thought I was. Think it's the first time in my life I've ever been complimented on *anything* at school. Or, well, most things. Hadn't really been sure what to say in response, but as I swapped books and walked down the hall to leave for the day, I kept replaying the memory: I ain't a failure to *someone*. She'd even said she wished I had another year or two left, could only imagine how much more I'd learn, and that I should look at additional Spanish classes in college. Fuck, she assumed I'm *going* to college — first time I'd seen someone make that mistake since like... Sai. And he'd been the first ever. Genuinely didn't know what to expect from my future, let alone what I might've wanted — it ain't exactly a problem I'd dealt with b'fore.

I pushed open the doors, seeing Kyle at her usual spot as she waited for me. Maya waved at her, likely heading off to work. As soon as Maya stepped out of hearing distance, that damn bitch approached Kyle. I increased my pace. I couldn't even fuckin' leave Kyle alone on the damn school grounds anymore, and I'm goddamn tired of it — at least the year's almost over, under two months b'fore this particular problem'd be *permanently* over.

"I'm sorry," Kyle said. I hadn't heard what Ashley'd said this time, but I assumed it's similar to every other bitching times past. Kyle's eyes're different from when she'd been cornered like this b'fore, though. For once, she didn't look away or down, didn't avoid Ashley as she instead met her eye to eye.

Finally near Kylie, I slowed my steps and stood to her side. I'd originally intended on jumping in, but I hesitated from the change in Kyle's usual demeanor during these incidents. Ashley didn't acknowledge me; usually if anyone else approached Kyle, she dashed.

"You're sorry? Sorry won't bring them back." How could she be such an ever-loving goddamn bitch? Like fuckin' goddamn. I knew she didn't know the truth, but who fuckin' blames someone for surviving a massacre like Kyle had? "Why did *you* make it, but no one else did?"

Kyle's lips pushed together as her eyes lowered. "I've asked myself that a lot too, honestly."

I remembered it too well — well, that's every damn thing now, granted — but it's the moment I realized why Rotanu'd always been pissed at me, what I should've noticed over a year prior: she felt guilty to be alive. Alone, unwanted, what'd brought attackers to the school, chaos to the people around her. She felt the only way to protect others's to not exist, a concept I couldn't fathom living through. But that day ain't her fault; she hadn't asked for any of this shit, never incited any of this goddamn mess. And she absolutely didn't deserve the bullshit Ashley gave her 'bout surviving.

"But guilt won't bring them back either, just like anger won't." Her eyes centered back on Ashley. "I won't forget, but I can only live for the people still here, not the ones that aren't. I'd suggest for you to do the same." Kyle turned to me and nodded, walking toward the school grounds' exit.

I said nothing to Ashley as I jogged past her while catching up to Kyle. "You okay?" I asked. I felt fuckin' proud as hell of what she'd said to Ashley, but she'd still been accused yet again and I knew it hurt her each time.

"I think." Her left hand moved to her absorption device, holding on to it as her steps slowed to a pause. "What feels the worst is that I prefer this year to last year. Even though so many people died, and I didn't kill them but being in the same room as me *is* what killed them, and Maya's almost died — *you've* almost died for that matter — but..."

It just emphasized how bad I'd fucked up last year. I hadn't caused all the problems, but I'd made 'em worse and maybe still didn't know how much I'd hurt her. If she preferred being in a school where she watched her class be murdered and then blamed for it the rest of the year, that said less 'bout her and more 'bout exactly how shitty things had gotten last year. I wanted to reach out, hug her and apologize to her and reassure her, but... I'd been part of the problem, so it didn't feel right.

"I, uh..." Really, nothing felt right, and I wished I knew something to say or do that'd actually help.

She still stared down, either at her absorption device or shoes or, hell, maybe even her hand. Fuck knew how her empathy hadn't given away my feelings — right then, yesterday, hell, near every fuckin' time we saw each other. It's simultaneously a blessing and a curse, a boundary I'd never push. That said, Maya's damn teasing stung like fuck; how'd *she* seen it so easily, so quickly, yet Kyle'd never noticed?

"Before Act, I didn't know what I wanted to do — just whatever Mom told me. I'd grown up hearing the same routine: get good grades to go to a college, take honors classes to get into college, take AP to get out of college faster. I just did whatever she said I should want and didn't think much about anything if it kept her off my back." Kyle's voice's calm, reflective even, not filled with anxiety or remorse like I'd expected.

"She just wants you to do well." Ms. Rae had *expectations* of Kyle, thought Kyle had a bright future, and of course she did. She was hell'va smart and capable. The fact she'd stomached the past couple of years while still carrying on showed that.

Kyle nodded. "I know. Mom loves me and wants the best for me. I really do know that," she said, her voice progressively growing fainter. Guess there's not any point mentioning emotions to an empath; she knew what Ms. Rae felt far better than I'd ever be able to. "But after the kidnapping... I kept wondering, what's the point? Why does school even matter? What good is college? I kept telling myself that I couldn't afford to think about the future when I barely survived the present."

I balled my right fist. She hadn't meant to attack me. In all the years I'd known her, she'd never been passive aggressive — if she had a problem, she said it loud and clear.

"Then this year..." This year she'd asked me to kill her, a mercy kill to save everyone around her.

"Yeah." Her voice's steady, but I couldn't get a read on if she's upset or not. "Not even a month in, the gym attack happened. People I'd just started knowing were gone or, like Ashley, hated and blamed me for surviving when people important to them didn't. I couldn't even say she's completely wrong because my classmates *did* die because I was there."

It ain't her fault. She couldn't lock herself in a room 'cause some damn bitches kept trying to kill her and the people around her. That ain't fair to her.

"You were the first one to say it wasn't wrong for me to still be alive. That's probably something I can't ever repay, honestly, just like I can't repay Maya endangering herself every day."

I didn't know how to respond, but not once had I ever thought she needed to *repay* me for anything. Hell, she'd been the only person willing to even *look* at me most of my life — first person to talk to me, to be my friend. For many years, our hangouts're the only goddamn thing I looked forward to.

"It's not..." She still faced away from me so I couldn't fully see her face, but I made out a smile that pulled at the corners of her lips as she nodded.

"I still don't really know what I want to do, but I think I want to try finding out. That's progress, isn't it? That's *something* compared to last year, when I couldn't even fathom thinking about the future."

Almost felt fuckin' tears come to my eyes hearing her say that. "Of course that's something. And it's not like I got all this shit planned out either. It's not just you unsure what the fuck to do from here."

Less than two months b'fore graduation, and I had no clue what my post-May plans're. When I'd started this year, I'd thought I'd work in the grocery store the rest of my life, and that'd be enough. Honestly, it would've been if I hadn't utterly failed at balancing magic and school and work. And without Sai, I wouldn't've had a choice, wouldn't've had a shot in hell.

She laughed, finally turning back around to face me.

"Mom had me put in all these college applications a few months back. I've gotten a handful of acceptance letters, which I guess has been great for my self-esteem, considering I felt like a failure at nearly everything lately."

I shouldn't't've been surprised she'd been accepted — *of course* she had, she's brilliant — but I rubbed the back of my neck as I mumbled a congrats to her. There's only one college in Opal Pines, and it ain't exactly one you worry 'bout getting accepted into.

"But I told Mom... I don't think I'm quite ready to leave. Not yet. So I'm going to go to Jenn for my first couple of years and then transfer. Maybe by then, I'll actually have a plan. It's not much, but it's more of an answer than I've had until recently. And it's because of you — well, you and Maya. So I just wanted to say, um... thanks. Thanks for being here for me."

# Chapter Forty-Three

## never again

It'd have been a lie to say I felt completely comfortable here after what'd happened the last time. But I'd had another short Saturday shift, so here I was back at this house with my sketchpad in my lap. I glanced up here and there as usual. There was a comfort to the routine this had somehow become. Despite my best efforts, I'd grown fonder of Jordan, let alone Kylie, than I should've. They provided a sense of peace I hadn't had in forever, shouldn't have at all. For the first time in years, I didn't have any scabs along my arms or stomach — there'd been no reason to slice across my skin to distract me, a strange realization in and of itself.

The door opened, Sai there again. I shifted, unsure if I should stay. Kylie turned her head to the entrance, longer than normal hair swaying in the braid as she stared at him a second before returning her focus to Jordan. Jordan nodded, but I wasn't sure if it was to me or her.

There was no reason to trust Sai, but the last time had shown I could trust Kylie and Jordan both to watch out for me, didn't it? Regardless, I still regretted coming once I saw him, a knot now in my throat that hadn't been there before.

He mumbled something, his form shifting to the one he usually was in here before he sat on the ledge beside me.

I didn't want to greet him after his behavior last time, so I said nothing and kept my attention on Kylie and Jordan. Jordan swung his sword at Kylie and she faltered, the blade piercing her arm. He immediately stopped, attempting to pull the sword out of her arm frantically and not particularly successfully. Kylie yanked the sword from her arm, her eyes clenched during the gesture. Afterward, she removed the glove on her left hand and covered the wound with her palm, her signature shades of blue emanating from her hand.

Hearing a "hmph" from Sai, I almost asked what his problem was. The answer wasn't that hard to see — he didn't like the frantic attention Jordan gave Kylie right then, though I wasn't sure why he hated Kylie specifically so much. I wouldn't ask him, wouldn't invite conversation after what had happened the last time.

"I don't get what he sees in her," he said. "Hundreds if not thousands of others like her." Real charmer. I was beginning to question Jordan's judgment in friends. "But he's damn determined with *this one*."

Did Sai really not get it? Jordan rather obviously had feelings for Kylie. I'd never seen him act on them, but he wasn't exactly *subtle* either. Or maybe he had acted on them in the past and had accepted rejection, given Kylie's poor insistence there was nothing between them when there very obviously was. He wanted someone he obviously cared about to live, and that wasn't wrong. I was envious Kylie had someone who cared for her so much, but really, Kylie had done the same for me, rescuing me every time I was in danger. I'd grown to trust her, and that was likely why I was there myself.

"I just don't get it. He's going to get hurt. That's how things work."

Why was he telling me all this?

"They've known each other since, what, childhood? He probably knows her better than us both combined many times over," I said.

He said nothing in response. Kylie and Jordan were back at it, this time Kylie working on telekinetics again. I'd yet to see Jordan work on something with fire and ice outside of shields and offensive magic. Kylie had mentioned something about temperature, but he'd just blushed and changed the subject; I assumed there was something he could have practiced there if he wanted.

"Oh," Kylie chirped. He cringed, and I understood why. Kylie *chirping* usually meant something with magic, and in a training session, that usually meant she wanted him to be the guinea pig yet again. "I was reading through my spell book the other night."

"Uh-huh." Judging from Jordan's bored and exasperated tone, we both waited for the inevitable.

"And I found out how they do the teleportation thing. I've been practicing it, and I can get a few inches!"

That sounded surprisingly not harmful to Jordan.

"Ah, that's great." How she missed the relief in his tone, I wasn't sure. For all her talk about empathy this and empathy that, she didn't catch some really obvious things.

Kylie tensed, then disappeared; she reappeared just a few inches from where she'd been — in fact, she could've walked there faster than the disappearing-reappearing — but she wasn't wrong in that she'd clearly moved by magic.

"I need to teach you, but maybe next week. I want a better handle on it first."

Distracting me from Jordan's response, Sai said, "He's the first that saw me as a human instead of some pawn or object." That was a rich explanation coming from a guy who clearly didn't see others as more than collateral to his needs. "He's so damn focused on her that he isn't watching out for anything else."

Was this his attempt at an apology? Maybe "apology" was too generous; this barely qualified as an explanation. I didn't look at him, keeping my eyes on Kylie and Jordan.

"You have valid points. But trying to force secrets from people is an asshole move," I said.

"Anyone could buddy up to them. Neither would notice a thing — too naïve." I also didn't disagree with that. Jordan interacted with him, after all. And even Kylie, she'd picked me out on day one somehow and never let go. For that matter, she'd been friends with Ashley originally, so her judgement of character wasn't exactly exemplary either. Yet...

"I don't think someone that's been almost killed multiple times in the past year would have great self-preservation instincts to randomly *buddy up*, all things considered." I would be more offended, but neither Kylie nor Jordan had ever implied suspecting me — only Sai, someone who I only needed one hand to count my interactions with.

He didn't immediately snap back, and when he replied, his response was a quiet "I know."

Knew what? That I'd almost died multiple times, and he'd still tried whatever that was? That it was wrong? That he shouldn't have attempted such a thing?

I hated Kylie's empathy, but from what she'd said and reasonably demonstrated, it wasn't like she had a choice in the matter, not yet at least. Jordan's memory didn't affect me one way or another. But something about Sai's ability thing was different: it had intention that neither Kylie's nor Jordan's magical ability things had.

"It's a big secret, right?" Kylie had been so terrified when she'd first used magic in front of me. She hadn't mentioned it in a while, but she'd said even outside of the women that had attacked her, attacked me, there were others who went after mages specifically. She and Jordan might've discussed magic here and there at school, but neither actually used any outside of emergencies — though how much of that was because of the barrier-thing, I wasn't sure either. "I could've said something for literal months now. Little late to be concerned about my 'trustworthiness' now."

"You're just a bitch too, aren't you?"

So keeping my eyes away from him pissed him off. Was that how his ability thing worked? "Not the first time I've been called one. Doubt it'll be the last."

He scoffed. "That's not... I'm *trying* to have a conversation with you."

And? Why should I give a damn? "I'm not going to tell

anyone. But that doesn't mean I'm going to suddenly be buddy-buddy with you, sorry." I wasn't actually sorry and don't know why I said I was.

"Don't you know who I am?"

Of course I didn't. "As you've already so intelligently deducted, I'm not from here. You're just a dick involved in the magic weirdness as far as I'm concerned."

What I hadn't expected was for him to snicker, laugh even. How was that *funny* at all? His reaction caught Jordan's attention as well and he barely dodged a swing from Kylie's staff.

Kylie's movements stilled suddenly as she uncharacteristically didn't follow up on her swipe. Jordan hadn't tripped or anything, so I wasn't sure why she paused. Her head twisted to the side, as if bracing for something. Jordan never used offensive magic without her prodding him, so I doubted she was bracing for an offensive attack from him. In fact, Jordan nodded at her even though she'd said nothing.

Something was wrong. There was a seriousness suddenly in the air, and I wasn't sure why. Kylie's posture straightened. "What, just stalking now?" Stalking?

She couldn't mean—

There was a woman suddenly, the same one that had attacked the day I'd found out about magic at Kylie's house. She was between Kylie and Jordan, facing toward Kylie. "I wasn't going to intrude yet, but I see you've gotten better with auras. I've gotten clearance, you know, *especially* after what you did to poor Zimihe. Our leader's *bored* with you now."

Kylie had yet to turn around. Sai slid off the counter where I still sat. Should I hide? But where? Sai didn't charge, he and Jordan meeting each others' eyes for a moment before Jordan nodded.

It was like an entire other conversation took place, one I had no understanding of.

Kylie's grip on her staff tightened. "Well, I better not disappoint, then." She rapidly turned around, swiping at the woman who blocked the staff with some type of sword. Kylie was already on her next maneuver though, backflipping as she gained some distance before the same water beams I'd seen her use against Jordan time and time again shot out.

For his part, Jordan hadn't remained still either, stepping right behind the woman who'd been distracted by Kylie's attacks. He stabbed her through the chest, face scrunching up in disgust as he pushed down, screams coming from the woman as she kicked backward, knocking him and his sword away from her. Little good it did as Kylie had already regained her ground, slicing the woman's head off as she panted. "Never again."

I didn't know quite what to say or do. Sai jogged over to them, attention more on Jordan than Kylie. Even though I jumped down from the counter, I didn't know how to approach them.

She was all right. Jordan was all right — *I* was all right, for that matter.

No one had almost died. Kylie had somehow recognized the attacker before she'd even arrived. My heart raced more now than during the event, which had been over in mere minutes.

"That was..."

A mild shake to her, Kylie straightened her posture. "She's never again hurting anyone."

# Chapter Forty-Four

## high school life

Among other accomplishments this year, I'd objectively gotten *better* 'bout being on time. Helped that I just ain't got time for detention: most days after school, I trained with Kyle, and even more than that, I'm at this school on an override. Sai'd not been subtle that he'd *not* bail me out if my ass got kicked out from me being late too much. Unlike other years, I *had* to care, and damn's it hard some mornings. I'm still as much of a morning person as ever so never had trouble getting up, but walking the whole damn town after dealing with whatever bullshit's up at home meant being far more prepared for said bullshit than I'd ever been before.

Jewel's ankle'd swollen kinda badly after Father's latest *outburst*. Ice'd been taking it down when I'd left, but still wished I could've stayed longer. A year ago, would've not given a damn, but I guess just had more capacity to care compared to then, not constantly overwhelmed with every fuckin' thing. Hell, I felt valued and even *wanted* for the first time in my life — teachers weren't sitting on their asses expecting to read a

285

headline 'bout me in jail one morning, actually thought I could *be* something.

Sai'd brought college up again last weekend, and he'd been just as bitchy as the other times it'd been brought up. Kyle said she's going to Jenn when she could be going damn anywhere prob'bly. Maybe... it's all right to ask *how* to put an application in, just on the off-chance they'd even consider someone like me.

The bell rang, yanking me from my thoughts. I hadn't paid attention to any of the morning announcements. For the first time ever, I'm on somewhat friendly terms with a few people I shared classes with, but there's no one in homeroom I'd bother trying to keep in contact with once I graduated. Even "somewhat friendly"'s so fuckin' strange since it'd never happened b'fore this year. I nodded to Theodore as I said I'd see him in English.

I'd accidentally ended up in AP history thanks to my hypermnesia, so second period's the first time since middle school I shared an actual class with Kyle and even Maya. Didn't bother swapping books after homeroom — unless I'm late, got my second and third period books while heading to homeroom — so I went straight for second period as usual to sneak a few extra seconds of talking with Kyle and Maya.

As I approached the entrance, I saw Ashley glare at me. Ain't done jackshit to her, but I'd rather her bitch at me over Kyle. She bumped into me, whispering, "You'll get hurt if you stick around her. Better leave now before something happens."

I rapidly turned around, but she's already gone somehow. Must've run as soon as she'd said that shit.

Guess since Kyle'd told her to fuck off, she's trying to fuck with me 'cause I'm close with Kyle. Damn bitch, couldn't wait to not see her again.

As I walked into the classroom, everyone looked normal enough. Kyle's talking to Maya, who I wasn't sure actually listened to whatever Kyle's saying as she sketched. I sat down behind Kyle, as I'd done since I'd transferred here. She turned around, eyes staring straight at me. Fuck's she so focused on?

"Did something happen?" she asked. "Were fine a few minutes ago, but..."

Goddamn motherfuckin' empathy. I didn't want her worrying 'bout this shit, but no doubt it'd put me in a bitchy humor and I should've known she'd catch it, 'specially with me sitting behind her.

"Ah, it's nothing serious. Just some random bullshit."

Her lips pressed together as she wouldn't meet my eyes. "Okay, if you say." She didn't believe me a damn bit, but at least she let it go.

Maya hadn't said anything, not even the routine greeting. "She okay?" I asked as I watched Maya sketch.

Kyle nodded. "Huh? Oh, yeah. She said she had to work late, so she didn't get much sleep last night."

That'd been me at the beginning of the year — would still be me, if not for Sai. I guess even... would still be me if not for magic given that'd been the link that caused me and Sai to meet in the first place. He'd asked a few times 'bout memories from past lives, memories I'd never gotten around to telling Kyle I had. Hell, didn't know how I'd tell her or what I'd say if I did; most memories I had're of her — of us, well, *them* — together. And it ain't like the things're fully fleshed out, just a sentence here, a smile there. The only one I'd placed with any of Sai's prior incarnations's when the actual reincarnation spell'd been cast. Takite didn't seem to have that much of a connection to Sai's original incarnation so I guessed that's why there ain't many memories.

"Just two more weeks," Maya mumbled. She sounded exhausted.

Two weeks, huh? That's all that's left of my high school life. I wasn't sure I'm ready for the change, yet... it's coming, regardless. Maybe it'd even keep getting better, as this year had.

# Chapter Forty-Five

## overload

Kylie | May 1
Rae Residence

I felt a stab through my stomach; a few minutes later, there was another stab through my left wrist. The fact I felt stabs at all meant this premonition wasn't "just" from Jordan's home life. It was yet another time I wished I knew how to *not* have premonitions, or that Sia still dealt with them in my place. Even worse, I understood enough of my premonitions to know they reflected injuries from myself or someone close to me.

Clenching my eyes shut, I winced. Why couldn't it all just *stop*?

I saw my phone screen light up. Who was texting me this late? It had to be around nine thirty at night. Jordan was usually asleep at this hour. Maybe Maya? That would be its own problem though, given she never texted outside of an emergency, especially not when we would just see each other tomorrow at school. Dani hadn't texted me in months, but I wished it was her just so I could ignore said message and resume attempting to sleep off this premonition.

Biting back a wince as I stretched my arm to the corner of my bed where my phone rested, I picked it up, seeing Jordan's name on the new message alert. But why? It was way past when he usually was up. As much as I hated to admit it, if he was just asking about tomorrow's training plans, he wasn't getting a response tonight. This was the third time I'd gotten this premonition today, and I already gambled that after so many today, tomorrow wouldn't be an encore. It'd been hard enough hiding the one that'd started toward the end of the school day, but Maya's work had kept her late multiple days this week so she'd been distracted and the attack had subsided enough by the time I'd met up with Jordan that he hadn't noticed.

*"U up?"* his message read.

Huffing — and wincing as I did so — I wished he'd just said what he wanted instead of asking a question obviously setting up another question. It wasn't his fault; he didn't know I'd spent all afternoon and evening having premonitions again.

I replied, *"Yeah, something up?"*

*"Meet @ training?"*

Why did he want to meet at the training house this late at night?

No... I knew exactly why, didn't I? He needed help healing something. It was the only explanation that made sense, and why I replied, *"On my way."* If he knew I was mid-premonition, he would tell me to stay home, so I didn't mention it. He'd only asked for help a few times, and little that it was, I wanted to be there like I'd promised. I knew I wasn't actually in shape to sneak out of the house and walk across town, but I'd make it work.

Changing out of my pj's, I slid today's t-shirt and jeans back on with my sneakers following soon after. I'd become proficient enough at teleporting that I didn't bother unlocking my window, instead levitating off the carpet and then teleporting onto the roof, still intentionally hovering a fraction of an inch above the roof's shingles. I wasn't sure if it was because I had a distraction or from the crisp night air, but my mind calmed as I walked across town. It also didn't hurt that most people were winding down or already asleep, so I felt fewer emotions than usual.

Arriving at the training house, I noticed Jordan's aura already inside, distraught emotions filling me. When I opened the door, I saw he'd only turned one lamp on in the corner, leaving most of the training house dark. The walk over here had been pleasant enough weather-wise, but I rubbed my arms as I stepped further into the training house — there must've been a ten or fifteen degree temperature drop compared to outside. Said temperature drop *had* to be because of Jordan, and he wouldn't have done it intentionally, given he'd always been more cold-natured than me. This deep panic and insecurity and sadness ate into my chest, threatening to knock the breath out of me.

I stepped closer, kneeling down to where he sat. He said nothing as he wrapped his arms around me, hands in my hair as he held on like I was a lifeline. I heard him sniffle, liquid dropping onto my shoulder. I finally felt some pain, but it was just a light throb compared to his other emotions. I'd never seen him like this before, so emotionally distraught from something that'd happened in his home life.

"H-hey..." I returned the hug as I felt his clammy skin against my own. "You okay?" I knew he wasn't but didn't know what else to say.

"S-sorry," he mumbled. "I just can't reach some spots I need healed, and..." He moved away, rubbing his eyes with his arm.

The dim light didn't matter. I felt his pain, each sob and ache echoing through my body.

"It's okay. You need someone right now." How had I missed something so obvious for so many years? I'd never thought twice about how timid and conflict-avoidant he'd always been, just assuming it was his personality despite him getting increasingly passive the longer I'd known him, the older we've become.

He sniffled once more as he shuffled away; I couldn't see how he shifted because it was just too dark with only that one lamp on. I shortcast a small light orb; it illuminated the nearby area, including Jordan's bloodshot eyes that he quickly turned to obscure from me. He took his shirt off, showing me a few sloppily healed bruises on his chest with more on the back of his shoulder that he hadn't attempted; maybe those were the ones he wanted assistance with.

I swallowed, doing my best to mask my emotions. He didn't need pity or remorse or whatever I felt. He'd asked for help with healing, and that was what I'd provide. My hand reached out, but he jerked away as my fingers brushed against his shoulder.

"S-sorry. Was colder than I expected."

That was a poor lie. He'd been startled and panicked from my touch. I didn't call him out and instead brought my fingers close, intentionally pausing before resting the pads of my fingers against his frigid skin.

"I haven't healed many bruises, so I'm not sure if this will hurt at all. It'll be over quick if it does." He'd know if it hurt to heal bruises far better than I would, so it was useless commentary, but I didn't know what else to say. What was the "normal" way to act for something like this? He kept his head hung as he nodded, shame filling both of our stomachs.

"I really don't mind you asking for help. It's better to ask than sit suffering—"

I felt a blow into my shoulder, but it wasn't a stab this time — more blunt, like knuckles into my bone. I'd experienced the sensation so many times through premonitions but hadn't understood until rather recently. Because I hadn't anticipated the hit, a gasp slipped from my lips. Squeezing my eyes shut, I did my best to refocus, to ignore the compounded throbbing from my empathy and this new premonition blurring together as my head pulsed. Jordan immediately noticed, anxiety's familiar stomach drop gripping me as it did him.

"Wait, shit, you ain't been getting premonitions on this, right? Like..." Sudden self-loathing led me to cough, his emotions consuming my mind because of the direct contact we had while I healed him. I winced as I felt my head slam against something in the premonition. Jordan's anger dug deeper through my skin. His hand gently pulled my fingers away mid-heal, interrupting the cast, none of the fury reflected in his touch.

"It's fine. You need these heals," I insisted.

He only felt more agitation from my attempt at reassuring him. "That's why you came, ain't it?" His tone was so defeated, as if I'd struck a blow against him. "You already knew."

That wasn't correct, at least not the way he thought. "I mean, I figured you asking me to come here at this hour probably meant... But I didn't have an attack earlier from this." I lowered my hand to my lap. He needed the heals but I wouldn't force them without his permission. I didn't want to say the reason I hadn't had a premonition over what'd happened at his house was because I'd had more life-threatening ones instead.

"Just now's the first one I had like that today. If I'd had one like it earlier, I would've tried to warn you, or..."

My heart raced as I barely prevented myself from hyperventilating, chills filling my body. "You had other premonitions today? Ones that didn't involve...?"

I lowered my eyes to my lap, nodding. I'd been caught, and as I'd suspected, he was none too amused.

"Three times so far today. I guess I can't have more than one at once, at least right now."

"Fuckin' hell." He shifted away from me. "You shouldn't've come out."

The temperature dropped further as his frustration grew. I bit back rubbing my arms to warm myself — I didn't want him to notice how bad he'd lost elemental control on top of everything else, but I felt goosebumps on my arms. I'd come out here to help him, but I'd only made everything worse.

"Why'd I even drag your ass out this late? Your mom'll be pissed if she finds out."

That was one concern I didn't have.

"She won't — she was already asleep when I left." I reached out, laying my hand on top of his; his skin was warmer than mine for once. I wondered if it was because of all the mana he accidentally burned through while modifying the training house's temperature. "Let me finish healing you. I'm already here, so there's no reason for you to sit in pain."

He paused all movement, a tangled knot deep in my stomach once more as he tensed.

"Shit, your empathy... I didn't even... I'm just fuckin' every damn thing up tonight."

I shook my head. "I could've said no. I made the choice to come."

He said nothing, but at least the temperature steadied instead of decreasing further. I took that as permission, moving my hand to his still throbbing wrist. As my fingers brushed against his right wrist, I felt the air be knocked from my lungs as a stabbing sensation shot through my left wrist once more. I

**293**

wasn't able to bite back a wince despite bracing for the inevitable pain.

"Is... it's still...?"

Shaking my head, I clenched my eyes shut — the other premonition had returned for round number four. "It's... It's not that. It's the..." Words hurt — my lungs stung as if they'd been pierced, filled with lead. "Other..."

"You gotta get home, like *now*. Your ass needs to be in bed." His fingers gently gripped my wrist as he pulled me upward.

I gasped, whimpering and wincing as a tear slipped down my cheek from the pain. "I-I can't. Need to wait it out. Don't... don't move me..."

He mumbled a curse under his breath as he instantly let go. "Sorry, didn't think 'bout how it'd..." I heard him take a deep breath, frustration and helplessness like sirens in my blood. "Is there anything I can do to help? I can leave, get outta your empathic range at least, so I'm not fuckin' you that way."

"Don't." If anyone were to attack right then, I'd be dead. If he left, I'd be alone in the dark in the middle of nowhere, and that was far worse than experiencing his emotions. "Just... just sit with me. Okay?"

My cheeks flushed. Was I struggling with elemental manipulation now? I didn't feel a breeze or more humidity. Maybe it was Jordan's mana burning finally catching up to him, our emotions so blurred together that I struggled to separate what was his and what was mine. Contrasting his cooling skin, his emotional warmth invited me closer, grounded me in the still-safe present instead of the dangerous future. I felt his chest against my side as my head rested on his collarbone. My cheeks flushed further as he shifted his arm to hold me.

"Oh, fuck." He tensed, a new wave of anxiety eating into me, my stomach dropping, heart racing. "It's worse when I touch you, ain't it? So like..."

"It's okay." All I saw were auras: just mine and his, nothing else around for easily over a mile. "The contact helps ground me away from the premonition, and it's nice to not be alone out here right now." It was support I'd never thought I'd have this time last year, and sometimes, support I still wasn't sure I deserved.

His anxiety calmed, something peaceful that I couldn't identify now his predominant emotion. The training house's temperature either finally stabilized or I'd burned enough mana from the premonition that my body temperature had increased because I no longer felt cold. I continued resting my head against him, no longer fighting the premonition as it passed through me like a violent wave. Once it played out, I'd be able to move on with my life. I just needed patience.

I wasn't sure if it was minutes or seconds or hours that passed as we sat huddled together in the training house, the intoxicating warmth from his emotions helping to dull out the remaining pain from the premonition. I shouldn't feel safe. We were both exhausted and extremely easy targets here with no one else around. But I did, his emotions tricking me into an illogical comfort. The pain finally dulled to where I could move, so I opened my eyes to only see darkness, blackness. Had Jordan turned the lamp off? When though? And what about the light orb I'd created? It shouldn't have expired yet.

"Kyle?"

Maybe I'd just misjudged how long we'd been there; I'd been distracted with pain, so it wasn't out of the question. "Why'd you turn off the lamp?" I asked.

He shifted, but I couldn't tell to where without the light on, just that his aura hadn't really moved. "Uh, I didn't?"

I closed my eyes, squeezing and then reopening them. Nothing. But why? Something wasn't right. Even if this was some poor-taste joke he played, even if my light spell had expired and I hadn't noticed, some moonlight should shine into the training house from the broken windows. I couldn't see even that though, just an absence of all light. But why — *how*?

"I-I'm blind."

"Huh? What d'you mean?"

Sensory precognition had caused this somehow, sending my senses into such an overwhelmed state I'd lost my vision. I kept opening and closing my eyes, but I still saw nothing. As far as I could tell, it was just sight I'd lost. I still smelled the grass around us outside of the training house, felt my skin against the warm concrete, heard myself and Jordan talk. Even my empathy and aura reading still worked somehow.

"The attacks, they must've..."

A second passed before he cursed. "You're not fuckin' around. You really can't..." It sounded like he moved further away. "You gotta get home."

Home wasn't some magical safety point. They'd attack me there just as easily as here, and either way, I couldn't fight like this.

"How?" My tone was sharper than I'd intended, my heart racing with my thoughts as I realized how vulnerable I was right then. "I *can't see* to walk back."

His aura quickly spiked before settling back down. "Here, I'll carry you back. Still not ideal but best we got, I think." Carry me? We were easily forty minutes from home.

"But..."

He ran my fingers across something leathery, a glove maybe? "I shortcast alt form. Should be fine." That was what had caused his aura to spike then, but I hadn't expected him to go into alt form without an emergency or someone asking.

"M-mm."

I heard more shuffling before he said, "Step forward. I'm right in front of you. Just wrap your arms around my neck."

Doing as he instructed, I felt the leather top of his alt form, his hair tied back. I felt his arms rest under my thighs, holding me piggyback style. We were such an easy target if attacked, but...

I didn't understand how he felt happy right then. I knew it wasn't because I was blind, but I didn't understand why it'd calmed him to hold me despite how heavy I was. With little else to do, I rested my head against his shoulder. Neither of us was comfortable like this, but the peace he had must've passed to me as I relaxed against him. His stride was steady, only momentary pauses as he'd adjust his grip on me. I wasn't sure how long had passed, but his arms ached; even though he was in alt form, he still had carried me for literal miles.

"Um, we can take a break if you need."

"S'fine. Just keep resting — maybe your sight'll come back sooner if you do." I doubted I was that fortunate but didn't argue with him.

Time blurred as crisp air filled my lungs, a pleasant breeze against my back. I felt more peace than I should in the middle of an empty street at night without my vision; even for normal crimes like theft, we were sitting ducks.

"Hey, uh, Kyle?" His voice was gentle, waking me from the passive nap I'd accidentally taken. "Any chance your sight's back?"

I opened my eyes but saw nothing, the absence of light everywhere. "Not yet." It wasn't his fault, and I didn't want him to even consider that it was, so I did my best to hide how insecure this made me. I needed to be stronger.

"Fuck..."

"What's wrong?" He'd stopped moving. I recognized the auras nearby — we were close to my home, Mom's aura in my scanning range.

"Doubt you can sneak in the front door, so, uh..."

I'd jumped down from the roof. Even if Jordan normally could've climbed up there, I seriously doubted he could do so while I hung on to his back. As it was, I always used air manipulation to—

That's it. While I needed line of sight for telekinetics, I didn't for the levitation of things I had contact with. The neighborhood was almost completely asleep, so as long as we were quick, maybe I could levitate us up.

"I need you to be my eyes for this, okay?" I said.

"Uh, sure, but what're you thinking?" Nothing he'd like, I was pretty certain.

"Let me stand. I need full alt form."

He lowered me to the grass cautiously. I felt the warmth from his skin still, which aligned with his aura being basically on top of my own. I transformed into full alt form, opening my eyes to still see blackness. I hadn't actually thought it'd work, but part of me had hoped that'd restore my sight since alt form's body wasn't mine.

"Okay. I'm going to levitate us both, but I need you to tell me when to stop because I can't see where we are." This was totally about to suck. I moved Jordan telekinetically during practice fairly routinely now, but never for more than like thirty seconds and never literal stories up. It wasn't even just his weight this time either since I needed to levitate both of us so he could guide me onto the roof.

"You can do that without seeing? I thought you needed line of sight?" He was mildly paranoid, likely from all the times I'd broken my line of sight while telekinetically moving him.

"Mm. It's different than telekinetics, so it should work." I'd barely formulated this plan and didn't want to consider needing a backup plan if this failed. Reaching out for him, I felt his arm and brought myself against his torso, hugging him. His heart raced, likely because of the admittedly many times he'd been dropped from far less dangerous heights than what I planned here. "I'm going to attempt levitating us to the roof, but you'll have to guide me because I have no depth perception. Tell me when I need to start slowing and then stop, okay?"

"Will do." His arms circled around me, that same contentment pulsing through him. I was glad one of us had faith this would work because he must be more confident than me about this whole thing. I focused on levitating, drawing mana and separating my feet from the grass.

"Fuck, you really..." he mumbled. "This's hell'va impressive, 'specially without sight."

Pushing more air into my lungs, I realized this plan was significantly more taxing than I'd estimated. "Thanks."

Sweat formed on the back of my neck, a mixture of exertion and humidity. I felt like alt form needed more showers than my actual body lately. "'Bout six feet away."

That meant absolutely nothing as far as my rate of levitation right then, but I assumed he meant to slow down. Levitating slowly upward was even rougher, no longer having bursts of rest periods like I had while raising us up more quickly. "Like this?"

"Yeah." Another second passed. "We're parallel to the roof, but like eight steps over." He guided me, and I soon felt the roofing under me instead of air. I'd never felt so thankful to feel my feet on something solid. "Your window unlocked?"

That... was an entire other problem. I shook my head, trying to gauge where I was on the roof. "Locked. I teleported out."

"Fuck..."

I couldn't teleport myself; I needed sight to place where I

wanted to land. Jordan could've handled the visualization, but he didn't know the teleportation spell and there was no point in him being in my room alone even if he had learned it. But... if I worked off his sight, maybe...

"I can teleport about three feet. If you're okay splitting the mana with me, I think I can get us both in, if you don't mind being my eyes for it."

"Oh, uh, sure I guess. How's that even work though?"

We need direct contact and, ideally, to be as close as possible to minimize both the mana needed and the chance of collision with anything once we teleported inside.

"Can you help me up on your back again? I think if I levitate us on the roof so that there's no sound and we get right up to the window, I can walk you through the visualization needed for teleporting while I handle the actual spell."

"Uh, sure, but I don't think it'd be a good idea trying to turn you around up here. Can I pick you up where you're at?"

I nodded, then felt him grab me around my hips and lift. When I circled my arms around his neck this time, I felt his warm exhales against my shoulder. I relaxed as he held me, that internal and external warmth back. My heart raced as I levitated us ever so slightly off the roof. Just a few seconds later, I felt cold glass near my left arm. We had to be right outside my bedroom window then.

"Ready?"

"Y-yeah. So it's like a mana transfer?"

I removed the glove from my left hand, which admittedly was a pain to do while being held and unable to see.

"It'll be like that one time at Asuza's, so it's probably easiest for me to stand and us split spell cost through direct contact."

He set me down as I lowered us fully onto the roof. I heard additional shuffling, his fingers touching mine as his aura spiked and then remained more illuminated. That must have been him full casting alt form.

"Like this?"

Sliding my fingers into his, my cheeks burned, and I was fairly certain his did too. It was strange to feel my hand in his, the calluses on his fingertips and palm. Bringing myself closer so my body pressed against his, I said, "Okay. Visualize us being right inside the room. I should be able to handle it from there."

His other hand moved against my back, as if securing me against him. I started the spell, pulling mana from him. Admittedly, I didn't split it evenly even though I probably should. But after the levitation stunt, I still felt winded and wasn't in a rush to expend a ton more mana so quickly. The air shifted from crisp outdoor currents to filtered and stationary. We'd made it, but I felt a sharp sting through my empathy, back around my left shoulder blade.

"Fuck, goddamn motherfuckin'..." To Jordan's credit, his string of curses was under his breath, but I still shushed him. His aura shone even brighter now, too. Wait, had he—

"Your wings are active?" My voice was as quiet as I could get it, but I wished I'd still spoken softer regardless.

"And yours ain't..." Even with a mumble, his lack of amusement and frustration more than came through.

Oops, I messed up on the conversion somewhere since he shouldn't have triggered his wings from that teleport. "Sorry..." As I released his hand, I felt feathers crowd us. I reached to them and stroked a few, noting how soft they were, pleasant against my fingertips. I wasn't sure if he'd triggered his wings before while I wasn't around, but I hadn't been around them since that day at Asuza's, and I hadn't exactly had the capacity to focus on them back then. This was the first time I'd felt wings from someone else instead of someone touching my own.

"They're soft." It was an obvious statement, but I wasn't exactly at the peak of my mental capabilities after my fifth — or was it sixth — premonition today.

His wing pressed against my fingertips, his skin suddenly warmer. The mana usage must've caused some amount of adrenaline to hit him. Regardless of his apprehension, my empathy showed he did relax from my fingers against his wing.

"You should get your ass in bed."

I couldn't get ready for bed until he left, still in my day clothes. "It'll be fine. I'll get to bed once you leave."

"Uh, your ass can't see a damn thing. No way in hell I'm leaving you to kill yourself by concussion up here."

My own cheeks flushed now, lightly gripping feathers as a fidget response. "Um, I need to get ready for bed though — like pj's and stuff, and um..."

"A-ah. Shit, uh..." Feathers brushed against my palm as he shifted. I didn't know why he hadn't dismissed them yet, but I wasn't complaining, the warmth from his wing comforting.

"I'll, uh, I'll turn around, then help you to bed?"

While I didn't doubt his integrity, it didn't change that I just wasn't comfortable changing with him in the room.

"I'll be fine, really. I know my own room."

"Kyle, you got shit thrown damn near everywhere in this room. No shot in hell you wouldn't trip." Despite his less-than-pleasing review of my organizational systems, I knew he was worried about me. He also wasn't wrong that I probably would trip on things here without anyone nearby, and I did *not* need Mom knowing something had happened to my vision.

Taking a deep breath, I sighed. "Okay, fine. It won't kill me to sleep in jeans for once, and with any luck, I'm going to crash." Granted, I'd been awake in the first place because the pain had been too much to sleep through. I wasn't exactly hopeful there wasn't a sixth premonition heading my way somehow that'd continue that trend. I bit my lip to prevent yelping as I felt my feet leave the floor, him picking me up and fraying the sense of orientation I'd established. I reached forward, hand against his shoulder and then wing, which I loosely gripped as my mind attempted to visualize how I'd been shifted. Something soft was under my butt, so I felt around me, noticing I touched my sheet. He'd moved me to my bed.

Another second passed, him growing increasingly embarrassed. What was going on? "Uh, Kyle?"

"Mm?"

"I, uh..." He paused before adding, "I don't know if I can get rid of, uh, *them* with your hand holding on so, uh..."

Oh. I'd forgotten I'd grasped on in the first place, my fingers still holding on to part of his wing. "Sorry." I released my hold as I moved my hand back to my side. Only a second passed before I no longer sensed his wings around me, his aura dimming back to its normal alt form intensity. Maybe one day,

I'd actually get to see his wings since I hadn't really both times they'd been out now. I kicked my shoes off, lying back down in my bed as I pulled and shuffled blankets.

He shifted again, this time pulling covers over me like I needed tucking in. "B'fore I sneak outta here, you need anything?"

While I wasn't excited about being alone without my vision, it wasn't like he could just stay here until it came back. Speaking of things that Mom would *not* handle that well, that was up there as nightmare fuel. All I could bank on was that sleep would restore my sight. I shook my head as I leaned back against my pillow.

"Though..." I didn't want his takeaway from tonight to be blaming himself — I'd still sneak out all over again if it helped him. After all, better for him to get help than us both suffer in silence. "I'm glad you asked me to come. Don't suffer alone, okay?"

His gloved hand rested against my forehead, cool leather seeping into my warm skin. "Even when your ass should've been in this goddamn bed."

"I mean it."

He chuckled, brushing a few strands of hair off my face. "I know you do, and it means a hell'va lot."

# Chapter Forty-Six

## senior antics

Maya | May 2
Matthews High

There were under two weeks left, then I could leave this place forever. Well, I guess I could leave Opal Pines itself too, but I mainly meant this high school building. I'd received an acceptance letter from the local community college, Jenn-whatever, and I'd gotten a state scholarship that would cover tuition with some of it left over. I'd been sleeping on the floor of my apartment for almost a year now and was thrilled at the idea that maybe I could use some of the leftover scholarship money one semester for an actual mattress of some kind.

Out of the corner of my eye, I saw Kylie doodling shapes in her notebook, bunches of dots and lines. Actually, it looked similar in style to what I'd seen in her spell book, and I'd seen Jordan write out different combinations of those same dots and lines as well, so they likely related to magic. Either way, she rubbed her eyes, looking less awake than normal for a Thursday morning. She'd more than emphasized she had never been a morning person, and it was rather common for her to struggle the further the week went on, so her fatigue wasn't particularly noteworthy in and of itself. I heard the bell chime, but neither of us moved since our next class was right here; that was a perk I'd miss in some ways.

I saw Mrs. Carslie step out of the classroom, something she usually did between classes. I wasn't sure if it was to get non-classroom air, a bathroom break, or give students non-teacher time, but I stopped complaining months ago about how it made her late every time and no longer minded a few minutes less of history lectures. We'd already taken our AP tests, so really, this class had become a glorified study hall since she lectured over material that we wouldn't be tested on.

Kylie closed her eyes as she laid her head on her desk. "That done?" I asked.

She didn't open her eyes back up as she nodded, covering her mouth while she yawned. "You don't know how tempted I am to ask Jordan to give me notes for later. But she'd totally notice if we swapped seats." Jordan sat behind Kylie, where Ashley had once sat during homeroom. Actually, speaking of Ashley, she'd yet to leave the room, instead lingering by the door with a smirk. Whatever caused said smirk, I wanted no part in.

"Jordan doesn't take notes though, does he?" He usually had a notebook out on his desk during class, but I'd never seen him write down anything related to the lecture; instead, he doodled those weird dots and lines or listened to the lecture without writing anything. From what I'd seen of his memory, I didn't blame him — why bother taking notes if he remembered it all either way?

Kylie huffed. "No. And his notes always sucked anyways." I liked she didn't ask me. She knew I wouldn't cover for her sleeping in class after all the times I'd taken my own notes despite working shifts that kept me out until midnight.

Jordan slid into his regular desk; his expression was surprisingly concerned as he watched Kylie. "Did...?"

Kylie nodded. "Yeah, woke up fine. Well, fine enough."

Had something happened? Jordan was lethargic for this time of the morning as well; he usually held up far better than Kylie throughout the week. "Did I miss something?" Neither of them answered, avoiding the question entirely; that wasn't the reassurance they must have thought it was. "Okay, so what happened?"

With a sigh, Kylie sat up, keeping her eyes away from me. "I didn't want to worry you so I didn't mention anything this morning, but I've been having premonitions the past few days. I found out last night that if they get too intense, it can short out my sight to where I can't see anything. But it's over now and everything's fine. Just tired."

I'd hardly call all of that "all right." I knew she meant well, but I wished she'd *stop* hiding when she had premonitions that likely involved me. If they both knew, I would like the memo too.

The door slammed shut, but the bell hadn't rung yet. Barely a fifth of the class was even in here, for that matter. I glanced up, seeing Ashley as the one who'd shut the door. Why was she even still in here? Usually she'd long since scattered off to whatever was her next class.

Jordan's attention was still focused on Kylie, but Kylie shifted her head in Ashley's direction. Following Kylie's line of sight, I saw Ashley hold a small white remote in her hand. I made out at least four buttons on it, her tapping one repetitively. Jordan coughed suddenly, as if something had knocked the breath out of him.

Had Ashley caused that somehow? "What're you doing?" I asked her.

Ashley glared at me, a smirk rising on her face. "Oh, you'll see."

That sounded less than reassuring. Why would she lock the teacher out? So help me if she did some dumb senior antic that would get us all stuck here longer — I'd already told work my hours were completely free starting the beginning of June.

Kylie's lips pressed together as if distracted, while she continued staring in Ashley's direction. "That doesn't..."

"What doesn't?" Ashley asked, her back to us as she lodged something near the door-handle, a clicking sound I couldn't identify. What was she doing? "Or is that a secret? You *are* so fond of those."

As Ashley turned back around, she ran her hand through her hair, strands shifting from their usual brown to bright blonde. She tossed her glasses to the tiles, stepping on them and shattering the lenses. Didn't she need those to see? I glanced over to Kylie, and the color had drained from her face as she mumbled, "How?"

Jordan had tensed as well, mumbling, "The fuck?"

Neither of these reactions were particularly comforting, but the other few students hadn't noticed anything — not yet, at least. While they probably assumed it was a senior prank, I had a sudden suspicion I only wished that was the case.

# Chapter Forty-Seven

## death count

Kylie | May 2
Matthews High

It made no sense. Ashley had become Lianne, brown hair now blonde as she no longer wore glasses, didn't seem to need them at all. I'd noticed aura similarities many times between Ashley and Lianne, but I'd been convinced they were just that: similarities. Hadn't Lianne been kidnapped after she'd walked out of my house last year, just like Amalia had been kidnapped? If Ashley *was* Lianne, why hadn't she ever said anything? Why did she have a disguise at all?

Biting down on my tongue, I ate the mana drain on a magipoten check spell — Ashley's magipoten was the same as mine, but how? No one else's — not even Jordan's — was that high.

"Nuh-uh," she said, a teasing tone as she pressed a button on the remote in her hand. I bit back a cough as it felt like additional weights dropped onto my lungs. The barrier was even more potent now. Somehow, she controlled it directly — but wasn't that something only Sase and Zimihe and their leader could do?

"You know, there's some people that rather *don't like you*, and they're willing to make some fascinating trades. Like this little machine here, bits of paperwork slid around there... Justifying a couple deaths... All just to *observe* the princess here."

Yet if she controlled the barrier, that could have only meant—

"You bitch," Jordan said. "You knew — *intended* — fuckin' all of it. That's why you kept fuckin' gaslighting..."

She brought her fingers to my jawbone. I didn't know whether to slap her hand away or be glad Lianne was here, hadn't been taken like Amalia. Nothing made sense. "Remember the many times I told you I hated liars... I bet you do too, now don't you? How does it feel, being lied to?"

I didn't know what she meant; this all had to be some big misunderstanding, between me, her, Jordan. "I don't..."

"'I don't know what you mean' you said, again and again. What a liar." I hadn't wanted the attention of people that hated mages. I had to protect myself, protect Jordan, had even wanted to protect her...

Jordan's anger threatened to consume me, but I shoved enough of it out of my empathic reads to see how *sadistically eager* Lianne was right then. Why?

"Not good," Maya mumbled, and I noticed the few other students in the room had turned toward us. Mrs. Carslie yelled through the door about how this wasn't funny. Emotions suffocated me, fatigue compounding with the higher-than-normal barrier threshold.

Lianne grabbed my hair, yanking me upward. Even though we were the same height, I'd still been sitting at my desk and hadn't anticipated the action. My thighs collided with the attached desk table before the whole desk tumbled to the side and I struggled to catch myself from tripping.

"Why do *you* get to graduate with the perfect little life? Look at how everyone loves you, supports you... even though it's your fault all those people died and that the ones here now are about to die too."

She'd had an attitude problem, but there was no way Lianne had organized all this. She wasn't a killer, just another classmate, a mage—

"The hell's wrong with you?" Jordan snapped. He yanked her wrist off of me, gripping me with his other hand as I stumbled and keeping me from falling. "So you were lied to? Grow the fuck up."

Lianne's eyes cut as she staggered from Jordan's intervention. She pushed that same button on the remote once more, my suspicions confirmed as it felt like air drained from the room. Jordan felt the toll too, his exhaustion slamming into my empathic reads as he panted.

"Don't touch me, you lapdog." I saw a knife appear in her left hand. It had to be her weapon, shortcast. She threw it at Claire, stabbing her in the leg and causing her to cry out. I bit back a wince myself, not expecting the sudden rush of pain. "Someone else injured, all because of *you*." Kendrick ran to the door, tried to bang on it. "Oh, it's not opening until I say it can." She'd sealed it with magic somehow, judging by her confidence.

I knew my options: use magic in front of others or watch them die. Hurt someone that hated me for being afraid to be honest or do as she wanted and just die. "If it's just me you want..." I stepped toward her.

I didn't want anyone else to die because of me. I wasn't worth it.

"Kyle!" Jordan hissed as he tried to pull me back. I broke his grip; the barrier had him struggling to breathe, his endurance sapped, so it wasn't hard to outmaneuver him.

It was fine. As long as it meant no one else was hurt because of me, it was worth it. Though... I guess I'd be alone for a while. I was more prepared this time. If Kisate could handle it, I could too.

The knife came back to Lianne's hand as she traced its blade around my collarbone, blood dripping from the action. I just stared ahead. Pain was fine. I'd been getting used to it. I just didn't want anyone else dying, hurting, because of me. Lianne licked my ear as she whispered, "How brave."

The pressure on my lungs eased — but Lianne hadn't anticipated that for some reason, so a rush of anger filled her. Hadn't she gotten what she wanted? What happened? She punched me in the side; I recoiled, struggling to gain my footing. I felt this deep puncture in my abdomen, but it wasn't from me.

*"You're* just damsel bait. Know your place."

When I looked up, I saw Maya had stolen the remote from Lianne, somehow using it to release the barrier back to its normal intensity. It'd come at a cost as Maya now bled from her stomach. Jordan rushed over to her — he couldn't heal her, not in front of people, what if one of them...

"Don't..." I mumbled. I didn't want him hurt, didn't want Maya to die, didn't know what to do.

"Now I'm pissed." Lianne punched me to the floor as she stepped on my arm, extra emphasis with the heel she had on as I felt a bruise form. Jordan's aura spiked, so he had to have healed Maya — but he couldn't... couldn't...

A stab into my neck, the pain instantly vanishing. Slices across my throat, suffocation clouding my mind—

As I stumbled to my feet, I watched as she killed the few classmates in the room. I couldn't save them, few as there had been. It was the gym all over again — so many dead. Maya was only barely conscious while Jordan was gasping, struggling to stand from how much that one heal had fatigued him. Lianne grabbed the remote that'd fallen by Maya's foot, the barrier's intensity increasing even more than it had earlier.

"Why?" I asked.

I said she could kill me. That was what she wanted, wasn't it? That was what everyone wanted.

She turned back to me, and her smile gave me goosebumps. "You know, before you took out Nimaka — *however* your inept self did that one — she taught me a few things. There really *is* an entire organization out there dedicated to *properly utilizing* people *like you*, and they can be surprisingly flexible with the right negotiations."

It wasn't that she'd been captured by them; she'd been *hired* by them somehow. But why? She was clearly a mage as well, so why would she have done that? Why would they have worked with her instead of capturing her too?

"Second. You know there's a pitiful existence out there that only exists to *counter* a high-powered mage?" I remembered Sia teaching me about those "counters," an *Anti-Existence* she'd called them. "You know, they don't get to have *anything* original about them. After all, they only exist to mirror the *actual* existence. How quaint." She kicked a chair onto the bodies of our classmates, as if everything and everyone in the room was discarded trash, beneath her. "One late afternoon, I started seeing colors. Suddenly, I understood classwork without any effort... all just one *random* March afternoon, two years ago."

My eyes widened. That'd been around my own Act. She implied *she* was my Anti-Existence, but—

It all lined up: we shared the same birthday, same heights, similar builds, sounded like we'd had Act the same day, similar aura intensities...

"Then why do you want to kill me? That's the dumbest thing you could do."

If I died, she'd have mana drain to the point of organ collapse, as if her symbol was destroyed. Killing me killed her. If she knew what an Anti-Existence was, she had to know that, didn't she?

Yet she just rolled her eyes. "Don't start with more lies. I know better. I'll finally get my *own* life once you're gone, no longer tied down as some shadow of you."

I shook my head. "That's not—"

She threw a knife at Maya. Jordan intercepted it with Nateka, but only barely. Maya herself was dazed and unlikely to move around much anytime soon.

"And you understood what a *plague* on society you were until these two showed up. Now you have *hope* and that's just terrible, considering the death count on your head, not to mention what a *murderer* you've become after what you did to both Sase and Zimihe, killing them so ruthlessly. You think you should get to be happy with how much misery you've caused?"

She dashed at Jordan, his movements so sluggish compared to normal. He'd never used magic in the barrier, so he hadn't known how bad the mana drain would be. She stabbed through his arm and I felt the blade pierce through his muscle. He tried to switch to holding Nateka with his left hand, but wasn't fast enough as Lianne held her knife to his throat, a desk blocking him from getting away from her. She drew blood from his neck. He winced and then threw a punch with his other arm.

**311**

I needed to help him. But if I died, if she died — I had to tell her Nimaka had lied. If she knew the truth, she'd understand how pointless this all was.

"Lianne, listen to me. Nimaka lied. If you really are my Anti-Existence, you'll die if I die. You can't—"

She stabbed Jordan in the chest, barely missing his heart once more. He couldn't heal, not in this barrier. Blood dripped onto the tile even though he'd done nothing, each breath a strained gasp as he gripped his desk as best he could to prevent falling forward.

A haze filled me, distance from the pain and even the barrier itself right then. It didn't matter what it would take: she wasn't hurting him ever again.

"Riyati." I'd never gone into alt form through the barrier; last time, I'd barely been able to get basic heal spells to Maya, let alone an entire glyph. It didn't matter.

Lianne threw Jordan to the tile, more and more blood puddling around him. The iron smell coated my senses as pain melded itself in, this haze further intoxicating my mind. This peace was like when I'd killed Zimihe, everything so *tranquil*, so *simple*. A growl came from my throat as I expended however much mana it took to get the alt cast through.

"What little trick are you trying this time?" She raised the barrier further.

I didn't care.

"Obey your mistress's command, activate withdrawal." I'd cleared the alt form, access to mana she couldn't have. Yet every breath took more effort than my normal body would. The higher magipoten came at a cost. That was fine. I didn't care if I lived, but she'd hurt him, and that was unacceptable.

"Isare, heed your mistress's call, summon forth." I felt the staff in my hands begging for her blood. I charged at her. She blocked my swings with a knife in each hand. Yet it took all her weight to do so, especially as I dropped Isare and kicked her jaw. She slid, maintaining her balance as she wiped blood from her mouth.

"Oh, change of heart. Let's end this then, shall we? You and your *prince dear* and *damsel bait* can all die together. Or will they assume you killed them all if you manage to make it out again? I wonder. We can only have so many *accidents* now, can't we?"

Whatever she said didn't matter. He'd make it, I'd assure it. I resummoned Isare to my grip and focused my mana further, releasing the blades. As Lianne charged me, I stared at her, generating a water beam from my right palm. It pierced through her shoulder, damaging the cinderblock in the wall.

"How?! You shouldn't be able to even breathe right now, let alone pull off a spell!" she shrieked.

No matter what she put the barrier at, I'd been right beside it all year, in my programming classes, during my so-called library trips. I was used to struggling for every breath, knew the limits of my body far better than she'd ever imagined. But he should've never experienced this pain.

As she held her shoulder, I rushed forward. She didn't have the practice I had, experience that I'd gained from sweating and bleeding, struggling to survive. She'd passively gotten my mana increases but nothing else. I stabbed her heart, and unlike her, I didn't miss or falter.

"H... heh..." she mumbled, leaning onto Isare as she coughed blood. "Should've... killed you ear... lier..." Her body fell limp, and I dismissed Isare, rushing to Jordan as I chain cast heal after heal. He was unconscious, and I doubted I'd be up much longer myself, that haze fading as I saw his breaths even out. I coughed up blood, releasing alt form as I saw spots.

I'd done the best I could.

# Chapter Forty-Eight

## path forward

Kylie | May 4
Crestia Regional Hospital

It was the second time I'd been admitted to the hospital this year, and I was more than ready for it to be the *last* time as well. While I wasn't discharged yet, at least I could walk around the hospital finally. Only with an escort and I had to use the elevator without leaving the premise of said hospital, but anything was better than lying in that bed. Maya was my escort, Mom not trusting me to be alone yet, deeming Maya *responsible* enough.

We stood in the elevator, silent as I had the dumb beeping thing attached to me again. Of course, it was steady. I was fairly certain I'd completely healed by now; at most, I had a bit of mana drain.

Two days had passed since the last attack. It was Saturday now. I'd woken up late Thursday, but they'd wanted me on *strict bed rest* until this morning. Maya had been released Friday morning. I didn't know how she'd pay for her time in the hospital, couldn't find the words to ask. She'd come to check up on me today, letting Mom go home and get some sleep for a few hours. I'd worried her again, even if I hadn't meant to.

The elevator opened, and I started down the hallway,

walking to room 259. Peeking through the glass, I saw Jordan, Richard in the room with him. They said he'd need to be here longer than me; even with the heals I'd done, he'd been in far worse shape. I knocked a few times before stepping in, Maya behind me. Richard sat in the guest chair, but no one else was here. Was his family getting stuff from home, much like Maya had allowed Mom to do? Or did they not even know anything had happened? Or...

It was probably better I didn't ask.

"H-hey," I said. He'd ended up here because of me, just like Maya. I didn't know how to apologize enough.

As it was, I barely remembered what'd happened once Lianne had stabbed him, my memory blurred. But I'd killed her, another victim on my list. This violence had surged yet again when Jordan had been in danger. It wasn't like it'd been for Sase, where I'd known what I was doing. Lianne's — Zimihe's — kill had been instinctual, like an animal—

"You hanging in there?" he asked, worried about me yet again. He had some light scarring across his neck, but the actual injury looked to have already healed over, thankfully.

I nodded, moving my eyes away. "Yeah. I'm fine now honestly, but they want to keep me one more day."

"Same here, am basically fine now but no one's said shit 'bout me being released." He was as poor of a liar as ever, ignoring my empathy gave away how fatigued he still felt. The heals he'd used on Maya within the barrier had overtaxed him when compounded with the injuries he'd sustained. I didn't call him out on his lie, not with Maya in the room.

Richard rubbed his eyes, let out an irritated huff, and snapped, "Can all the *excitement* with that damn high school *stop* already?"

Even if I didn't like him, I'd caused trouble for him too somehow.

"Sorry," I said.

Maya shifted closer beside me. "When I went to work to explain things, they said the news going around is the school's cancelling the rest of the year; any remaining finals are omitted from grades, and they'll look at rescheduling the ceremony to walk in a few weeks."

Oh right, I'd ruined everyone's graduation ceremony too — mine included.

Richard snorted. "Yeah, 'cause it's going to take a week alone to bleach the classroom and clear the whore's corpse and guts off."

"Not. Helping," Jordan mumbled, a comment I don't think I was meant to hear. Surprisingly, Richard actually didn't add anything further, and it might've been funny to observe had I been in a better mood. Jordan's attention shifted back to me. "It's not your fault."

I nodded. While I didn't believe him, I didn't have the energy to argue either. "I'm not at the police station, so that's something, I guess."

I never would've expected Richard to shift his posture, avoiding looking at me— pity from him, of all people. Normally, I would be offended to be pitied by *him*, but I didn't have the energy to complain about it right then.

"Currently being called a murder-suicide by what's-her-face, since she's the one they have on camera locking everyone in from the hallway cam. Fact you three lived's being considered god-tier luck, but since you're all various degrees of fucked up, assumption is she got careless and didn't notice you'd all lived — apparently paramedics almost missed you in particular." He stared at me.

Even if the high-powered spells had been used in alt form, just getting alt form through the barrier likely had used near all my mana.

"Any fingerprints are assumed to be self-defense too, I'd bet," Maya said. "Even more so, given that Ashley didn't even look like Ashley, so makes it even more suspicious for her to have been there."

Somehow, we'd made it out. Our five classmates hadn't, all dead, but I'd been able to save Maya and Jordan this time.

That meant something, didn't it? It wasn't enough, but it was *something*.

"I still..." Everyone who wanted me dead was gone now, right? I could be a *normal girl* if I wanted. "I still want to practice. To be safe."

Jordan sighed, nodding. "Yeah, yeah, gonna go slam my ass

into a few dozen more walls." I really hoped to *stop* doing that with telekinetics soon. Just... eye contact was far more important than I'd realized when originally learning from Sia.

I wasn't sure if I walked the path Sia and Rota had meant for me, for Jordan. But I was still alive, and more importantly, so were Maya and Jordan. Seeing him rub his neck, ice-blue eyes staring at me, made me think maybe it was okay to want to be around people still. Unlike this time last year, I felt wanted.

"Are you both done training then? I'm going to have more shifts, but until the fall, I'll still have far more free time and can stop by if so."

Jordan motioned his head toward me. "Ask her. Like hell am I signing up for more torture, but like that's stopped her so far." Despite myself, I chuckled. "At least you can't complain about it being *too cold* anymore."

This was the path forward I'd chosen, and these were the people I wanted with me on this path.

# thanks for reading!

Thank you for reading until the end! If you enjoyed this story, please consider leaving a review on Goodreads, TheStoryGraph, BookBub, PageBound, or on your favorite book retailer — as you've likely heard many times, reviews are exceptionally important for indie authors, and each one both means a ton and is super helpful in helping others decide if this book is right for them!

Check riyati.ink/ripple for a handy list of review sites & retailers!

# acknowledgments

While previous *Riyati* books' acknowledgments started with me thanking Krishna for his endless dedication to sleeping on my feet, I'd like to start this acknowledgment section by switching it up: this time, Hari the very orange old man took point supervising, and I'm somewhat certain a good 20% of the manuscript's chaos came from having an orange supervisor (which is not to understate the role Krishna still played, but this time, he slept in his box next to me instead of on my feet, which meant less direct involvement in the creation process). I'd next like to once again thank my husband — for supporting me through the ever-winding publishing process and continuing to support my dream of writing, even when I don't always believe in it myself — and my close friends for lending their ears and shoulders when I need someone to confide in.

As before, numerous individuals assisted me in getting *Riyati Ripple* out, and I'd like to take the time to thank them here as well: first, I'd like to thank both Alli Rense (yet again!) and Liz Sauco for their valuable feedback during the beta'ing stage; their feedback helped to refine and expand originally confusing or vague aspects of *Riyati Ripple* that I would have never thought to give a second glance to. I'd also like to take the time to thank Isabelle for her phenomenal editing — I can say with certainty that despite its size, *Riyati Ripple* is the most polished *Riyati* book to date and that is 100% Isabelle's doing! With regards to the graphics, logos, and all non-character illustration art, I'd like to thank Liz Sauco for the numerous hours she's spent teaching and guiding me while I've learned how to Do Graphic Design (kinda); the covers the series has now would literally not have been possible with Liz and Dax Murray's expertise (they sat with me many evenings as I got everything lined up and are most definitely why we don't have scribbles for covers now). Speaking of covers, I'd also like to once again thank amagren for his amazing glyphs, used in both the standard cover and for the deluxe edition's foiled cover and sleeve. Compared to previous *Riyati* books, I commissioned the help of two artists for *Riyati Ripple*'s character art (hosted on Riyati's Library Archive): Kylie, Jordan, and Maya's shoulders-up art was illustrated by cingaja; the striking Lianne and Ashley art meanwhile was illustrated by aucrowne.

Finally, though certainly not least, I'd like to thank the readers of *Riyati* — both if you started with *Riyati Ripple* and if you started with one of the earlier books in the series. It's been incredibly humbling how many people have enjoyed the series thus far, and I hope that you enjoyed this book as well! It's been an adventure to release the series up to *Riyati Ripple* so far, and it's one I hope to continue doing through the support of readers like yourself.

Sincerely,
Kai Zeal

# *about the author*

Kai Zeal (she/her) is a queer, disabled writer, academic, gamer, cat mom, and, most recently, content creator. She got her start writing fanfiction as a child, creating an awareness of tropes, characterization, and the importance of retellings. From there, she refined her analytical skills both in academia and through fandom with critical analysis of media to gain a better understanding of how the parts of a work come together to form its whole.

She has degrees in psychology, writing, higher education administration, and is pursuing a PhD with a research focus on critical disability studies through a queer, feminist lens. In her free time, she's a lifelong gamer, particularly of JRPGs, many of which have shaped her storytelling strategies and love of media.

Want to know more? Check out her personal website & sign up for her monthly newsletter at https://kai-zeal.com/. For *Riyati* specific information, check out https://riyati.ink/

# *interested in more riyati?*

If you'd like to further explore Opal Pines and the *Riyati* universe, sign up for my newsletter to receive *Riyati Origins*! You'll also receive behind-the-scenes updates, previews, and deals for *Riyati*. If you're more of a Discord fan, join Riyati's Official Discord server — on top of a great community and instant Riyati updates, subscribers get access to Riyati's Archive Library, a *Riyati* hub for bonus short-stories, alternative PoV chapters, and character art!

Newsletter: https://riyati.ink/newsletter

Official Riyati Discord: https://riyati.ink/discord

**Long before Kylie Rae ran into the forest that fateful day, there lived another woman — Kisate Riyati, crowned princess to the Royal Kingdom of Riyati. This is her story, of how kingdoms fall and dreams are dashed.**

Just before Kisate's twenty-second birthday, she received word that the man she'd secretly loved for many years was now arranged to be her eventual husband, Takite Tanoti. Yet this news sets in motion a series of events that would not just be life changing, but ultimately instigates the destruction of the kingdom she was to rule. What was meant as a kindness to Asuza Nuueti, her primary servant and a man that long since had unrequited feelings toward her, will both save her and damn her.

Explore the beginnings of the Riyati universe, back when the Ancient Kingdom of Riyati still thrived — and see Kisate, Takite, and Asuza as they once were, long before the events of *Riyati Rebirth*.

**Get *Riyati Origins* for free today @ <u>https://riyati.ink/newsletter</u>!**